"Don't open the first page of this novel unless you're prepared to sacrifice all other commitments for the next forty-eight hours or so! This is Riggle's best yet. Compelling, believable, and full of delicious twists, this story will forever change how you relate to strangers, friends, and even family—reminding you that everyone you meet might be carrying her own secret struggles." —Katrina Kittle on *Things We Didn't Say*

"With ease and grace, Riggle walks the fine line between sentimentality and comedy, and she has a sure hand in creating fun, quirky characters." —*Publishers Weekly* on *Real Life & Liars*

"This delectable read is both irresistible and fulfilling. . . . Riggle mesmerizes and enchants with this hope-filled, honest and remarkably raw tour-de-force. *Things We Didn't Say* is a beautiful account of modern family that resonates, restores and charms." —examiner.com

"*Real Life & Liars,* Kristina Riggle's sumptuous and rich debut novel, examines the complications that arise in family and marriage, love and heartbreak. With lush writing and nuanced, relatable characters, this book is a must-read for anyone who has ever been both grateful and driven mad by the people they love most: their family." —Allison Winn Scotch

"*The Life You've Imagined* is a richly woven story laced with unforgettable characters. Cami, Maeve, Anna, and Amy will snag your heart as they explore the sometimes wide chasm between hope and reality. A beautiful book." —Therese Walsh

—Keepsake—

Also by Kristina Riggle

Things We Didn't Say
The Life You've Imagined
Real Life & Liars

—Keepsake—

KRISTINA RIGGLE

wm

WILLIAM MORROW

An Imprint of HarperCollins*Publishers*

P.S.™ is a trademark of HarperCollins Publishers.

HarperCollins books may be purchased for educational, business, or sales promotional use. For information please write: Special Markets Department, HarperCollins Publishers, 10 East 53rd Street, New York, NY 10022.

FIRST EDITION

Designed by Diahann Sturge

Library of Congress Cataloging-in-Publication Data has been applied for.

ISBN 978-0-06-200307-2

12 13 14 15 16   OV/RRD   10 9 8 7 6 5 4 3 2 1

To Sam and Avery, my own genuine treasures

Chapter 1

The stranger gave me an empty smile. It was flat and mechanical: the forced grin of someone who delivers bad news all day long. She was holding out a business card, and I was refusing to take it.

Ayana Reese, the card said. What kind of name is Ayana? On her left hand, which was clutching her notepad, I saw no wedding ring. I could bet every shingle on my roof that this girl was barely out of college and had no children. She would have a pamphlet and a workbook and seminars, but she'd never pushed a child into the world and felt what I felt both times I did it: that our bond was powerful and perfect and would not be broken. By anyone.

Yet here she was, this tiny black woman with a huge messenger bag, holding out a business card with the words *Child Protective Services* as if my child needed protecting. From me.

I made to close the door but she stepped forward. I stopped the door only an inch from her face. She flinched, and I was glad.

"I don't want to come back here with the police, Mrs. Dietrich," she said. I detected in her voice a drawl she was trying to hide.

I considered Jack's reaction to the police pulling up here, knocking on this door.

I reminded myself that no one could love a child more than I love mine. So there would be nothing to hide. No matter what that busy-body Urgent Care doctor must have thought when he looked at Jack's shoulder last night.

I swung open the door and stood aside to let Ayana pass. I slammed it hard behind her, but she did not react.

The empty smile, however, was gone.

"I didn't know you were coming," I said.

"That's exactly the point," she replied. "We received a report about your son's injury and came to investigate his living environment."

"The doctor, huh? And I thought he was just making conversation." I should have known. As a cop's daughter I know what a "mandated reporter" is. But a broken collarbone from an accident at home? Worthy of a report?

"We're not allowed to say."

If Ayana was disgusted by my messy house, she didn't show it. She probably dealt all the time with meth heads and gangbangers who had loaded guns on the coffee table and shit on the walls. Some clutter wasn't going to faze anyone with an ounce of sense.

"Mama? Who's . . ." Jack appeared from his room, where he'd been reading. He stopped in midstep, one foot trailing behind him. "Oh. Miss Ayana."

"You know her?" I asked him, my palms slicking with sweat.

Ayana, still looking around and taking notes, said mildly, "We talked at school today."

"How dare you!" I exclaimed, then bit my lip: *Pull back, Trish. Don't frighten Jack.* I patted his head, told him it was fine, told him to return to his reading. He glanced back over his shoulder with widened, curious eyes before retreating to his room.

Ayana wound her way through my living room, jotting notes on a yellow pad.

"I don't know what you think you'll find," I said.

"Show me your son's room, please."

Panic was now snaking up my spine. What was happening here? What would I be saying to Jack about this? *"Honey, this lady says your home is dangerous and thinks you shouldn't live with Mommy anymore."*

This thought made tears prick at my eyes, and I clenched nails into my palms until I felt pissed off again.

She stopped in the hallway in front of Jack's room.

His door was open, as always. He didn't like to be separated from me by a closed door. He was sitting in what they used to call "Indian style" on the one clear space of his bed, the rest of its surface mounded with clothes I hadn't gotten around to folding and putting away. His drawers were stuffed with other clothes, anyway.

Jack looked up from his book. His face had that spooked look he would get from watching the Harry Potter movies, when things looked bad for the boy wizard and his friends. No matter how much I reassured him the hero would have to survive, that's the way things worked, he never believed me until the triumphant music played.

The pile of fallen things had not been cleared up just yet, except for the path I'd dug through to reach Jack. I pushed away that memory in order to focus on the real threat: this intruder with a clipboard, this . . . adolescent bureaucrat.

"This is what fell?" she asked, jotting again. She took out a camera and snapped photos.

"I didn't give you permission to take pictures."

She made another note—"uncooperative" maybe?—and resumed clicking. Then she turned her lens on the rest of his room.

"He doesn't sleep in there," I said, seeing her notice his bed that was piled with clothing.

"Where does he sleep?"

"With . . . In my room. On what used to be my husband's side of the bed. He's got plenty of space."

Ayana stepped away from Jack's doorway, deeper into the hall, cocking her head to get me to follow her. As I did she said under her breath, "He's seven years old. A seven-year-old should have his own bed"—here she began to tick off reasons on her fingers, as if reading from a chart—"for privacy, appropriateness, even hygiene."

"Hygiene? Are you telling me I'm filthy? He gets afraid at night."

"That happens sometimes," she said, her voice empty of conviction, already looking away.

She put a hand on the door across the hall from Jack's room. "No!" I shouted before I could stop myself. "That's just storage." I could hear the strain in my own voice.

She turned the knob and pushed, then shouldered the door open. She drew back slightly, her first visible reaction to my home since she'd crossed the threshold. She said nothing, only clicking a few pictures, before pulling the door closed again.

She repeated the same routine in my room. While she was snapping pictures I noticed some bras and panties I'd left lying out, and I shouldered my way in front of her, snatched them up and said, "Do you mind?" Ayana was passive, her face masked by the camera.

I had nowhere to put the underwear, not being able to reach the dirty clothes hamper, so I balled them up in my hand and followed her back to the living room.

Ayana turned to me. The empty smile was back. It made me feel cold down to my toes.

"Mrs. Dietrich, can we sit down somewhere, please?"

I led her to my couch. There were some shopping bags on one end, so we had to sit very close. Our knees were almost touching. "I interviewed your sons this morning, at school."

"How could you? Without my permission!"

I knew as soon as I said it what her answer would be. She replied something about official protocol when a report has been made. "I also spoke to your ex-husband."

"How dare you!" I said again, other words sputtering on my tongue, at a loss to express this betrayal, this sneaking and treachery.

"This is not a healthy environment for your sons. The fact is, Jack was injured by a pile of falling debris and there are many more such piles in this house. Further, he has no room of his own to sleep in. Even if he had no nighttime fears, there is no other bed for him here that he can use. A child deserves a place to sleep."

"He has a place to sleep."

"Irregardless . . ."

"Regardless. You mean 'regardless.' "

She drew herself up straighter on my couch, her eyes narrowing the tiniest bit. Then she blinked, back to cool and professional. "In any case. We have a problem here, and we need to help you address it."

"What . . . What are you going to do?" I settled back onto the couch. My bravado was crumbling. I wanted to stay pissed off because to be pissed off was powerful. But fear was outpacing anger.

"I'm going to file a report. We're going to refer you for a psychological evaluation and follow-up counseling."

"A psychological . . ." My vocabulary evaporated in the heat of my outrage. "I'm not crazy!"

"No one said you were. I'm also going to come back on a weekly basis to help you stay on track with cleaning up this environment. It's extremely hazardous not only for your children but for you as well. If something fell on you and if you were home alone, what would you do?"

She was exaggerating, twisting reality to suit her purposes. She'd made up her mind about this place before she even knocked on my door. I'm sure my older son didn't help matters. He'd turned on me long ago.

"What happens if I don't do it? If I refuse to go get *evaluated*. If I refuse to spill my guts to some shrink. What happens if I *can't* clean up, because if I could keep this house neater, don't you think I would? I'm a single mother, as you obviously already know."

"Surely you have some relatives who might be able to help you? Like I said, we can provide you support."

"There's an 'or else' here, I know there is. You're not just here to hold my hand. If I don't do what you say, if I don't get the house cleaned up, what will you do?"

"In theory, your case could be referred to a judge, but that's something we all want to avoid."

"And then what? What would this judge decide? What are you driving at, young lady?"

"Ma'am, I have a master's degree in social work so I'd appreciate it very much if you didn't call me 'young lady.' As to your question, the judge could issue a temporary order of removal until you clean up this house."

"Removal? To . . . to where?"

"That would be up to the judge. Likely to a family member such as the children's father. Maybe your parents."

"Father. I only have a father," I corrected, my voice trailing off as I pictured Jack being told he had to leave me. I had to fight for deep breaths as I imagined my little boy's fear and grief at being taken from me and the only home he's ever known. A perfect home, maybe not, but we made the best of it.

"I don't want that to happen, Mrs. Dietrich. I'd rather help you clean up your house. Don't you want that, too?"

"I do the best I can," I gulped out. "I'm not perfect."

As I knew she would, she handed me booklets and pamphlets, plus a business card for the psychologist I was apparently required to call, if I didn't want her to run to a judge to take away my kid. She then said she had some questions.

I heard her like we were underwater—distant, distorted—while I turned the business card over and over in my hand, the shrink's name spinning in and out of my vision. She asked me questions about my own history, probing questions about whether I'd ever been abused (no) and mental health problems in my family (no, I said, because it was none of her business) and, weirdly, whether I was Native American (duh). She reminded me to call the psychologist, who will determine whether I might need medication. At the state's expense, not mine, she assured me. I thought, *Drugs? This child who doesn't even know me is talking about drugging my brain?*

She offered to rent me a large garbage Dumpster for outside, and when she came back she would show me some sorting techniques.

"I'm not an idiot," I barked, jolted back to life by the thought of my things in a Dumpster. "I know how to clean, but I don't have time. Great, a garbage bin; can you also use taxpayer money to hire a cleaning crew to do the work because I'm a single mother with a full-time job! What I really need is time!"

"We don't expect perfection, Mrs. Dietrich. We do want to see progress. Please call me if you have any questions." At my doorway, she paused. Turned back. "Believe it or not, ma'am, we're not the enemy here. We are trying to help."

She closed the door behind her, and I listened to the crunching of her shoes across my gravel driveway. I held the papers she'd given me in my hands, not knowing where to put them. I was also still holding my underwear.

I was still standing there when I heard Jack's bedsprings squeak as he got up to come out to the living room.

I jammed the social worker papers under a grocery bag and threw my panties under the coffee table.

"Hi, pal!" I said, reaching out to hold him in a hug, carefully avoiding his injured shoulder.

"Hi, Mama."

"Was school okay today?" I wanted to ask, but knew I shouldn't, *What did you tell that social worker?*

"Fine. Everybody thought my brace was cool. They were bummed they couldn't sign it, though, like a cast."

Jack was wearing a white Velcro contraption that fastened his left arm to his side, bent at the elbow. The rigging pulled his shoulder back to the proper position to heal a broken collarbone.

"And, um . . . Did you talk about how it happened?"

"Yeah." He looked down at the worn toe of his sneakers. His feet were almost busting through. He wore out his cheap shoes so fast I had a stockpile of spares. "They thought it was cool, like a cave collapsed on an explorer."

I imagined the circle of boys, Jack at the center, telling this story, his towheaded bangs bouncing as he elaborated with his one good arm. He always could tell one helluva story, that kid. I imagined a playground aide overhearing, trading looks with another adult, over the boys' heads.

"Um, pal?" I ventured.

"Yeah?" Jack leaned back on the couch. He sat with one ankle crossed over the knee, just like Ron always used to, in that exact same spot on the couch.

"I don't think everybody needs to hear that whole story, do you?" I strained to sound casual. "I dunno, it just . . . It sounds kind of bad. That my things fell on you. Especially if you go making it sound very . . . dramatic."

"I'm sorry, Mama. I already told Ayana, cuz she asked. You always taught me not to lie, right?"

"I didn't mean you did anything wrong, I just . . . I just . . . Some things are not other people's business, is all."

Jack was saying, "I told her I didn't like how it was messy. She asked if I could wave a magic wand and fix anything what would I fix? And I said I'd want the house cleaner. And to have Daddy back here. Did I do something wrong, Mama? She said I shouldn't lie to her. Lying is bad, isn't it?"

"You're right, of course it is," I said, pulling him toward me gently to hold him, so he wouldn't see the tears snaking down my face. "You did fine. Just fine."

He nuzzled into my side, and I closed my eyes to drink up the moment. Before long he wouldn't let me hug him anymore, I know. Most of Jack's classmates already seemed so tough and masculine, their ages not even in double digits yet. And Drew might never come home again, given the events of the last two days.

"I think we should clean up around here, though, don't you, pal?"

I could feel him nodding. "Yeah. That would be good."

"I'm sorry it's so messy."

"What do we always say, Mama?"

I smiled, eyes still closed, and we sang out softly together, "Mommy's not perfect!"

After Jack drifted off for the night and I came back to the living room to watch TV, I heard a rattling at the front door. I yelped at first, then crept past a pile of storage crates to try to get a look out the front window . . .

The door swung open and I was terrified and then saw it was Andrew.

"Drew! You scared me out of my mind!"

"I texted you I was coming."

I whirled around, trying to remember where I'd put my cell phone. "I wish I'd known; I'd have put sheets on your bed."

Drew snorted, tossing his hair as he did so. "Like you can even see my bed. I just stopped by for a minute. I need my report card. They mailed them, and I have to get you to sign it and take it back to school."

He brushed abruptly past me without even a hug. It stung, this contrast between sweet Jack who will still nuzzle me, and my older son who doesn't even live here anymore, truth be told. Just like Mary did to our mother, he hightailed it out of here. Every night, he sleeps at his girlfriend's parents' house. Why her parents allow that I haven't the foggiest idea but if he creeps in her room and gets her pregnant, I will bash his punk rock head in.

He grabbed papers off a stack on the kitchen table. In the yellow kitchen light his blackened hair glowed almost blue. He was such a handsome young man, always was, and then he had to go and ruin it by putting all that black stuff everywhere. Even his fingernails were black, which would get a boy's ass kicked back in my day. His high sharp cheekbones gave him a hungry, hawkish look, just like his biological father had.

"By the way, I had an interesting day at school," he snarled, still snapping his way through my papers.

"How so?" I asked, though I already knew.

"A social worker came to talk to me. Now that was a laugh riot. They called me down to the office, and I could see all those office ladies staring at me and wondering why a social worker is coming to visit me at school."

"I didn't know they were going to do that," I offered weakly.

"She wanted to know if I'm doing drugs, if I'm drinking, if anyone beats on me. Not that she said it exactly like that, but I get the idea. So after a while she's leading me to talk about the house and it dawns on me—oh, that's how Jack hurt his arm. Not roughhousing on the playground, right, Mom?"

I shifted under his intense gaze. "No. Not roughhousing. Some things fell on him here."

"Well, you'll be glad to know that I didn't tell her you lied to me about what really happened. But I also didn't tell her that home was a fabulous paradise. I figured she knew better than that already or she wouldn't have pulled me out of English class. Fuck, I can't find anything in here." He threw down a fistful of paper and turned to me. "So now the doctor reported you, and if you don't clean up they'll take Jack away, is that about the size of it?"

"They're not going to take Jack away. I'll just do some cleaning and it'll be fine."

"*Some* cleaning? You'll need a fuckload more than 'some.' "

"Watch your language."

"Where are they gonna send him?"

"Nowhere! I'm gonna clean!"

"You've 'cleaned' before, Mom. And know what happens? You buy a bunch of storage bins and you decide you can't part with anything and nothing changes. They'll probably make me live with someone else, too, you know. I'm only seventeen. So unless Miranda's parents become my guardians, then what—I get shipped off to my dead father's relatives I don't even know? Or to Ron?"

"I doubt it, and anyway, you'll be eighteen soon . . ."

"Almost a year from now. And even assuming you *want* to clean this time, how are you gonna do it? You can't do it by yourself."

"You can help me, right?"

"I've got school! And you work all day! You gonna hire some magic cleaning elves?"

"Andrew Dietrich, don't you start with me."

"I don't know why I bother to start." He shook his head at the table. "Forget this, it's hopeless. I'll tell them the dog ate my report card and pick one up at the office. I'll stop by your work so you can sign it."

With that he started toward the door.

"Andy!"

"You know I like 'Drew' now."

"Drew, then. How is your report card? Do you know?"

"All A's, probably. Just like always."

With that he slammed out of my house and stomped to his rattly old car, back to his girlfriend's house, leaving me alone with my things.

Chapter 2

When at last I recognized the man on my porch, I thought, *Trish is dead; it happened again.*

At first he was a stranger to me. When I drew closer, I noticed the leather jacket I'd seen in photos, graffitied as it was with Sex Pistols patches and anarchy symbols. My nephew was seated on my porch steps, hunched forward, his head drooping low like he found it too heavy.

I approached slowly, my arms weighted down by a cardboard box.

He looked up. Those were still Andy's deep brown puppy eyes, but now they were ringed with black eyeliner and set in a face that was hard and sharp, with a shadow of beard on his chin.

His soft brown hair was dyed an angry black and hung half over his face. He raked his fingers through it—nails also painted black—and stood up.

So tall!

There was so much of him there on my porch that I suffered sensory overload. With some quick mental math I determined he must be seventeen.

"Andy," I finally said.

"I go by Drew, now."

"What's wrong?"

I shifted the box in my arms. Its contents rolled and rattled, and I nudged it back up with my knee.

"I didn't have your number," was all he said. He shoved his hands far down into his pockets. His black jeans were ripped.

"It's a long drive from Grand Ledge."

"Not so long."

My feet throbbed in my work shoes, and my shoulder bag slipped down to my elbow, yanking at the box and nearly spilling it. I wished Andrew would offer to take it.

"Did something happen to your mother?"

"Not yet," he replied with a scowl.

"Well, come in, I guess," I said, clumping up the steps with my unbalanced load.

"Gee, thanks," he replied. I winced, and I hoped he would interpret that as a grimace of effort.

I plopped the box down on the small cement porch near a mat that said WELCOME bordered by cheerful daisies.

His presence unnerved me so much that I bobbled my keys.

A nauseating swell of panic churned as I contemplated letting this young man—my nephew, yes, but a virtual stranger—into my home. I exhaled slowly, from the abdomen, and shoved the door open.

He picked up my box and brought it inside. He stood like a delivery boy just at the threshold. My nephew looked at the box and then asked where to put it with a light, silent shrug. I pointed to a spot along the wall.

He grunted as he deposited it and looked at me with his eyebrows quirked as if to ask a question. I pretended not to notice.

"Can I get you something?" I asked. Really I had no idea about hospitality. It was something I'd seen people say in movies and TV shows, and it made a certain kind of sense.

He shook his head and lingered in the entryway.

"Sit down for goodness' sake. And, Andy, tell me what's going on."

"It's Drew." He scanned the room looking for a place to sit. I realized that I should have indicated one for him. I froze in the moment of deciding which chair would be best.

Without waiting for me, he opted for a kitchen chair, so I joined him there, kitty corner to where he sat at my table. I tried not to drum my fingers as he worked up to tell me what the hell brought him to my town house, unannounced, after all this time. . . . I hadn't seen him since his hobby was doing tricks on his BMX bike.

"We need your help," he said, worrying a hangnail next to one of his black-tipped fingers. I thought, bizarrely, he was going to ruin his nail polish doing that.

"Help with what? Is she sick?"

"How long has it been since you've seen her place?"

I tried to think. It must have been . . . eight years or so. When Jack was born.

"It's been a good while," I answered, seeking comfort in being vague, not sounding quite so awful. I reminded myself Trish had never been to my home. So if we were keeping score, I was still ahead.

"It's gotten worse," Andy—*Drew,* that is—said, for the first time meeting my eyes directly.

He didn't have to say what "it" could be.

"How bad?"

"Jack got hurt. Broke his collarbone."

"Oh, God."

"That's not the worst part."

I realized I'd been holding my breath, as if I could freeze time and stop myself from hearing this. It's amazing how when you wake up some days you have no idea that your life will be inside-out by sunset.

"The doctor reported Mom. If she doesn't clean up, they're going to take Jack away."

I tried to comprehend Trish's reaction to this. I lacked the imagination to register her grief.

"Where . . . where would he go?"

"To Ron, probably." He said it like "prolly." He'd been looking so much like a grown man I'd forgotten that he himself was actually still a kid.

"And you?"

He shrugged, slouching down in the chair, crossing his feet at the ankles. That's when I noticed a glob of dirt slide off his Converse onto my cream-colored carpet. As casually as I could manage, I rose, turned to the kitchen, and pulled a piece of paper towel off the roll. Meanwhile, Andrew said, "I stay most of the time at Miranda's house. Her parents are cool. I'll be eighteen next year anyway."

I crouched down next to the dirt spot. Andrew yanked his feet back as if I were going to tie his laces together or something. I picked up the dirt gingerly, fearing that if I disturbed the integrity of the blob that more would spill. It could get everywhere.

"How can I stop that from happening? I'm not a lawyer or anything." I dropped the paper towel in the trash can and exhaled.

"You've gotta help her clean. It's too much for her to do alone."

"Well, I mean . . . When?"

"Now. Tomorrow. It's the first time since before Ron left that she even acts like she might want to try to clean up. If we don't act now, we'll lose our chance forever."

And he was back to sounding like an adult again. I shook my head, raised my hands, helpless. "I can't just drop everything and fly to her side."

"Forget it." Andrew stood up, bashing the chair back into place so hard I jumped and my gaze went right to the table, looking for marks. "I don't know why I bothered, *Aunt Mary*." His mocking tone highlighted how seldom he'd had occasion to speak those words.

"No, wait, I didn't mean . . ."

"No, forget it. You're right. You shouldn't have to be bothered. It's not like your nephew's welfare should concern you at all, or the fact that your own sister could die just like her mother."

With this he was striding across my floor, so tall and fast that he was out the door for that last vicious phrase.

"I'll come! I will, maybe not tomorrow, but . . ."

He was already climbing into a car I hadn't noticed before, parked in front of the next town house down. He threw his arm back at me, too aggressively for a wave. I didn't think I'd seen a middle finger. Rather, it looked like he was swatting away an annoying bug.

He didn't burn rubber. He pulled away carefully, even signaling before he joined the light flow of traffic on my sedate suburban street.

My box remained where Andrew put it next to the wall. I hefted it up again and brought it to my kitchen table for sorting. As I passed the spot on the carpet where Andrew's feet had been, I noticed a smudge. A tiny dot of ashlike dirt remained.

I left my box and went to find my cleaning supplies. OxiClean carpet spray, yellow gloves to protect my hands. I gave the spot a squirt and then a few more, then sat back on the carpet to let the chemicals work their magic.

The shadow of the box felt strange, off-kilter. I'd have to move it soon. I'd have to find places for these work things I used to have at the store, break down the box, and put it in the recycle bin. My work things had to become home things, I supposed. Maybe some of the things wouldn't be able to transition, and I'd have to get rid of them.

My nephew's arrival had startled me so much that for a few minutes I'd forgotten about George, and the bookstore, and my sad little cardboard box.

George had looked incongruously cheerful when he opened up the store for the last day of business. I wondered briefly if he was high, or drunk, or something, though that would be out of character for him.

But he called me Mary-Mary with a big gorgeous smile as he swept by me, depositing a steaming coffee at the checkout counter where I was getting the registers ready for our last day. Mary-Mary was his nickname for me, short for Mary-Mary-Quite-Contrary, which other people had tried to use and I always squashed, angrily enough they wouldn't try to persist. I was well aware of the irony of being cranky about that and would entertain homicidal fantasies every time someone felt pressed to point it out.

George said it with a sense of cheery irony, I thought. Like calling a fat guy "Tiny."

So I sipped that coffee and watched the hands spin around the clock all day, a fluttery sensation building in my chest, and even in my hands. I dropped lots of things. I did not dread the closing of the store. I rather anticipated talking to George at the end of the day, finally and at long last no longer his employee. Interests no longer conflicting.

My giddiness increased when he walked by me near the end of the shift and murmured in my ear, "Let's talk in my office after closing."

He'd nudged me as he went by, having dive-bombed this invitation to me, and I allowed my heart to leap. A little experimental flight, to see how it would feel.

So we said good-bye to the last weeping customer and I almost slammed the door on the back of her heels. Some of the people who'd been saddest about our closure had never spent more than $3 on a latte per visit and read our magazines without paying. I wished on those types an uncomfortable rash in a place they couldn't scratch in public.

I followed George to his office, nearly skipping, feet barely tethered to the ground.

He sat down on his side of his desk—he hadn't cleaned his off yet—and folded his hands. He beamed out at me, and I sat on my own hands not to leap across his desk and throw myself into his lap.

"I'm getting married," he blurted.

I became a mannequin on my chair, my expectant smile frozen to my face.

He took a picture frame that had been sitting on his desk, and he turned it to face me. A lovely young woman with short dark hair in feathery curls smiled out at me from under George's arm.

"Her name is Melissa. I'll send you an invitation. You'll have to make sure you tell me if you relocate so I can get your new address." With this he scribbled on a piece of paper. He slid it across to me. I grasped that it was an e-mail address, but a fog of stupid had gathered in my head.

How had he met, courted, and fallen in love with someone without me ever knowing?

I asked something to the effect of why we hadn't met her at the store.

She's a nurse, he said, she works weird hours. "And I assume," he continued, still with that jaunty smile I'd grown to love, grown to imagine he'd saved just for me, "that your next word will be 'Congratulations.'"

"Of course," I mumbled. I detected no sense of embarrassment from him, no recognition this might come as a shock, or unwelcome news. I'd been Miss Moneypenny for years to an oblivious James Bond.

He chattered about the wedding date and his father's plans for a new business venture for him, and I started to remember, like a trauma victim whose amnesia is fading, various mentions of a girl named Melissa. So this would be why he was so ebullient this morning though his beloved store was closing. His rich father's money would catch him like a fireman's net, and he could marry his one true love while the rest of us stood on the unemployment line in the worst economy any of us could remember.

He finally noticed that I wasn't beaming with happiness.

It was a lucky break that I could pretend my distress was related to my joblessness and the closure of the store where I'd worked for thirteen years as manager, one of George's first hires when he had the brainstorm to open his own bookstore. Back then, we were both U-M grads and booksellers at the original Borders. I was trying to figure out if I could afford grad school and panicking each time I pondered having to teach undergrads, and he was dabbling in writing a play. So when George told me he wanted me to manage his store, I was relieved to have a plan, and more than that, what washed over me was an unfamiliar sense of specialness. After all, I'd been chosen, hadn't I? Out of the whole crop of young booksellers there, he'd picked me to start the store with him. For that he could call me Mary-Mary and I would never object.

I always knew the store could close, but I'd thought that would happen early, and when it didn't . . . I couldn't imagine George ever letting it go.

Yet here he was, looking at me with pity. George came around to my side of the desk, crouched down next to me. It was an awkward positioning. He was much shorter than me this way. He took my hand, and part of me wanted to yank it back.

Mostly I wanted to savor this last time he would ever touch me.

"You'll be OK," he said. "I've written you an amazing letter of reference. I'll talk to my connections; maybe we can get you a position with one of the publishers, as a sales rep or something. Anyway, you're better than this store. You're brilliant."

"Brilliant," I muttered, now, out loud in my silent home. I scrubbed in the OxiClean, pushing hard and taking pleasure in the white foam squirting up around my paper towel.

George was wrong. I'm not brilliant in the least. Brilliant things shine, stun you with their glow. Whatever intelligence I have is the manila envelope of smarts: perfectly adequate and unnoticed.

I stood up from the carpet spot after wiping it dry with another paper towel and then stood back to survey the dining area carpet. Yes. Definitely gone. I tugged off the gloves and laid them carefully next to each other on the kitchen counter to dry.

With this I retreated down the hall to my room, with its neatly made bed and organized bookcase. No one from work had ever been in my room. They'd no doubt be stunned at the neatness of my shelves. Everyone was always complaining about the avalanche of advance copies we get and the books bought with our discount. I've always been careful about what I bring into my home, however.

I peeled off my work pants and my lilac blouse and dropped them in the laundry bag in the adjoining bathroom, yanking the drawstring tight.

Having slid into my after-work uniform of yoga pants and a big T-shirt, I returned to the living room, sweeping my eyes across everything, catching on the out-of-place box.

In the dining room, my eradication of the dirt blob had created a new problem. Now that part of the carpet was distinctly lighter. I looked away and looked back, to see if it had been a trick of the eye. No, it definitely was lighter there. Now the whole rest of the carpet in my whole entire front of the town house was clearly a dingy gray, and I hadn't seen it before. Thank goodness Andy brought in that dirt.

Well, I told myself, time to abandon my plans for the evening and get out the carpet cleaner.

As I wrestled the machine from the closet I reflected on that: plans. What plans? No schedules to figure out, no job applications to review, no inventory to order, no work e-mail to answer.

I filled the reservoir of the carpet cleaner with soap solution at my sink and pondered what I'd earlier said to my nephew about Trish. That I couldn't just drop everything and fly to her side.

Well, now I had no job. I'd have to find a new one eventually, but with unemployment benefits, the severance pay that George was able to provide, and my own savings—having no one in my life to spend money on, I quite simply didn't spend it—there was no urgency to that effort and I didn't relish starting. In my town house I had no pets— urine, pet hair, dirt tracked in from outside, no thanks. Not even a houseplant.

As I plugged the cleaning solution into the machine and fired up its whirring, sucking motion on my dingy carpet, it occurred to me that in actual fact if I spontaneously combusted at that exact moment, the most significant impact would be the mess on the floor.

The machine sucked the solution back up off the carpet and I noticed all the dirt swirling around. *Aha!* I told an invisible someone who was telling me that cleaning my carpet for one piece of dirt was stupid and crazy. *Look at all that filth!*

Filth like what Trish would be living in, or more to the point, little Jack. Filth bad enough to cause my teenage nephew to scrounge up my address from somewhere, drive himself all the way here, and lie in wait for me.

Chapter 3

Jack bounced his way out of the school doors, with his backpack flopping off one shoulder, and my heart got its daily shot of joy at seeing him so happy to see me.

"Mama!" he shouted and grabbed me around the hip with his one good arm.

I settled for a kiss on the forehead and an awkward squeeze around his middle instead of my usual bear hug, which would hurt him right now.

"Hey, pal. How was your day?" His day was not only a full day in school but a couple of hours at after-school day care in the building. I worried like any mother about all the time away from me and his adultlike schedule, but what else could I do? Unless my ex decided to swoop in and marry me again, or I won the lottery, there was no choice to make.

Thinking of Ron reminded me of those text messages and voice mails I'd been ignoring. I shoved down thoughts of the man who left us, and I smiled at the one boy in my life who still loved me.

Jack dropped his gaze. "Fine." I craned my neck to try to get a peek at his face.

A parent honked in the carpool drop-off behind me, and I stuck out my tongue at her. Jack giggled. "That's Olivia's mom. I don't like Olivia very much because she says I'm weird."

"Sticking out tongues isn't very nice, I know. But what do we always say?"

"Mommy's not perfect!" we sang out together as I helped him into the car, buckling him since he couldn't do it himself.

I pulled my beat-up Chevy Malibu into traffic, the rattly exhaust making it too hard to talk while I accelerated.

Out on the road, I tilted the mirror to see Jack's face. He was nibbling on his fingernails again, just like his brother. "Pal, fingers out of your mouth."

"They're not *in* my mouth."

He put his hand in his lap, but within moments his hand drifted up again.

"Jack, so what happened in school today? You seem a little down."

"Don't worry, Mama, I didn't tell anyone else about it."

"About what, pal?" I asked, even though I knew.

"The stuff in our house. I just said I fell."

Just yesterday he'd told that social worker the full story, and now, after talking to me, he was already editing the story for public consumption. What kind of mother . . . Car taillights, far too close, grabbed my attention. I had to stomp hard on the brake to avoid rear-ending a truck stopped for a left turn.

Jack cried out, and when I looked back, he was bent over, free hand on his hurt shoulder. I pulled the car over and released him from the seat belt. I sat on the grassy outlawn of a strip mall, hazard lights on in my Malibu, holding him as he cried for his sore, broken shoulder, pinched painfully by the shoulder belt. We were still ten minutes from home on a patch of brown grass in a cloud of vehicle exhaust, but I ignored all that. I rocked him back and forth, as my car chimed *ding, ding, ding* to tell me my door was open.

* * *

I hurried through the front door, glancing back over my shoulder before I closed it, looking for people on the road who might see inside my house. But it's spacious out here, and wooded. An easy place to keep secrets. Also, easy to get lost.

Hot, panicky rage bubbled up again at the memory of Ayana's visit, her interviews of my children without me even knowing, calling my ex. Eventually I'd have to take his call and deal with the shitstorm this Ayana girl had started. But I sure as hell wasn't going to do that at my desk at work.

To think they could take my son away, and for all things, a messy house! Maybe the TV guys were right, the government really was out of control, now threatening to take away my child if I didn't do what they said, not to mention making me see some shrink who might decide I need medication. As if the government had any right to decide what I put in my body. That was only yesterday, but it might as well have been a whole other era. B.A. for Before Ayana.

I reached out to help Jack step over some clothes on the living room floor, but he shrugged off my hand. "I can do it, Mom," he protested, voice spiky with irritation. He sat down on the couch and took out his homework, arranging it in his lap, and reaching into his bag again for a pencil.

Without asking if he needed it, I grabbed an old record album—*Slippery When Wet,* Bon Jovi—and slipped it under his papers so he'd have a hard surface.

He was already staring at the paper, his brow creased with deep thought about first-grade math.

I found my cordless phone on the recliner arm, and my heart quickened.

Two new messages.

I ran my thumb lightly over the phone buttons and reviewed my options again, same as I did last night after Drew stormed out. I could hire a lawyer. With what money? And how would I find one anyway, in the Yellow Pages under "bad mother attorneys"?

Run away. Pack a change of clothes, close the door behind us, and never come back. A tempting fantasy, but I'd never do that to Ron and the boys. I'd never split them up, whatever had passed between us as adults.

Clean up. The only thing left to do.

A glance around the whole of my house made my throat close up, so instead I turned to the pile on the kitchen counter in front of me. I would need this cleaned up anyway, to get dinner ready.

The first paper was Jack's spelling test. His teacher had written, "Great work!" though Jack had written a couple of his letters backward. I reveled for a moment in his penmanship, how carefully he formed the "w" with its precise little points, and fingered the scratchy brown school paper. Many things had changed, but they still used that grainy brownish paper . . .

I shook my head. This would never do. *Concentrate, Trish.*

I put Jack's schoolwork on a pile on the kitchen table behind me for saving. Someday he'd be a grown-up teenager like Drew and not take spelling tests or draw stick figures or ride a bike anymore. This scratchy brown paper was a snapshot of time. A keepsake.

The next thing was an announcement about a field trip coming up next week. I glanced around, and then slipped that one on top of the microwave. Would have to keep that handy so I'd see it and remember to send him with a sack lunch for a trip to the zoo.

School newsletter. It had some calendar dates on it, which I'd have to put in my datebook.

Where's my datebook? It might have been in the car, because I called that stupid shrink on my cell while cowering in my car so my boss wouldn't overhear. But I could have sworn I brought it in . . .

I left the pile and started to rummage in the table papers, which then fell in a swoosh onto the floor.

The phone ringing made me yelp a little. I couldn't see the caller ID number from here.

"Mama!" called Jack from the couch. "The phone's ringing!"

I snatched it up quickly, scrunching my eyes shut as I answered, "Hello?"

"Hi, um, Trish?"

I opened my eyes. "Yeah? Who's this?"

"It's Mary."

"What happened? Is Dad OK?"

"Nothing. He's fine."

"Oh. Are you OK?"

"Yes, I'm perfectly fine."

"Well, then. That's good."

Jack had turned on the TV. Had he whipped through his homework so quickly? Some days I thought I should homeschool him, because he just flew through his work so fast like he never even had to think about it. . . . But I'm a single mother. I've got to work. Anyway, where would I find space for homeschool stuff?

"So, Trish, is everything OK?"

"Fine, why?"

"Um. Andy came to see me."

"What? Why in the hell would he do that? How does he even know where you live?"

"I don't know. I didn't ask him. He told me that Jack got hurt."

My knuckles burned as I gripped the phone. My own son, turncoat and traitor. My first baby whose diapers I changed and who I nurtured alone after his father . . .

"Trish, are you there?"

"Yeah."

"He said you need some help. Do you need some help?"

My instinct was to scream no and hang up on her. My sister was always one to criticize even when things were better.

I looked at the papers in front of me, the piles not at all smaller, only shifted, and the new avalanche that had cascaded from my kitchen table. I still didn't have my datebook. But Mary? The perfect one, coming in here to scrutinize this? *That'll be the day,* I thought, but said, "Things are fine here. I can handle it."

"How about if I come over? I'm free tomorrow."

"Not here. But maybe we can meet for dinner. You are my sister, I guess."

"Dinner would be nice."

I told Mary I'd get back to her about the time once I figured out what to do with Jack. I had a distinct feeling I wouldn't want him eavesdropping on whatever it was Mary would have to say. I hung up and stared at the phone with its "two new messages" blinking at me. I clicked a few buttons without listening and made the blinking go away.

How long had it been since I'd even seen her? I tried to think. . . . When Jack was born. Almost eight years ago. She'd come to visit, bringing with her a picture book called *Love You Forever,* which would become one of Jack's very favorites, and mine, too, truth be told. But that day, she spent the whole visit as close to the door as she could, only peeking at her infant nephew, declining an offer to hold him. Something about her seemed desperately uncomfortable, and as full of the hormone storm as I was, aching from the birth and the sleepless nights already, I was in no mood to dig through her defense mechanisms. Some old friends from high school dropped by then, and she slipped out with barely a word.

My house was only run-of-the-mill messy at the time. Baby equipment, new diapers, wipes, receiving blankets, boxes of nursing pads. All over the place, yes, like someone had ransacked Babies "R" Us, but I'd just given birth! Was she expecting me to clean up for her while I was still bleeding, for God's sake? That would be the frickin' day.

If we were a normal family, I might have still seen her at holiday dinners, but after a few strained and painful gatherings in the wake of Mom's death where we all exhausted ourselves faking family unity, Mary became too busy at the store to break free for a Thanksgiving meal or a Christmas Eve church service.

I texted Drew to call me.

"Jack, honey, what do you want for dinner?"

"Pizza."

I turned the oven on to preheat and was glad I didn't have to use the burners tonight.

On the kitchen wall calendar I saw a date circled in black. Spring break was coming, creeping up on me. That meant a week without Jack. Ronald would take him to his parents' place, a condo along the lakeshore. Jack would tell me how bored he'd get in an old people's place where they had hardly any toys and how he wasn't allowed to bring much because they didn't have much space.

That's where Ronald would always go with Jack. He never did know how to be alone with his son, so he would make his mom do the motherly type things I always did. Pauline had raised her own kids with a "let them entertain themselves, toss them in the playpen" school of thought, so I know damn well that Jack wandered through the rooms and cried himself to sleep every night, though Ronald always tried to sugarcoat it and pretend being on the lake made it all better, and that Jack liked his grandma Dietrich's cookies.

Every time I dropped off Jack at Ronald's place, we'd all have these huge, sad eyes and I'd think, what are we doing this for, anyway?

If Ronald would come home, we could put an end to it. He can't, he told me.

Can't. Bullshit "can't." He meant "won't."

My phone chimed. Drew texted back, *What.*

Dammit. I'd get him on the phone if I had to make his phone ring every five minutes for the rest of the night. He'd better not be getting that girl pregnant.

I was throwing the pizza in when Drew picked up, sounding a little breathless. "What?"

"Don't 'what' me, I'm paying for that phone and when I tell you to call me, you better frickin' call me."

"So cut off the phone, then you can't harass me when I'm busy."

I closed my eyes, put the phone to my chest, and mouthed a blistering streak of swear words at the ceiling before putting the phone back to my ear.

"Drew, why did you go see my sister?"

"You know why."

"Well, now she wants to talk to me, so you have to watch Jack."

"What? I'm busy! I've got studying!"

"So study while you watch him. He's not that high maintenance."

"I'm not coming over there."

"You mean your *home*?"

His voice dripped with derision. "That's not my *home*. It's a box filled with garbage."

"I did not raise you to talk to me that way. Do you enjoy hurting me, Drew? Do you have any idea what it does to me to hear you say these things?"

A part of me knew that wasn't fair. That maybe it was dirty pool to manipulate my child, but it's not manipulation if it's true. He killed me every day.

He'd been silent a moment. "I'll pick him up and we'll go somewhere."

"Not to Miranda's!"

"Why not?"

"Because I said so. Take him to the library to do your homework, both of you, and when you're done, you can take him to McDonald's or something. I'll pay."

"No, I got it."

Drew had started a side business building websites and was making quite a bit of money, for a teenager.

"Fine. I'll text you with the time."

I pulled out the pizza and balanced the pan on a box resting on top of the stove burners. Slicing it on this unsteady surface was tricky; the pan shifted and singed my arm.

"Shit!"

Jack appeared in the kitchen entry. "What, Mama? You swore."

"I know. Mommy isn't perfect. I just burned my arm a tiny bit, hon. Grab the paper plates, OK? If you can?"

"Yeah, I can," he said, sighing heavily. He'd already gotten pretty good at moving around one-handed.

He fished some paper plates out of a grocery bag near the garage door. I finished slicing and grabbed us each a Sprite from the fridge and we returned to the living room.

"Oh, not SpongeBob again, Jack."

"You think he's funny."

"Nuh-uh."

"Do so. I saw you chuckle at Patrick."

I looked over at my Jack, with his white-blond flop of hair and gap-toothed grin, and the laughter broke loose. "OK. Busted. But don't tell the grown-ups at school I like SpongeBob. I'll never admit it in public."

"Don't worry, Mom. I can keep secrets," said Jack, balancing his paper plate on his knees, holding his pizza one-handed, as we ate our dinner on our island of a couch.

My cell phone rang again, and I sighed with resignation as the caller ID flashed my ex-husband's name.

Chapter 4

The sky was teasingly bright, but cold. My Corolla wound through the streets of Grand Ledge, and I kept missing the address Trish gave me, distracted as I was by the façades in the tiny downtown. A flat, slow stretch of the Grand River threaded through the heart of the town, and the well-preserved old buildings put me in mind of ladies with bustles and parasols. Quaint would be a word for it, like that little Christmas town our mother used to put up around the base of the tree. She got so excited about all the little buildings that the town soon fell victim to suburban sprawl and became bigger around than the base of the tree itself, exploding around the living room. It got so we would have to step over the tiny post office to go upstairs to the bathroom.

I chuckled, remembering the time Trish and I pretended our Barbie and Ken dolls were nuclear-mutated giants and had them "walking" about, kicking over the little Christmas town houses. When Mom saw, she was livid and I cowered before her anger. Trish tossed her hair and laughed it off. Right up into our adulthood I remained in awe of her ability to stand firm in the face of Mom's fury. Why did she get all the strength? If I could have only borrowed some from her like I used to wear her favorite sweaters, maybe I would have dared get another job, rather than cling to the safety of that bookstore like a kid holds on to a frayed blankie.

I parked the car near a riverside walkway to study the map I'd printed out to find my way here. I imagined my mother crying at how separate we sisters had become—yes, I'd even say estranged was the better word. But she wasn't here to hold us together anymore, and her death had in fact driven us further apart.

There had been no final showdown, no phones banged down in the heat of argument. It would be easier to patch things up, in a way, if there had been one clean break. Instead, our relationship wore out like an unraveling sweater.

Trish was mad at me, I know, for not making it to family dinners. She huffed and sighed, broadcasting her irritation and disbelief when I said I had to work every time the family planned a painful charade of togetherness for Thanksgiving, or Christmas, at Dad and Ellen's condo. But I enjoyed the overtime pay, and the younger employees who had families were as grateful as panting puppies every time I took over a shift.

The last time I was at Trish's, I'd brought my favorite picture book as a gift for tiny baby Jack, just born. I'd walked up her porch steps determined to say something comforting about the absence of our mother, how she was smiling down on little Jack, though I didn't really believe that kind of thing. I was going to reach across the divide and be kind to her, as a way of making amends for skipping those awful holiday dinners.

Once I stepped inside, she barely acknowledged me. She was barking orders at Ron to fetch her this and that, she was burping the baby, she was rubbing cream on his reddened cheeks, she was talking to little Andrew about school. She smiled at the book for a mere heartbeat before tossing it aside—a literal toss, it became briefly airborne before settling on top of a grocery bag out of which spilled diaper cream and baby wipes—and then she was reaching into her bra to whip out her breast right in front of me as the baby began wailing.

When a passel of girls she'd known in high school came in with balloons and flowers and a casserole, I told her good-bye and let myself out. All the way home I wondered why I hadn't thought to bring a casserole.

We were Facebook friends, though. That's how I found out about her split with Ronald. When she changed her relationship status and there was a little icon of a broken heart, I thought, *too bad,* and *poor Trish* and, *really, Facebook? A broken heart?*

I did not call her. She did not call me.

I looked up through the windshield and decided just to walk the rest of the way. It couldn't be far, as the center of town was little more than two intersections.

On foot, I finally spotted it. I hadn't thought to ask what kind of company it was—I once had known, but had forgotten, and she might have changed jobs and hadn't told me. As such I hadn't known what to expect.

The façade said KENDRICK AND ADAMS in spare Helvetica lettering on a small brass plate, which is why I'd driven past it several times. Suite two.

I stepped into a narrow hallway and followed it back past the street-facing shop, which was some kind of crafty store with cute little knick-knacks jamming the display window.

I found the Kendrick and Adams door. When I pushed it open, the door made a *hush* sound brushing across thick carpet. The lobby was a tiny nook, in the center of which was a reception desk.

Trish sat behind the high desk, a phone headset over her frizzy hair, which was grayer than I'd remembered. She glanced up at me and gave me an "I'll be right with you" look, which made me wonder if she recognized me.

"Let me see what I can schedule with Angela," she said into the phone, her voice smooth and efficient, like a television news anchor. Her fingers clacked away at a keyboard I couldn't see.

A window next to the entry door faced uselessly into the dark hallway. I snuck a peek into it to see if I looked so different from eight years ago. Straight, flat hair cut shoulder length and with a sharp line of even bangs across my too-high forehead. A long, narrow nose that I never liked in profile. No reason she shouldn't know me. A few extra crow's-feet certainly wouldn't throw her.

I might even have worn this shirt eight years ago, or something very much like it.

As Trish finished up her task, I took my time observing her. Her hair was still frizzed out and curly, having inherited that from our mother. It had been brown once upon a time, but now was shot through with gray. She was wearing a blazer that looked strange on her; I was used to seeing her in embroidered tunics and flowy skirts. It was like she'd gotten cold and borrowed someone else's coat.

She hung up at last, clicked a few last keys, then turned to me.

For a half second I held my breath.

"Mary," she said, and then swung around the desk to greet me. She was wearing, I could see now, a flowy skirt indeed, and brown high-heeled boots. She swept over to me and squeezed me in a hug.

My hands got caught in her hair when I hugged her. There was so much hair! Her tub drain must get constantly clogged.

She sat me back at arm's length. "You look great," she said.

"No, I don't," I responded, then looked down at my feet. "Thanks. Hi."

Trish was about to say something else when a voice cut through the air like a trumpet blast. "Patricia! What's going on out there?"

"Sorry, Mrs. Adams, my sister stopped in."

The woman who must be Mrs. Adams emerged from the recesses of the office. She was weirdly petite for such a frightening voice, and she propped her tiny doll-hands on her slim hips and stood akimbo.

She looked like someone who'd spent much time trying to seem bigger than she was. Like a puffer fish, or one of those lizards with a big frill.

I bit the inside of my lip to keep from bursting out laughing about this because my sister looked abashed and a little pale.

"It's almost closing time, so she just came in to wait."

"Yes. *Almost* closing. If you can't finish your workday with her here, then ask her to wait outside."

Mrs. Adams stomped back to her office, or she would have stomped, had she the mass necessary to make a sound against the thick carpet. She never once looked at me.

Trish was already moving back behind her desk.

I took the hint and sat quietly in a chair near the entry door, leafing through a *Newsweek* from the tiny table. I looked at my watch: 4:55 P.M.

For the next five minutes, the phone didn't ring. No one came in. Trish didn't look at me. Instead she busied herself behind her desk, but with what I couldn't see. She seemed to be moving things around. At one point I saw her take out a squirt bottle and a lemony fragrance wafted over to me as she wiped something down.

The minute hand ticked up to the twelve and Trish sighed. She shed her blazer and hung it over the chair and reached down somewhere to pick up a battered leather jacket and her purse, a denim thing with leather fringes swinging off it.

She shot me a look and called, "G'night, Mrs. Adams!" over her shoulder before escaping into the hall. She didn't look at me as we darted through the passage. I half expected to turn and see the woman chasing us on her tiny feet for another scolding.

We burst into the sunshine and I could finally breathe.

We faced each other on the street for a beat too long. "Hungry?" she said at last. "Cuz I am."

Without waiting for a response, she headed off in the direction of a Mexican restaurant in a vast brick building. I'm not keen on Mexican food, but I didn't want to start an argument. As we walked, her skirt rippling behind her like a flag, I asked a little breathlessly, "What was that all about?"

"Mrs. Adams is overcompensating. If she were a guy, we'd say she has a tiny dick."

I choked out a laugh and glanced around to see if anyone had heard.

Trish charged into the restaurant and took over the mechanics of getting seated.

"Did you have a nice drive?" she asked, once we'd settled into a booth.

It had taken not quite two hours from Ypsilanti. "Yes."

"So what is it you do, exactly?" I ventured, stirring my ice in my plastic water glass with a Pepsi logo. Trish ordered a margarita.

"I'm a receptionist," she answered.

"Well, obviously, but what does your boss do?"

"Whatever she wants. Like that gorilla joke. What does an eight-hundred-pound gorilla do? Anyway, whatever, you're asking about the business." She cleared her throat and said, in the same smooth voice she'd used at work, "Kendrick and Adams designs process streamlining solutions for the modern information technology sector."

"I'm sorry?"

"Yeah, I know. It means that other businesses pay them to find wasteful habits. It also means she doesn't tolerate inefficiency in her own office. You know, inefficient things like going to the bathroom, talking, excess breathing."

"Wow." I thought of George and the time we'd spend chatting when the store was slow.

"You still at the bookstore?"

"I was. It just closed."

"Sorry to hear that."

"Yeah."

We ordered. I selected a salad, which seemed a likely candidate for me to pick off stuff I didn't like. Trish ordered a burrito.

We stared across an eight-year chasm.

"So," I asked, uncomfortable under her direct gaze, "how are the kids?"

She laughed, then shook her head. As she did this, I noticed her earrings were long and silver. "I didn't mean to laugh, but really, Mary? My older son, who you saw, fancies himself quite the punk rocker, or maybe he's a Goth kid, or whatever. I don't know, but he hates my guts and spends all his time with his precious girlfriend at her family's perfect house. And my younger son broke his collarbone at my house, and now we fear a knock on the door at any moment for the Gestapo arriving, so yeah, they're perfectly swell."

I started folding my napkin in half, and half again, smoothing the crease each time. "I don't know what to say."

She sighed, fluffing her hair out behind her shoulders. "I know."

"I can help you clean up, you know."

At this my sister took a long drink of her margarita, staring into the golden pool in her glass as she did so.

"I don't let anyone in my house, and you . . ."

"I . . . what?"

"It's not like we're close. And you have a habit of judging."

"I do not!"

By way of riposte she just plunked down on her elbows, one eyebrow pulled up, her hazel eyes locked onto mine.

"I won't say a word," I said, raising my hand like the Girl Scout I used to be. "I swear."

She snorted. "We'll see."

Our food arrived. My salad was massive, and I regretted ordering it. I already wasn't feeling well, but I tucked in anyway, so I wouldn't have to say anything else wrong.

* * *

I followed Trish's taillights as we left the quaintness of downtown Grand Ledge and headed into the rural wilds. The sun was sinking, and whatever fake warmth there had been in the air was gone entirely now; winter was reasserting itself. My car's heater blasted away to keep the windshield clear.

She'd explained how she'd sent the kids out for the evening but they'd be back soon. She'd said that I could agree to help only after seeing what we were up against. I could tell she assumed I'd run screaming, and her problem would be solved. It made me nervous, which forced me to pretend I wasn't nervous. I was failing at this; I'm a lousy actress.

We were on our way to the house that her husband, Ronald, had built; literally, he'd built it himself with his crew, being a contractor and all. She'd explained this to me back when we still kept up the pretense of connection.

I wondered where Ronald lived now.

We turned onto a long gravel driveway leading into a stand of naked trees. The house revealed itself as being a perfectly normal house. Trish got out of her car wordlessly and only glanced back long enough to see I was there. A motion-sensitive floodlight clicked on and put us in spotlight. As we approached, I noticed funny bulges in the curtains, which were drawn closed and in places pressed to the inside of the window.

Trish closed her eyes and sucked in a breath as she shoved the door open and hit a light switch.

My hands flew to my face, to cover my shock and also my mouth and nose from the intense musty, mildew odor. It was a smell with substance. Three-dimensional. It was like walking into a wall.

Towers of junk teetered around us, hemming us in. Two paths wound around the perimeter of the living room to meet at a couch, which was clear but for piles sprouting on the arms and along the back.

Trish nudged me inside so she could close out the cold evening, and as she did so, a shivery feeling crept up my spine. My ill-advised taco salad burbled in my gut, and my heart worked harder. I swallowed, reminded myself to breathe. I reached for something to support me but could find only precarious towers.

I was driven to find more space, and with the door shut behind me I wandered to the couch, and then took another path until it led to the kitchen.

No relief here, either. Every counter space was jammed with shopping bags and piles of paper. The sink was overrun with dishes, themselves crusted over. All around my legs were more bags. I stumbled away from that mess and down the hall to the bedrooms . . . the hall was made narrower by stuff along its edges. Each bedroom I looked into was crowded with piles; they looked like Indian burial mounds.

I felt hot, my skin prickled, and my breathing shallowed despite my efforts to settle myself.

I battled back through the hall. Trish, having followed, wheeled herself in reverse ahead of me. I couldn't see her face; my eyes were darting for more room, space, air. . . . I turned back through the kitchen, a dining area, all this stuff, and came across a back door. I yanked it open only to be blocked in by a wall of things, the entire enclosed back porch was jammed full. I whirled around again and stumbled back through the front of the house, past the narrow entry and over the front porch where I folded down to my hands and knees in front of a garden. My body shook and I breathed slowly, swallowing hard, rocking slightly, to keep myself from retching onto the soil. At this close view, I could see the green shoots of early flowers, daffodils or crocus, nudging out of the earth.

When my breathing had slowed and my stomach settled, I sat back on my heels, daring to raise my face to Trish.

She was on her porch, sitting much the way her son had. Her head was resting on her arms, and she stared into the enclosed space created by her drawn-up knees.

When she looked up at me, I could see in the yellow floodlight her face was wet.

"Oh, my God," she said. "You have hives."

I touched my face and became aware of an itchiness that had been in the background of my fear of vomiting in Trish's garden. Trish took a compact out of her purse and handed it to me, as if I doubted her.

I looked. Sure enough, bright pink, raised splotches spread across my face, neck, and collarbone above my shirt.

I handed back her compact, staring, openmouthed. She took it from me, snapped it shut, and tossed it roughly back into her bag. "You're allergic to my house," she said, putting her hands to her temples now. "It makes you sick."

I wondered where I could get some Benadryl. I rubbed my face and tried not to scratch it.

Trish looked down again at her skirt, and I tried to reconstruct what I'd seen just moments ago. What *was* all that? In my memory it was just indeterminate shapes, mostly in bags.

The image of Trish's house conflated with my last memories of Mother's house.

As the initial shock of seeing her home receded like a wave, a new thought crashed in. She'd gotten as bad as Mom. And little Jack was living here.

Trish was getting up to go back inside. She closed the door, leaving me in her front yard.

What did I do? I kept my promise and said nothing. I couldn't help my body's physical reaction.

I drew myself up and knocked.

Trish answered and rolled her eyes. "You don't have to say anything to me. It was nice having dinner, good night."

She started to close the door, but I slapped it back open.

"I can't leave you like this."

"Why not? You left Mom like this."

She slammed the door and left me in the yellow light.

Left Mom like this, she'd said, as if at fifteen years old I'd been my mother's guardian. Did Trish think I skipped out of there happily, whistling show tunes? Did she think it was easy, in the white-water rush of puberty, to leave my mother's home to go live with my father in the two-bedroom flat he'd rented? We'd sit there every night at our Formica kitchen table pretending not to notice the jagged edge left where we'd torn away from the rest of the family.

I hadn't even meant to do it. To leave, that is. It's just that Mom took us girls to the amusement park, and the fun we had that day was so rare and bright that it was like an eclipse that burned away the reality back home. I was sitting on a bench in my wet bathing suit, having zoomed down a waterslide with Trish, both of us in an inflatable tube and shrieking with the lack of self-consciousness that comes with youth and the fake terror of such things as waterslides. Then we took a break and sat down to eat corn dogs and slurp sugary pop. We were teasing Trish about the cute boy she'd been flirting with the whole time; somehow this kid kept popping up every time we were waiting in line for a roller coaster or something . . .

And Mom said, "You'll have to get his number and call him when we get home, you minx, you . . ."

Home. We had to leave this place and go back home, where the air reeked of cat urine and rotted food. Where we had to ignore the skittering in the corners that I only hoped was spiders. Where her junk had begun to cross the Maginot Line of my bedroom threshold, because at school all day, or off at my part-time job at the mall, I could not stand guard. Where Dad no longer came home after a workday to ask us about our classes and listen, really listen, not just fake-listen over the newspaper.

"I want to move in with Dad," I'd exclaimed. Mom dropped her corn dog and turned as white as the puffy clouds above us. And though I wanted to take it back as soon as I said it, seeing her face, I knew it was too late anyway. Something had been fractured just at the utterance of the words. And so I did move out, and Trish chose to stay. I'm not sure "chose" is the right word because that implies two options weighed and considered.

But she did leave, eventually. She grew up and moved out as we're all supposed to, right? Why was I the only one who betrayed Mom?

I stood on Trish's porch so long, wondering what to do, that the floodlight winked out with my lack of motion.

Chapter 5

I waited for my sister's car to drive away. I listened to her walk across the gravel, open the door, and close it, but she did not start the engine.

I wanted to open the curtains to look, but that would be impossible, given the wall of boxes and bags.

She said she wanted to help me clean, but that would last about two days, then it would be just like with Mom; she'd turn her back and leave, and go back to her insulated life.

Or maybe she wouldn't do that. Maybe she would stay and use me to make amends for neglecting our mother to death. Fuck me for being her charity case. She could take her hives and her barfing and never come back.

I stretched out on the couch, turned to face the back of it, away from the mess.

"Ronald," I sniveled, letting a tear run onto the crusty upholstery.

The Ronald I missed, of course, was not the same Ronald who bellowed at me last night over the cell phone about why CPS had called him.

"You told me he tripped and fell at home, and she's saying a pile of junk fell on top of him. He could have been crushed, Trish!"

"He did fall!" I'd insisted in a hissing whisper, down the hall so

Jack wouldn't hear me. "Some books fell on him after he tripped, but that's not the same as being crushed by a pile of . . . debris, or whatever. It was just an accident. I'm allowed to be imperfect, you know. Remember that time you were watching Drew and he fell down the stairs and got three stitches above his eye? He's still got a scar."

"Something you weren't exactly calm about back then, *dear.*"

"I swear to you, he's safe here. That doctor was young, he's probably naive and earnest and thinks he has to report every bump and bruise. I'm handling it."

The doctor was actually about my age, but I had to keep talking, to settle Ron down.

"So if I drop by there unannounced someday, I'm going to find a nice clean and safe house?"

"Jesus, Ron. I would never hurt Jack. You know how much he means to me. You also know how hard it is for me to keep up the house, especially since I had to start working full-time after you left me." My voice was breaking up like melting ice.

He sighed and I knew I had him. I'd hit the guilt button dead-on.

"Just keep me posted, OK? And answer your damn phone when I call you."

I sat up from the couch's scratchy upholstery and wiped my face roughly. The Ron I loved and married never would have ordered me to answer my damn phone. He was supposed to love and protect me. Not leave me, then boss me from afar.

I heard a car pulling up, and then Jack's chirpy voice. I wiped my face again, smoothed my clothes, and ran my hands over my hair.

In they came through the door, all three of them. They'd let in Mary, too.

"Mom! This lady says she's Aunt Mary," Jack said, slinging his bag onto the couch before coming to give me a one-armed hug.

"Well, she is Aunt Mary. She was just heading home, though."

I glanced at her over the top of Jack's head. She was studying her folded hands as if she'd never seen them before. Drew was burning a glare straight at me.

I met his gaze with a challenging stare of my own. I diapered his skinny ass and he was not going to intimidate me, even if he was almost six feet tall and dressed like Halloween.

"Aunt Mary and I talked," he began, at the moment sounding so much like his biological father I got chills, "and we thought this weekend we could clean. Jack could visit Ron and Grandma Pauline."

"No!" shrilled Jack. "No! It's not their weekend!"

"But, Jack, you don't want to be here while we're cleaning, do you?" my sister asked, bending herself partway over, using that falsely high, sugary voice that those without children always use, as if all children are just tall babies who know nothing about anything. "Wouldn't that be boring?"

"No!" he shrieked, dashing down the path to the hallway. "You're not touching my room!"

I threw a glare at my idiot sister. "Thanks a lot for that. Now I'll have to spend twenty minutes calming him down." I addressed the pair of traitors at once. "You two seem to have this all figured out, but neither of you knows how to handle Jack. He can't be just handed off like a house pet when he's inconvenient. Don't I get a vote in this? His mother? My own house? Or are you planning to kick me out, too?"

I didn't wait for an answer.

I found Jack in the center of his floor, arm wrapped around his favorite stuffed animals. He'd also pulled up some of his treasured boxes of Legos and action figures to gather around him.

I moved some old clothes out of the way and settled down next to him. He whimpered as I dislodged some of the toys surrounding him.

"Pal, they're just talking; they're not going to do anything without my say-so. I'm the mom and I'm in charge. You don't have to leave if you don't want to."

"They won't take my stuff away?" He cried a few more tears into the top of his threadbare Cat, named simply Cat ever since he was two and naming everything in the house.

"Of course not," I said, stroking his hair, which still had baby-soft fineness.

"I can help clean," he said, sniffing hard and taking a shaky breath. He looked around his room. "I think it's probably a good idea."

I looked around, too. There were baseball posters and a wallpaper border behind the piles, but you'd never know it. His closet was blocked, so he got clothes out of the laundry piles, same as I did. Or sometimes I just bought new clothes. It was easier, and he was growing so fast anyway.

"Yeah," I agreed, ruffling his hair. "It's probably a good idea."

I scrunched my eyes shut as I kissed his forehead and tried to wish away my haughty sister and judgmental son, who I knew were still hovering in the doorway, plotting.

I left Jack reading a Magic Tree House book and in the hallway took a deep breath, which set me to coughing as I inhaled some dust.

When I came out of the hallway, my sister and son were on the couch. Drew was slouched way down, his knees spread wide, arms folded. Mary was next to him sitting primly on the edge, knees together, as if she couldn't bear to let her ass touch more of my couch than she had to.

I wanted to knock her block off.

"OK, fine," I said. "We'll start cleaning this weekend. But I'm not sending Jack away. He can help."

They traded a look.

"Stop that!" I snapped. "Stop this . . . conspiracy between you. You barely even know each other; I mean, when was the last time you even saw him, Mary? Before he showed up at your house."

She flushed pink and I felt satisfied, but also a little ping of discomfort registered. It's not as if I tried to stay in touch either.

Drew chewed on a black fingernail. "She wants to help."

"That's a switch considering she turned her back on your grandmother."

Mary had picked up a piece of paper and was creasing and smoothing it. "That's not true," she said softly. "Not the whole story."

I snatched the paper out of her hand. It was a shipping receipt for a tablecloth I'd ordered. "I don't know what the rest of the story is that you think made it OK to walk out on her." I could still picture Mom's paling, crumpling face when Mary announced it, her intention to move in with Dad. How she'd picked a day out at an amusement park to lob that mortar round, and how Mom dropped her corn dog onto the pavement and it was so ludicrous I almost laughed, when I really wanted to shake my sister until her teeth rattled. The ink was barely dry on their divorce papers, Mom was so depressed most days she could hardly brush her hair, and then her youngest daughter jumped ship, too? When Mom turned to me with moist eyes and asked if I wanted to go, too, there was no other answer to give.

"I couldn't live like that anymore." She raised her eyes to me. I'd forgotten how much they looked like mine; I could tell because they looked so much like Jack's, that odd pale hazel color that seemed to alter with the light. She went on, "You said you couldn't stand it either."

"But I stayed as long as I could. I supported her."

"I stayed as long as I could, too. I just didn't last as long."

I looked at Drew, appealing to him to see it my way. I could see only revulsion. Anger.

I put my face in my hands. Would this be Jack at seventeen? No, it wouldn't be, because Jack understands me. Jack would never hate me. At least that I could cling to, when the whole world turned on me.

But if I lost Jack, maybe he would hate me after all. If my mess forced him to live away from me, in Pauline's sterile condo or that bachelor apartment of Ronald's. The rest of the family would blame me no doubt, and with Jack living there all the time, that's all he would hear, how bad of a mother I was. . . . I'd not only lose him physically, I'd lose his love.

I'd blow my brains out. I really would. And that would teach them all.

"I care about you," Mary said, and she flushed as soon as she said it, like her words had just slipped out. Like she'd farted at a dinner party.

Jack wandered out from the hallway and wordlessly wrapped his good arm around my waist. I settled on the couch and he curled into my lap. He fit awkwardly this way, all lanky limbs, but he shrunk into an approximation of his old toddler snuggling habit: head sideways on chest, just under my chin, body coiled in my lap. I put my hand on his back and the other on his hip to avoid his broken shoulder and rocked him lightly with my eyes closed.

Regardless of their traitorous reasoning, regardless of the unfairness—*whoever told you life was fair?* our mother used to say— the cold fact remained that if I didn't do something, they could take my Jack away.

I heard a muttered good-bye from Mary and nothing at all from Drew but footsteps as they went out the front door. At last, when two engines puttered away, I exhaled.

Jack dropped off to sleep next to me as he always did, in my bed. The other thing little Ayana Reese disapproved of.

But try explaining to a seven-year-old why grown-ups get to sleep with someone even though they're big and brave, but scared little kids have to sleep alone. And I have a big old bed with no one to fill the other side. The other choice was listening to him cry in his room, alone, and being mean and making him stay in bed and fighting with him for an hour about it before he eventually passed out from exhaustion.

Or in fifteen minutes he could fall asleep with me, no trauma.

I gingerly slid my arm out from under his neck. Jack sighed in his sleep and nuzzled Cat but didn't wake up.

I got back up out of bed every night, because though Jack is like a part of my own body, so essential was he to my very existence, I also, like any human being, needed a little bit of solitude.

I got myself a bowl of mint chocolate chip and went back to the couch. I left the rest of the room in darkness and let the television be the only light. I was in a private little cave here, where no one could bother me, enjoying my ice cream and stupid TV shows about "real" housewives.

The housewives couldn't keep my mind away from recent events, like that humiliating call I had to make to the psychologist's office to set up an appointment, the lie I had to tell my boss about seeing my gyno because I sure as hell wasn't going to tell her the state was forcing me to get my head shrunk.

If I had to march through a charade to get the state out of my life and keep Jack with me, so be it. But I'd be damned to hell every which way before I'd give my boss, my neighbors, my family, or anyone else a front-row seat to my humiliation.

And then my sister! Mary had some balls coming here, acting the savior after she brushed off Mother—and me—like dust. She moved in with Dad, barely talked to me at school, and took her honor roll and National Honor Society off to the University of Michigan to go read dense novels by dead people. I remembered sitting there at her high school graduation with Mom. Dad sat two rows behind—no Ellen yet, he sat with his brother, our uncle Howard—and Mom murmured to me with admiration that she was off to college. I set my jaw and asked her what was wrong with what I'd chosen to do with my life, to make a go of a jewelry business while office work made the ends meet. Oh nothing, she'd insisted, patting my hand. Nothing at all, your jewelry is beautiful. But her eyes were on Mary, who was crossing the stage and choosing that moment to try to adjust her mortarboard, which fell off in front of the principal trying to hand her the diploma. And I saw it in my mother's face then, in her smile and shining eyes: Mary was still the favorite. She'd abandoned us in Mother's hoard, but she was still the special one. The fragile one, the one to be protected and sheltered, and now she'd also be the educated one. The one Mom would talk about to her friends with pride, and when asked about me, she'd have to strain to make me sound important and successful.

"Maybe I'll go to college," I said then, not knowing if I meant it.

Mother had stopped clapping, as Mary thumped down the steps with her mortarboard and diploma pinned with one elbow; with the other hand she was trying to fix the barrette in her hair.

Mother turned to me and clasped my hand in hers. I looked around like I was still in high school myself instead of two years out, reflexively worrying if I'd look like a dork. She squeezed my hand to get my attention. "You are a special woman, Trish, with uncommon vitality and creativity. They don't teach that in college. You jumped into your life with both feet." Mother searched the crowd of graduates—still holding my hand as the principal continued droning names—maybe looking for the back of Mary's head. It was impossible; they all looked identical from the back. "Some people aren't ready for that yet. Mary's college education doesn't make her better than you, and don't you ever think that."

I stirred my now-melted ice cream as the tears leaked down my face again, which still felt tight and dry from the earlier crying. Fourteen years later, would I ever again be able to think of her without weeping? Dammit, at forty years old I still wanted my mother.

I called up in my memory her tight embrace when I told her that Drew's father wanted nothing to do with me, or his unborn baby, at the time just a bulge at my waistband.

I pictured my mom—stout and round and sunnily cheerful—in her kitchen basting the turkey, overseeing the side dishes, on Thanksgiving. Clutter was there then. But it was just stuff around her house. It hadn't yet begun to creep up the walls in stacks, or spill out of her fridge in rotting sludgy piles.

They thought I was just as bad, I could see it in Drew's sneer, in Mary's hives and heaving. But my house does not have rotten food, ever. I do not have pets to leave their poo in places I can't reach, no matter how much Jack begs me for a dog. It might be dusty in here, but it's dust, not cat shit. It's just dust.

Dust never killed anybody.

But, I thought, as I spotted my wedding photo in its frame on the wall, just peeking out from behind a tall stack of storage bins, *Mother and I did have this much in common. Our husbands left us when they could no longer stand the stuff.*

Chapter 6

I walked back into my town house and savored a long, deep breath of clear air. I turned on all the lights. I lit a candle and let the scent of vanilla unfurl.

In the bathroom mirror I could see my hives had receded, but if I looked carefully, I could see the faint outlines of the splotches.

And I had just volunteered to willingly go back in there. Where I wasn't even wanted. Trish saw me, and Drew, as invaders. Betrayers.

I braced myself on the bathroom counter, letting my head droop. Hopeless. Utterly, utterly hopeless.

Trish didn't want help any more than our mother did. She was only permitting us in her house under threat of losing the only thing that might matter more to her than stuff, little Jack. I say "might" because I would have thought our mother would have ranked her daughters over things but she did not. In the end, she did not.

I was still living there when her things began to creep down the hall, and one day I found a box of hers in my pristine room. We held a battle over that box. I kept putting it out, and I'd go off to school and it would creep back in.

One day I came home to find a pile of shopping bags in the corner of my room, right on top of my beanbag chair where I liked to read.

I wouldn't have thought Trish would blame me for leaving. She was mad, too. She complained all the time about the mess and the stink and how humiliating it was. Mom cluttered the yard, too, for the whole world to see. We were forever fending off nuisance complaints from City Hall via our disgusted neighbors.

No one ever called social services about us. Maybe it wasn't the thing to do then. Or maybe no one cared if a pile of stuff crushed us, or if we got sick from all the bacteria and cat urine.

In any case, I left before any of that could happen. Trish left, too, eventually, so why was this my fault?

I wanted to call George. If the store was still open, I'd go into work early and we'd hash it over with some coffee before opening the doors for the day, and he'd be sympathetic and listen and agree that yes, it's terrible.

But now I'd have to invade his private home space to hear his voice, and he's probably with his lady love.

I thought about calling Jamie, from the store. She was always my favorite. She looked like a punk kid but was wonderful with the customers and knew the location of just about any book we had, instantly.

I walked to the kitchen phone and dialed her number by heart.

"Hello," she said distractedly, with a little bite in her voice. I looked at my watch. Oh. Much later than I'd thought.

"Hi, Jamie. It's Mary." Pause. No response. "From the bookstore."

"Oh. Yeah, hi. What's up?" Jamie sounded wary, like she was going to get called on the carpet. Now that I thought about it, I couldn't recall a single other time I'd called her at home that wasn't about work.

"I just . . . I wondered . . ."

"Yeah?" Jamie prompted.

"I'm having a bad day."

"Unemployment can do that."

I heard a voice in the background, Jamie hushing it. In the silence when I tried to marshal some words, I heard her hiss, "my old boss."

"Sorry to bother you," I muttered into the phone and hung up.

Jamie and I used to talk, didn't we? Laugh sometimes, even? That made her friendly, but not a friend.

I set the phone down on my counter and looked up. I could see there on my refrigerator a postcard from Seth, sent from a psychology convention in New Orleans. In our college days I sometimes had a coffee with him in the dorm, or ate lunch in the cafeteria with him, but since graduation our contact had dwindled to postcards and birthday phone calls, the latter tradition emerging when we discovered we shared a birthday, along with Ralph Macchio and Walter Cronkite. It was many months away from November 4.

And then I felt thirteen years old again, hanging around the cool kids' lunch table, listening to their plans for Saturday night at the movies and waiting for one of them to say, "Hey, Mary, you should come."

It was too late to call Jamie or George or Seth, but not too late for my dad, the chronic insomniac. His wife, Ellen, would be in bed already by now, one of those greet-the-dawn types.

He picked up with his constant greeting, "Hey, Peaches."

"Hi, Dad."

"How's my girl?"

"Fine. How's Ellen?"

"Getting along OK."

We chatted about the store's last day, which he'd already known about. When my dad and I could pretend we were the only two people in the world, our chats went very well. But sometimes we were forced to acknowledge the people around us who complicated everything.

"I saw Trish," I ventured in a lull, during which I could hear the squeaking and shouting of a basketball game.

"Yeah?"

"It's pretty bad."

"I expect it is." Dad sighed as he said this, a great whoosh of air.

I caught him up on recent developments, all of which he listened to silently, until he said, "This feels very familiar. Too damn familiar."

"I know. I'm going to help her clean, though. She says she'll take the help."

"Don't get your hopes up too high, Peaches. Remember when I took Mom to Florida?"

"I know. I don't think she's there, yet. Anyway, this is different."

"I hope it is."

"Want to come and help?"

"You think she'd stand for it? She'd chase me off her property."

"Maybe not, Dad. She's a little desperate."

"If she asks for me herself, I'd come. But hey . . . Maybe Jack shouldn't be there at all. If he got hurt and now she's being investigated?"

"What do you mean?"

"Maybe he should come stay with us. Or with Ron."

"He doesn't want to be away from her, Dad. He's already away from his dad most of the time, and Drew doesn't even stay at the house most days. Trish is all he has."

"And for that Trish just has to look in the mirror."

I sighed. "Maybe you're right. Maybe it's better if you don't come."

My dad continued, "Honey, take care of yourself. She's gonna turn on you at some point. You have to decide how much you can take."

"It's for Jack, Dad. Your grandson."

There was a silence. I heard him take a shaky breath. "I know," he croaked.

We said our good-byes. "The week Mom went to Florida." Our family euphemism for when it all blew apart.

I decided to make myself go to bed and read something old, dense, and classic, something so removed from my own life I could pretend the real world didn't exist. I was turning pages in *Anna Karenina* until past 3:00 a.m., which upset me until I remembered I didn't have to go to work.

No one was expecting me anywhere.

──────────── Chapter 7 ────────────

The loudspeakers at Target were playing Mötley Crüe, and I was crooning along softly "*I'm on my way-ay-ay . . .*" and the sheer pleasure of the nostalgia, the cheery store lighting, the cart full of useful things, and Jack bouncing along merrily next to me with his tasty shopping bribe all helped me to forget two things.

That the rebellious music of my youth was now soothing music in my favorite store.

That soon my family would descend on me to start getting rid of my things.

"*Home sweet home!*" Jack chimed in with Vince.

I was pushing the red cart out of the cleaning products aisle. I'd already loaded up on paper towels, cleanser, trash bags, rubber gloves, and in deference to my sister's apparently delicate constitution, breathing masks. On the way out I'd pick up more plastic storage bins. To help organize.

I noticed jeans were on sale in Jack's size. He was so hard to fit, so thin and lanky. I grabbed a couple pair, then a couple more. He was tough on his clothes, always wearing out the knees. Spring was coming soon, so I picked up a couple of bright T-shirts, too. I noticed socks on sale—another thing he wore out constantly—and threw a few packs into the cart.

I strolled past the home decor section, my mind popping with bright images of my tastefully decorated, clean home. That whimsical clock with the oversize numbers would look so cute on the living room wall. I peered at the price tag. On sale! Twenty-five percent off! And there was only this one.

I slid it off the shelf and tucked it on the bottom of the cart, underneath the basket.

My whole body hummed. This clock would be my treat for finally getting my home in order. And surely when Ronald saw all the progress I'd made, he'd not only lay off me about the home's "safety" but maybe even come home again.

I wheeled past the baby section, looking away from a cooing bundle peeking up from an infant seat. "Mom . . . wait up," Jack said, trotting along, his sack of miniscones pinched awkwardly under his elbow.

"Here, let me hold that," I said, taking it from him as I selected a checkout aisle.

Target was busy and we had to wait. A woman in line in front of me with silver spiky hair turned to Jack and gave him a little frown. "Oh, too bad about your arm, kiddo. Did you have an accident on the playground?"

"Yep," said Jack, looking at the floor.

"I was a teacher for thirty years," the woman declared, still staring at Jack. "The way these kids play on the playground it's a surprise they're not hurt more often. You rambunctious boys!" She turned to me. "I only had girls and I counted myself lucky when they were his age. But then, as teenagers! Not so lucky anymore." The woman laughed at her naive younger self. "Do you have girls?"

"No," I said, swallowing hard. The store felt hot then, the store lights overly bright. "Excuse me, I think a line just opened up."

I yanked the cart back so fast the clock started to slide out of position. I bent down to push it back and cracked my head on a candy shelf. The woman was saying, "I don't see an open line . . ." and Jack was saying, "Mom? Are you OK?"

Jack trotted to keep up with me as I shoved the cart as far away as I could, to a different line with oblivious teenagers in front of me texting and talking and buying clothes.

I dared not look back at the woman and what she must have been thinking about this crazy lady with the injured son, a freak who panicked and fled from her at the simplest conversation.

Jack reached up with his good hand to hold mine and squeezed.

They're here!" crowed Jack, stumbling over the pile of Target bags by the door. The large, flat clock was balanced on the pile of blue storage bins next to the television.

I was not prepared for them just yet. I was still working myself up to the idea of them coming in here and touching my stuff.

I opened a box of donuts, which I'd placed on the stovetop between the burners, and fished some napkins out of a shopping bag on the floor. They were bringing coffee, they said.

"Hi!" I heard Mary call with fake cheer. Drew didn't announce himself, just shuffled in. I heard another high-pitched voice, and I froze in the act of wrangling my hair into a bandanna.

I stepped out of the kitchen to see Miranda, her fingers twined into Drew's. When I spotted them, she was planting a kiss on his cheek for no obvious reason, the kind of gesture women make when they're proving to the world they own their boyfriend. Like a dog pissing in his yard.

"Hi, Trish!" she chirped. "I wanted to help."

Drew stuck out his chin at me. This was my first test, so it would seem. Mary caught my eye and gave me a quick cringe-face. So at least my sister wasn't in on this. Also, though she looked pale, she wasn't vomiting or going into anaphylactic shock. Progress.

"Hiya!" Jack said, skipping over to Miranda, this girl, and hugging her. I wanted to rip him out of her arms.

Her hair was dyed an aggressive orangey red. She was wearing a long shirt over tight leggings and flats, the same kind of clothes I wore at her age. All she needed was a Swatch and DayGlo socks.

I looked away from my son's aggressive stare and his perky girlfriend and counted backward from ten in my head. "Want some donuts?" I called, now using my own fake-cheer voice.

We busied ourselves with treats and coffee for a few minutes, jammed together in my kitchen by the wall of bags at our feet. No one mentioned anything about it. We prattled about exams and spring break. Miranda mentioned her family was going to Gulf Shores and she was hoping that Drew would be able to come, too.

I swallowed and said, "We'll see," and realized if he did this, I'd be entirely alone for the week of spring break.

"Well," Mary said, wiping sugar off her hands over the sink. "Let's get going."

She led a procession of us out to the bags of supplies I'd plopped in front of the garage and started handing out plastic gloves. The weak March sun was not yet above the thick, leafless trees. Our breath made clouds in the air.

She handed out garbage bags to all of us.

"What are you getting these out for now?" I asked. I'd pictured the dirty paper towels going in there. Used-up dust rags.

"Trash, Mom," announced Drew, as if I were a moron. "Hence, trash bags."

Mary interjected, "For really obvious garbage, you know. Food wrappers and whatever. Stuff that's too ruined to use."

"Do you think I'm some kind of pig that I'd have food wrappers and ruined stuff?"

Everyone froze like that childhood game where you can't move until someone taps you.

No one talked, so I kept going. "Look, what's the plan for stuff that's not garbage? Because, believe it or not, I don't live in a landfill. We're not just going to dash in there and start whipping things into bags."

Mary and Drew traded looks again. Mary said, "Um, OK, there's a tarp in here? We'll put stuff we're saving on the tarp."

Drew nodded. "And we can put donation stuff in the driveway."

"Donations?" I said. "Who said we're donating stuff? If it's perfectly good and usable, we'll just organize it and put it back."

Drew was opening his mouth, but Miranda tugged on his arm, and when he turned to her, Mary jumped in again. "Let's just put stuff in the driveway if we *think* about donating it. We can always change our minds; it's not permanent."

"So you're using the royal 'we' now?" I shot back. "Don't say 'we' when you mean 'You, Trish, the disgusting slob pig.'"

Mary flinched and I bit my lip. We hadn't even started yet. I said, "No, never mind, fine. The driveway is fine. Let's just get going here." Ayana would be back Tuesday.

To prove to them I was not a total lost-cause loser, I went back in the front to the first pile and started throwing papers into the bag. I looked at the first few, then got impatient and used my arm to sweep the whole pile into the sack.

I pointedly marched out, shouldering my way through the trio of them, and tossed the bag onto the grass. "There. Happy?"

With this I grabbed a new bag and plunged back into the house, the rest of them following behind me, silently.

A system emerged as we began cleaning. One of them would call, "Trish" or "Mom" and I'd look up and say "keep" or "toss" to whatever they were holding up.

While we were doing this and I made myself recycle years-old *People* magazines, a thought kept twisting around in my head like an earthworm trapped on a hot sidewalk. What had really been in that bag I filled all hasty and carelessly, just to show off?

There could be photos in there, old photos of my kids. . . . And not necessarily digital photos I still have copies of, either. I was scrapbooking in that room for a while. I did see an envelope of scrapbook paper in there.

No. I forced myself to inspect a bag full of yarn right in front of me. The yarn had gorgeous color and texture, and it had been a steal on clearance. True, I hadn't yet managed to learn to knit, but if I did, what gorgeous sweaters I could make. Or if I couldn't use it, maybe someone I know could. I must know some knitters. Or! It would sell at a garage sale. I'm sure it would.

My heart was lugging in my chest like an engine in low gear. I hauled the yarn bag to the Keep pile on the tarp, and then looked over my shoulder. No one right behind me.

I knelt in front of the trash bag and fumbled with the knot on top. I'd yanked it too tightly in my haste before. I ripped it open at the top, hoping to knot it back up without anyone noticing. I started combing through the papers.

I found a flier from my cell-phone company telling me I could get an upgrade, a drawing of Jack's, and while no pictures, I spied an ATM envelope. I seized it and opened it to see $100 in twenties.

I clutched it to my chest. I could not afford to throw away money, certainly.

"Mom?"

I looked up to see Drew looming over me, with the rest of them trailing after.

"What the hell?" he shouted.

"Look!" I held up the ATM envelope. "There's a hundred bucks in here I almost threw away!"

He grabbed the cell-phone flier. "And this? Is this worth a hundred bucks to you?"

"Why, yes it is," I shot back, standing up in my circle of papers. "I could save that much on a new phone so, yes, give it to me."

"Is it worth losing Jack?"

"Stop being so dramatic. It is one piece of paper, one! And I need to save money!"

"You just tore through a bag of garbage!"

"And I found a hundred dollars!"

"By the way, what was a hundred dollars doing in a pile of junk in your living room?"

"It was an accident, I didn't mean to leave it there."

"Hey," interrupted Mary, "you know, it's cold out here, and we've only got so much time."

"Right, so quit interrupting me!"

Drew held up the cell-phone flier over my head, grasped the top of it in his fingertips, and tore it right down the middle. "Andrew Michael Dietrich!" I shouted at him, but he didn't move. He brought the two halves together and tore again.

"No! Stop it!"

I heard it in the trees before it happened. It whistled through the branches, and I looked up and saw the trees swaying. The March wind grabbed my papers and scattered them across the driveway, as if Drew had planned it that way to spite me.

I shrieked and started running after them. Mary started scrambling too, and from the corner of my eye I saw Jack doing his one-armed best to pick up scraps.

When the gust died away and we returned to the torn bag with what we managed to grab, I could see even Miranda had picked up some paper, though she looked at me sideways, like how she might regard a snarling, frothing dog.

I sat down next to the bag, pinning the papers I wanted to keep under my knee. From the corner of my eye, I could spy bits of paper clinging to bushes, tree trunks. I resumed combing through what we'd saved. The stillness around me caught my attention.

"Go!" I shouted without looking up. "If you're not going to help me with this bag, just . . . go. Do something else."

I heard shuffling, and then Jack squatted down next to me. "I'll help you, Mama."

He held the papers down I wanted to keep as I combed through the contents. I found a birthday card from an old college friend, a receipt for some lampshades I would be able to return once I found them.

"Mama?"

"Yeah, pal?"

"What did Drew mean when he said, 'Is it worth losing Jack?'"

I stopped sorting and looked him in the face. His chin was tight and lips pursed, like always when he tried not to cry.

Chapter 8

I sorted through a pile of shopping bags near the couch, paying closer attention now to things I'd ignored at first: random envelopes, a half-crumpled small shopping bag. I hadn't yet turned up $100, but I didn't want to be the one to throw away Trish's money.

When I'd first walked in today, the musty smell nauseated me again and I worried about an encore performance of the hives and the heaves. However, I'd loaded up on Benadryl preemptively in case of hives, and I concentrated on sipping slow, deep breaths of cool outside air. Then I'd plunged inside quickly, as if jumping into a cold lake.

I was gradually acclimating to the cavelike darkness in the house. With the curtains drawn and the piles reaching high, little outside light penetrated. The dust was making me cough, though I didn't want to resort to the mask yet. I could just imagine Trish's face if we all started suiting up like hazmat workers. Even though she'd bought the masks herself.

To say she was a little touchy would be to say a land mine was a little dangerous.

Murmuring voices floated by me. I glanced up to see Drew and Miranda in conference on the couch. Miranda was squirming, tossing her hair, looking at the ceiling as she talked.

I looked back down to the bag I was working on and tried to tune them out. But it's not like there was privacy to be had in Trish's cave.

"Bye, Mary, nice to meet you!" Miranda called out and almost skipped out the door and down the driveway.

Drew started banging things into bags.

"Careful," I said.

"Like I'm going to break her old *Reader's Digests*? This is so fucked up."

I felt like an aunt should address the language, but authority over children was new to me. I was never the one in the bookstore telling kids to stop climbing the shelves. George was great at that; he could always get them to stop without making them cringe or cry. They were usually laughing by the time he convinced them to stop using our store as their personal playland.

"Where did Miranda go?"

"She was feeling *uncomfortable,* she said."

"I know the feeling."

"But you're still here, I notice."

"This is pretty major to deal with."

"God, stop sticking up for her."

I recognized this conversation suddenly. Countless times Trish and I would fight and she'd be angry, so angry, but in her eyes you could read the hurt if you dared look her straight in the face.

I looked at the papers on my current stack. Purple crayon scribbles swirled all over a coloring book page from a Disney movie that came out years ago. Jack's old handiwork, doubtless.

I'd just put it in my trash bag when I became aware of Jack's feet running toward me. "No!" he cried.

He yanked open the bag with his good hand, started digging down inside it, but as a flexible trash bag it swayed under his reach and his fingers scrabbled above the paper.

"Aunt Mary, those were mine!"

He yanked the bag down hard, throwing it to the floor and scrambling around inside it, trying to hold one side with the immobilized arm braced to his side. "Ow!" he said as he must have moved his shoulder when he shouldn't.

"Jack, those pages were from preschool, must be . . . years and years ago." I crouched down to try to take the bag from him, because I didn't want him to hurt himself more. Maybe he'd even rebreak the bone if it had started to heal.

He spotted the pages and snatched them up with his good hand, crumpling them as he did so. He clutched them to his chest and sat down on the floor as Trish came back in through the front door, her cheeks pink from the brisk air outside.

"They're mine," Jack said again. He was panting with effort.

"Slow down your breath, honey; do you need an inhaler?" Trish said.

"She's a thief," he announced, turning away from me as if I'd mug him for his coloring book pages.

Now Drew reached for the pages. "Jack, you were, like, four when you did those."

"So? They're special!"

"Why?"

"Because they are! They remind me of Miss Kelly and how nice she was!"

Drew glanced at his little brother, then faced his mother with a glare so hard I winced to see it.

Trish ignored Drew. She crouched down to be level with her youngest. "Pal?" she ventured. "We can save nicer coloring pages than this. These got stained." She tried to tug them away, and he gripped harder.

"No! They're mine!"

"Oh, let him keep the damn pages," Trish blurted, standing up. "It's just a few sheets of paper."

"Right," muttered Drew. "That's all any of this is."

Jack scampered off down toward his room, no doubt to hide his treasures from us.

I looked at the living room again, carefully. I detected a few more square feet of space near the front door, but otherwise you couldn't tell we'd accomplished anything in two straight hours.

I sighed as I started scooping the papers back into the bag, and in doing so, some dust caught in my throat.

I coughed lightly a few times, which seemed to only increase the tickle in my throat. Soon my eyes were watering, spilling over, and my hacking was more pronounced.

"Oh, Christ," muttered Trish, as if I were coughing on purpose to make her feel bad.

I heard Drew walk away from me and I thought maybe he'd given up too, gone after his girlfriend, but he returned in moments with a plastic water bottle.

I gratefully accepted it and swigged down some water, finally able to settle down and wipe my eyes.

I sat back on my heels and looked at Trish directly. She was on the floor, cross-legged, hands open on her knees like a Buddha.

"How are we going to do this?" she asked, her gaze unfocused. Sitting on the floor as we were, the piles seemed like skyscrapers.

"We need more hands," I agreed.

"I know what you're going to say. Don't waste your breath."

"We can't afford to be picky."

"Not after what he did before. I won't give him a chance to do the same thing to me."

Drew interrupted, "Will you two stop talking in secret sister code?"

I looked up at Drew. "I was thinking of calling your grandpa."

He brightened. His whole face looked years younger without the scowl. "Yeah! Totally! Why didn't I think of it? It's not like he's all that old, right?"

Trish put her head in her hands. "I can't do it."

There was a knock on the door then. We all traded quick looks of confusion.

"Oh, God," Trish muttered. "Not now, I'm not ready. No, not yet . . ." She scrambled to her feet and made for the back of the house, toward Jack's room, and I wondered if she meant to flee through a window and disappear.

The knocking continued.

Drew's face was grim now, and he looked old and tired beyond his years.

"Coming!" he shouted, and he stepped over me with his long legs to open the door.

Chapter 9

I came upon Jack in his room, curled up on the center of his bed, holding his drawings, faced away from the door.

Because of Drew's big frickin' mouth I'd had to explain to Jack that some people were worried he'd get hurt even worse in our house and that if we didn't get it cleaned up, he'd have to go live with his dad for a while. "I don't want to leave you," he'd cried and I told him, "I know, that's why we're cleaning up."

Then the unexpected knock. Maybe Ayana, early. Or Ron, deciding he didn't believe my story after all. I thought of snatching Jack up and running. But footsteps were coming down the hall.

"Oh God, no . . ." I said softly, and Jack turned toward me, his face puckered up and questioning.

"Trish," Mary called. "It's OK. It was just the UPS man. Of course, I had no idea where to tell him to put his delivery of several boxes from Crate and Barrel."

I braced myself in Jack's doorway, my knees having gone weak and my legs trembly. Jack was still here, he was. My heart was still throbbing away so hard my chest hurt. I wondered whether I could survive another knock on the door.

"Trish?" prompted Mary.

"Gimme a minute," I snapped, and I heard her footsteps recede.

Jack hadn't let go of his drawings. I snaked along the path to the center of his room and joined him on the bed, which was partially obscured by his clothes.

I sat cross-legged and leaned against the wall. Jack wriggled like an inchworm until his head was in my lap and he could still clutch his old artwork. I toyed with locks of his hair as we sat in silence.

I pictured the room the last time it was empty, when Ron and I moved in. I hadn't even known he was building us a house. He'd always said that we had to save up more money, that he had enough debt just operating his construction business and couldn't take on more for a house of our own just yet. So we were living in a rented trailer, this patched-up family made of my new husband, my preschooler from an earlier ill-advised one-night stand, and me. Ron would go off every day to wield a hammer and try to build his life and business. I'd spend my days sketching and making jewelry to sell at craft shows as Andy scurried along the length of the trailer, wearing a path in the thin carpet.

The trailer had been neat. Most of the sentimental stuff I'd saved was in storage at my mom's house. And since we were saving money for a house, I didn't buy much, just the baubles I needed for the jewelry, and most months I could make that back selling it either at the shows or on consignment in shops.

About a year after Mom died, Ron took us for a drive. I hadn't thought much of it, figured maybe we were going to pick up some lumber or something. I liked to go along on his errands, and in fact I always found him sexiest in his Carhartt work pants and steel-toe boots. That gear always made him look powerful and capable.

That day he turned onto a gravel road in the middle of nowhere, and I looked at him, confused. He smiled a little, kept driving, and refused to say anything else.

He pulled up the truck to a house. I didn't really look at it, assuming we were there to give someone a quote on siding or some such.

He turned to me, one arm up on the steering wheel, and smiled. "Welcome home, baby."

I could still picture his reddish-blond stubble glinting in the sun and smell the burning leaves of a rural October. I stepped out of the pickup truck unsteadily, and Ron had to help me down.

It was a brick ranch-style home with an attached garage. The brick was mottled in various colors of red, an exterior I'd admired on a home I saw more than a year ago. He'd remembered. All that time, he'd remembered. The window frames and porch railings were clean, bright white. The door was a rich red, like rubies.

Andrew, by then five years old and officially adopted by Ron, was tearing around the yard in high gear, and out of reflex I was going to shout at him to slow down so he didn't dart out into the road, or someone else's yard, but then I realized, wait. He was still several yards from the road, or anyone else's home. He could zoom out here until he fell down from exhaustion, no harm done.

Ron walked me through the house, explaining every detail with the pride of a craftsman. I fell in love with him again over crown molding and a bay window and recessed lighting and a master bedroom skylight.

Andrew's room had already been painted blue and decorated in a nautical theme because he loved pirates.

There was another room painted creamy yellow. He put his arm around me and said, "For the baby."

Baby? I'd sorely wanted another baby, this time doing it right, with my husband. The trailer was so small we hadn't started trying yet.

He turned me around by my shoulders. Across the hall was a room in spring green. "And for another baby, someday. But for now, how about a special room just for your crafts and stuff."

Jack's room to this day was still creamy yellow, not that I could see it behind the boxes and piles of toys and clothes. The green room across the hall was now closed off. It had been years since I'd looked inside for more than a second.

The room Ron and I shared was "christened" in a most passionate fashion on moving day when we got Ronald's parents to watch Andrew. We just had a mattress on the floor, cartons of Chinese food next to us. We gaped, amazed at the size of the place and wondered how we'd ever have enough stuff to fill it.

A powerful surge of longing for Ron, for my oldest son's return, for the safety of my youngest, pulled me upward, and filled my limbs with an itchy need for action. I patted Jack's head. "I've gotta get busy, pal. You can stay here and rest, though."

He bolted up. "No! Something else might get tossed!"

He scrambled down from his bed, and together we wound our way back to the living room.

Mary and Drew each greeted me with a box of things they'd run across.

I looked in Mary's box first.

She had a stack of scrapbooking paper with Christmas trees and mistletoe visible on some of the pieces. Once the house was clean I could get going on the Christmas scrapbook. "Keep."

A cobalt blue coffee mug with a broken handle, and the handle itself. I love blue; it could easily be glued. "Keep."

Some blank notepads from my bank. Always useful. "Keep."

Votive candle holders I'd gotten on sale last Christmas season. "I forgot I had these! Keep."

I made to look in Drew's box, but he yanked it out of view. "Forget it. It's all gonna be 'keep.'" He stormed past me

"But this stuff is usable! Those votives will be great Christmas gifts."

"I don't want a votive," Mary said, blinking at me.

"Not you, ninny. I'm talking about for Jack's teacher, his school bus driver, people like that."

"Can't you buy them something else? Christmas is eight months away."

"You think I'm made of money here that I can afford to get rid of good stuff?"

Mary opened her mouth, then shut it again, shoulders drooped with defeat. Score one for Trish.

I followed them out, suspicious Drew might toss the things he found into the trash can.

Instead I saw a growing cluster of things on the Keep tarp. Now that my things were spread horizontally, instead of stacked in boxes and bags, the sprawl of items seemed greater. Especially compared to the modest space we'd cleared inside.

Drew tossed the box down to the tarp with unnecessary force. I flinched as I heard things clank against each other. He cocked a brow at me and said, "Do the math, Mom," pointing at the tarp.

"Mama!" exclaimed Jack, skipping out of the house. "Look what I found!"

He was holding up a baseball glove with the tag still on it. I'd bought it for him last year at Christmas and lost it before I could wrap it.

I sank down to the grass of my front yard, the morning's dew now dried as the distant spring sun kept climbing the sky. I flopped onto my back and stared into the branches until my vision blurred and all I saw was a kaleidoscope of color.

Chapter 10

I t's pointless!" Trish bellowed at me.

"It's uncanny," I murmured in response, not realizing I'd spoken aloud at first until Trish hollered back at me asking what was so frickin' uncanny.

She looked so much like our mother. I had just enough sense not to say that out loud. But she did look like Mom, especially with the bandanna tied over her wild hair, her full, flowing skirt replaced with blue jeans. My mother and her clutter were one and the same to my mind, and more than anything it was this setting that inspired the comparison: seeing Trish defensive of her stuff, barricaded by clutter, hands on her hips. It was Frances Granger right in front of me again.

When I didn't answer about "uncanny," Trish resumed her argument against calling in reinforcements in the form of our father. "You know what he'll do. He'll judge and yell and insult me."

I doubted the yelling. Our father was not a yeller. I didn't respond while I tried to marshal an argument that would make sense in her brain. Trish's brain was a place I'd never understood, and that was before.

"We need more people. We just do. More hands."

I had my own concerns about Dad's presence, but now that I'd seen the sprawling mass of stuff and how slow our progress was—what with Trish demanding the final say over every single object—I couldn't see any other way to make progress.

Trish shook her head, strands of her graying hair springing out of her bandanna. Jack had accompanied his big brother into town to pick up pizza, so for now we were alone.

I needed some kind of leverage. I held my breath and stepped into a breach I'd dared not cross in fourteen years.

"What if I give you Mom's ring?"

This yanked her out of her furious, full-body refusal.

"You mean you will *bribe* me, by giving me something that was mine in the first place?"

"It was Mom's in the first place."

One of the squalls that eroded our sisterhood had been the issue of the Ring, one of the few of Mother's things to have survived. It was a simple diamond solitaire in a shape like a pointy oval, the technical name for which I never knew. The thin gold band curled up on each side of the stone. It was what my beat-walking cop father could afford, and one of the few precious items Mother managed not to lose in the rising tide of her junk.

Our father had given it to me, reasoning perhaps that Trish already had her own wedding ring and husband. Trish swore it had been intended for her, as the oldest. My mother never made a will, so one could only guess.

"I can't believe you," Trish sneered.

"Do you want it or not?"

"Not like this."

"Are you waiting for a miracle, here? How do you think this is going to get done?"

"Next you'll tell me to call my ex-husband. And anyway, it's not that bad."

"If this is 'not that bad,' I'd hate to see your definition of 'bad.' "

"Maybe I don't need your help at all. A couple weeks of working in the evenings and I'll be done here anyway."

A couple of weeks? After work?

After furiously working all day, we still hadn't reached the outer ring of junk along the walls. The Keep tarp outside held enough items to easily fill the floor space in the room, so really all we'd managed to clear was air. And where would she put the items for "sale" until she got around to selling them?

Trish used to rage at this kind of thing in our mother, the blinders through which she could not see reality. The funny thing about denial, though, is that you never know you're doing it.

I'd been wearing yellow gloves, and I peeled them off and tossed them on the nearest pile. I kicked one bag out of childish spite as I left the kitchen, swung past a fuming Trish, and made for the front door.

Stupid of me to think that she'd take her dumb little sister seriously enough to listen. Maybe it wouldn't be so bad for Jack after all. It would be hard for him to move in with his dad, but it's not like he'd be tossed into foster care with strangers. With Ron, he wouldn't be hurt by falling debris. He could breathe clear air, have room to play, have actual, real live friends who could visit him.

I glanced back at the kitchen where Trish was staring pointedly at a piece of paper, her back to me. Her piles stood around her like sentries.

Jack and Drew were coming in the front door with pizza.

"Aunt Mary!" Jack called as he struggled his way out of his coat, one-armed, until I came over to help him. "We got mushrooms cuz you said you like 'em."

"I'm not sure I'll be able to stay after all."

I always wondered where the word *crestfallen* came from. If Jack had a crest, it fell right then. I hadn't guessed he would care. I barely knew him. Maybe he was starved for connection outside his home.

All the more reason he should move in with Ron, who, after all, was a good guy, as far as I ever saw. Stable job and all that.

I met Drew's eyes then, and he just nodded. I knew that he wouldn't last on this shrinking cleaning crew either. He'd go to Gulf Shores with his redheaded girlfriend, and Jack would go off with his dad over spring break and maybe not come back.

And if I left too, that would leave Trish here alone. Just like Frances.

The boys picked their way through the junk to the kitchen where they laid out the pizza on the cold stove burners, digging through the shopping bags for plates, napkins. I watched them work at this and wondered whether my presence here made one jot of difference, or whether—as with George at the store—I was just another body, breathing the air, taking up space.

"Call him," Trish said at my ear, startling me badly. I nearly toppled into a pile of boxes at my elbow. I hadn't noticed her approach.

"What, who? Dad?"

"Yes, doofus. Call whoever you want. Call CNN. I might as well be thoroughly humiliated."

"Why would you be humiliated?"

She gave me that classic "are you a moron?" Trish glare, a combination of sneer and stare that from our earliest adolescent arguments could make me flush with embarrassed anger from scalp to soles.

"We're not going to humiliate you."

"Whatever. Call him."

She turned and stalked back to the kitchen.

I excused myself to the car for the phone call, the only place I could be sure of privacy. As my dad's house phone rang, I realized I wasn't sure he'd come. That would be worse yet, to have Trish capitulate to me in asking him, only to have him refuse.

Ellen answered. "Well, hi, Mary," she said. "To what do we owe this pleasure?"

Ellen was southern by birth, though she'd been living in the Yankee north for over twenty years. Dad married her after I graduated from college, so I never lived with her. In actual fact I didn't know her very well other than as a voice on the phone and a hostess of awkward, infrequent dinners. Sometimes I imagined she put on her accent like some people put on perfume.

"I need to talk to Dad."

"Sure, honey. Let me just get him for you."

"Y'ello," Dad answered. "Hiya, Peaches. What's up?"

"Trish wants your help," I blurted. When I planned what to say, it never worked out any better; maybe blurting was the way to go.

"Does she? Or did you badger her until she caved?"

"Hardly any badgering. I only got here this morning."

"I'm not interested in getting screamed at."

"Me neither. Think of your grandson. You said you'd do it if she asked."

"You're the one calling me, not her." He paused, and I braced for his refusal, already rehearsing how I'd explain this to Trish, then enduring her subsequent rage and indignation. "But anyways. All right," he said. "See you later then."

I put my phone back in my purse and found myself unable to get out of the car for several long moments. I wanted Dad to help, got Trish to agree, and he agreed to come.

I could not reconcile this supposed victory with a heavy rhythm of foreboding drumming away in my chest.

Chapter 11

When I found my box of tapes, I squealed like a ten-year-old girl.

"Mary! Look at this!"

My sister stumbled over a sliding pile of paperwork as she forged a path to me. I'd found a cardboard box crammed with old cassette tapes, as luck would have it, next to a portable tape player, what we called back in the day "a boom box" or sometimes "a ghetto blaster," which was hilarious for white kids who mainly played Debbie Gibson or Wham!

Mary finished her trek to me and laughed, reaching into the box to flip through the cases. "No way." Her teenage phrasing, headband, and laugh . . . Suddenly I saw her as fourteen, wearing fingerless lace gloves trying to be like the cool girls. I could still cringe thinking of her announcing that she loved the song "Like a Version," to explosions of laughter from my friends. And me, too.

I saw twin theater masks on a cover and whooped. "Theater of Pain!"

I scrambled through piles of stuff to uncover a power outlet and plugged in the old boom box. I fast-forwarded to my favorite song, second track, and started wailing along with Vince Neil and Mötley Crüe about smoking in the boys' room . . .

I leaned back against a cleared space of wall and closed my eyes in a nostalgia haze, feeling as warm as if I was making out with Bobby in his car, for real. With a little Boone's Farm in a travel cup and my cute boyfriend beside me, everything seemed so perfect.

This was what the rest of them could never understand. Sure, I could have sold or donated these tapes years ago. I'd have about—I opened one eye to gauge the size—one square foot of space more. But I wouldn't have this! This moment!

I could taste the ChapStick Bobby used, smell the Polo cologne. In the middle of my messy house, in my spongy forty-year-old body with graying hair and stretch marks, I soaked in that scary delight of first love, that top-of-the-roller-coaster feeling that is so intense and gone so fast, forever. Only it didn't disappear for me; a physical object was all I needed. I had a time machine and fountain of youth all at once and they wanted me to throw that away?

What I needed was to organize. A storage unit for some things. Ron had always put his foot down about that, saying it was dumb to pay rent for junk we never used, which was why it was in storage. But Ron left, so he shouldn't get a vote anymore.

Vince suddenly stopped shrieking, and the silence made me jerk my eyes open. My father straightened to full height above me, apparently having punched the Stop button.

"You never could hear a thing when you played that god-awful crap."

"Hi, Dad." I tried to unfold gracefully, but I'd nestled myself into a rather small space. Dad stuck out his hand and I took it, and its familiar roughness came with a pointed realization that it had been a long time since we'd touched each other.

He pulled me in for a hug. "Hi, Patty Cake."

He was the only one who was ever allowed to call me Patty, much less Patty Cake, and he hadn't done even that since before I grew boobs. In my Mötley Crüe, teased-hair, silver-skull-jewelry phase I'd put a quick stop to any and all girlishness.

By the time I might've softened, he'd hightailed it out of there. Along with Mary.

Dad let go of me and I could see Mary behind him, and the high of my time travel faded away. Thick as thieves, they were. Same fair coloring, same wiry slenderness, same judgmental attitude that let the whole world know they were better.

I noticed that Dad hadn't yet looked me in the eye. I also noticed the tightness of his jaw and the way he stood ramrod straight like he was at attention.

"What's wrong?" I asked.

He met my eyes then. He cocked one eyebrow at me, not a single other muscle moving anywhere.

"It just got a little out of hand," I offered.

"Come with me," he commanded, and walked away, refusing to pick his way carefully through the mess and in doing so, he left boot prints on some old newspapers, a sweater, and an unidentified shopping bag.

I followed, but I lifted my chin as I walked past Mary. I didn't cower as a teenager, and I certainly wouldn't now.

Whatever he had to say—he was in my house, this time.

I followed him out through the garage and joined him in the backyard. He stood with folded arms, legs planted firmly at shoulder width, looking out over my property like the lord of the manor.

I stood next to him, folding my own arms and regarding the woods. *My* woods. "Do you have any idea," he began, "what it's like for me to see that?"

"I don't suppose it feels good," I allowed.

"No. It damn sure doesn't feel good."

It was almost dinnertime; the sun had reached its peak, teased us with a notion of what true spring would be like, and now the air was growing cool again. An animal rustled in the distance, maybe the neighbor's hound dog, and reminded me of Jack's pleading for a puppy all last year.

My dad cleared his throat. "I thought you hated living like that with Mom."

"I stayed, didn't I?"

"It would have been hard to leave your own mother."

"Mary didn't find it so hard."

I remembered Mary packing her things at the tender age of fifteen. Mary always was more fragile, buffeted by any problem that blew through her life. Delicate, our mother always said. She couldn't take it, so she left; they both did.

I took it. I took it for years.

"Point is," he continued, "you used to tell me all the time how much you hated it. How embarrassed you were about the house."

I couldn't deny that truth.

"Why didn't you tell me Jack got hurt?" he asked. I risked a glance at him and could see his fingers digging into the sleeves of his flannel shirt as he folded his arms.

"It's under control and healing nicely."

"That's not the point now, is it?"

"I'm cleaning up. You're here, aren't you?"

"Yep." He turned on his heel and gave my shoulder a firm, masculine clap before he led the way back into the house. "Let's get to it."

In minutes my father commandeered the helm of my ship. He created an assembly line. Drew and Mary would pick up items and hand them to me alternately, I would determine their fate, then he and Jack would cart them out to their proper location.

In this way we got through several living room piles until we had almost reached the couch. Everyone's faces brightened. My dad started telling funny stories from his days as a Lansing cop.

All this was swell and should have been freakin' fantastic, only an invisible hand was turning up the volume on my panic.

When I said "keep" on some old paper towel rolls—they could have been used for crafts—my dad's glare could have peeled paint off the walls. I shook my head and said "toss."

An out-of-style sweater passed through my sister's hands and as she held it up I said "keep"—Ron bought that for me our first Christmas—and Drew coughed out an irritated sigh and I grumbled, "fine, donate," and then several bags passed under my eyes but I didn't have time to really search. If they held a bunch of papers and receipts, they'd barely slow down before waiting for me to squeak out "toss" and whisk them out of my view.

I kept looking at the cleared carpet, thinking, *progress progress progress,* but my heart was thudding and sweat was pooling in my cleavage.

I watched Drew hoisting a box to his shoulder that had held clothes of mine from several years and three dress sizes ago, and my father hauling out a box of Christmas ornaments—mostly broken—which Ronald and I had purchased together, and the room felt too hot suddenly, and I lost my sense of which way was up and then all of them faded to black.

I opened my eyes to see my eldest son's face, and for a moment I thought he'd taken to wearing white makeup in addition to the black eyeliner and hair dye. Then I saw how stricken he was, his eyes were reddened even, and it hit me that he thought I was dead or something.

"I'm OK," I mumbled, and tried to sit up and realized my dad was already propping me up.

"Told you this place was unhealthy," Drew murmured, the color rising to his face again.

"It's not the house; it's me," I mumbled, but my lips felt funny, half numb like at the dentist. The stars were still swimming around the edges of my vision.

"Should I call 911?" That was Mary, from somewhere unseen.

"You do it and I'll kick you in the head," I shouted.

"Well, all right then," she replied.

I pulled myself fully to a seated cross-legged position. My dad still had not spoken. His hand was at my lower back and I shrugged it off like it was a bug. I put my head in my hands.

"Mama, that was scary," said Jack. He scooted close to his brother, and Drew wrapped a protective arm around him. I wanted to swoon again with how sweet that looked, despite Drew's punk rock gear.

"Sorry, buddy, this is a little overwhelming. I think I was going too fast."

"If that was too fast for you, we have a problem," my father muttered.

I twisted around to look at Dad, who had stood up again. He said, "I think we all need a break. Mary, could you take Jack and Drew to dinner, please? My treat."

Mary replied, "No, I got it, Dad. Come on, kids."

"No!" I clambered up unsteadily, batting away Drew's hand and ignoring Mary's. "They're my kids, and I get to decide about their dinner. Andrew Dietrich, don't you dare roll your eyes at me. I saw that."

My dad folded his arms. "I'm just trying to give them a little breathing room. And I'd like to talk to you."

"Let's go, Aunt Mary," Drew said. "I'll drive because I know where everything is."

Drew led the way and Jack snuck in for a hug. "Bye, Mama. I'm hungry anyway. Can I bring you something back?"

"I'm not hungry," I replied, forcing a smile and kissing the top of his head.

And just like I didn't matter more than chewed-up gum on the bottom of their shoes, my sister and my kids walked out the door.

My dad was doing his military man thing again. A stint in the army, years of the army reserves, working as a beat cop, then as a police sergeant until retirement had all taught him that discipline was everything. No wonder he was so disgusted with our mother, and now, me.

"So." I was shaky but standing. Good enough. "What did you want to talk about that you had to send my kids out of the house?"

"I'm taking Jack home with me."

"No, you're not!" My heart started racing like a spooked horse. I steadied myself on a nearby plastic storage bin. "If you try to take him out of here, I'll call the police!"

"That would be quite the scene, now, wouldn't it?"

"You would forcibly try to remove my son?"

"I would invite my grandson over to visit. It's been a while. He loves Ellen's cooking."

"You will not. In fact, you better get the hell out of here. I don't need you coming in here to take over everything like I'm not even here."

"I'm not leaving here without Jack. It's not safe here for him. He was hurt already, and now that all this stuff is getting moved around, it's only going to get worse."

"He's fine!"

"Now that I've seen it with my own eyes I cannot in good conscience leave him in this mess. He is coming home with me."

"Over my dead body."

"I'm sure the doctor reported this, didn't he?"

I couldn't reply. I was concentrating on not folding like a lawn chair again.

"They're mandated reporters so I have to assume they did."

He paused, and I still couldn't answer. Swells of nausea were rolling through me. He might as well knife me as take my son away. My own father. And I knew him well enough to understand that he would do what he said. He would take Jack home with him, even if Jack caused a tearful scene, even if I called the police to say he'd run off with my child. And if I really did it, if I called the police, it would be more official eyes on my house. Another report for Ayana the social worker.

He had me in a corner, and he knew it, the cold, self-righteous bastard.

"I have no choice," I croaked out. "But after this, you're dead to me."

My father's stern expression cracked open.

I said, "What, you thought I'd fall down at your feet and thank you for taking my youngest son away, the only person in this world who still loves me? And I'll have to beg you to get him back, I know. I'll have to prove to you that my house is in perfect condition. It's not much different than if a government bureaucrat came in here and took him, only it's you, my own father, my last living parent."

"You think I don't love you?"

"Spare me the heartbroken parent shit. You had plenty of chances to be a father to me, and you gave up on that by moving out when I was fifteen, when I most needed my dad."

"Not true," he said softly. "You were the one who shut me out."

"I'm not the one who abandoned my mother to die in an inferno."

He flinched again, and I worried I might have gone too far. But the next thing he said wiped away any remorse.

"I'm making sure that doesn't happen to Jack." He grabbed a trash bag and snapped it open. "We gonna do this or what?" He grabbed something. "Keep or sell?"

I could barely see through a haze of rage and didn't answer.

He shoved it in front of my face. It was a dusty clear glass vase that had once held flowers Ron had sent to me on my birthday. I grabbed it from him and threw it past his head with all my might toward the kitchen, where it smashed against the sliding patio door. The sound of raining glass was like wind chimes.

Chapter 12

Drew slouched low in his seat, texting. Based on his tragedy-mask frown, it was a fair bet he was texting with the absent beauty, Miranda.

"Everything OK?" I asked.

He snorted in reply.

Jack was stirring the ice in his water glass and looking more worried by the moment. We'd picked an all-day-breakfast-type diner after ruling out Mexican, pizza, and McDonald's. I was not in the mood for heavy, breakfasty food. I wasn't hungry in the least.

The waitress came back to top off my coffee. I tried to put my hand over it to stop her and nearly got scalded. The kids ordered pancakes, I ordered an omelet.

Jack scowled at the table. In our bubble of silence in the busy restaurant, I scanned the paper placemat with its local advertisements for auto salvage, a charity golf outing, propane, an excavating service.

"What's on your mind?" I finally asked Jack, and he shook his head.

Drew was no help, still deep in whatever conversation he was having, hands below the table.

"How's school?" I ventured.

"Fine," Jack answered.

"You could draw on the back of your placemat."

He shrugged.

I looked up at the ceiling, searching my mental files for anything that would amuse and distract a seven-year-old. My old college friend Seth came to mind, probably prodded out of my gray matter by the eggy smell of the diner. We'd spent many a Sunday morning at Denny's laughing at the hungover specimens we saw dragging in for eggs and coffee. I didn't go in for excessive drinking, and neither did Seth. He was too busy studying.

"Hey, Jack, watch this."

I picked up a liquid creamer cup and stabbed through the foil top with a fork. This action caused Drew at last to pull his eyes up away from his phone screen. I turned the container upside down over my coffee and squeezed rhythmically, the creamer shooting out in white streams.

"Cow," I explained.

Drew allowed himself a smirk that almost, not quite, barely reached the level of smile, before returning to his phone. Jack tore loose with laughter and made me repeat the trick with every creamer on the table until my coffee was a sickly beige. I drank it anyway, happy to have done something useful at last.

Once Jack's giggles subsided and our food arrived, we ate in silence for several minutes until Jack unloaded with a question that caught me with my mouth full of egg.

"Am I gonna have to get a new family? People I don't even know?"

Drew had finally put away his phone to eat, so he started to answer while I choked down my food.

"No," Drew said. "No way. If anything, you might have to go stay with your dad for a while."

Jack's face crumpled up. "I don't want to."

"Why not?" I asked, finally able to speak.

"It's boring there. He's always working. We go to Grandma's a lot, but she never plays with me."

Drew and I traded looks again.

"That's why we're helping clean up," I said. "So you can stay put."

"I want to stay put. I love my mom."

"Of course you do."

Drew shifted in the booth so he could address his little brother. "Buddy, you know you can love Mom and not live with her for a little bit."

"You only say that because you're always at your girlfriend's." Jack pouted, and as he slouched down, he looked so much like a pint-size version of Drew it was a time warp.

"I kinda have to be. I can't even *see* the bed in my room anymore."

"If you really loved her, you wouldn't leave her."

"I didn't leave her," Drew said, turning back to his plate. "She drove me out."

"She did not!" Jack insisted.

A few heads nearby swiveled toward us. The waitress at the next table glanced our way as she set down someone else's coffee mug. My skin prickled under my shirt at all the attention.

"Jack," I said, "if he didn't love her, he wouldn't be spending his weekend sorting through garbage—"

"It's not garbage, it's her things. And my things, like my coloring you tried to throw out. Why does everyone else get to be in charge of our stuff!"

Drew put his arm around Jack. "Come on, pal, let's go outside a minute."

"I don't want to go outside! I want to go home! Take me home!"

More waitresses had paused in their serving. I was aware how obviously I was not his mother.

Drew was telling Jack he hadn't eaten nearly enough, but Jack was dissolving into hiccupy crying and tears. Finally our young, ponytailed server hustled over, and with impressive authority Drew asked for the check and to-go boxes.

The boxes and bill appeared with miracle speed, the staff no doubt wanting to be rid of us as fast as possible.

I had to wrestle with Drew for the bill. I couldn't let a teenager pay for me. I finally sent him out to the car to get Jack buckled in. I balanced three to-go boxes of still-warm food and my coat and scrambled to pay at the register.

"Rough night?" said the gray-haired woman behind the counter, peering at me over wire-rimmed reading glasses.

"I'm his aunt," I said, stupidly.

"Kids are tough," she replied, fingers flying over the keys.

"I noticed," I mumbled, leaving the warm diner for the cold March night and the disappearing sun, my two nephews already seated and sullen in Drew's beat-up car.

J ack and I walked back into the house alone. We'd finished our meals in the car on the way back, and Drew stayed in his car to finish his and, I suspected, to call his girlfriend.

Jack's face was still shiny wet, as if he'd sobbed quietly the whole drive home.

I worried Trish would see how upset he was and blame me for it.

Trish hugged Jack when she saw him but didn't question his tears. She was down on her knees so they could be nearly level, and she had her arms wrapped around his waist, away from his injured shoulder.

She rocked him in that stance, and he sniveled on her shoulder. Jack seemed young then, more like a toddler than a kid in grade school. He was so brittle—so quick to spin away into crying.

In seeing their bond, I imagined it broken, that Jack called someplace else home—unwillingly—leaving Trish alone in her hoarded cave.

It would kill her.

It would be physiologically impossible to die of heartbreak, of course. But someday we'd get a call. A fire, or perhaps a collapse of stuff on her head. Or she'd take to pills or drinking to numb the grief and go too far. She could trip going down her basement stairs and break her neck. For that matter, she could lie trapped and broken on the steps, alone and away from her phone, until she starved or bled to death.

Then Jack, as he matured without his mother, would cope with the pain in the ways that teen boys do, something poisonous or dangerous. And I'd get another call.

Trish finally released Jack and wiped the tears off his face with her thumbs. "Pal, listen, I think it would be a good idea if you stayed with Grandpa and Ellen this weekend."

He shook his head, looking at the floor.

"Because this is a ton of work here, pal, and I'm afraid that one of these piles could fall again, or you could trip, because you can't balance as well with one arm, right? And Grandpa will make it fun. He said he'd take you to see any movie you want."

"Any?"

"PG or less, anyway." Trish smiled, but her eyes were dead. "And you can have popcorn and stay up late. It'll be a lot more fun than working here."

"I guess," Jack said, his face showing how torn he was between the hedonistic fun he was promised and his attachment to his mom. "But . . . will I get to come back?"

"Absolutely," Trish said, pulling him into a hug again. "I promise. I swear, in fact."

"Pinky swear," Jack said, holding out his good hand.

They wrapped pinkies and smiled at each other.

My dad finally appeared from a back room, carrying a Spider-Man backpack and a ratty old stuffed cat. Good-byes were managed with just a few tears, and soon my dad's Chevy puttered off in the night. Trish never looked at our father during this exchange, and she never said good-bye.

"I think this is a good idea," I told Trish after their taillights had disappeared down the rural road. "We'll be able to go faster if we don't have to worry about Jack underfoot."

"Fuck off," Trish spat, storming past me to the farthest corner of her living room that her hoard would allow.

Chapter 13

Drew stood before me, his hair limp with sweat from hauling my crap around. He'd spent the last half hour putting tarps over my stuff outside and moving some valuable Keep things into the garage.

"So. I'm gonna go, then."

"Back to Miranda's."

He kicked at the gravel in the driveway with his Converse sneakers. He'd drawn an anarchy symbol on one toe, and a pentagram on the other, in black permanent marker. I was surprised that the parents of perky Miranda weren't upset by this. Maybe they thought they could do a better job of parenting him. Save him from his Satanic punk doom.

He turned away as I was getting ready to hug him, striding over the drive with his lanky legs, just like his late father. I felt guilty once again that I'd been even a tiny bit relieved about Greg dying in an ATV accident before Drew's first birthday. Greg and I hadn't even liked each other, really, and he definitely didn't want to be a dad. He rarely saw the baby and usually just dropped off some diapers or formula as his half-ass form of child support. He had only come to the hospital for the birth because his parents dragged him there. I thought they'd keep in better touch with Andrew themselves, but they faded away after some strained and formal visits. They still send birthday cards. I suppose after losing their son, seeing his young doppelgänger might have been too unsettling.

This meant Drew never got to have his biological dad in his life, but it also meant he was spared the effects of Greg's deliberate absence.

Greg might have matured, though. Unfair to judge what he might have been, considering he never got the chance.

Then Ron adopted little Andy and we were a family. For a while, anyway.

Andy even started calling Ron "Pop," though since the divorce I'm not sure what he calls him, if anything. They have made their own visiting arrangements entirely separate from what I might have to say, or whatever the court papers said, which I can't even remember now.

"You can sleep on the couch," I said to Mary when I came back inside, noting that it was already past 9:00 p.m. We'd cleared a nice wide swath up to the couch. The junk was retreating to a barricade along the walls in this room. I tried not to think about the large Keep tarp outside.

Mary looked like she'd been slapped. "What? No, I couldn't possibly."

I knew from her tone what she meant by "couldn't possibly." And she wasn't talking about not wanting to be a bother.

"You're gonna drive all the way back to Ypsilanti?"

"It's not Timbuktu. But, no, probably not; I'll . . . stay in a hotel. Or something."

"You just lost your job you said."

"I won't pick anyplace fancy. I'll be fine."

I muttered, "I hope you get bedbugs," and sat down on the couch. "I'm exhausted. I'm so done I'm like a burned turkey."

Mary sighed and joined me on the couch, still perching on the edge like a prissy little bird. "Yeah. I think I'll sit for a spell before I hit the road."

I grabbed the clicker and flicked channels. Sitcom, sitcom. *American Idol.* Grisly crime show. Creeping into the cable channels we passed a cooking show, and one of those design shows where they turn a shitbox apartment into a showplace. I paused, admiring the warm peachy-orange color the designer was slathering on the wall.

"You ever watch any of those hoarding shows?" Mary asked.

I snorted. "No. Why would I?"

I could feel her staring at me now. I kept pointing the clicker at the TV. Spring training on ESPN, home improvement, cooking show, some lady wringing her hands on the Lifetime channel.

"You don't find them . . . educational?"

I tossed the remote to the floor and finally turned to face her. She was folding her hands and staring down at them. I wondered if she was praying.

I prayed for strength not to wring her self-righteous scrawny neck.

"I am not a hoarder," I said. "And those shows are exploitive trash."

Mary turned to me and slowly raised her eyebrows, saying nothing else.

"Oh, shut up. I'm not like those people, and I'm not like Mom. I do not leave food lying around, I don't have cat shit everywhere."

"Thank goodness for that." Mary nodded.

"I just got . . . overwhelmed, OK? Divorce will do that to a person. I'm sure you've got all the time in the world to alphabetize your spice rack, but some of us have a life."

"I don't like spicy food."

I put my head in my hands. "Stay with me here, Mary. It's just an expression."

"So I don't have a life, then?"

"I'm just saying when you're single without kids . . ."

Mary stood up, smoothing her shirt. "No, I get it. You're right. I have no life. I would get up and work and come home and clean and go to bed. Alone. Thank you for pointing it out so carefully." She picked up her purse from the floor near her feet. "I lead a sterile existence. But I would like to point out there are plenty of people who have busy, full lives whose piles of junk don't crush their children."

"How dare you."

"How dare I what? Surely you can't tell me that everyone lives this way. You're not crazy."

"Oh, thanks for giving me that much."

"I mean, look at this, really look!"

"We've made progress, here. It's not that bad."

Mary set her lips in a thin, grim line. I knew that face. Mary may have been the quiet one, but she could get just as pissed off as any of us.

She turned away from me and headed down my hall. Because I understand her weird little brain, I knew just where she was going.

"No! Stay out of there!" I slipped on some magazines, so she was faster. She pulled open a door to the Green Room.

There was a wall of things higher than our heads. It nearly reached the top of the door frame.

"We don't use that room," I said, by way of explanation.

"Clearly."

"It's a storage room."

"So it seems."

"Storage rooms can be messy."

"So what do you store in here, then?" she asked, reaching out and pulling a shoebox off the top of the pile. She lost her grip on it and it tumbled to the floor, spilling postcards, letters, and an old composition book down onto the carpet. She made to pick up the book.

I grabbed her by the shoulders and pushed her away from the door, turning her so her back was against the hallway wall. "Don't you ever, ever! Touch anything in that room."

Mary squirmed in my grip, but I wasn't done. "You have no right to come charging in here telling me how crazy I am and touching things that don't belong to you."

She pushed back against my shoulders with surprising force, until my back slammed into the opposite hallway wall. "For God's sake, Trish! Maybe you are crazy!"

I slapped her snotty little face.

She was already striding away from me, but I pushed her from behind, speeding her down the hall, giving her a final push into the living room, which made her stumble forward into a pile of things, causing that pile to slide down and cover a good chunk of carpet we'd spent the day clearing.

Mary grabbed her purse again off the floor and ran out, not bothering to close the front door behind her. I slammed the door hard as she hopped into her car and sped away. I could hear the gravel spraying out from under her tires. I figured she'd drive all the way back to Ypsilanti and I'd probably never see her again. Not until Dad died or something.

For a few exhilarated moments I felt victorious. I'd expelled an intruder. I'd saved the sanctity of my home.

Then I thought of the things in the hallway and knew I had to get them off the floor. They didn't belong there; they could be ruined.

I scrambled back to the hallway and put the letters and book back in the box as a highlight reel in my head played back what just happened. Had I really slammed my sister against a wall? And slapped her? It seemed unreal, like something from a movie I'd watched. I'd never raised my hand to her before. Not to anyone, in fact. I don't even like violent movies.

My hands were shaking so hard I could barely keep my grip on the box. I replaced the lid with trembling hands, watching the cursive name written on the front of the notebook disappear under the cardboard: *Frances Van Linden.*

The furnace was running, I could hear its *whoosh,* but right then a cold bubble of air settled around me.

"Mom?" I whispered, then felt foolish. It was a draft, that's all. Houses have drafts all the time.

I pictured our mother, and what she would think of me hitting Mary. She'd have been horrified. She never once raised a hand to us. To my great irritation she was always defending Mary, though now that I have both an older and a younger child I understand why. And Mary, though only two years younger than me, seemed leagues behind in knowing how to navigate the messy, confusing world.

Not only have I failed to protect my baby sister, I just attacked her and forced her out of my home, for the great crime of touching a box. A box of mementoes that she had as much right to as I did.

"I'm sorry, Mom," I whispered, not feeling foolish this time. "I'm sorry I did that."

I sat in the hall with the box in my lap. Whether I truly felt her presence or was making it up in my sick little head, I sat there anyway, saying "sorry" in rhythm with a ticking clock, the only other sound in my house.

Chapter 14

I'd intended to drive all the way back to my town house and leave her to rot with her garbage. Jack was with our dad, Drew had made other arrangements, and whatever happened to Trish, she'd chosen for herself.

I didn't like hotels. Especially not cheap hotels by the side of the highway advertising their rates in red lights.

But I couldn't even focus on the road and kept seeing vague outlines of deer along the highway, which might dash out and cause me to swerve and die in a fiery wreck.

I steeled myself for the inevitable and pulled into the parking lot of someplace advertising rooms for $55.

I rushed into the lobby, blinking in the inhumanely bright light, my cheek still stinging.

If the hotel clerk thought anything about my pink cheek and zombielike demeanor on a Saturday night, she didn't show it. As we walked through the mechanics of getting a room, I tried not to look at the peeling wallpaper on the wall behind the desk.

At the room door, I sucked in a breath and shoved in quickly, eyes closed tight.

I opened them and surveyed the room. It was standard-issue high-way motel stuff. I hadn't been in a place like this since our last family vacation as a kid. A rush of sensation hit me as I pondered all the people who'd been in here, what they would have been doing in here. I imagined maids rushing through their work, onto the next room, paid too little to care about being thorough.

I walked to the bed and yanked back the never-washed comforter and sank onto the scratchy sheets, which at least would have been washed before me.

I gazed at the popcorn ceiling and put one hand over my heart, try-ing to will it to slow down before I had a heart attack and died all alone in an EconoLodge.

It hurt when Trish slapped me, no mistake. But worse was the surge of fear. My sister never would have done that to me, no matter what our differences. It's true that for our whole lives I've shrunk down in the face of her temper, her sneering dismissal of me. It's true that even as I was charging down the hall, propelled by frustration, part of me wanted to reel myself in and revert to cowering and deflecting.

But I never dreamed she'd hit me.

So this wasn't my sister in that house. Hoarding had taken her over, possessed her.

I imagined Trish still in there somewhere, fighting the demon, sometimes emerging for a few minutes to clear a path in the hoard, then the demon would surge up again, turning her into someone who could attack her little sister.

It occurred to me, what if Jack hadn't been injured by stuff? What if . . . ?

No, not her little boy. Never.

But then, I never thought she'd hit me, either.

I pulled myself off the bed and squinted into the mirror in the bath-room. The unforgiving light put my cheek in spotlight. The red had faded. I saw no signs of a bruise. It was, after all, an openhanded slap.

Not a punch. I pushed up my sleeve to inspect my upper arm. I could, in fact, see some bruising there, where she'd grabbed me and slammed me against the wall so hard my teeth clacked together.

I returned to the bed and lay down, curled on my side.

I was no exorcist. I could sort her things and I could carry bags of trash, but I couldn't drive out this demon. She'd need the mental health version of a priest with holy water. She'd need a shrink.

I sprung upright on the bed. A shrink! Seth! Maybe he could help her.

I sank back down to the mattress as quickly as I'd been inspired. Trish would never stand for such a thing. The demon wouldn't let her. The horrific catch-22 of mental illness.

M y eyes popped open to the jarring metallic blare of my cell phone. I scrabbled around the bedsheets for it, finally springing up and grabbing it from my purse on the nightstand. The curtains had not been closed all the way, and a knife of bright sun slashed across the dim gray of the hotel room.

I'd barely assembled the previous day's events in my head when I answered sleepily. "Hello."

"It's Trish."

"Oh."

"Look, I wasn't myself yesterday."

"True."

I bit my lip in an effort to keep myself from blurting out apologies.

Sorry, I said to the woman in the parking lot who banged her cart into my car, leaving a scrape in the paint. Sorry, I said to a date when I happened to glance at his cell phone as a text from his ex-girlfriend came in. Sorry, I said to a coworker at the store when she reneged on her promise to cover a shift for me.

I could hear Trish swallow hard. I did not relish her discomfort, and every old habit was primed to launch a "sorry" out of me, first.

"I need you to come back," Trish finally said. I closed my eyes and sagged with disappointment. Of course she needed me. That's what prompted the call, not true remorse.

I remembered the demon and struggled to forgive the real Trish.

"I don't know," I managed.

"There's something I need to show you," she continued. "Something that belonged to Mom that you need to see."

This piqued my interest at last. We'd given up hope of finding many of Mom's possessions intact after the fire; the ring's survival in a box in her underwear drawer had seemed like a miracle. She'd had a storage unit, but her most special things she kept close to her at home: her wedding dress, family photos, childhood mementoes. The storage unit was filled with old broken toys and flea market "finds" and at one point had flooded. Mother still hadn't wanted us to clean it out; Dad had thrown away the molded, warped junk over her protests, and she'd sulked for days.

Indignation surged on the heels of my curiosity. "You've had something of Mom's all this time? And you never told me?"

"It never seemed to be a good time."

I said, "True," because it was. "Fine. I need a shower and then I'll come back."

"Where are you?"

"At an EconoLodge. I didn't get very far." I opened my mouth to say good-bye and hang up when I heard Trish say, "Oh, Mary? I'm sorry."

She hung up first. I could imagine her gearing up to say the words, and then spitting them out fast, like ripping off a bandage.

While I was letting my hair dry—and if I were being honest with myself, stalling—I thumbed through my cell-phone contacts until I landed on the only person listed who was not a relative or co-worker.

Once a year, on our joint birthday, my cell-phone display would light up with his name. We'd share a memory or two of college and give each other the highlight reel of our past year. Seth would tell me about the conferences he attended and where he'd moved this time. He told me when he found a business partner and set up his own practice, when he got married, the birth of his daughter. I'd tell him I was still working at the store and then, for lack of anything else to say, would talk about my latest favorite book.

Occasionally he would send me a postcard from one of his professional conferences. Once, as a joke, I sent him one from Lansing. "Wish you were here," I'd written, intending for him to read it with an ironic smirk, though as I dropped the card in the mailbox I realized I'd written in earnest.

The only time we'd violated this pattern of our strange and ongoing friendship was the death of my mother. Seth came to the funeral, and said, "Call if you need anything."

That was fourteen years ago, and I'd never called. Hadn't needed anything. Correction: hadn't *thought* I needed anything. Hadn't *wanted* to need anything.

It would be bizarre to call now, wouldn't it? To violate the pattern? He'd said to call if I needed anything, but that was years ago, an offer he made when I was in the throes of my grief. What if his wife got angry? What if she barely tolerated our birthday calls as it was? What if she'd gotten the "wish you were here" postcard and torn it up? Our traditions made sense to the two of us, but I had just enough awareness to know this habit of ours was odd.

He probably wouldn't answer, I told myself. I could just leave a voice mail and see what happens.

I almost hung up in a panic when I got a human voice.

"Hello?"

"Seth?"

"Mary?" His voice was questioning, and I gulped hard.

"It's Mary Granger."

"Yes, I see that on my caller ID. Wow, I didn't expect to hear from you this morning."

"I didn't expect you to pick up."

"So you called to flirt with my voice mail?" Despite the banter, something about his voice sounded robotic and forced.

"No, I just . . . I was going to leave a message. I didn't expect to get you in person."

"It is Sunday morning and I'm a heathen."

"Oh, right. I mean, that it's Sunday, not that you're a heathen. I mean, I know you're not religious but I wouldn't say—"

"Breathe, Mary."

"Right. Hi."

"So let's start over and pretend you got a machine. OK, ready?" He cleared his throat. "Hello, you have reached the voice mail of Seth Davis. I'm either on the other line or away from my phone. Please leave a message after the tone." Then he performed an uncanny imitation of a voice-mail beep.

"Hello, Seth; it's Mary Granger," I said, smiling into the hotel room mirror across from me. "I know it's not our birthday or anything, but I've got a problem and I hope you can help me. Call me back when you can."

I almost hung up right then, as if I'd really been leaving a message.

"What problem?" he asked, his voice guarded again.

"It's my sister. You remember what happened to our mother?"

"Yes, I do."

"It's happening to her."

"Oh, no. I'm sorry. But what can I possibly do?"

"You're a psychologist, Seth. You gave me your card, remember? If I needed anything?" Maybe he didn't expect his offer would last for fourteen years. Or maybe it was never a genuine offer at all, more like an expected gesture, part of the unwritten funeral rites performed by us all.

"Well, I'm kind of . . . I'm on a sabbatical of sorts."

"Well, it's not like you put your clinical brain on the shelf, right? You still know what you know."

"I'm not so sure about that."

"What's going on?"

"I can't talk about it." All the larkiness was gone. I could picture his jaw tightening and his hands drumming the table, just like during exam week. I could almost hear it, in the background, in fact, a rhythmic light hammering.

"Seth, are you OK?"

"I'm fine."

"If I call you a liar, will you be offended?"

"Why don't you try it and see what happens?"

"I'm sorry I bothered you," I said, just then detecting a slight hurried tone to his voice, betraying impatience. I could feel a pink flush creep up my face, at my presumption for having called him at all. Irretrievably weird: that's Mary, all right. He dated my roommate. We shared coffee in college diners. He came to my mother's funeral. He owed me nothing, least of all free mental health advice for my crazy hoarding sister. He probably got this kind of demand all the time. I was no doubt only the latest in a parade of freeloaders asking him to psychoanalyze for free while he wrote massive checks to pay off student loans.

"You weren't bothering me," he said unconvincingly.

"Sorry, talk to you later, bye," I blurted in a rush, punching the cell button but missing it at first, so that I heard his voice saying "Mary?" before I managed to actually hang up.

It occurred to me I was running low on people to turn to for help.

I'd already summoned my father. George, whom I'd thought of as a close friend, and potential romance, was gone with a poof along with my job. Seth was busy living his life.

I steeled myself to venture back into Trish's house. I might have chosen to live with my father, but my heart never left her. Even if Trish and my mother both refused to believe it.

Chapter 15

Mary and I were on the couch again, our mother's diary on the table in front of us. My sister, as I could have predicted, was angry. In her muted, Mary kind of way.

"This is incredible. You've had this for fifteen years?"

Mary pressed her mouth into a thin line, waiting for me to justify myself.

The diary was a composition book, actually, with a marbled black-and-white cover on which was lettered in the precise, careful cursive my mother used for her entire life: Frances Van Linden.

I couldn't look at the diary without thinking of the day it ended up in my possession, though I didn't even know I had it, at first. Mother had just handed me a box of old clothes, saying, "You might want some of these. I wore this stuff in high school. Maybe you could wear it to a costume party or something." I'd rolled my eyes and she replied, "Look through the box. You never know, there might be something in there you like."

I was living in the trailer with Ron and Drew by that point and didn't want more stuff, not then. So I crammed it in a closet and forgot about it. I assumed this was one of her attempts to cut down on her clutter by passing it off on us. It wasn't really "gone" if it was still in the family, she figured.

Then she died. And we began moving into the house Ron built for me. She'd been gone a year, and in a fit of grief I yanked open the top and sobbed into the musty cardigans and skirts. It was in that process I saw something on the bottom of the box that wasn't clothing.

I opened the front cover expecting to find some homework assignment or other. *Dear Diary,* the first line had read, and I'd tossed it away from me, gasping.

This was the story I'd told Mary just now. This was what made her so angry.

"When she was first gone," I began, trying to explain myself, ". . . I couldn't read it. Andy was so young, Ron and I were just married, and I was grieving so hard. It was a terrible time."

"Granted, but maybe I could have read it."

"Things between us were so . . ." I pedaled my hands in the air, trying to grab the right word.

". . . fraught."

"Sure, that."

"But all those years, Trish."

"Fine, I suck. I'm a selfish bitch living in denial. I'm also a horrible mother and a disgusting person."

"You're not a horrible mother."

I rolled my eyes. Thanks for that much, Mary. "I can't turn back time. I called you, didn't I? I told you about it today, at least. I didn't have to do that; I could have put it away again and never breathed a word."

"And I could have gone home to my nice clean house and refused to take your call today."

"Well, aren't we both a couple of freakin' gosh darn holy saints, then."

This made Mary laugh, and I smiled, too. She was so pretty when she laughed, her pale face flushing with rosy color, her light hazel eyes crinkling up, shining bright. Pity she laughed so rarely.

Her chuckle subsided and she looked at the diary again, the mirth falling away from her as she pondered it, thinking of our mother. I wondered if Mary was doing what I often did: calculating what her age should be now, mentally slipping her into family events past and future. I imagined her helping to blow out the candles on Jack's last birthday. I imagined her clapping as she watched Drew cross the stage in his cap and gown next year.

Conjuring up my mother was impossible, though, without thinking of her clutter, and for that matter, the smell. When I finally moved out, she took in the first cat. At least I drew the line at animals.

Some line, though. I stared around at my partially excavated living room. The curtains were open in here for the first time since well before Ron left, and the natural light should have been refreshing and cheerful. It was always so bright this time of year, before the trees leafed out and shrouded my home with their cool shade.

The light was an indictment. I couldn't imagine the piles as vague shadows at the fringes of my vision anymore. Every shopping bag and piece of paper could be seen in bright color, high-definition 3-D reality.

"Are all the pages full?" Mary said, brushing the notebook with her fingertips. "I'm tempted to sit right down and read it all."

"I'm afraid to," I said.

"Why?"

"I'm afraid . . . I'm afraid we don't know our mother like we thought we did. I'm afraid of what we'll learn."

"Mom probably didn't even know she gave it to you. She never knew where anything was. She could have looked inside the top of the box, seen a bunch of her old clothes, and handed it off to you."

"I don't know."

Whether a premonition or a paranormal event or just a hunch, I felt that cold bubble of air settle on me again.

"How about this," said Mary, folding her hands on her lap and turning to me like a schoolteacher. "We parcel it out. Reading it can be an incentive for cleaning. We clean, we read a few pages. We clean some more, we read a few pages. It will be easier for you if we don't read it all in one go, and for me it will spur me on."

"Spur you on? You're staying?"

"I guess I am. I hope you promise not to hit me again, though."

Mary startled as I reached for her, but I only wanted a hug and to say I was sorry again. She was stiff in my arms, finally relaxing on my shoulder for half a heartbeat before releasing me and smoothing down her hair.

"Can I ask you, though?" she ventured, fussing with the hem of her T-shirt. "What is it about that room?"

I shook my head and would give no other answer.

"Shall we read an entry, then?" Mary said, reaching for the note-book. "Just to get us started?"

April 4, 1961

Dear Diary,

Lots of girls here are getting pinned, but I don't seem to be asked out very much. If anything, a bunch of us go out to the diner and I always end up sitting by Wally. I think he's got a crush on me, but I just think he's nice is all. I don't feel any of this powerful emotion that other girls seem to. Well, Mom always said I was a late bloomer. Anyway, I feel like I've known these boys my whole life. When you've seen a kid wiping snot on his sleeve in third grade, it makes it hard to think of him as attractive in eleventh grade.

This is exciting. My mom has started going to the mi-grant camps to help Doc Wilson vaccinate the children. I guess he started hearing about little Mexican kids getting really sick with preventable diseases, so he decided to do something about it. They don't have cars, and don't like going into town, so he's going to them, in a little trailer he pulls behind his truck. My dad is not so sure about this. He said she'd be "vulnerable." Mom scoffed and told him she'd be with the doc and would be perfectly safe, and anyway, what about the children? Why should they get sick? Mom said. It's the Christian thing to do. And that got him. He couldn't argue with that. It was exciting to see Mom standing up to my dad like that. Mostly she doesn't argue with him, just nods and lets him ramble on. I know for a fact, though, that she voted for Kennedy. She told me, when I asked her, but said not to tell Daddy because she didn't want a fight.

I've been thinking about what I want to study in college. I think my dad just wants me to find a husband and get married and he thinks I can find a better type of man in college than I can working as a secretary. And I do want to find a husband, eventually, somewhere, and have beautiful babies. But as long as I'm there, I want to learn something! Maybe I'll be a nurse like my mom. She loves caring for people, and so do I. Or a teacher. I could be a good teacher. I just really like kids. I mentioned this to Daddy, and he said a woman shouldn't work after marriage. I know it was sassy, but I couldn't help but point out that Mom works. Daddy scowled and said if he had a better station in life, there's no way his wife would work and that he wants me to improve over the quality of life we've led so far. That's what every father wants for his children, he said. A better life.

I snuck a look at Mom and she was very carefully cutting her meat into teeny tiny pieces, not looking up. I think she's glad she has to work.

That's when Margaret, of course, had to pipe up and agree, saying to be a wife and mother was plenty work enough for any woman. But she's only a kid, so what does she know?

I dropped the subject to keep the peace. I could see Daddy getting riled, and a funny vein was standing out on his head. I think he felt we were criticizing him by saying he didn't make enough money. I didn't want to make him feel bad. He really is a good father. He takes very good care of us.

Good night for now,
Frannie

Mary was a faster reader, always had been, so she was sitting back with her hands in her lap while I was still getting to "Frannie."

"Wow. I didn't know any of this," she said.

I finished the entry and sat back on the couch, my eyes still drinking in our mother's handwriting. We got a glimpse of her again, but she's still gone to us forever. I tried to remember mentions of our grandma Joan ever even having a job, much less as a nurse, much less volunteering to vaccinate children of the Mexican migrants who picked blueberries and cucumbers.

Mary said, "Mom didn't go to college, right? We would have known that, if she did."

I shook my head. "No, she didn't. She went to a secretarial school, I think. She did shorthand and whatever until she met Dad."

"I wonder what happened."

"I'm surprised Grandpa would have been able to even think about sending her. It's not like they had much money."

"Maybe that's what happened. Maybe they didn't have the money, in the end."

"She thinks she has a chance, though, here." I sighed for my optimistic teenage mother, blissfully ignorant of what lay in store for her years later.

"She sounds like a whole different person."

"Weren't you? When you were seventeen?"

I caught a rueful smile, almost a sneer, on Mary's face. "Yeah. Maybe."

Mary and I invited no one else over to help. Neither of us suggested it. I suspected Mary was uncomfortable around angry Drew, and our dad was watching Jack, and who else could we approach? Coworkers? Hardly. I had only my pint-size bitch-on-wheels boss, Angela. Neighbors? No thanks, they didn't need to see how I lived in here.

I could tell Mary disapproved of the large Keep pile growing outside. She said nothing, but she'd press her lips together firmly each time I said "keep" even for perfectly usable things, things still with tags on, some of them. And a broken vase could be glued.

My phone rang at almost lunchtime, and I couldn't get to it as I vaulted over piles. The caller ID when I finally reached the phone was for my dad's house and I dialed him back with a lump the size of a baseball in my throat, wondering if Jack was OK.

When I got him on the line, I was almost crying. "Dad? Is Jack all right?"

"Sure he is, Patty Cake. He just wanted to say hi."

"Hi, pal!" I exclaimed when he got on the phone, burying my fear with cheer. "Are you having fun?"

"Yeah, I guess so. We had tin roof sundaes and watched *Star Wars* and then this morning we played Wii."

"We what?"

"Wii, you know, Nintendo where you wave the thing around to play. Ellen says she bought it cuz her daughter has one and it's really cool."

We couldn't have a Wii. Not only did we have no money to spare, there was no room in here to be swinging our arms around. These were all things that make up a kid's idea of paradise on earth, but Jack sounded flat.

"What's wrong, pal? All of that sounds really fun. Does your shoulder hurt?"

"Nah, not really. I just miss you lots."

"I miss you too, pal, but you'll be back tonight. You'll have school in the morning. It won't be long."

"I guess. But Grandpa asked me if I wanted to stay. For a while. He said he could take me to school."

I had to force the words out; my throat felt swollen and thick. "Would you want to, pal?"

"It's pretty OK, here. I'd miss you, though."

Rage burned through my limbs. I gripped the phone harder, concentrating on choosing my next words.

"You don't have to go anywhere you don't want to, honey. Of course you can come home if you want." I made myself say the next words: "Or you can stay at Grandpa's if you want."

"Grandpa said we can go to Chuck E. Cheese tomorrow after school. That would be kinda fun."

"Pal, can you let me talk to your grandpa? I need to straighten this out."

"Yes?" my father said when he picked up the phone, relaxed and casual, like we'd been discussing a round of golf.

"You cannot do this," I hissed. "You cannot bribe my child away from me with Chuck E. Cheese and Wii and ice cream. He is my child and I want him home."

"I'm trying to help," he said coolly. "Jack is little, and he's injured, and he needs tending to. You have a big job ahead."

"Spring break is coming. I can work then."

"And in the meantime Jack is still having to stumble over things and breathing in all that dust."

"Do you want me to beg? Is that what you want to hear?"

"I want to hear you put your child's interests ahead of your own dependence on him."

"On him? I'm dependent on him?"

"You damn sure are. I think he doesn't sleep in his own bed because you want the company. I think that's why you're in no hurry to clean up his room."

"You son of a bitch. I'll show you. I'm going to clean up his room tonight and you will bring him back to me or so help me I will call the police and demand that you bring him back."

"You'd subject your child to that kind of scene?"

"I wouldn't be the one subjecting him. You are the one who has him and are refusing to give him back to me."

"He's not a toy to fight over."

"It seems I'm the only one who knows that. You're using him to punish me."

"I'm trying to protect him so he doesn't get hurt anymore. It's him I'm thinking of. Dammit, Trish, don't you get it? If that stuff landed on his head instead of his shoulder, he could have been killed."

I gasped, and my father continued, his voice cold and even. "This thing killed one person I loved, and I will not let it take anyone else. Do you hear me?"

Do you hear me? His famous words delivered at the end of a lecture on not smoking, on studying hard, on my above-the-knee skirts making me look like a streetwalker.

I concentrated hard on breathing so I wouldn't faint with my suffocating anger. "I will clean out his room and you will return him to me because his own room will be clean and the living room has enough space to walk through comfortably. If I have to get Ayana to use her resources—including cops, including a judge—to make you give him back, I will do it and don't think I won't."

"Only if the room is clean. If it's not, I'd say it's likely Ayana would be on my side, don't you think?"

I banged down the phone, and as my breathing slowed I hoped that my father had had enough sense to move where Jack couldn't hear him for that little exchange of ours.

The phone rang again and I picked it up with a curt, "Hello."

Jack shouted into the phone, "Oh, Mom, please don't get rid of Scruffy!"

I recovered my calm Mom voice with effort. "Oh, honey, I wouldn't; I know how much he means to you. We're only going to get rid of junk. Clothes that don't fit, broken toys, toys too little for you . . ."

"But, Mom, what if you have another baby? My baby brother could use those toys."

I clenched my fist, glad that Jack couldn't see me. "Honey, I'm not having any more babies. But look, let's not talk about this now. I promise not to get rid of anything really special."

"Pinky swear?"

"Pinky swear in the air." I waggled my curved pinky in front of the phone as if he could see.

"Love you, Mama," he said, and then just before hanging up he asked, "If I come home tomorrow, can we still go to Chuck E. Cheese?"

"We'll see," I said, my hand over my hammering heart. "We'll just have to see."

Chapter 16

Trish gripped a stuffed animal. It was a frog and was wearing what seemed to be a tutu. The green of the frog was frosted with a layer of gray, reminding me of volcanic ash, like those news segments about the Mount Saint Helens eruption I remember seeing as a kid.

Jack's treasured preschool-era Scruffy we'd already given a place of honor on the couch in the living room, that cleared space now to serve as the staging area for the emergency cleanup of Jack's room.

"He is not staying there another night," Trish had pronounced, fairly sprinting down the hall as she said so.

Trish's face contorted now as if she were suffering physical pain. Her knuckles were visibly white. I wondered how special this frog was, resting as it had been under Jack's bed. The edges of its little frog feet seemed to be flecked with mildew, but other than the dirt it looked almost new, that is to say, unused. Not well loved and snuggled like Scruffy, whose eye had fallen off and whose plush had been worn thin with love. And what little boy wanted a frog in a tutu?

"I bought this for him in his frog phase," Trish said, answering my unspoken question, or maybe just talking to herself. She seemed barely aware of my presence. "I knew it had a tutu but I thought Jack wouldn't mind. Or that I could snip it off and he'd never know. He had frog jammies, and frog toys for the bath, and a toothbrush with frogs on it. Even Ron brought home a notepad from a customer once that had a frog design on it. Jack used to put throw pillows on the floor and pretend they were lily pads and hop between them." Her eyes misted over.

"But Jack never played with this one."

Trish's head snapped up and she glared at me. I recognized the demon flickering in her gaze. "He loved this toy because he loved that I bought it for him and encouraged his interest. It sat on his bed for years."

I looked at Jack's bed, piled with clothes and stuffed toys. Trish followed my gaze and flinched away.

"Why is this so hard?" she moaned, still holding the frog in one hand and propping her head in her other hand.

"I don't know," I replied.

She snorted, and then said, her voice thick, "I wasn't asking you. Do you know you always answer rhetorical questions?"

"Yes."

It took me a minute of listening to Trish's half-sobbed giggles to figure out what was so funny. I had to allow a smile. Oh yes, a rhetorical question I answered.

Trish regarded the frog again. "What would Jack say if he were here?"

"Is that one rhetorical?"

"No."

"He'd want to keep it."

"You seem awfully sure."

"Remember the coloring pages? The only stuff he was OK with pitching out yesterday were things of yours. Anytime we happened across something of his, we put it in here." I pointed to a small mound near the door, with less dust than the rest of the room.

"So I should keep it," Trish said, but she sounded unsure.

"Is he likely to remember this particular frog?"

"You would not believe this kid's memory about where things belong. I swear it's photographic, which is the only way he can find anything in this jungle."

"We can't keep it all."

"It's only one frog."

"Any one thing is only one thing."

"He'll hate me."

I wished for Seth. He might have known how to walk this knife edge, being tough on her without making her shut down. Or attack.

"How will he feel if he can't come home at all?"

"He likes Dad's house. Dad can get him to school." Her earlier determination was gone from her voice.

"I don't mean that. I mean, if he can't come home, ever. If the social worker comes in here and sees this and . . . they take him away from you."

The anguish returned to her face, and she doubled over as she sat. I wondered for a moment if she were about to vomit.

She sprang upright, carrying the frog around its neck like she was strangling it. She took it to a box we'd already filled with old books for the charity pile and marched her way outside. She put it on the charity pile in her garage, then she folded the box closed. Then she stacked other things on top of it. She stared at the pile sideways, as if trying not to let the box know she was looking.

She finally tore herself away, but braced herself on the outside of her garage, leaning on the siding, her breathing slow but shallow.

"I feel like I'm gonna be sick," she said. "And my heart is freaking out, feel this." She grabbed my hand and smashed it flat against her chest. I could feel it, thrashing away far too fast, flailing almost. I drew back.

She sank down to the ground, tipping her head back against her garage and saying into the air, "I'm never gonna survive this. Not if an old frog Jack never played with nearly kills me. We haven't even gotten to the hard stuff yet."

I suspected she meant that barricaded room. I sat down across from her, the rocks from her gravel driveway digging into my bottom. "We'll think of something," I told her. "We have to, so we will."

In my head I rehearsed a conversation with Seth that would convince him to come help us.

As the sun continued to sink, Trish got faster, but more agitated. She was making quicker decisions, but she would gasp and flinch as she threw out old clothes from Jack's toddler days, or when she ran across something too small and never worn that was going into the Sell pile.

Still, the room gradually cleared. I almost did a cartwheel when Trish came upon a cache of scrapbooking supplies she'd stowed away in there and with only the briefest glance said, "Toss, it's mildewed."

We'd cleared off the floor in Jack's room and the clothes off the top of the bed—these were clothes he wore, and Trish ran them through the washing machine, along with his bedsheets—and then we both knelt down next to Jack's bed to inspect the underbed clutter.

At first, Trish and I just yanked the pile into the daylight, not really looking at the items. But then, we both slowed down, exchanging wordless glances.

School papers. Birthday cards. Birthday party invitations from other children. There were objects, too, besides just paper. Little pieces of detritus that were dirty and scuffed up and unrecognizable. Odd bits of metal and plastic. Some rocks and acorns. More coloring pages were at the bottom, back when coloring was a novel thing for him, obviously, when it didn't matter if Mickey Mouse had a purple face, and coloring inside the lines wasn't important. There were photocopied worksheets with shaky, uneven letters scrawled barely inside the manuscript lines.

I could tell by the look on Trish's face she hadn't known about any of this.

"Now, what?" she breathed.

I shook my head. I was sure both of us were replaying that movie in our head of the time Mom came home from Florida and saw what we'd done.

As recently as yesterday morning I would have told her just to trash it, that he'd never know, or even if he got briefly upset, the bigger goal was a clean space. That he had to learn to let things go.

But yesterday morning I hadn't yet seen Trish nearly vomit over an old mildewed frog. I hadn't yet felt her heart thrashing in her chest. And she was a motivated adult, not a sensitive little boy with an injured arm.

Would Seth know what to do? As a professional?

"Maybe we put these things in a box," I ventured. "And show them to him when he gets back and help him choose."

Trish nodded, head bobbing gently like a marionette on a string.

I continued, reaching out to touch her, bring her back to me. "Let's get him a scrapbook. He can put the best things in the scrapbook and store it on his shelf. He can display his things, we'll tell him. Be proud of them, not just shove them under his bed."

Trish fingered the mangled edge of one of the papers. It had a distinctly chewed look and I tried not to think about what chewed it.

"Look, why don't we go get something to eat. Jack's room is almost done. We're hungry. We can go eat and pick up a scrapbook at the store. He'll feel better if we respect his stuff, right?"

Trish came back to life then. "OK, yes. Good idea."

As she left Jack's room, she stared hard at the pile next to his bed, walking out backward, transfixed until I pulled her away by her elbow down the hall, toward the outside world.

Chapter 17

My heart lifted as that bright red bull's-eye came into view. Target! Target of the cheap but trendy, where the middle class and even the nearly poor can afford Isaac Mizrahi. Target of the whimsical commercials and catchy jingles. Target, which has pulled me out of a funk more times than I care to consider.

Shallow? Well, duh. However, it's not like I was shooting heroin. Retail therapy is a time-honored tradition and though Saint Mary over there would never cop to it, I'd bet my filthy house that she's bought herself a lip gloss on a bad day.

Mary lagged behind me walking into the store, her arms folded around her, hands tucked under her upper arms. We really should have gone to a craft store, but the ones I knew of in town were closed on Sundays.

The store was crowded with shoppers, and we had to step lively to avoid being bumped. It was like highway driving, pushing the cart.

"Why do we have a big cart?" Mary asked, as I swung around a mother fussing with her baby and its pacifier.

"I need a few things," I said, paying careful attention to navigate the red plastic cart around someone stopping to fondle the scarves near the jewelry counter.

"You need a few things like you need another arm."

"I don't know, another arm might come in handy sometimes." I paused by the shoes. My dressy boots for work were wearing down in the heel, and these were on clearance, making way for sandals and such. I nudged my tennis shoe off with one foot and bent to find a size eight.

"You've got to be kidding me."

"My old boots are wearing out." They had black and brown, both in my size. I mentally reviewed my work clothes, trying to weigh which would be better. Then as I pulled on a brown boot I realized that with the clearance price I could buy them both for the price of one pair. Nearly, anyway.

Mary grabbed the box as I made to put it in the cart.

"No."

"I'm sorry, did you just tell me no like you're my mother?"

Both of us stood on opposite sides of the cart, holding the boot box. She was lightly pushing it back toward me, toward the shelf.

"You cannot buy more things now."

I shoved the box hard, downward, so that it smacked into the cart. Then I grabbed the black pair as well and dropped that in, too.

"These boots matter more to you than Jack, I see."

"Oh, for God's sake. Every time I make a decision you don't like, you all throw my son into it, every one of you. Like it's really so simple, if by choosing these boots I'm sending him away. Am I not allowed to have anything, then? At all?"

"You don't need them!"

"My boots are wearing out!"

"They're not worn out yet, are they? Until you walked by these boots you didn't think you needed any. You didn't say, let's go to Target and buy boots. If these boots hadn't been here, if we hadn't come here, you never would have thought of new boots."

"I just needed to be reminded."

"Let me remind you of Mom's purses."

Drew had complained about a secret sister code and he was right—we did have a language between us, a shorthand of phrases that only we truly understood.

Mom was notorious for hoarding purses, and the sick thing was, they were nearly all the same: large, black, with a long strap. Dad used to ask aloud how many variations could there be for a black bag? Before Mary and Dad moved out, I'd gone batshit crazy over seeing one more purse come into the house. I'd started screaming at her, yanking purses out of her closet until I'd made a pile of them in the middle of her bedroom floor. Mount Handbag. And Mom screamed back at me, things like, *how dare you?* As if I had no say over what she was doing to the house we all lived in. Now that I have a teenager of my own, I see what she meant, though. Once you've squeezed a child into the world through a hole no bigger than an orange, cleaned up vomit and fretted over homework, and waited up past curfew, there's a special kind of gall it takes for that very child to try to run your life.

Mary was still staring at me. Shoppers were starting to turn and gawk at our standoff.

"I don't have a dozen pairs of boots," I told her. It was not the same as the purses. It just wasn't.

"No, you have bags of yarn and broken coffee mugs and outdated clothes and paperwork."

"You are not in charge of me."

"Mom said that one, too."

"I'm not going to end up like her over one pair of boots."

"How do you know you won't end up like her?"

"Because I'm careful. Because I don't burn candles next to giant stacks of paper like Mom used to, trying to cover up the smell of cat piss. Because I don't have any pets."

"Where are you going to put these?"

"In my closet, obviously."

"We can't even see your closet right now."

"But we will."

Mary threw up her hands. Tipped her head back as if stargazing. She blinked several times and if I didn't know better, I'd have thought she was crying or something.

"Whatever. Let's get the scrapbook, get dinner, and get out of here."

I tried to hide my smile as I pushed the cart away, so she wouldn't think I was being smug. I always could outlast her. That much had never changed.

W e were in a restaurant booth eating lukewarm burgers when my ex-husband called me.

A large woman was trying to get her kids to settle down at the table across from me, and she was blocking my exit. The rest of the place was jammed with families and dudes watching basketball. So I answered the call in front of my sister, who, thank goodness, looked away and pretended she couldn't hear me.

"Hi," I said, trying to act like all was normal.

"I called the house and there was no answer," Ron said, sounding puzzled.

"What, I went out. I can't leave the house on a Sunday afternoon?"

"I guess. It's just different, is all."

Sunday used to be our family day together. Ron's jobs would often bleed over into Saturday, so Sunday was the day we refused to make plans for anything but spending time together, even if that meant dragging our boys along on errands. I'd had trouble filling up those long Sundays after Ron left, and I often found myself driving to Target, especially on days he had Jack.

"Everything OK?" Ron continued.

"Everything's fine," I said, looking down at the table and pointedly away from Mary.

"Can I talk to Jack?"

"He's visiting my dad and Ellen."

"Huh."

"What, he can't visit?"

"No, that's fine. It's just . . . odd. Usually you keep him with you. You don't like to be apart from him on your weekends."

My weekend, his weekend. I always hated the possessiveness of those weekends.

"I'm just doing some cleaning up at the house."

"Because of that social worker?"

"Because it *needs cleaning,* Ron. I told you that was no big deal. It's already over with, if you must know."

"If you're cleaning, why aren't you home?"

"I'm taking a dinner break. Do you need something, or did you just call to grill me about my Sunday activities?"

"I, uh . . ." He coughed into the phone, and my body tensed. That was Ron's nervous noise. He coughed before he told me he was leaving, in fact. Divorced or not, I knew every nuance of his personality, every hill and valley of his body, every scar and birthmark and secret fear.

He continued, "I thought over spring break I'd like Jack to meet Summer."

"Summer what?"

"Summer. The girl I've been seeing."

It felt like someone turned up the volume in the restaurant. No, that was a ringing in my ears, obscuring the chatter, the TV sports, and Ron's voice growing tinny. I grabbed the edge of the restaurant table.

"Sorry, I lost you for a minute there," I said when the ringing subsided. "I've never heard of Summer before."

"Well, it's not something I like to share with you. My dates. But now we've been seeing each other a while and she'd kinda like to meet Jack."

Dates. Plural. "Who . . . who is she?"

"Her name is Summer, like I said. She works out at Belding Supply with her dad."

"You make her sound about sixteen!" I laughed, as if this were funny.

"Naw, she's not sixteen."

I noticed he did not supply her actual age.

"Well, fine, if you want him to meet her. That's fine. That's good of you to check with me first."

Ron usually was a good ex-husband. If one had to have an ex.

"We thought we'd take him out to . . ."

I couldn't hear any more. The use of "we" so casually had interrupted any hope I had of following the conversation. Ron sounded relaxed now, like the storm he'd feared had missed him after all. Made me wish I had freaked out on him. It would have been cathartic.

"I can't hear you," I told him. "You're breaking up. Call me later."

And I hung up, rejoining the world of the restaurant.

Mary had finished her burger. She'd draped a napkin over the top of the dirty plate like drawing a sheet over a corpse.

"That sounded difficult," Mary said, folding her hands on the table.

"I thought he left me because of the stuff. The clutter." I pushed my own plate away. "But now he's got a new girl."

Mary had that look on her face, where she wanted to say something but knew it would come out wrong.

"What? Spit it out."

"How long have you been divorced now?"

"Only two years."

"Only two?"

"Two years is like . . ." I snapped my fingers. "Hardly any time. It's been fourteen years since Mom died and do you miss her any less?"

She flinched, as I knew she would. I reminded her, "I loved that man more than almost everything."

Mary wrinkled her forehead at me, and I heard her loud and clear. I jabbed my finger across the table at her and said, "Don't you say it.

Don't you dare say that I chose the clutter over him. It's not that fucking simple. Anyway, what would you know about it?"

"About what?"

"Marriage."

"Thanks for reminding me that I'm a cold, lonely hag. I'd forgotten for about thirty seconds."

"I didn't mean that."

"Sure you did. I'll have you know I've been in love for years." Mary flushed pink from her chin to her hair.

"What? With who?"

"Don't sound so stunned."

"I just . . . You never said anything."

Now it was Mary's turn to look at me like I was the moron, reminding me with just a tilt of her head that we'd barely spoken since Mom died. Then she shook her head, brushed nonexistent crumbs from her shirt. "His name was George, and I worked for him for thirteen years."

"Thirteen years? And you didn't get married or something?"

Her mouth twisted into a smirk on her pale oval face. "He never returned the favor of loving me back. Oh, I thought maybe he did, you know, secretly. Then I found out otherwise. So actually, you were right, Trish, in assuming I don't know anything about human relationships. I withdraw my earlier remark."

I tried to drum up sympathy for her. But years of pining for your boss doesn't compare to a marriage dissolving, children caught in the middle, and now a new girlfriend named Summer. Who wanted to meet my boy.

I waved our waitress over.

"Let's get the hell out of here," I said.

"Daylight's burning," added Mary, prompting me to look at my watch. We were not yet done with Jack's room. Monday was bearing down on me with my psycho boss and its long workweek, the return of

Ayana with her notebook and camera, and that appointment with the fucking government shrink.

Bitter resentment rose up into my throat at the box they had put me in. They were always against me, the whole lot of them, just like they lined up against Mom, who defied them all at every turn.

Mary paid the bill and crooked her finger for me to go, and I followed, silently, allowing myself to be led and bossed and ordered around, for the privilege of keeping my own son.

Chapter 18

Jack's room had been cleaned of clutter, but what remained . . . a layer of dust covered everything. The walls, too, seemed to have a coating of mysterious grime. With one swipe of the sponge we'd realized just how thick the dirt had gotten.

As the sun fell to earth again, Trish's determination became a frenzy.

Trish assigned me the task of sweeping the baseboards and vacuuming, and I tried not to think about the cobwebs in the corners, and what must have been lurking nearby. I tried not to pay any attention to the black flecks of half-eaten bugs trapped therein.

Living with Mom, I'd battled back a case of arachnophobia as a matter of survival. It was simply not possible to freak out over every spider, when spiders seemed to love the dark crevices created by her piles of junk.

Years of living on my own, keeping everything clean and just so, had eroded my resistance. So I pretended I didn't notice the scurrying motions as I jabbed the broom at the corners, though a gasp snuck out of me before I could stop myself.

The carpet was mottled and uneven. It seemed to be stained in spots, bright yellow in others where boxes had hidden the fibers from the fading effects of sun. The stains, the grime, were a mystery to me.

Whatever Trish may have hoarded always seemed to be paper, objects, items. Never rotted food. No pet waste.

It's as if dirt floated through the air, looking for a place to settle, and hid itself in the places Trish would never be able to reach. Mindful, crafty, like the spiders.

This thought set my skin to crawling. I feigned a need for the bathroom and fled the room.

The bathroom was not much better. She'd started plopping her most recent papers in here, when she ran out of space on the kitchen table.

Despite the chill air outside, I shoved open the window to let the cold rush in and surround me with its bracing reality.

I stood in the vortex of the outside air and imagined the cold sanitizing me. Protecting me, as if I could wear it like armor back into the rest of the house.

I wanted Seth. We needed more hands, and Seth wouldn't be carrying all our Granger family baggage. I could pretend he was just a friend who had some time off and could lend us a hand. And maybe Seth could ask a pointed question now and then, or talk her down if she started having an attack. She wouldn't even have to know he was a shrink.

Seth was always so great at that: asking the most perfect question, the one you hated to answer but needed to hear. And that was just when we were college kids. Now he's got an education and training. Maybe he could make a difference, battle back the hoarding demon, even in an unofficial capacity.

Because Trish was motivated now, for Jack's sake. Drew was right when he showed up at my house. This was a rare window of opportunity to save Trish. And my old friend is a shrink, and on sabbatical, too! I couldn't waste the opportunity.

I closed the window reluctantly and stepped into the hall, my feet already knowing where to pick a path through the mess. I was beginning to see how it could start to feel normal, how the sides of the piles could start to seem like mere walls, and maybe the hallway became a little narrower, but you could forget the stuff was stuff, and not part of your home itself.

When I returned to Jack's room, Trish's face was wet, with sweat, or maybe tears, probably both. She was panting and beaming. She'd somehow scrubbed the walls almost entirely clean of the brownish film. We'd put the freshly cleaned sheets back on his bed. His own hoard we'd moved to a box on the couch next to the scrapbook supplies. The treasured Scruffy was on the center of the pillow.

If you didn't look too hard at the carpet, you'd never know anything had been amiss.

"Wow," was all I could manage. Then, "I'll call Dad and tell him to bring Jack over."

"No," Trish said, smiling. "Let *me* call."

She flounced from the room, radiating triumph and pleasure. I made note of her mood, to remind her of this moment when her will-power flagged, as of course it would.

I had my own call to make, and this time I wouldn't let my own bumbling mess it up.

If Trish could clean, then I could be persuasive. Bold. Charming, even. Stranger things have happened, as Mom used to say.

When Seth picked up the phone, he sounded warmer, less wary. "Hi, Mary," he said, and then immediately, "I'm sorry I was so abrupt before. I tried to say something else, but you hung up."

I started to apologize and explain about my own stupidity but remembered my goal was to charm and cajole. "What was the 'something else' you wanted to say?" That came out more coquettish than I meant it to. I'd been going for charming. It came out as breathy Mae West.

He chuckled before he answered, the sound producing a funny

elevator-dropping feeling in my gut. "I wanted to direct you to some resources and give you a referral. I have the information right here, in fact."

"You didn't call me back?"

Seth explained how I sounded upset last time, and he didn't think I wanted to talk right then. I told him he was right. He was always right about that kind of thing. About me.

I took a deep breath and plunged ahead. "I've called to throw myself on you. Your mercy, I mean. Throw myself on your mercy."

I balled up my fist, thumping myself on my knee a few times as if I could beat the stupid out of me.

"What makes you think I have any of that?"

"Isn't it a job requirement?"

"You'd think." There was that funny tone again, I noticed. A sour tinge.

"I've called to ask you a favor."

I was perched on the couch next to Jack's stuff. Trish ducked into my peripheral vision and gave me a double thumbs-up, smile wide. I relaxed my shoulders, not realizing I'd been tense. That meant that Dad was bringing Jack home without any fuss. Trish vanished toward the back bedrooms again.

"What favor is that?"

"We really need extra hands here. Can you come help us? We had my dad here, but it blew up in our faces. We don't work together well, really."

"I can't treat your sister. It's called a 'multiple relationship,' and I could get fined and disciplined."

"I'm not asking you to do that. You said you were on sabbatical. And I got fired, so isn't that a nice coincidence?"

"You got fired? I'm sorry to hear that."

"That's not really the point now. Will you help?"

"She really should see a professional. In fact, I'm surprised the social worker hasn't lined up an evaluation for her. I used to do that kind of work myself. I've got these resources—"

"We have no time for resources! The social worker might take Jack away, and even if she doesn't, my father will make sure of it, unless we make progress, like now. Right now. We can take her to a shrink later."

"I can't."

"Why not?" My attempts to be cool and charming were melting away. "Seth. Please."

"You might not want me there if you knew the whole story."

"I don't care about the whole story. We need your help."

"Why me, specifically? If you don't want me to treat your sister like a patient, then why does it have to be me? Ask someone else."

"There is no one else," I said, letting the shame of it overtake me, my wretched loneliness. "There is literally no one else I can ask. My roommate's boyfriend from twenty years ago is the only person I can turn to."

"No one at all?"

"Is it all that shocking that stupid Mary Granger should end up alone?"

"You sound like you think you deserve to be alone."

"If you're not allowed to treat people outside the office, don't do it to me on the phone."

I slumped on the couch and tipped my head back, letting the tears run into my ears. It felt funny and ticklish, and I almost laughed at how stupid it all was. Me, a jobless lonely hag in my crazy sister's hoarded house, crying on the phone to my college roommate's boyfriend I hadn't seen in almost fifteen years. Who, if not for the coincidence of our shared birthday, would have drifted away like all the other college kids I knew. Every one of them forgot about me as soon as they turned their tassels.

He said something, but I didn't even hear him, treading water as I was in my own ridiculous life.

He spoke up louder, and I finally heard, "Mary? I said I'll come. Are you there? Are you okay? Mary?"

Instead of answering Seth, I could only think of myself as an old, old woman, still sitting on a couch and crying, nothing around me ever changing.

Chapter 19

J ack froze in his doorway, his creamy yellow room looking nearly the same as it did when we moved in. I'd hoped for excitement and feared a freakout. But his statue act was unnerving.

"Pal? Jack?"

I'd asked Mary to wait in the living room. She looked wrecked herself, though I wasn't sure why. I'd thought the call she made was something unimportant, some busywork part of life we all have. But when I came back to the living room, she was on the couch like a broken doll, limbs limp and face staring up, the phone loose in her upturned hand. Her eyes were all red and her face was shiny.

So probably good she just stayed away for now. One emotional crisis at a time was all I could handle.

Jack was still staring. "Is it all gone?" he asked, his good hand clutched around Cat, which he held up to his heart.

"Of course not, pal. The things from under your bed we saved in a box and we'll sort through it together. The rest of the stuff that we took out of here was all clothes you don't wear anymore, broken toys, or things you never play with."

"Maybe I never played with them because I couldn't see them anymore. Maybe I would play with them, now."

"Don't think about that now, pal. Think about how great it looks in here. And you can sleep in your own bed like a big kid!"

He glued himself to my side when he heard that, thrusting his good arm around my hip. He shook his head. "It's too . . . big in here. Empty. It's scary."

"Honey, this is what a room is supposed to look like. It's not empty, it's neat and clean."

"I don't want to sleep alone. Why did you work on my room anyway? The kitchen is more important, so we can eat." His voice sounded muffled. He'd turned his face away from his clean room, into my side.

I was tempted to blurt out the ugly truth: because your grandfather was going to keep you away from me until I did your room. When Dad drove Jack home, he walked inside and raked his gaze over every part of the house he could see and then each corner of Jack's room, like a soldier on patrol. He nodded and grunted at me by way of approval, in such a way that declared loud and clear: *So far so good, but you're on notice.*

I edited reality for my son, as I always had. "We wanted a safe place for you."

"I was safe in here."

"The pile of stuff fell on you in here, pal."

He shook his head.

"Kiddo, it's late. We should get you to bed."

"No!"

I slumped with defeat. "You can sleep with me tonight. We'll talk tomorrow about sleeping in your own room."

Jack's face brightened at this, and he allowed me to help him put on his pajamas. He managed bathroom and teeth brushing with minimal help. I lay down with him in my bed and curled around him like a fortress. We didn't speak. He seemed pale and frail. This had probably exhausted him. After the cleaning we tried back home, my mother was spent for about a week, dragging herself around the house.

Lying there in the dark, I remembered Jack's injury.

I allowed myself to review it in my head. It hurt, but I deserved this hurt. In fact, I lingered over the details of it, soaking in the suffering I'd earned.

I'd been in the basement, stuffing laundry in the machines. A sound came to me faintly, but I'd thought it was the television. I finished cramming the clothes into the machine, then I picked my way carefully over the mounds of clothes, through the winding path in the basement and then up the stairs, narrowed by things I'd meant to put away somewhere downstairs, but "away" turned out to be the steps themselves.

How long had it been since the time I first heard that faint noise and the time I made it all the way up the stairs, through the kitchen where I finally heard the crying? Maybe as much as ten minutes. Everything seemed to be taking me longer lately. My energy level was poor on the best of days. And that day had not been the best, even before . . .

In the kitchen I heard the crying, and it was alarming in its softness. It was the weak, thin crying of someone on the brink of a terrible fate. Resigned that no one is coming to help.

At the time, I didn't think exactly that. It was later, in one of the times I went over this in my head, that I realized why I ran like my hair was on fire to Jack's room.

I screamed, and at the same time Jack's whimpering drew energy from my presence and he began to wail, "Mommy!"

Now I squinted my eyes shut in the dark, inhaling Jack's hair. In reality, the scene I came upon lasted only a split second before I dove forward and hauled things off him. But in my replaying of this incident, I had plenty of time to linger over the details captured in freeze-frame.

His legs jutted out from a pile of things. One sock was half off. His legs were scrabbling uselessly, like he was trying to run sideways. I could not see his top half. I could only hear him crying, sounding distant, like he was in a deep cave.

I fell on the pile and threw things to the side with both hands, excavating until I reached him. His head, arms, and torso had been buried by papers, and by then he was coughing and wheezing, hysterical screaming having worn out his lungs, combined with dust from all that junk. He shrieked as I lifted him up. I later learned his collarbone was broken there. He'd landed on his shoulder as the pile collapsed on him.

He later said it was his own fault for trying to brace himself against that pile to reach a stuffed animal he'd glimpsed, a panda bear he'd forgotten about. He should've known it wouldn't hold him, he told me later as I insisted again and again he not blame himself.

As I held him, and he sucked on his inhaler, he asked between gasps, "Why didn't you come? I was scared."

I told him I didn't hear, and I apologized for so long he finally told me to stop saying it, once his breath had regulated. Then he said, "Mama, my arm really hurts."

Now, in the dark and safe under my protective arm, I realized Jack's breath had slowed. He wasn't shifting or fidgeting. I peeled my arm off him, pulled my body away. Yes, asleep.

With my eyes adjusted to the dark, I could see the piles now all around my bed, obscuring any moonlight from outside. It was truly like a cave in here. Did Jack want to sleep in here only to be with me? Or did he actually want the cave itself?

"I'm sorry I did this to you," I whispered, wishing suddenly Jack were more like Drew. I might have preferred a second angry, indignant son to the realization that I'd created another hoarder out of this innocent little boy.

M ary had pulled herself together when I came back out.
"I thought you fell asleep in there," she said, not accusatory. She was pulling a brush through her hair. "So what's the plan now?"

"I have to work tomorrow," I said with a groan.

"Can't you take any time off?"

I shook my head. "My boss has a strict policy about notice for vacation time."

"Can you call in sick?"

"That might work for a day, maybe two. Any more than that she'll want a doctor's note and preferably an amputated limb to show for my absence."

I gulped to think about the lies I'd have to tell to get to my government shrink appointment on Wednesday.

"Well, then . . . Now what?"

I shrugged. I felt empty. Withered. I was seized by a bizarre desire for my dad to stride in and start ordering us around. Not even an hour ago when he dropped off Jack, I'd had to resist the urge to push him out my front door so hard he'd fall down the steps.

"You said spring break is coming."

I nodded. Speaking words aloud seemed to be too much now. I sank down into a chair that only this morning had been covered with papers. The chair smelled terrible, but I sat there anyway.

"What if you do what you can in the evenings or whatever, and then I come back over spring break and we just . . . go crazy. Clean like dervishes. I've got a friend who says he can help."

"Who?" I said up to the ceiling. I closed my eyes.

"His name is Seth. I used to know him in college. He happens to be on sabbatical now."

"Fine," I said. "Okay."

Mary didn't say anything, and I wished for the magical ability to poof her back home and myself into my bed with teeth brushed and face washed and finally write "The End" on this ridiculous day.

"Should we read the diary again?" Mary asked, and I shrugged, all the caring about anything having been sucked right out of me.

"Maybe I'll read it out loud," she said. I heard rustling of paper.

April 10, 1961

Reading *King Henry IV* in English, and it's the most boring thing. Leave it to old Mrs. Schultz to skip over all the romance and blood and guts in Shakespeare plays and go for the dull political intrigue. Though Falstaff is funny.

Mom came back from her first day visiting the migrant camps and said it's the most pitiful thing she's seen, some of those kids with ear infections so bad they have these huge lumps behind their ears. But the doctor is treating them nicely, and the farmer didn't seem to mind or anything. But here's the exciting part. Mom wants me to come help her! Apparently it's pretty hard to keep the little ones entertained while they wait their turn, and sometimes Mom could use an extra hand to hold a vial or whatever. Daddy is skeptical, saying my schoolwork could be affected. I think he doesn't want me mixing with "those" people. My mom gets away with it because it's her job and her job brings in money (though she doesn't get paid extra to do this and it's after her normal hours; I think Daddy doesn't want her to disappoint Doc). He says the Mexicans might whistle and jeer at me. Like I've never been whistled at before by a white guy. I survived the experience perfectly well, thank you.

I hate how he thinks I'm so helpless. My boy cousins can do whatever they want, whenever they want, with whoever they want. Meantime it's like Daddy thinks I'm walking around in a corset and waving a little fan in front of my face saying, "My stars!" With ruffians ready to ravage me at every corner.

I know he wants to send me to Hope College, because it's so close. Not that there's anything wrong with Hope, I'm sure it's fine. But I want to go to the Univ. of Michigan. Or maybe—dare I imagine it?—out of state? If I end up at Hope, I'll be living at home and it will be like nothing's changed at all. And if I meet a local boy there and get married, I might never see any part of the world except our little chunk of the lakeshore. Which would suit Daddy just fine, I know.

Anyway, I think volunteering at the migrant camps would be a wonderful experience. I've spent my whole life in this little white house in Holland, Michigan, never doing anything more exotic than wearing wooden shoes in that stupid parade every year. Why shouldn't I see how other people live? Other people who haven't been as lucky as us? Maybe I can even learn to speak Spanish. If I'm going to be a nurse like Mom, that would come in handy.

Wally has been hanging around me a lot lately. I think he wants to ask me to prom. I guess I don't mind that. It would be better than sitting at home. I hope if he tries to kiss me, though, he has sense enough to suck on a breath mint first.

I'm getting sleepy so I'll sign off now.

Frannie

Mary closed the notebook gingerly, with the care she'd take with a holy relic. "I wonder why we never heard any of this. Mom volunteering at a migrant camp? That's fascinating."

"She was seventeen years old. By the time we came along, it probably wasn't important in the scheme of things."

"I wish we'd asked her."

I sat up in the chair then and looked at Mary. Her gaze aimed at the far corner of my house. She continued, "I wish we'd asked her more about her life."

"Oh, Mary, don't beat yourself up. No one's interested in their parents until they get old and decrepit themselves and start thinking about life and the past and mortality and crap."

She nodded, pursing her lips, and I could tell what she was thinking as clearly as if I were reading it off a screen. She was wishing we'd had the chance to start getting old with her still on this earth.

Me, too, kid, I thought. *Me, too.*

Chapter 20

A s I parked the car within sight of my town house door, I felt the knotted rope in my shoulders go slack. I'd made it.

I had my key almost in the lock when I noticed a heavy package on my neighbor's doorstep. The quiet inside my town house beckoned me, but instead I tried a knock on Harriet's door. I heard rustling and a faint, "Just a minute!" I felt that I'd missed a birthday, standing there waiting for Harriet to open the door. Then I heard the many clicks of her many locks.

"Oh! Mary, dear. This is a nice surprise on a Sunday night."

I pointed down to the box. "I see you have a package here. Would you like me to bring it in for you?"

"Oh, that would be lovely, sweetheart."

I bent to pick up the awkward box, which reached almost to my chin. "What do you have here?" I asked as I carried it inside and set it where Harriet pointed, on her kitchen island.

"Some things for my grandchildren. I'm going to visit them next week so I did a little online shopping. I might have bought a bit much, but then, what are grannies for?" She raised her glass to me. It was a tumbler filled with wine. "I probably shouldn't shop in the evening when I'm having one of these. . . . Would you like a little something?"

"No, thanks. I was just coming home from a weekend away when I saw the package and thought you might want some help."

Harriet started talking about her grandchildren, and as always I had a crazy déjà vu feeling in this neighboring town house. It was just like mine, but reversed, so that right was left and left was right. Like facing pages in a book. Another difference: Harriet covered every inch of her home in doilies and framed photos of the cherubic grandbabies who also wore her upturned button nose.

So much stuff, yet it was so neat. My mother would have loved it. It's probably what she thought she was going to achieve, each time she brought home another beautiful thing she just had to have.

Harriet was still going. If it weren't so late, I'd sit down and let her talk; the poor thing seemed so bored since moving in here after her husband died.

I yawned theatrically and stood up. Harriet, bless her, took the hint and ushered me out.

Unlocking the door to my own place again caused a wash of comfort and relief. The dim living room still smelled faintly of OxiClean. I locked my outside door, then flicked on the light in my foyer.

The silence was pure. Not so much as a dripping faucet.

The aching began, as my muscles remembered all the lifting and hauling I'd been doing this weekend. And I'd just agreed to do it all over again, for five straight days or more.

I walked through my living room, drawing my curtains shut against the outside. Each time I shut out the world beyond with a snap of fabric across the curtain rod, I felt more secure.

If someone had asked me—not that anyone would have—if I was happy, as of last week, I would have said, yes, I'm just fine. I had a job I enjoyed, a lovely home, and plenty of time to read and exercise. It wasn't just losing my job that had me unsettled now; it was that all this emptiness that I'd found so comforting and calm just days ago now seemed painful and shrill. My ears started ringing in the silence so I flicked on the television, just for noise. I'd never been prone to do that before.

I sat on the couch, my mouth open in wonder at this emotion. It felt just like envy, for Trish. I could surely recognize envy, because I'd felt it often enough growing up.

But why on earth should I envy her now, with her pathological hoarding and garbage and her troubled sons and her marriage over?

It was unmistakable, though. That little pang in the chest when I thought of her followed by a chaser of bitterness.

"Everything's gone all crazy," I said out loud, and the ringing of my own voice in the still air gave me goose bumps.

The week passed as if it were a year. With no time clock at the store and no regulation to my day, the empty hours piled on me like bricks, and each time the hour hand ticked forward I'd push a brick off, feeling relieved when it got late enough I could reasonably go to bed.

I often caught myself wondering what George was doing now, with all this extra time. Wedding planning, no doubt. Being dragged along to cake tastings and floral selection. I imagined him relaxed in a tuxedo with a tasteful boutonniere, getting married and giving me not a second thought.

I watched my favorite old DVDs in succession: *Sleepless in Seattle, Guess Who's Coming to Dinner?, The Princess Bride, Four Weddings and a Funeral.* They didn't have the same allure as they used to, and for a few days I didn't know why, just that they barely held my attention, and I started sorting through my cabinets and restacking all my dishes while I listened to the familiar dialogue. Then I reflexively imagined George sweeping me into his arms, and with a punch it hit me. I'd been daydreaming my own fairy tale every time I rewatched these sappy old things, and look what happened there.

Meanwhile, Seth and I exchanged text-message arrangements for him to help at Trish's house, but our conversation stuck with logistics. I longed to talk to him in detail, from small-talk boring things to asking him what was wrong, why was he not working? But he never seemed to provide a window for such talk. It had been fourteen years since I'd seen him, and other than the funeral, our talks had been airy and inconsequential. It's not as if he would spill all his secrets even if I asked.

On Wednesday, the phone rang and I dropped a dish on the floor. I made myself stare at the ringing phone, right there on the kitchen counter just inches from my hand, for two full rings before I picked up. It was my dad, letting me know he'd parked the camper at Trish's house and gotten it all cleaned out and stocked up for me. I started to decline, but soon the logic of his plan made all too much sense. Silly to throw away my savings on a hotel when I found hotel rooms creepy anyway. It went without saying I wouldn't want to sleep in her house. Even in Jack's cleared room.

Dad then reminded me of something I'd forgotten in all the fuss. Sunday was Easter, and he was inviting us to his and Ellen's place. All of us.

"Trish, too?" I asked, trying to remember the last time we'd all gathered for a holiday. From what I was told, once I started working all those holiday shifts, Trish began to spend her Easters and such alone with the boys, unless it was Ron's turn to have them, in which case she ignored the holiday completely. Dad and his bride had taken to visiting Ellen's relatives in Georgia.

"Well, sure, I think it's about time, don't you?"

"Did she say she'd come?"

"Yep. Then Ron will pick up Jack for spring break."

I ticked off on my fingers: my dad, Ellen, me, Trish, Jack, and maybe even Drew if he deigned to come. "Wow, six of us. Is Ellen ready for the stampede?"

"You know her. She's already planning the menu and stenciling place cards."

I made plans to join them for dinner, then leave from Dad's and follow Trish back to her house, so we'd be ready and raring to go come Monday of spring break.

When the arrangements were all made, I still had too many long days remaining, especially with Harriet off visiting her children. I checked out a book from the library on hoarding and watched some of the TV documentaries Trish had dismissed as "exploitive trash."

I took up jogging outside, instead of just on my treadmill. I'd never done that working at the store. In the morning, it was too dark and I feared being snatched off the street by a maniac. In the evening, after work, I'd simply been too tired.

I found that I rather liked covering ground, though I never really went anyplace, always ending up right back on my own front porch.

Chapter 21

I snuck back into the office, opening the door barely enough for me to squish through, like I was some kind of ninja and Angela wouldn't notice.

That'll be the day, when Angela doesn't notice.

"Patricia!" she blared. "Are you back?"

I bit my tongue not to retort, *Nope, I'm still in my car, driving, you ignorant cow.*

"Yes, ma'am," I replied. I nudged the mouse to wake up my screen and cringed at all the new e-mails.

Angela appeared in the lobby, just at the edge of the hall. "That seemed to take a very long time for a simple doctor appointment. You will need to work through lunch to get caught up. Everything is fine, I trust?"

"Just fine," I answered reflexively, and I wished I'd thought to make up an ailment. I still had to find a way to stay home and clean next week.

She looked me up and down over the edge of her glasses. "You're not pregnant, are you?"

"No!" I blurted.

"Good. I hope you're being honest with me. Because if you're pregnant, obviously that's your business, but I would need to start training a replacement."

"Replacement? You can't fire someone because they're pregnant."

"I meant a temp, Patricia. Don't be paranoid. And anyway, you're not pregnant, you said, so you don't have to worry about it."

She threw a pointed glance at my midsection and stalked back to her office, calling over her shoulder, "Make those follow-up calls today!"

I plunked down in my chair as I exhaled a sigh. So maybe I shouldn't have told her I was going to the gyno. But I sure as shit wasn't going to tell her the truth about the government shrink, and the gyno seemed the most likely way to head off follow-up questions. Who wants to know about what's going on with an employee's lady parts?

My stomach rumbled and I sipped from my smoothie. Angela frowned on eating at a receptionist's desk. "It's the public face of my company and I won't have you chomping like a cow out here," she'd said the one time I'd brought a salad to my desk.

On one plane, my brain cruised through the e-mails, filing them rapidly and answering the ones requiring action, my hands flying across the keys.

On a lower, gut level, I relived my all-morning shrink ordeal.

At home, beforehand, I'd had to fill in page upon page of paperwork about myself, ticking off boxes about how much I drink, how much I sleep, how anxious I am, whether I have persistent unwanted thoughts, whether I've ever been suicidal. I'd been so irritated having to spend my evenings taking my own inventory after a long day of work that I'd ripped through the paper with my ballpoint pen at times. So ridiculous. Like a drunk would be honest about how much they drink, or if a single mother ever happened to have a suicidal thought once in a while, on a really low, lonely night, she'd ever check that box for a shrink who could report to a judge.

Dr. Tom, the man had called himself when I arrived. I'd bridled at that. Jack used to call his preschool teacher Miss Kelly. What was I, a toddler? We couldn't use proper last names like grown-ups?

He asked me questions about my past, how I feel on a typical day. He echoed some of the questions on the form, which made me furious for my wasted time. He got around to asking me about my living environment. I said it was messy.

"How messy?" He tapped his pen against his lips.

I didn't answer, and the moment stretched like taffy until I couldn't stand it anymore. "Very messy. It is very, very messy."

"How much does it interfere with your daily life?"

"I manage."

"You manage easily? You manage with moderate difficulty? Severe difficulty?"

"Moderate."

"Your son was injured."

"Yes."

He asked why I was so quiet, and I said I was tired. Which I was. Weren't we all?

On his office walls were framed photos of grown children with yellow-blond hair and blue eyes. The boys had square jaws with dimples. The girls had acres of wavy gold tresses. A digital picture frame near his desk rotated through pictures of their weddings, and sports prowess, and school dances.

I wondered what kind of picture I'd hang up if I were allowed to do so at my desk at work. If I had a job with an office of my own. Look, here's my older son, scrawling a pentagram on his sneakers. Look, here's my younger son, reading a book hiding in a cave made of clothing.

As I answered "Dr. Tom's" questions robotically, I thought there should be a rule about show-off photos in the office of a psychologist whose job it is to see people whose lives are circling the drain.

He asked about hoarding in my family history. He said "hoarding" like "measles" or "heart disease."

I told him my mother was also messy.

On a scale of one to ten? he asked.

I answered: twelve.

You?

A six.

I uncrossed my legs, squared my posture, looked him in the eye, and repeated, "I'm a six."

He smiled mildly and jotted a note.

What was it about these people and smiling?

I endured more questions. I studied the spines of the books in his bookcase, wondering if he ever opened them or they were for show. To make me feel that I was in the office of someone educated and competent.

Then there were more tests. Personality quizzes, which brought to mind the ones in women's magazines with titles like: *Are You a Lover or a Fighter?* Or *Take Your Bedroom Temperature: Hot or Not?*

Then I was back before Dr. Tom again and jiggling my foot impatiently, staring at the clock and imagining Angela's growing anger. He said he'd look over my paperwork and his notes, and he'd like to see me next week for a follow-up. No, I'd told him. It's spring break.

"Oh, you're going out of town?"

"Yes," I answered automatically. "On vacation."

I made an appointment for the following week with an impossibly perky office lady, whose glasses hung from a whimsical beaded chain, the kind I used to sell at art shows.

The phone rang at my desk.

"Kendrick and Adams," I answered in my office voice. "Oh, hi, Kristy, I can answer that, actually."

Kristy was a secretary for a banker in Lansing, Peter Mason. Peter was on the board for the Boys and Girls Club, and he was planning a fund-raising dinner. That is to say, he was making Kristy plan the fund-raiser while he did whatever bankers do.

Kristy was asking about the centerpieces for every table at the dinner. Angela had volunteered to be in charge of decorations, which meant I was in charge of decorations.

"No, we got those donated. Yep, gratis, every last one. And we are auctioning them off in a silent auction, too. They're going to do gorgeous arrangements, not just carnations in a cheap vase."

I'd pitted area florists against one another, playfully teasing them into competing to see which arrangements would garner the most money in the silent auction.

"Sure, I've got the list right here," I said, and I opened the file drawer at my knees and grabbed the florist list. I began rattling them off to her.

Having worked so long together on the fund-raiser, Kristy and I had gotten together for drinks once or twice after work.

Then one day she'd invited me to join her book club and I started to enthusiastically accept. . . . Then she explained that the club meets in rotating fashion at the members' homes.

So much for that.

"Oh, you're welcome," I said to Kristy's gushing thanks. She told me in a stage whisper that Peter had been all over her about the decor today, grousing that he wasn't going to have "naked tables with a doily on them" at "his" gala.

We shared a chuckle. "His." Right. And that night there would be a round of applause for the chair of the event "who worked so hard to make it happen."

We said our good-byes and I knew I'd hear from her again soon, the minute Peter remembered something else he just had to make someone do for him.

I slipped the florist list back into the file and turned to open the mail, which had arrived in my absence. I whipped each piece open with the opener and sorted quickly: action items, junk, file. File, file, file. Junk. Payment. Invoice returned to sender, must investigate what happened there . . .

My phone buzzed in my pocket for a text. I looked down the hall to see if Angela was approaching. No, I could hear her bellowing into her phone. I looked out the door. No visitors and no appointments due.

It was Drew. I also noticed an earlier text I'd missed. I'd muted my phone completely at Dr. Tom's.

Where were you this morning? From Drew.

What's wrong? I thumbed back, wincing at the soft beeping of each key. I should have asked Drew how to shut that off.

I was feeling sick.

Shit. Poor kid. *Sick how? Are you still sick? Do you need me to come get you?*

stomach hurt. okay now. just wondered why you didn't answer.

I exhaled. *I'm sorry. I had to shut my phone off for a meeting and forgot to turn it back on.*

I called work and you didn't answer.

It was an offsite meeting.

Gotta go to class. Bye.

"Patricia!"

Angela startled the phone out of my hands.

"I do not pay you to be on Facebook, or whatever you're doing."

My head remained bent toward my phone, which seemed unharmed on my desk, landing as it had on the large paper calendar. It had landed smack on next Monday. The beginning of spring break. The beginning of the Big Clean.

"Did you hear me?" Angela barked.

I smacked my hands flat on the desk and pushed myself up to stand. I met her eyes. "That was my son, who sent me a text because he wasn't feeling well. I know this is inconvenient for you, but I do have actual living, breathing children who at times need my care and attention, even when it's not quitting time. He's fine now, actually, and in the time I've been back at work, I've opened and sorted all the mail, responded to all the new e-mail, and dealt with Peter Mason about the centerpieces for the fund-raiser. All while sipping a smoothie instead of eating actual food."

Angela stepped as close to me as the tall reception desk would allow. "I will allow for that little tirade because it's out of character, and because you managed to do so much work this morning. Besides, training a replacement is a hassle. But you are on notice."

"What kind of notice?"

"In this economy, plenty of people would do your job happily and not talk back."

I watched her retreat to her office, and for the next few minutes, I entertained a delicious fantasy of tackling her scrawny ass, grabbing a fistful of her hair, and bashing her face into the closest hard surface I could find.

Maybe that's a question they should have put on their psychological evaluation form. *How often do you have homicidal fantasies about your boss? Never, Rarely, Sometimes, Often, Always. Choose one.*

Chapter 22

On Sunday morning my eyes popped open earlier than usual, and I felt giddy, like I did as a kid when we once went to SeaWorld and had to start driving before dawn. I made my bed as usual, but decided to have breakfast on the road so I wouldn't have to wash dishes.

I felt more energetic than I had all week, despite that I'd gotten up extra early. I supposed it was a thrill having someplace to finally go. My thoughts also kept wandering to Seth, and what he looked like these days. I'd be seeing him Monday for the first time since he came to Mother's funeral. I'd been in a fog back then, and now I could barely remember what he looked like. The last time I'd seen him before that we'd hugged, giddy, minutes after graduation. My funny graduation hat had fallen off backward, and he'd bent to pick it up for me.

Seth and my roommate of the time, Rebecca, had dated in high school. We ended up hanging out as a trio some nights when he'd stop by on his way home from a night class, or they'd bump into me in the dining hall. Rebecca never seemed to mind including me, though we'd been randomly assigned as roommates and our friendship seemed born of necessity more than anything. They struck me as a comfortable old married couple, laughing at in-jokes and relaxing with that easy physical intimacy that must come from knowing someone for years. She'd be sitting next to him and throw her legs over his, and he'd cup her knee in his hand. And it wasn't sexual, or it didn't seem to be. Comfortable. I looked at them and dreamed of having a boyfriend like that, a connection like that.

They broke up, quite suddenly, near the end of sophomore year. He showed up at our door with blue hollows under his red eyes asking for her, saying he needed to talk to her. She'd gone home early for the weekend, I told him. She'd left a note saying she'd be back Sunday night.

It was a balmy spring night and stuffy in the dorms. I had our windows thrown open and a box fan braced on the sill to get some air moving. I asked him what was wrong and he bit his lip.

I convinced him to come in, and he sat on our little college-issue sofa, upholstered in nubbly orange fabric. He put his head in his hands, gripping his forehead like he had to hold it together with his hands alone. I sat across the room in my desk chair, not knowing what to say, wondering why I'd invited him in.

Then he just started talking. About how she'd broken up with him at a picnic the day before. That they'd been sitting on the blanket, leaning against a tree, and he was playing with her hair and she was tucked up under his arm and he was just thinking about how long he should wait before asking her to marry him. How young was too young, how long of an engagement she would want, whether he could borrow money from his dad for a ring.

And she sat up abruptly and said, "I have to tell you something."

Seth said he thought she was going to say she was pregnant—that she'd forgotten a pill—and he felt both fear and elation at the idea. Then she said, "I don't think I love you anymore."

He leaped up from the blanket like it was on fire and stared at her. And she started talking about how the passion had gone out of it for her, and she'd known him so long she felt stifled, never having discovered who she is without him.

In one of the only times he looked up from the floor that whole time, Seth said, "It was like something she read from a script."

As she kept talking he started to wonder how long she'd been planning this, whether the previous night when they had sex in his apartment she'd already known that would be the last time.

He asked her if there was someone else and that made her furious, he said; she started screaming at him about how dare he accuse her of cheating, only he said that's not what he meant, he just wanted to know if she *liked* someone else, is all . . .

That felt staged, too, Seth told me. How far she'd flown off the handle. It was unlike her to be so sensitive.

I let him talk for hours. I didn't say much. I opened a bottle of vodka Rebecca had left, and we mixed it with Dr Pepper.

The conversation wandered from there. Seth started talking about how it was always like this with him, that important people left him all the time. He talked about his dad who, after his parents' divorce, seemed content to ply him with money and trips to the movies but never any actual parenting.

He looked so broken that I sat on the couch next to him and touched his knee carefully, like I might approach a dog I didn't know. He shocked me by snatching up my hand and clutching it there on his knee, while with his opposite hand he roughly rubbed his face.

"Fuck," he said quietly, with no heat. Then he turned to me and looked me in the eye. I hadn't seen his eyes so clearly before; he was much taller than me and we rarely had occasion to be so close. He had long, long lashes and his eyes were a pale blue. "I'm just doing my best. Why isn't that ever enough?"

That's when he leaned close to my face.

I didn't understand what was happening at first, then I did, and I closed my eyes. The first contact was like a buzzing jolt that made me jerk backward.

He slid away from me down the couch. "Sorry," he said. "I shouldn't have . . . Sorry. I guess I'm . . ."

". . . drunk," I finished for him.

He got up and made as if to go, but he was wobbling all over and I insisted he stay on the couch. I had a loft bed way up high on the other side of the room, after all. He seemed dubious and indeed pained to stay in our room without his girlfriend, but when he couldn't manage to even put on his jacket correctly, he nodded that maybe he'd better sleep it off.

I retreated to my loft in my unsexy floral cotton jammies and wondered why my heart was hammering so hard. I couldn't sort out even for myself what was going on. Did I jerk back because I didn't want to be kissed? No, that didn't seem right. I liked his lips on mine very much, however briefly. Did I do it out of loyalty to my random-assignment roommate? That seemed less plausible yet. After all, she'd broken his heart. Fear of getting caught? We had left the door open, though the couch was not visible from the doorway.

I went to bed in a riot of confusion and lay awake for long, silent hours. Seth passed out almost immediately.

He was gone by morning, leaving a scribbled note that said only: "Thanks."

I held my breath for Rebecca's return, suspecting that someone in the dorm would have spotted Seth leaving our room in the morning and report that to my roommate. Would she be angry? Even though she'd dumped him? Anger was always like kryptonite to me. Even unjustified anger rendered me pathetically helpless as I scrambled to get back into good stead with the offended party.

Rebecca was distracted upon her return, hardly seeming to notice my presence. I wondered if this was the silent treatment, and when I could take it no longer, I cleared my throat and said, "Um, Rebecca? I wanted to tell you . . ."

"Oh," she said, waving her hand like she was batting away a fly. "Seth explained it to me. Thanks for letting him stay over when he'd had too much to drink. The last thing he needs is a DUI."

"So you don't mind?"

"Why would I care if he slept on the sofa? It's not like you fucked him, right?" She laughed. "Ha, I can just see that. Mary Granger, sex kitten, seducing poor brokenhearted Seth." She shook her head, smirking. "Though I shouldn't joke. It wasn't fair of me to do that to him. I just had some kind of commitment freakout, you know? I've already taken it all back."

"Took what all back?"

"Breaking up. That would be stupid, wouldn't it? To drop such a terrific guy for basically no reason?"

"Yeah," I'd replied. "Stupid." And I'd gone to bed with a headache for the rest of the day, skipping all my classes.

Rebecca never did marry him. He told me in the first shared-birthday phone call the November after graduation—which shocked me like bad wiring when I answered the phone, having not heard from him since school—that they'd broken up because he was going to grad school in California. He'd reported this to me in a matter-of-fact way, the same tone he used to explain his off-campus apartment and his part-time job. He'd asked about me and I'd told him I'd gotten promoted at my bookstore job and was trying to decide about grad school myself.

"So happy birthday to us," he'd said warmly.

"Happy birthday," I'd replied. "It was good to hear from you."

As I hung up, I realized that "good" was an understatement, that I felt like a light had gone out when I flipped my phone shut. But he was all the way in California, which might as well have been Mars.

The phone calls continued yearly, and then postcards began arriving. He moved several times, trying to find a city where he felt most at home, he said.

Once on our joint birthday, I'd opened a bottle of wine by myself and was a few glasses into it when the phone rang. *When Harry Met Sally* had been on, and a half-eaten chocolate bar was in my hand.

I was feeling unusually verbose and told him a goofy story about someone coming into the bookstore asking for a reference on how to start his own escort service and because I could think of nothing else to do, I took the man seriously and guided him to the "small business" section.

He laughed and my stomach swooshed like I'd been on a merry-go-round. In the pause, a thought formed in my head and I prepared to announce it: *I miss you between calls. Once a year isn't enough.*

Then he said, "Hey, I have some news. My girlfriend and I are moving back to Michigan."

Instead of speaking, I picked up my wineglass and took a long, deep swallow.

My car wound through the streets of suburban Lansing to the brick-and-siding condo owned by Ellen and Dad. Well, really Ellen. It had been her late husband's and was not so unlike my own town house.

I was the first to arrive, not surprisingly. I looked at my watch and noticed I was a full hour earlier than I was supposed to arrive. I'd been so eager to get out of my place for a change I'd gone and been early to the point of being incredibly rude.

But there I was. In fact, I could already see where Ellen had parted the curtains in the front window and noticed me sitting there.

My dad opened the front door and I did a double take. Was he wearing a cardigan? Like Mr. Rogers?

He saw me notice. "Hi, Peaches. It gets a little chilly in here sometimes." He pulled me into a hug and then guided me through the door. "They say it's going to warm up today, though, finally."

In their foyer, I glanced around. Even more country knickknacks had invaded since I'd last been here, at Christmas. More dried flowers, and wicker, and embroidered cutesy things on the walls. But it was all meticulous, all the level surfaces neat. Everything dust free. Much like my neighbor Harriet.

"Ellen is just putting on her face," he explained. Normally she'd be embracing me, too, drawling and squealing.

"Sorry I'm early," I said.

"Oh, Peaches, you're family. There's no early or late. You can be here anytime."

I didn't bother correcting him that I was not really Ellen's family, and she might not feel the same. A hostess doesn't like the guests to see her without her face on, or without the table set, family or not. Stepfamily or not.

We settled in the living area, where I had a view over the dining room table to the wooded back lot shared by all the condos. I was struck by how little of my mother there was here, and how that was insult and relief at once. She felt erased in this household, yet I don't think I could have stood to see framed photographs everywhere, or to eat off their wedding china.

The first holiday after the fire had been Thanksgiving and we'd gone out to eat. The following month Christmas dinner took place here. Ellen twittered about in an apron and chattered to fill every dead space. The rest of us sank into wine-soaked silence, clutching her tasteful stemware with whimsical wine charms labeling each one of our glasses as our own.

Now it was Easter, years after the fire, and I still could not get comfortable in a holiday without Mom. Having no children of my own to squeal over eggs or chocolate rabbits, honestly I'd just as soon skip the whole damn thing.

Dad and I made excruciating small talk until Ellen emerged, her silver hair swept back from her smooth, powdered face, her lipstick as ever applied neatly, never bleeding into the cracks around her lips. Large silver hoops peeked out from beneath her chin-length haircut. "Mary, darlin'!" She swept over to me and I rose to greet her, pressing my cheek lightly to hers, having to dust some of her makeup off me when we parted.

The doorbell rang, and we all exchanged tight smiles.

Here we go.

Trish came in wearing an ill-fitting floral dress made from a shiny fabric in a bright turquoise that pulled tightly across her bosom and her middle.

"You look lovely!" exclaimed Ellen, clearly lying, pressing her cheek to Trish, bending to squeeze Jack, and straightening in time to see Drew slope in after them, toting a bag of things, probably toys for Jack. "Well!" she cried, eyes wide, faking delight when actually she was probably alarmed. "Look who's here!"

I hid my face behind my hand while I smiled. It seemed that no one had warned her about Drew's punk rock transformation. At Trish's house I'd run across a picture of Drew that couldn't have been very old; only a year or two ago, he'd looked like any ordinary kid with mousy brown hair, braces, and blue jeans.

My dad reached out to hug Trish, but she stiffened so visibly, and narrowed her eyes, that he dropped his arms and cleared his throat, reaching down to ruffle Jack's hair.

Then there was immediately a welcome bustle of hanging coats, and small talk about the drive, and then Ellen flitted around offering drinks. By the time she vanished to her kitchen to glaze the ham, we were arrayed about the living room holding beverages as neatly as if we'd been dolls in her own personal dollhouse.

Jack had buried his nose in a Magic Tree House book, and the rest of us adults and one uncomfortable teenager stared at one another with rigid grins until Trish said, "Oh, for the love of God, stop smiling, everybody."

We tittered uncomfortably, and all tried not to stare at Trish. I wondered how on earth she ever managed to hold an Easter egg hunt at her house. I'd think she'd be afraid to hide eggs in there for fear you'd never find them again. That would be quite the smell.

Then Dad went ahead and asked, "So did the Easter bunny visit your house today?"

"There is no Easter bunny," Jack intoned into the pages of his book.

"Well, aren't you all grown up, now? Practically a man," my dad continued, undaunted. Trish was drumming her fingers on the overstuffed arm of the plush chair she was sitting in, gaze on the floor.

My dad said, "Did you hunt for eggs?"

"No," was Jack's simple reply, face hidden behind his book. On the cover, the *Titanic* was going down, and some kids and a dog were scrambling around on deck. I knew how they felt.

Drew cleared his throat. "I thought we could maybe hunt eggs later, here. Jack could go in the other room, and then the grown-ups could hide them. That's what's in all those bags."

Ellen ducked in from the kitchen. "Eggs? We'd better refrigerate them!"

"Plastic eggs, Ellen. They have jelly beans in them and stuff," Drew said. "None of us really like eating real hard-boiled eggs."

I pictured Trish in a store in front of an Easter display and bit my lip to keep from visibly cringing. I could just imagine her grabbing everything in sight. She always was a sucker for holiday merchandise. The last day I was at her house I'd uncovered a trove of Halloween party paraphernalia, for some grand gala that never came to pass. There was a punch bowl shaped like a skull. She'd put it in the Keep pile, and I'd snuck it onto the Sell tarp when she wasn't looking.

"I got the good jelly beans," Drew continued. "The really juicy fruity ones. Yum."

And then I saw an unabashed smile from Drew, so big I could see his canines, which seemed very sharp. His smile was bright and white, especially compared to all that black he was wearing. Jack finally peeked out from above his book, prairie-dog fashion, and I detected a smile in the corners of his upturned eyes.

Drew had said "I got," which meant Drew went shopping. I wondered, then, if Drew had done all the planning for the festive part of the holiday.

In contrast to punk rock Drew's big smile, Trish looked like someone had pulled her plug, slumped in the chair as she was, unmoving.

I wondered at the dress she was wearing, something years out of date, and a few dress sizes ago. Not that I could claim to be the exact same size as in the bloom of youth myself, but it was unlike Trish to dress in such an unflattering way. She was always buying new clothes, and we hadn't thrown out her best things, I know we hadn't. I noticed her hair seemed stringier than usual, too.

Ellen trilled from the kitchen she could use some help with the potatoes. Drew and I leaped from our chairs. Trish didn't budge. Dad turned on the television and started clicking. I hoped he wouldn't settle on cable news. The last thing we needed was drama from the outside world.

Ellen set Drew and me to working on a fruit salad and potato peeling, as she stepped into the dining area to lay the table. That's what she always said, "lay the table." It sounded fancier to me than what we always said growing up, "set the table," or later, when we had no visible table, "grab the plates" or "unfold the TV trays."

"What's wrong with your mom?" I asked him.

"You mean more than usual? I don't know." He cut his eyes back over his shoulder, toward the living room. "Ever since I stopped in to see her on Wednesday, I've noticed she'd gone all, robotic, kind of. Listless. That's a good word for it."

"Had she been cleaning?"

He shook his head, frowning hard at the potato he was trying to chop into bits. "Nothing looked different, anyway. Not worse, though, either. I tried to talk to her, but she claimed she was 'just tired.' "

"Our mom used to say that. Sometimes she seemed more aware of the mess than usual. Some days she'd deny anything was wrong with her house at all, that she just had a tiny bit of clutter here and there. Other days, without saying it out loud, you could tell she was feeling it, a taste of what it was like for us."

"I don't know. Something else happened, I think."

"How do you know?"

"Jack said she'd been on the phone to Ron a lot. And I tried to text her Wednesday morning, and she didn't get back to me for hours."

"Really? That's odd." I was thinking of the new girlfriend, name of Summer, age indeterminate. "It won't do for her to curl up in a shell now," I said, chopping some onions with energy, enjoying the solid *smack-smack* rhythm and sound on the cutting board. "We've got so much to do."

"Do we, now?" I gasped. Trish was right behind me, opening the refrigerator. "I'm right fricking here, you know." She slammed the refrigerator shut. "Drew, if you have an issue with me, you should talk to me about it, like the adult you like to pretend to be."

"Like the adult who actually did the shopping so Jack could have a frickin' Easter for once."

"Oh, 'for once,' like we've never had an Easter at the house."

Drew never stopped chopping, never looked up as he continued,

"Last year he went with Ron for Easter, and I stayed with you and ate takeout so you wouldn't be alone."

"You're too old for Easter baskets, c'mon."

"And the year before that? Remember that? He didn't find out about the Easter bunny because someone at school told him, or because he just got old enough to figure it out. He knew when all the eggs were 'hidden' right on top of everything, in plain sight."

"That's not fair to put on me."

"He looked right at you and he went, 'Mom, you put the eggs out' because they weren't actually hidden, because you didn't want to lose any."

"Stop it!"

"And then you lost the Easter baskets you bought, so his Easter basket was a plastic ice cream tub you'd washed out."

"Shut up, damn you!"

Ellen popped her head into the kitchen from the dining area, her eyes wide, hoop earrings swinging. "Patricia?" she asked, her voice tinged with anxiety and maybe a bit of irritation, too.

Trish ignored Ellen. She said to Drew, "You think you can do a better job parenting than I do? With your store-bought Easter baskets and Starburst jelly beans? Have at it, pal. Good luck to you."

At this she pushed past our father who'd appeared in the opposite kitchen entry and slammed her way through the front door.

Drew gaped at me, finally with his knife stilled. "Did she just, like, resign? From being a parent?" he whispered.

My dad shot me a look. In the instant of his stare, I could read it all. A lifetime of living in a screwed-up family will do that, will make a person fluent in silent looks and body language. *See? I knew she wasn't up to it, and now she's gone and ruined Easter for her little boy.*

He turned away and boomed out, much too loudly, "Hey, Jack, I challenge you to some Wii bowling. I'm gonna top your high score this time. I've been practicing with Grandma Ellen."

I put down the knife and retrieved my jacket from the front hall. Drew was still too stunned to move, and anyway, he'd be the last person she'd want to see just now.

I might be only second to last. Third, behind our dad.

Ellen called out behind me as I went out the door, "But when will we have dinner? The ham!"

I stopped in the doorway to turn back to my stepmother. "Screw the ham, Ellen."

Chapter 23

I knew without turning that it was Mary behind me. She had an unmistakable gait when she was in a hurry, a pitter-patter of feet, on her toes, like she didn't dare run without her jogging clothes, special shoes, and a water bottle.

I wondered if she'd run if an axe murderer were chasing her, or if she'd still do that silly prance.

Her shadow was in my peripheral vision, and her stride slowed to match mine, which was more of a plod.

So I hadn't had the energy to rustle up a holiday. What no one seemed to understand was that I had cleaned Jack's room totally—only to have him refuse to sleep in his bed—then I had to submit to a humiliating government shrink with the threat of losing my son hanging over my head. And I almost got fired by my dragon lady boss. After that, something settled on me like that heavy blanket you have to wear at the dentist while getting x-rays. Every step was harder to take. Even words were harder to speak. I saved what little energy I had for Jack, and I feared he could tell how hard it was for me.

Early spring was always hard in recent years, since I closed up that one room. I used to try to talk to Ron—some of what I was going through he understood all too well—but as patient as he tried to be, this time it didn't help.

"Drew thinks you resigned from parenthood," Mary said, still puffing from her attempt to catch up with me.

"Jack didn't hear that, did he?"

"I don't think so. He was busy in the other room. He's playing Wii with Dad now."

"Let Drew think I quit. Maybe if he ponders what it's actually like to be a parent, he'll quit being so judgmental. Not to mention maybe he won't knock up his girlfriend."

"You think he would?"

I stopped and stared at Mary through a curl of hair that had fallen out of my ponytail. "Duh. He's seventeen and he's always at her house and her parents don't get home from work until six. What do you think he's doing in all that time? I gave him condoms, so I hope he's smart enough to use them."

Mary grimaced slightly. She shook her head as if to clear her thoughts. "Anyway, Trish, he's just being a teenager. He's frustrated."

"Join the club."

"You had a rough week?"

"Ding ding! Mary wins the prize! You are correct!"

We'd left the town house development by now and turned onto a busier street. We had to stop in front of a church whose occupants were spilling out of the doors, and the parking lot, such that we had to stand and watch them go rather than cross the drive.

The sun was climbing higher. I reckoned it was probably sixty degrees or so. The women and girls coming from the church wore pastel dresses and pretty, delicate shoes. The men wore suits, or at least natty ties and dress shirts. I wondered how many of them went home to a hoard of objects, or some other dreaded secret. A husband who might hit them when he drank. A wife addicted to pills. A son surfing porn. Why did everyone have to look so perfect all the time and make you think your life was terrible? Couldn't the screwed-up people look the part at least so we wouldn't feel alone?

"What was so rough about your week? Like, in particular, I mean."

I wasn't about to tell her about Dr. Tom and his perfect blond children.

I sighed. "Ayana came back."

"The social worker? Was she pleased with your progress?"

I shrugged. "She liked that Jack had his own room cleaned, but I had to confess he wouldn't sleep in it, because I knew she'd ask him anyway and I'd just get caught in a lie. I saw her jot that on her notepad and wanted to shove her pen in her ear. Her ear if she's lucky."

"Then what?"

"She stayed and tried to help me sort, but it was so stupid. She just doesn't get it, what it's like to be a parent. She kept saying that his old keepsakes weren't important, like a ribbon he won for field day."

"He won first place?"

"Well, no, it was a participation ribbon everyone got. But that's not the point! I can't ever get that time back, but if I keep some tokens, I keep some of little Jack with me. Otherwise he really is gone forever, my tiny little boy. And before you know it, he's grown up to be a man who's gonna leave me. Another one."

"But he's going to grow up whether you keep it or not."

"So Miss Ayana says," I retorted, unable to keep the sneer out of my voice. "You think I'm stupid, too?"

Mary shook her head.

"Anyway," I continued, finally turning away from the church with all its perfect people, heading back toward where we came. "I moved half the stuff we threw away back out of the garbage bins. She has no right to force me to give up my own things."

"Well . . ."

I wheeled on Mary. "No right! None! Don't you start, too."

We walked along in silence. I would have enjoyed the warm day if not for my cluttered, broken life. Tree branches were speckled with green buds, but I felt as dead inside as withered autumn leaves.

"What are you going to say to Drew when we get back?" Mary asked.

"I'll apologize. Thank him for buying the Easter things. Ask him to hold his gossip for when I'm not in earshot. Same goes for you, too, sister dear."

I froze for an instant when I felt her touch me. In the next moment, I recognized the gesture. She'd put her arm around my shoulders. We'd walked like this as little kids, when we were going somewhere fun, like to get ice cream, or over the dune to get to the lake.

I should have slipped my arm around her, too, just like old times.

I couldn't muster the enthusiasm, but I allowed myself to marvel at my bumbling younger sister, trying to take care of me.

For all my indignation, the Easter egg hunt turned out to be almost fun. We'd turned it into a boys-against-girls contest with us girls doing the hiding and my dad, Drew, and Jack trying to find the eggs. I drew from energy reserves I didn't know I had to pretend I wasn't furious with my father and his ongoing threat to take Jack from me and act like I was having a fine time. We gorged on jelly beans and foil-wrapped eggs to the detriment of our teeth and to the chagrin of Ellen, who'd made an angel food cake no one wanted.

Then came the doorbell, and my heart sank. I'd been trying all day not to think about the moment, which is why I'd also neglected to tell anyone but Jack what was coming.

Dad looked up from his rummaging under the couch for the final egg—none of us could remember where we'd put it—and they all exchanged confused looks.

"But I'm not done with the egg hunt yet!" wailed Jack.

"I'll get the door," I said, heaving myself up. "It must be Ron."

"Ronald?" asked Ellen. "Oh, dear, I guess I could make him a plate."

I ignored her and answered the door. Ron was wearing khaki pants and a button-down shirt. He must have gone somewhere nice for Easter with his girl. He also smelled good, but foreign, wearing a scent I didn't recognize.

He gave me a hug, but it was distant, more arm-and-shoulder than an embrace. "Is he ready?"

Jack called out, "We haven't found the last egg!"

"Honey, your dad's here to pick you up; we can find it later."

Ron shrugged. "I ain't in a hurry. I can wait."

"Your girlfriend isn't in the car?"

"Naw. I'm not going to introduce Jack in the car. That doesn't seem very pleasant."

"Well, come in then. Don't just hover in the doorway like a deliveryman."

The greetings all around were warm and friendly. My family always liked Ron. This made me set my jaw in remembering how they all lined up against me after the split, more or less. I mean, no one came out and said, "He was right to leave you," but I didn't get as much sympathy as your average wife left by her husband. And Mary, she didn't even call me.

True, I never called her. But I figured Dad must have told her, and wouldn't she reach out then? Wouldn't she want to see how I was doing? Why didn't she care?

And why did she care all of a sudden now?

Everyone cheered as Jack yanked the final egg out from between sofa cushions with his one good arm, and he held it aloft like the Olympic torch.

Oh yes, that was why. This was all for Jack, in the end. It was still true that no one gave a good goddamn about me.

Chapter 24

When I opened the door of Dad's camper Monday morning, I came upon Trish surrounded by boxes in the driveway. Her hair was pulled up in a frizzy ponytail, hands on her hips. She stared hard at the boxes, biting her lip and shifting her weight.

I stepped out and blinked in the slanting sunlight. The air seemed brighter with the promise of spring, like a drug to us soggy, cold Michiganders. But wet leaves blanketed much of Trish's yard. The wind carried a sickly rich and sweet smell of rotting plant life, like a big pile of mulch, or compost.

"Hi," I said, trying to catch her attention since she'd not yet looked up.

She waved at me, eyes still on the boxes.

"Are you watching to make sure they don't run away?" I asked. I could gauge her mood by this. If she smiled, great. If she snapped my head off, well . . .

She cocked her head like a spaniel. "I just . . . These are Ron's. Old tools. I don't know what to do with them."

"Have you talked to him this morning? About how Jack's doing?" The parting at Dad's house last night had been tearful, for both Jack and Trish, though she tried to hide it. I thought I'd seen some dampness in Ron's eyes, too. Then I'd followed Trish back to her house, and I sat with her watching television in her living room until the scattered remains of her hoard made me feel jumpy enough I retreated to the camper, my home-away-from-home for this cleaning week.

"No," Trish said. "I haven't heard from Jack yet."

I found myself surprised by how much I was used to seeing the little guy. A pang snapped like a rubber band at how many years I missed because we weren't speaking, Trish and me. And here I thought we were only hurting ourselves.

"What about Drew?"

Trish shrugged. "He hasn't shared his plans with me."

"So he's not going with his girlfriend on vacation?"

"I said I don't know."

"Sorry."

Trish sighed, looking up at the sky. "Whatever. Never mind, OK?"

"Sorry."

"If you say sorry one more time, I'll knock your block off."

I bit my lip. "I'll just, uh, brush my teeth, I guess."

"What time is your friend getting here?"

"Any time now, I'd guess." *Hurry, Seth,* I thought, knowing that Trish would at least try to make nice in front of someone new.

I stalled inside the camper, rearranging my few toiletries on the tiny bathroom counter, straightening the inside of my overnight bag. I used to be able to navigate the ocean of Trish. That is to say, yes, I'd run into storms, but I'd usually know they were coming. Like when we were kids and I'd try to horn in on the fun she was having with her friends in the school cafeteria. That would set her off. Or when I'd go running to Mom for support when Trish told me what an idiot I was. I didn't seem to know anymore where the dangerous currents were.

I sank down onto the camper's narrow bed, remembering Mom's funeral, and all the family members who crowded around and swore to keep in better touch. Cousins I hadn't seen in years, the uncles who'd once helped clean her house rafters to cellar, church friends and family friends and neighbors and former teachers.

Trish and I, though we'd been distant since I moved out, stuck close together those few days. We seemed to have been appointed Chiefs of Grief, being the daughters and thus her closest kin. It might have otherwise been Dad, but in divorcing her he'd bumped himself down the ladder somewhat.

The relatives accosted us the most. Trish seemed to, well, not *enjoy* the attention. But she did seem comfortable. She gratefully returned the tearful embraces and cried on other people's shoulders. She found times to laugh through her tears when someone would try to cheer us up. One of our cousins had a baby, and Trish spent as much time as she could making googly eyes at the baby, being rewarded with drooly toothless grins.

I stiffened every time someone hugged me. My return hug was an awkward pat on the back. I tried not to visibly blanch at them coming at me with tissues soaked by tears and snot, the way they touched me all over my clothes, even my hair sometimes. For some of them I was still four years old and thus available for manhandling.

I went to the bathroom so often anyone who noticed would have thought I had a bladder infection.

I would close myself into a stall, sit on the toilet, and then sob silently into my hands. The effort of sobbing so hard, without sound, made my throat feel raw and heavy. Then someone would come into the bathroom, and I'd have to get up because if I stayed too long they would eventually notice and wonder what was wrong and come after me.

It was one of the few times people seemed to keep careful track of my doings, and instead of welcoming the attention, I resented it. I wanted to scream, *Don't you people know I'm grieving here?* But of course they did know, and in a way that made sense to everyone else in the world but me, they were helping. So on went the hugging.

After the service, a grim receiving line of sorts formed as people filed out across the front row of the funeral home, past us Chiefs of Grief, giving us platitudes and pats and, for God's sake, more damn hugs.

When I got home, I threw my funeral dress in the garbage, along with the pantyhose, underwear, and shoes I'd been wearing, though all of those things represented more than $100 of my own hard-earned money.

I wonder what Seth would say about that; what would he write in his little shrink notebook if I were a patient?

He'd come to the funeral, too, the only welcome face in that entire grueling ordeal. He hadn't been able to fight his way through the scrum of mourners to get much time with me, but when he did, he embraced me tightly. *Call me if you need anything,* he'd said. His hug was the only one I'd returned with feeling.

Many nights I stared at my phone, thinking of Seth's offer as sleep eluded me, but it was always in the wee hours of morning, and by dawn it no longer seemed like a good idea to violate our annual call tradition and intrude on his regular life.

So I finally did take him up on his offer. True, it was fourteen years later and outside the scope of the kind of help he thought he was offering, but even so. He'd honored his offer, like the true gentleman he'd always been.

Chapter 25

I watched Mary retreat into the camper, head down, and I thought, for the love of Pete, if she'd learn to stand up for herself once in a damn while, she might not be so infuriating. Her and her "sorry" all the time. She must think she's being so sweet and nice, but the thing is, there's a dark side to it. It's her sneaky way of saying, *You are so mean to me, you make me feel bad all the time.*

Maybe she does feel bad all the time. She always did shrivel up in the face of conflict.

Am I mean? I wondered, regarding those boxes again. Did my stuff make me mean?

I considered Ron's tools, this old stuff he had when we were first starting out, before he was able to buy newer, nicer, faster things. Seeing the tools made me think of him in his grubby work pants, his big strong hands, his reddish hair not going gray at all. The way he used to smile at me, just for me. Because all in all, he wasn't a real smiley kinda guy.

Would Ron want these tools anymore? If it were me, I'd keep them as a memento of how things were when we were just starting. I'd remember buying those tools full of hope for the new business. They'd symbolize how far I'd come. I was so proud of him when he could finally buy a new truck with money from his jobs! His dad had always been running him down, saying he wasn't ever gonna make it because he didn't have a head for figures and all he could do was bang a nail. But Ron taught himself figures, well enough to get going anyway.

These tools were still good, too. He could keep them around the house, for home-type repairs.

I bent down and shoved the boxes to the side of the garage. Pulled a Sharpie out of my pocket and marked them as Ron's things. He'd have to decide. I certainly had no right to make the call about his stuff.

Why couldn't everyone have that respect for me?

My phone chimed. A text from Drew.

Called to check on Jack. Seemed cheerful. All OK.

I couldn't hardly let go of Jack last night. Jack was wiggling around like a little worm while I hugged him. Normally he's not embarrassed, so I don't know why he was so bothered. I just wanted to hug him extralong, I said, to store up extra for a few days.

Drew had been coughing and shuffling his feet, his own coat in his hand, planning to make his hasty exit at the same time. I made to hug him, too, but he gave me only a quick one-armed squeeze and he was gone like a puff of smoke. He was never too good with good-byes.

I couldn't resist texting Drew my question. *Are you coming back today?*

The answer came back immediately.

Nah. Stuff to do.

So you're not going on vacation? Or what?

No answer. I stuffed my phone back in my pocket. How was it OK that he wasn't going to tell me his plans? My own child and I don't even get to know if he's going to be in the state or not.

Nor could I say what Jack was doing right this minute. I sat down in my garage on an old broken office chair and wondered how the hell this happened, that a once-married woman with two children ended up so goddamn alone.

* * *

W hen I heard tires crunching on the gravel, I was in the kitchen, feeling dizzy with the papers in front of me. They all seemed equally important. Receipts would be needed for tax purposes. Jack's school papers mattered to me, showing his progress as they did, and in fact—I should have thought of this before—Ron should see them, too. No reason he should be updated only twice a year on report card day.

I dropped the papers and beelined for the door, catching myself amazed again I had a straight path instead of a maze to navigate.

My shoulders slumped. Not Drew. A shiny black car, looking to be a . . . Lexus? Not sure why that would surprise me, but it did, even so. And I couldn't help but wonder what kind of job Mary's friend had that he was off work in the middle of the year with nothing better to do than go help a stranger clean a house. And if that work pays enough to drive a Lexus, how can I get that job?

Mary had been sorting in the garage. My piles had started to meld together the way spots of mold will, so she'd been pushing them back apart again. We both made it to the driveway at the same time to see this guy, this Seth.

"Mary, it's good to see you," he said. She looked down at the ground, of course, not having enough sense to smile back or look pleased.

"Thanks so much for coming," she said, like a Realtor at an open house or something. Honestly.

"I'm Trish," I said, holding out my hand. Seth was bald, but it was the purposeful kind of bald that men our age do when a retreating hairline gets too embarrassing. I could see plenty of fine stubble. He had a nicely shaped head for it, at least. His eyes were a faint blue, and he looked like he didn't get very much sun. He wore glasses, the kind with the rims that are practically invisible. He was wearing track pants and a shirt advertising some kind of 5k run.

"Seth Davis," he replied. "Glad to meet you."

"I really am glad you're here," I said, as earnestly as I could, to make up for the time coming soon, no doubt, when I'd lose my temper in front of him. "This is such a big job, and it's great to have some help."

I caught Mary staring at Seth. "What happened to your hair?" she asked.

He startled, grabbed his head, affecting a look of shock and horror. "Oh, no! Where did it all go?"

For half a beat Mary looked horrified, too, then she turned pink and giggled. Giggled just like a twelve-year-old. Seth dropped the act and ran his hand over his head. "Would you believe it's cheaper than shampoo?"

Then we all stood there like three morons, glancing at each other.

"OK, well," I announced. "So here's what I'm doing. I'm sorting papers in the kitchen, and Mary probably needs help in the garage getting those piles straightened up. We'll need to package up some of the recyclables. It's garbage day tomorrow. And, uh . . . we'll see after that."

Seth nodded and moved to follow Mary into the garage.

"Oh, one more thing? Just so you know? Don't throw my stuff away without asking. Even if you think it's junk. 'One person's trash . . . ,' right?"

I watched Mary freeze and try not to react, try to stuff down whatever she was going to say. This time I was glad she kept her mouth shut instead of giving me crap.

Chapter 26

In almost fifteen years, his hair had disappeared. His eyes had fine lines like arrows pointing at the corners, partially hidden by the stems of his eyeglass frames, though his smile hadn't aged a day. He was both so much the same and so different that I was rendered mute and helpless, grappling with how much time had rushed past me like so much river water.

I finally managed to explain what I was doing, trying to neaten up the piles.

Neither of us commented on how large the Keep pile was compared to the Sell and Donate piles.

He asked me how the cleanup had been going, and I answered, "Fine," reflexively. He asked me about work and I told him the store closed. I could hear him pause in the hefting of boxes to look at me, but I kept working with my back to him and asked him instead about his daughter, who, according to the last postcard, was in grade school by now.

In this way small talk continued, and I snuck another look at him.

He looked stronger than I remembered. I could see defined muscles where his T-shirt sleeve stopped. His baldness made him look older but not in a decrepit way, rather seeming to connote wisdom. As if he were too smart to bother with hair.

When I felt sure Trish was busy enough inside that she wouldn't come out for a while, I walked up to him, screwing up my courage. Seth put the box down he'd been holding and stood watchfully next to me. I was so close I could smell the minty tang of his aftershave.

"Thank you. For helping."

He nodded. "Of course."

"And . . ." I said, my voice as soft as it could be without whispering. "Trish doesn't know what you do. That you're a psychologist."

He just stood there. Waiting.

"So," I continued, "I don't think we should tell her."

Seth rubbed the back of his neck, sighed, and stared up at the rafters of the garage. "I don't want to lie."

"I'm not asking you to come out and lie. I'm just saying that you don't want to treat her or anything anyway, right? It's unethical? You said you're only here as a pair of extra hands."

"So why can't we be honest? Why the subterfuge?"

"She'd flip out. She'd accuse me of treachery. She would never believe in a million years I didn't do this on purpose."

I caught my breath and held it. Seth could insist on coming clean to Trish, and she could throw him out. He could be upset with my duplicity, spin on his heel, and walk right out. I could lose the last friend I had, right here.

"It's manipulative," he said, folding his arms. I didn't know if he meant manipulative of him, or of Trish, but I dared not ask.

"I'm just trying to help her," I said, aware of the begging in my voice, and not minding, because if it's one good thing about having very little pride, it's being able to humiliate yourself for a good cause. "She could lose her little boy over this."

He dug the toe of his running shoe into a crack in the garage floor, staring down, silent.

Finally, he looked up. "She needs to get some help. When we've avoided this imminent disaster. Because if she doesn't, no matter how clean we get this place, she'll do it all over again."

"You think so? She's so motivated this time."

Seth said in a detached, cool voice, almost reciting, "When the threat is gone, the fear will fade. If fear is the only thing keeping the house clean, it will not last."

"I guess you're right."

"So I'll only agree to this if you promise me, and I mean swear to me, that you will let me refer her to someone when this is done. And not me. She needs someone who specializes in OCD or hoarding. Like I said, I'm surprised the CPS people haven't already lined something up for her."

"OCD? She's got OCD?"

"Sort of. The latest thought is that compulsive hoarding works in a similar way. The difference is that people with OCD don't enjoy their compulsions, they're just trying to rid themselves of an intrusive thought. But hoarding brings a kind of enjoyment. So I've read, anyway." For an instant I flashed back to Seth with hair, scooping in eggs at the dorm cafeteria while Rebecca slept off a hangover, telling me about something really cool he just learned in his psych class.

I cast a glance around at the dusty, smelly piles. Enjoyment? Then I remembered the way she lit up at Target, the way she fought me to buy those stupid boots. Well, cocaine is pleasurable too, in some ways, I supposed.

"I thought you said this wasn't your area."

"It's not, but I did some reading."

"I thought you didn't want to treat her?"

"I don't. But I wanted to be prepared. So what do you say? I'll keep quiet about my job if you promise you'll talk to her about getting real help from an expert."

"It's a deal," I said. "I promise I will. I'm out of my depth here."

"You and me both," muttered Seth. He turned away and retreated to the far corner of the garage.

* * *

At lunchtime we gathered back in the house, with Seth following us in. With him behind me, I couldn't tell what he thought of the house. I looked at it again with the eyes of a newcomer.

The living room had once been a waist-high mass of clutter with curved paths in and out, like an ant farm. The shades had been drawn tight against the outside. Now the remaining piles were pushed back to the walls in the living room. A coffee table was visible, though I noticed it was sprouting new piles I hadn't remembered last week. Fresher papers, it looked like. Mail, some newspapers. A plastic grocery bag. The carpet, a tan Berber, was visible under our feet. The wear pattern was strangely uneven, and it was faded in unusual spots.

Boxes, full of things Trish hadn't quite sorted yet, were stacked up along the walls. The kitchen table was still coated in a thick layer of paper, and new piles on the floor represented Trish's latest attempt at sorting.

I saw Trish stare at Seth, gauging him. Seth walked in the house as if he'd been here twenty times, striding to the kitchen. "I'm just going to wash my hands," he called to us.

I saw Trish's shoulders relax, and she smiled sadly. She cast me a look that seemed like gratitude. But I could have been mistaken.

I followed into the kitchen and saw Seth drying his hands with paper towel. An open roll peeked from a shopping bag. He was looking around as he continued to dry.

"Oh, put it here," Trish said, dumping some things out of a plastic shopping bag and holding it out. "The regular trash is full anyhow."

She dropped the shopping bag on the floor and then turned to the refrigerator, yanking the handle.

A block of cheese fell out and Trish jumped back, nearly banging into Seth who was standing too close behind, but he had no choice as his feet were hemmed in by bags. I realized that in my visit last weekend we'd eaten out the whole time. We'd never eaten anything from inside Trish's house.

I peeked into the fridge and stifled a gasp. It was almost a solid wall of food. An odor wafted from it as well. Sour, pungent. I stole a look at Seth who was now puckering up his forehead and peering inside with intensity.

Trish shoved the block of cheese back into the gap from which it had fallen, and then she retrieved some lunch meat from the crisper, and some mustard from the door. She bashed the fridge shut with her foot and bopped it with her hip for good measure. I wondered what she'd say if I told her most people don't have to slam their fridges shut just to keep from being buried in a waterfall of expired food.

Seth caught my eye and glanced down at the lunch meat. I remained confused for a moment until it registered; he wanted me to check the expiration date. I had to be the one to raise the question.

I picked up the turkey and turned it over, searching.

"It's not rotten," Trish barked, and I dropped the package. She'd been pulling some bread out of a bag on the floor. "I'm not disgusting. I'm cluttered. There's a difference."

By the end, our mother no longer could distinguish between good and bad food. It was one of the lowest moments. Until the fire, of course.

"Oh, I know," I said, lying badly. "But, um, the fridge did smell. Just a bit. A little."

Trish scowled, digging a plastic knife and plates out of yet another bag. "Well, I'm sure there are things I haven't gotten to back there that should be thrown away, but in case you haven't noticed, my son had to be rushed to urgent care and I'm a single parent and I do work full-time, so you'll excuse me if I'm a little distracted."

This time it was me looking at Seth. I wanted backup. All my life I've needed backup. It used to be my parents who would take up for me, mostly Dad toward the end of the time I lived at home, but even

Mom would say, "Oh, Trish, leave her alone." Even though I knew it made Trish hate me a little more, I needed it. God, how I needed someone on my side.

Seth shook his head so gently I might have imagined it. I slumped, but I knew he was right. He wasn't going to be some shrink referee in our sister fights. Not fair to even ask him.

So we ate our sandwiches standing in the kitchen, wordlessly, taking turns reaching into an open bag of chips on the counter. All last week, I'd been counting the hours until I could leave my silent home. Now I found myself counting the hours until I could retreat to the camper outside.

W hen we'd dusted chip crumbs off our hands, we confronted the kitchen table.

It was mounded with a pile of papers. Trish reached out to pick one up and caused an avalanche down the side. This made her curse and stare at the ceiling, blinking rapidly.

"What can we help with?" I asked, quite sure she didn't want us to just sweep the whole mess into a garbage bag, though I sorely wanted to.

"I don't know. I mean . . . These could all be important. I have to sort through them one by one, myself."

"Oh, Trish, that'll take too long. And what will we do while we wait for that?"

"Straighten the garage piles?"

"We did that. They're straight."

"I don't know how else to do it."

"Why don't you let us help? Just tell us in general what you're looking to keep and what you're looking to recycle?"

I'd been watching those hoarding documentaries on TV and read a self-help book from the library. Some experts said the hoarder should set ground rules so other people could help.

Trish sighed. "I guess we can recycle old newspapers. And junk mail. But open it and look, don't just throw away the whole thing un-opened. One time I thought a piece of mail from my bank was a life insurance offer or something and it turned out to be my escrow state-ment and I paid my next mortgage bill wrong and it was a huge night-mare. So look at every piece. Every single one."

She grimaced at the memory of that bank envelope going awry.

"But what about Jack's school stuff? A lot of this looks like school stuff."

"I'll do the school stuff myself."

She'd never accept otherwise. I was only glad she agreed to let the newspapers go. I was tempted to call the *Journal* and cancel her subscription. There was a new paper on the doorstep I saw when we came in.

Seth and I got to work on the papers. We dutifully opened enve-lopes and looked inside. We took to ripping them in half, the credit card offers. There were so many! Most people got a bunch, but she seemed to have an enormous amount. I began to wonder how many cards were in her wallet. How many times she'd looked at one of these offers and thought that low, low APR sounded like a brilliant idea.

I noticed Seth watching Trish when he thought I wasn't looking.

We observed the agony on her face as she confronted each piece of schoolwork. It was like someone was digging a sliver out of her toe. A huge stack was growing next to her.

"Trish," I said, trying to sound gentle. "You can't keep them all, can you?"

"But Jack did these. Some of these are from kindergarten, and I just loved them. Look at this, it's a self-portrait. How cute is that?"

"Where are you going to put them?"

"I'll store them."

"Where will you store them?"

"Dammit, Mary! You don't understand! You don't have kids, so you couldn't possibly."

"I understand," Seth interjected, softly, calmly.

Trish and I froze in our sorting and fighting.

"My daughter is ten and, believe me, they create a tidal wave of paper. And it all seems really crucial, doesn't it? Aurora went through an artist phase where every day it seemed like she scribbled something on a piece of paper and presented it to us like it was the *Mona Lisa*. And we praised her like crazy, we were so proud to see her showing an interest in something."

Trish was glowing, listening to him. She smiled, eyes bright. She nodded along rapidly.

"And for a while we had stacks and stacks of it everywhere in the house, and she just kept making more. It got to be where me and my wife, we almost dreaded her getting out the art supplies."

Trish now appeared on the brink of tears. Her eyes shone, and she bit her lip.

Seth continued, "But then you know what? We realized something. Aurora is not 'in' the artwork. If we discard a piece, we're not discarding 'her' or her effort. Her enthusiasm for art is still there, Aurora herself is still there." He chuckled to himself, smiling. "So we saved the best ones in a scrapbook. We got some mattes and some inexpensive frames and we hung others, and we rotated the freshest drawings into the display. We dedicated part of our dining room wall to her gallery. My wife even made a sign that said 'Aurora's Gallery.' And the rest, we just recycled. We felt lighter, I tell you. And we stopped dreading the art supplies. We could enjoy her art again."

Trish was holding a piece of finger painting, from the look of it. "But Jack would be upset. I know he would be. I mean, what did Aurora say?"

Seth shifted, turning his attention back to the papers. "Well. She's not very verbal."

"You must have known how she felt about it, though. She must have said something."

"Aurora has autism."

Trish gasped and held her hands to her face, and I felt my own eyes widen. "Oh!" Trish said. "I'm sorry. I mean, maybe sorry isn't the word, I'm just . . . Oh, no."

Seth shook his head. "Don't worry about it. She was diagnosed a long time ago. We cope."

"We can't keep you away from your family all week!" Trish exclaimed.

Seth shook his head. "You're not. It's my ex-wife's time with her."

I blinked hard and looked down at the papers in my lap to mask my surprise. The "ex" part of ex-wife was new to me, too. I started to ask myself why Seth had never told me about his daughter's diagnosis in all those phone calls, why I didn't know he'd gotten divorced. Then I answered my own question. Those calls must have been just a silly tradition. Lightweight and meaningless. To him, anyway.

For his part, Seth reached into the paper pile, took out an envelope, and opened it calmly as if he'd said nothing at all.

Trish stared at the pile of artwork for long moments, then got up and trotted down the hall to her room. I heard the door slam.

"Seth," I ventured. "Thanks for that. And I'm . . . I'm sorry."

"Don't be."

"I'm just really grateful that you . . ."

"It's fine, Mary. Do you have another bag? Mine's full."

I handed over another bag and watched him continue to inspect papers, noticing a wavy furrow deepen across his forehead.

I'd seen that before.

Once, in college, Seth's father had a heart attack. He'd been in California and Seth couldn't get there quickly; his mother had told him to stay put and wait for news. Rebecca was on a weekend trip with her parents. Seth called me—this was before the drunken kiss—and came to the dorm room sober, but wrecked and worried. I sat next to him and let him wring his hands and fret. I told him several logical things about how he shouldn't borrow trouble, and his dad was at a great hospital and plenty of heart attacks turned out fine. Seth had that same furrow then that he has now. Back then, I'd given in to the temptation to brush my hand across his brow, trying to smooth it out. I was briefly tempted again. Instead I ripped open an envelope, the sharp edge of the paper slicing my finger.

"Damn," I muttered, sticking my finger in my mouth.

"Are you OK?" Seth asked.

No, I thought, but answered, "Yes. Just fine."

Chapter 27

I tried to imagine this Seth fellow, his autistic daughter handing him paper after paper of her scribbles. I tried to imagine his joy at cracking her shell. The hope he must have felt that she found a new way to reach out to them.

And he could just . . . toss that away?

Not all of it. He kept the best, the most special pieces. He gave her art a place of honor in the home.

I pictured Jack's art in a mountain on top of my table. That wasn't honoring his work, to be sure. And did I ever lovingly admire his efforts? Of course not. If anything, I'd catch a glance of the mountain and feel like I was suffocating. I'd find more in his backpack and feel like Seth must have: *Oh no, not more.*

I remember coming across a huge stack of my own childhood artwork during that fateful Florida trip, when Dad whisked Mom away for a sunny vacation, and me, Mary, and the uncles and cousins descended on the house.

I was in my heavy-metal, skull-and-crossbones phase then. I came across a My Little Pony coloring book that week and I sneered and threw it away. I found stacks of my old artwork in the same box, most of it yellowed with age, some of it dampened by moisture. Some of it was kinda cute, I recognized even then. I was already showing how much I loved color, and where most kids would make their pictures small, using one-quarter of the available space, I would turn every piece of blank paper into a mural of color and design. But I was past all this! Stupid to keep all these dumb projects from first grade when I was making clay sculptures, sketches, acrylic paintings. There wasn't any room to display my new work because of all this old crap. So I threw it all away. I remember stepping on the art with my foot to crush it into the bag, watching it crinkle up.

Now my cell phone rang: Ron's number.

"Hello?"

"Hi, Mommy."

"Jack, baby! How are you, pal?"

"Good. Daddy said I could call you anytime I wanted, and I said I was lonely so I called. I used the phone all by myself. Can I have one?"

"A cell phone?" I asked, laughing. "I don't think so, buddy. Maybe when you're in double digits."

"Three years? That's too far!"

I pulled the phone away from my head and frowned at it. Unlike him to whine for something. "Kiddo, let's not talk about it now. You can just use my phone, or your dad's."

"Summer said I should have one."

My hand tightened on the phone. "I'm sure she was just joking with you. Anyway, it's not up to her, it's up to me. And your dad." I scowled, glad he couldn't see my face. "Are you having fun? What are you up to?"

"We took a walk along the lake. And oh! Summer has a dog. He's really cute. He's a beagle, and his name is Snoopy."

"Real original."

"Huh?"

"Nothing. Did you find any good rocks?"

"Yeah, but Grandma said I couldn't keep them because they were just junky old rocks and that you wouldn't want me bringing back a bunch of junky old rocks."

I could hear him trying not to cry. I wondered if he cried when she told him no.

"Well, we are trying to clean up here." I clenched my fist, wanting to scream at that stuffy old biddy what harm could come from letting him take home a stupid stone. "We don't really need more things."

He talked a little longer and seemed calmer. He handed the phone back to his dad.

"Hi, Ron," I said, and couldn't stop myself from saying, "So Summer thinks he should have a cell phone?"

"She wasn't really thinking. She's trying to make nice."

"Well, now she's got him whining for one, thanks a lot."

"I told you she didn't mean anything by it. I told him we'd have to talk about it."

"Oh, real authoritative, Ron."

"I'm doing the best I can here. I'm not perfect either."

"Just talk to her, OK? Tell her not to promise my kid the moon."

"I will, I will. Would you prefer she didn't like Jack?"

"No, of course not." My voice cracked. *Dammit, Trish.*

"Hey, he won't ever love any girlfriend better than you."

"Thanks, Ron. I've gotta go."

We hung up and I curled over on the bed, trying not to picture the three of them playing fetch with a dog, or playing a board game at the table, or anything else I couldn't do in my stupid house.

When I emerged from the bedroom, I gasped.

My dining room table. Clear! I stepped forward slowly and ran my fingers along its surface.

The table itself was nothing special. Some cheap thing that came in a flat box from Target and we'd had to screw its legs on. Ron had been promising me he'd build a table for me and stain it beautifully. Then I buried the old one in paper, and the subject was never raised again. The last time we'd had a meal around this table, Ron was still living here and Jack was using a booster in his chair to reach his plate. Drew was still Andy and his voice was cracking.

"I can't believe I'm crying over a stupid table." My hands shook as I wiped my face. Mary approached, sidelong. Cautious. I reached over and threw an arm around her shoulders and laughed. Seth stepped back to the periphery so I couldn't see him even from the corner of my eye.

"Where did it all go?" I asked.

Mary pointed to six large bags behind us in the living room. "That's all recyclable stuff." She also pointed to a stack of papers along the wall. "Those are school papers. Seth and I put the nicest stuff on top but I know you wanted to look through it all. Anything that looked important we put here." She pointed to the kitchen counter. "The papers from . . . well, the state, I guess. They're on top."

I felt a plummeting sensation, like on an elevator when your stomach drops. CPS, threatening to take my kid away. Good thing I'd put the shrink's card in my wallet. No one needed to know about that particular humiliation.

Mary squeezed me around the waist. "Hey, we've made great progress, and we've still got most of the week. We can do this. He'll be fine."

I nodded, not sure I believed it. And anyway, even if Ayana was appeased, our father could swoop in at any time and demand Jack for another "visit."

"I've been meaning to ask," Mary said, stepping away from me and fussing with her headband. "Have you read any more of Mom's diary?"

I shook my head. "I wanted to wait for you. Didn't seem right to read it without you."

"Weren't you terribly curious?"

I shook my head again. That diary filled me with dread. I couldn't help but wonder if she'd meant to give it to me. Though it was buried in old clothes so that it seemed accidental, maybe it wasn't. Perhaps she wanted me to uncover it, but couldn't bring herself to just hand it over. And if that was the case, what did she need me to know?

"I think we should read some now," Mary said. "As a prize for clearing the table. In fact, we should read *at* the table."

I went to fetch the diary, which I'd placed on top of the cleared entertainment center for safekeeping, while Mary explained about its discovery to Seth.

"I'll take these bags out to the recycle bin," he offered, then paused. "If that's okay with you, Trish."

I sucked in a deep breath and stared at my clear table. I'd seen them. They really had been opening all the envelopes. They didn't even fight with me about it.

"Yes. Yes, it's okay."

Seth nodded and grabbed two bags.

"OK," Mary said. "Should I read it out loud?"

April 16, 1961

I visited the camp with Mom and it was amazing! I've never heard so much Spanish in my whole life. I already picked up a few phrases just in being there a few hours. They seem to get a kick out of trying to teach Doc and me and my mom how to speak it, and they giggle at our accents, but not in a mean way.

A few of them spoke English, though, and that was a big help. One girl was named Inez, and I think she's in her twenties. Not much older than me but already so capable and grown up. It was very impressive the way she came in with her baby sister. The poor little baby was so sick with fever.

I got to talk to Inez a little bit while she held the baby and Doc and my mom saw to another child with an infected sliver in his finger. She said they live in Texas some of the year but come up north to make money in the spring, plus it's cooler up here. I wanted to ask if she was illegal but didn't want to be rude. Her accent was lovely, like music. I could have listened to her talk all day.

When it was Inez's baby sister's turn, I held her tiny hands while Doc took her temperature in her little bottom, poor thing, and Inez cooed and made sweet noises in Spanish to distract her. We were quite a team, and it made me feel very proud and mature. Doc gave her some antibiotics, just for free, handed them over, and said to bring her back next week and to call him if she got worse.

Inez smiled at me when she left and told me she'd see me next week. In that few minutes I felt more warmth from her than I've gotten from my own sister in a year. Margaret is so prissy all the time, so competitive. She tries to set the table better than me, she points out every mistake I make, and she's always brushing that soft blond hair she inherited from our mother while I'm stuck with this kinky brown mess.

Inez was so caring and sweet to her baby sister. But then, it's easy to be nice to cute babies.

Mom and Doc said I was a big help, and that made me feel proud too. I knock myself out at home to get fantastic grades and all Dad ever does is complain if I take too long doing my chores. It feels so good just to be appreciated.

And to see my mom in a new environment is exciting, too. She seems to glow when she's working, and she's so efficient and competent. Of course she's efficient at home, too, but she just doesn't seem to be *alive* when she's, say, cutting up a chicken for dinner.

I can't wait to come back next week. Dad said this will

make a great essay subject for college applications, so he
seems to be warming up to the idea.
    Wally asked me out for this weekend so we're going to
a movie.

I chuckled as Mary finished reading, comparing Aunt Margaret to
a Mexican migrant laborer named Inez. From what I heard of their
growing-up years, it wouldn't have been hard to be nicer than Margaret was to our mother. They made up as they got older, but when they
were kids . . . Mom said Margaret cut her braids off once and she had
to go to school looking like a boy for weeks until it grew out.

For our part, we remembered Aunt Margaret as being pleasant
enough but never warm to us, a condition that extended to our cousins,
who tolerated us but didn't seem to care if we were there or not. We
seldom visited.

"So much enthusiasm," Mary said, closing the diary. "I don't remember Mom ever getting that worked up about anything."

"Except a garage sale."

"Yeah, except that."

Mary folded her arms and put her head down. "I didn't think I'd get
so emotional about an old teenage diary."

"It's like having a little bit of Mom back. And yet, it's not really her.
Not the Mom we knew."

Mary turned her head on her arms, so she was facing me. She looked
very tired, and older than she should. "You know, I've been doing some
reading. And watching those hoarding shows this week."

"Hmmm." I was not looking forward to hearing her next thing, her
armchair diagnosis based on some stupid television show.

"And it seems like in every history of every case, there was some
traumatic event."

I rolled my eyes. "Mary, please. It's a TV show. They make *sure*
there's a traumatic event. It's a formula."

"But all the events *were* traumatic. One woman actually shot somebody in self-defense, another one was raped. In one case, it was 9/11 . . ."

I rose from the table, wishing Seth would come back because maybe Mary would shut the hell up. "What's your *point*?"

"What happened to Mom?"

She didn't ask what happened to me. Maybe she assumed I was just playing out our childhood again. Yep, that's good old Trish, doomed by her upbringing. If she only knew. If Mary had only bothered to ask.

"You're quite the expert now, after watching a few tacky documentaries."

"I'm just wondering."

"Well, wonder yourself into the kitchen and find some garbage bags. We'll clean my fridge that you find so disgusting."

"Why are you so angry all of a sudden?"

"Because you're so annoying all of a sudden."

"I'll never understand you."

"What's to understand? I'm a bitch and a crazy hoarder. I should get T-shirts made."

"I didn't . . . Who called you a bitch?"

"Mary, just get the garbage bags. Better yet, go get your boyfriend out there. Let him know it's safe to reenter my lair."

"He's not!" A pause where I looked at her with my *good grief* face. "Oh. Real funny."

Mary sighed and walked back out to fetch Seth. I leaned in to sniff my refrigerator. Crowded, yes, but it seemed fine to me. It smelled like a refrigerator. Maybe my nose isn't so refined as theirs. La-di-frickin'-da.

Chapter 28

I tried so hard to avoid using the face mask. I knew it would set Trish off, and how could it not? I'd be offended too, if someone had to cover her face to keep from throwing up at the smell of my kitchen.

But that refrigerator! Once we'd sequestered her few fresh things in a cooler with some ice from the ice maker—even though the ice itself smelled funny, too—the smell of what was left just about knocked me down.

Seth was better at hiding his reaction. I bet that's because of his job; he probably has to hear shocking things all day long and not react. There must be a cost to that, though, all that stuffing down of your own feelings.

Seth managed not to gag or choke or turn green, but I couldn't do it. When we came upon a jar of applesauce with a fuzzy layer of green crawling up the sides, I audibly choked.

Trish turned pink at the tips of her ears, and her whole face tightened up. I was so relieved to have Seth there with us so she'd make the effort not to tear into me in front of him.

I dashed outside with my hand over my face, breathing shallow, as if I were actually inhaling the filth into my body and wanted to keep as much of it out as possible.

In the cool outside I braced myself with my hands on my knees and forced myself to breathe enough not to pass out or throw up on the driveway. Stars speckled the fringes of my vision, and anxiety in my chest struck up a jangly, dissonant tune. I'd gotten so good at my old childhood habit of pretending not to see the clutter—to acknowledge it would have been panic on a scale I couldn't even imagine—that I'd been taken aback by the refrigerator.

I tore through the bags until I found the masks Trish had bought two weeks ago. When I came back in, Trish was slamming the food into the trash bag held by Seth as hard as she could, muttering to herself.

"What was that?" I asked.

She slammed a container of yogurt into the trash in such a way that it exploded. Even Seth flinched.

"I said I'm fucking furious that I have to do this with you here."

I blinked, reared back. "You asked us to stay. Didn't you? Don't you need the help?"

"I mean, it should be Ron. My husband should be helping me. Not my kid sister and some strange bald guy. No offense. But Ron's off on spring break with my little boy and his new girlfriend having a grand old time while I sit here in our house surrounded by garbage, all alone."

I blinked again, as if that would make me understand her, if I just stood there and blinked enough times. "You just said . . . I mean you were just complaining you were not alone. That we're here."

Even Trish flinched at whatever she discovered in the distant back of the refrigerator. She picked up another garbage bag and wrapped it around her hand, glovelike. "I'm just pissed. I'm completely pissed about everything. I'm pissed when I'm alone, and I'm pissed when you're here. I'm pissed that I inherited this stupid fucking . . . thing."

"Why are you mad at us?"

"I'm not."

"Then why are you taking it out on us?"

"Stop personalizing everything. I'm taking it out on the refrigerator."

Seth shook the bag he'd been holding for Trish, so the contents settled deeper, making more room. "You're taking it out on yourself, too, a bit."

Trish whipped her head toward him. She raked bits of her loose hair off her face and squinted at him. "What the hell are you talking about?"

"Nothing. Never mind. I spoke out of turn."

Trish turned to me in irritated disbelief, a look of *can you believe this guy?* She snatched the nearly full trash bag from where Seth had been holding it open for her and knotted the top roughly, so much so her ring snagged in the top of the bag and nearly spilled the whole reeking mess onto her kitchen floor.

I dared peek into the refrigerator. A yellow film seemed to cover everything. There were tiny flies buzzing inside. I hadn't realized fruit flies could live in that kind of cold, though I suppose in the center of the mess it probably wasn't that cold at all, but somewhat insulated, even. Various brown spills smeared the glass shelves.

An itchy sensation crept over my hands. It wasn't a topical itch, nothing I could treat with Benadryl or cortisone. It was the way I felt when Drew showed up at my town house and dropped a clod of dirt on my carpet. I'd never felt it in someone else's home before. I wondered at myself, as I stormed around to find the cleaning supplies she'd bought a couple weeks ago, now in search of gloves and Soft Scrub and Brillo pads. I wondered if I'd been in Trish's home long enough to have some proprietary feelings over it, and that's why I had this now powerful urge to clean the refrigerator.

I shoved my head inside and squirted lemony, bleachy Soft Scrub all over everything I could see.

"Mary?" I heard Seth say, but he sounded distant because of the cavelike effect of the fridge.

I answered him with cleaning. The shelves rattled with the force of my scrubbing. With each stroke of the sponge, each erasure of a bit of filth, I felt less crazy, less itchy, less frantic.

I heard Trish calling my name, and I ignored that, too, working on a stubborn bit of sticky brown that might have once been honey or perhaps maple syrup. Finally I tired of hearing my name called and yanked my head out, banging it on a shelf. "What?" I barked, and they both drew back.

Trish gave me a look I had rarely seen. She looked wary and shocked. Seth was studying me, I could tell. "What?" I repeated, feeling anxious again with the job half done. "What's the problem? I'm cleaning it out."

"You just seem," Trish began, proceeding with uncharacteristic caution in her speech. "A little . . . crazed."

"We're in a hurry, yes? So I'm hurrying."

"Well, it's not a race or anything. And we've made pretty good progress, really." Trish swiped her hand through the air, indicating expansive progress.

I glanced around. The dining table was clear, and the living room had gone from "crazy hoarder" to looking like someone just moved in and still had boxes all over, so yes, that was progress of a sort. We'd managed Jack's room, though Trish admitted he hadn't yet started sleeping in it.

But Trish's own room, Drew's old room, the cluttered master bath, and the mysterious spare room had not been touched. That didn't count her basement, which I hated to even consider, or the enclosed back porch, the garage.

I sat back on my heels and asked Trish, "How do you think we're going to get this all done? If we meander along?"

"Just don't, like, brain damage yourself with the fumes, OK?"

I debated telling her I rather liked the smell of Soft Scrub, but my role as the less-crazy sister suited me just fine and I did not intend to give it up.

Chapter 29

M onday raced by like one of those fast movies they used
to show in science class of flowers blooming and snow
melting. My kitchen counters were clearing, and the tarps
in the driveway and garage were filling up. At one point a Dumpster
arrived, after Ayana had called to report she'd rented it for me. This
monstrosity loomed in my driveway like a sleeping beast and I thought
we'd never fill that whole thing. How much junk did she really think
I had?

I'd struggled to sound grateful, and I grimaced when she'd said,
"See you soon."

Rural neighbors tended to mind their own business, but I did notice
a few cars slow down as they drove past my house, and Alvin from next
door looked like he wanted to talk to me when I bumped into him at
the mailbox, but I scurried away and pretended not to notice.

Progress came at a price, and that price was spectacle.

Besides the giant Dumpster, we had the camper. It was parked
along the garage, and Mary stayed there last night, with the generator running for heat. We also had the garage floor lined with objects,
and although we planned to close the garage at night, it was open all
day like a gaping hole for anyone to gawk into. We couldn't bring all

the other things lining the driveway itself, so we just planned to drape them with tarps to keep off the dew, or frost.

I figured it was only a matter of time before neighbors got curious enough to send someone over to ask what the blazes was going on.

As we cleaned, we fell into a habit of reading Mother's journal when we'd cleared some definable area, like the kitchen counter. Seth would always find something to do in another part of the house, or he'd step out to make a call.

So we read along as teenage Frannie dated a young man named Wally—chapped lips, bad breath, and all—and continued helping out at the migrant camps. She struck up a friendship with Inez. Because she spoke English, Inez had been appointed as a sort of representative of the mothers at the workers' camps, and she'd bring the sick children and then take them back and translate the doctor's instructions.

Frannie wrote about how she'd been teaching Inez some American expressions, like what "driving me batty" meant, or "the whole nine yards." Inez was teaching Frannie basic Spanish, and when her mother wasn't paying attention, some dirty words, too.

I imagined the writer of these letters as "Frannie" as opposed to "Mom." She seemed so remote from the mom we knew, anyway. I lapsed into thinking of Inez and Doc as characters in a book. I'd look forward to the next installment of their adventures, and then there'd be some reference to reality as I knew it—to Aunt Margaret, or their white house in Holland—and it would snap me back to life: these people were all real. Likely Inez was out there somewhere with a family of her own. Those little babies cured by the doctor were our age, having babies and taking them to doctors themselves now. I wondered if those babies were picking blueberries, or if they'd escaped that life, as their parents must have hoped.

As the day drew to a close my body was aching like I'd been pelted with stones. I doubted Mary was faring much better. She kept kneading her arms, sore from lifting and no doubt from scrubbing. No sooner did we uncover a surface than she leaped into action with the rubber gloves. Seth was stoic, but none of us was twenty-two anymore. I'm sure he felt it same as we all did.

I'd ache and I'd watch them ache and think, *They're doing this for me.* I needed to remember this, even in my angry times, or I might drive them all away.

I was basking in this gratitude and trying to brush my hair out of my face when I heard a distant rumble, something like a truck. Only there were no truck routes out this way, and the Dumpster was already here.

"Shit," I said. "A storm!"

We all ran to the sliding glass door, now accessible since we'd cleared most of the dining room. A flash made the trees seem to come alive for an instant, and then it was merely dusk again. Immediately the roll of thunder boomed, and we all realized how close the storm was.

I cursed myself for not paying better attention to the weather, especially in a Michigan spring when it could snow on Monday and be sixty on Friday.

We hustled out the front door to pull tarps over the driveway items. Wind had kicked up, as if to clear a path for the storm, blowing dead leaves and papers out of the way. The three of us struggled with the tarps, trying to hold them down with our feet long enough to grab a rock out of the garden or a hammer from the garage. We weren't speaking, any of us, just rushing and panting or with the occasional grunted command.

Rain began to pelt us in thick, heavy drops. It spotted the driveway before my eyes, and before long, the spots all melded and we three plus the driveway and the tarps were thoroughly wet.

We didn't have enough heavy things to weigh down the plastic. The last two tarps kept whipping up in the wind.

I held my hands up to Mary, helplessly. She shrugged back, looking all around the darkening yard for something else, anything. Seth was pointing back toward the house. Thunder made me jump with its closeness. It was the kind that started like a bone snapping and rolled into a roar. I could feel it in my chest.

Bouncing headlights illuminated the tarps, and I recognized the pickup truck of my neighbor, Alvin. Without saying anything, he leaped down from his cab with more speed than you'd think possible for a man nearing seventy. He pulled more tarps from his cab and pointed to the back. There were cinderblocks in there, and sandbags. We jumped into the truck bed, pulled them out, and started weighing down the corners of the other tarps.

Just as suddenly as he'd shown up in my driveway, he climbed back in the cab. "Go on inside, now!" he shouted over the rain, which was now coming down so hard it had a noise of its very own, hissing static. "Not safe with all these trees!"

And before I could even thank him, he slammed the truck door, backed down the driveway, and retreated to his own house.

Seth, Mary, and I scurried back inside and stood dripping in my living room, blinking at one another.

"Who was that?" Mary asked, wiping water off her face, trying to twist it out of her hair.

"My neighbor. He lives across the way." I was so wet I couldn't even conceive of getting dry. We were all soaking my wretched living room carpet. "I better find some clothes for you."

"I have some," Mary said, and I reminded her they were in the trailer, and she'd have to go outside to get them. I offered to get her something and told Seth I was sure I could find something of Ron's if he gave me a few minutes. "It'll take some time, though. I have to do some digging."

My heart pounded in my ears, and I wondered why I felt so queasy and shaky. Disaster had been averted.

But it hadn't, not really. As I moved across the living room, leaving a trail of rain behind me, I remembered the last few minutes and saw the rain blasting down on my things, the record albums I'd bought as a teenager, their covers now soaked. There had been at least a few boxes of books, some scrapbooking supplies, and yarn.

Ruined. Almost assuredly. I told myself not to fret, those were items going to charity out there, the things I decided to let go of. But I had consoled myself with the notion of someone else enjoying them as much as I had. It made me sick to think of them wasted, worthless.

I shouldered open my basement door and snuck a look behind me. They hadn't followed, thank goodness. They didn't need to see this just yet.

I fumbled for the light switch, and the anemic lightbulb splashed pale light on formless heaps all around the cool, dank space.

Jack refused to come down here for anything, and I couldn't blame him.

It was the first space I filled, and the first chink in the wall of my marriage. Ron had always planned to finish the basement and make it a rec room, when we had more money. By then I'd filled it. The fights we used to get into after the kids were sleeping! He'd holler at me for all the junk, and I'd tell him that basements were supposed to be for storage.

From my vantage point now at the top of the steps I surveyed the mounds, looking for what I remembered to be old clothes of Ron's that one day had been destined for Goodwill but never made it. Some of my clothes from the dryer would suit Mary, temporarily. I spotted the boxes I thought I remembered in the far corner, near where a workbench used to be. Well, it still was there, I supposed. Under the things.

As I began my descent, something rustled in the corner and I gasped.

Then I was tumbling, objects smacking and scraping me, the room whirling in my vision until I smashed into a wall of full plastic crates and landed faceup and flat on the cement floor.

Air wouldn't come for three long heartbeats until I finally sucked in a deep breath, which expelled in a weak sob.

I tried to pull up on my elbows, but my body had no strength.

I wiggled my toes. Thank God for that much.

Sharp pain was blazing in my wrist. I turned my head to the side, accusingly, at the stairs, and saw that I'd tripped on one of my small piles at the edge of the steps. A stack of cosmetics boxes had gotten somehow knocked right across the very step I'd been trying to navigate, then something had moved in my basement where nothing should be moving at all. I was distracted, I said to myself. Anyone could fall down the stairs when distracted.

Other body parts were blaring now, joining my wrist in a riot of pain: my head, my elbow, my back. I could finally pull up to my elbows, and I looked down at myself.

A thread of blood ran down the side of my leg from knee to ankle. I touched my face, which felt wet in a different way than rain, and my fingers came away red.

I tried to manage sitting, but the effort made the room start to come unmoored, and I lowered myself back to flat.

"Mary!" I called. "Mary? Can you hear me?"

I listened for the sound of running feet, but all I could hear was my own frantic pulse and shallow breath. A faint booming penetrated the basement space: thunder. What my mother used to call "angels bowling" to get us to calm down.

Mary and Seth were all the way at the front of the house. I could see from down here that the basement door had swung shut behind me. That plus the rolling thunder and the slashing rain would make for a noisy upstairs indeed. Perhaps they wouldn't hear me until the storm rumbled away.

I thought of my son, clutter raining down upon him. Then my mother, buried in her hoard as it burned around her.

No. No, stop being dramatic, Trish, I lectured myself. *You're just a little banged up, is all; it's not a fire.*

They say it was the smoke that got Mother, not the burning. This was meant to be a comfort, I think, a better way to go. But the fact is they didn't find her in bed, peacefully asleep. They found her in what had been the hallway, underneath an avalanche of newspapers that were blackened and soaked by the firemen's hose. They must have been heavy, all those papers stacked as they'd been against the wall.

We knew there'd been working smoke alarms in that house. Mary and I always made sure of that much, at least.

Mother had left a candle burning, they decided, and I could fill in the rest. One of the cats must have knocked something onto it, or knocked it over. Mother would have heard the alarm and tried to make her way from her bedroom. The newspapers knocked her down and she lay there, pinned to the floor as fire leaped up the walls in her kitchen, breathing in smoke until she suffocated, watching her home and her cats and her keepsakes burn.

Knowing this was supposed to comfort us. That the smoke got her before the fire.

"Mom," I said now, my voice weak in the stale basement air. "Jack. I'm sorry."

Chapter 30

S eth and I stood dripping in Trish's entryway, staring everywhere but at each other. I had my arms crossed over my chest,
seeing as I'd been wearing white and was therefore an unwill-
ing entrant in a wet T-shirt contest of one.

I gripped my elbows, too, to keep from shivering too hard.

Seth cast glances about the room, and his gaze lighted on an old afghan. "Aha," he said, and he shook some dust off and draped it around
me. His hands rested briefly on my shoulders as I pulled the afghan
more tightly around me.

I looked up at his face then. He had some stubble growing in. I saw
a scar on his cheek from a rock-climbing accident senior year on spring
break. The intensity of his eyes on mine made me feel overwarm in my
afghan, but I dared not cast it off after he went to the trouble of finding
it. Not to mention my soaked shirt.

We just regarded each other, then, our eyes searching. What was
behind this look? I wondered. What was it about my wet hair and wet
face that was suddenly so interesting?

"Are you OK?" I asked him.

He swallowed hard, looked down. "I hope Aurora is OK. She hates
storms."

I couldn't say *I'm sure she'll be fine* because how would I know? "Such a pretty name."

"We thought we'd call her Rory, that it would be adorable."

The look on his face suggested the nickname never came to pass, that very little about his situation turned out to be adorable. "It's a beautiful name as it is," I offered, having nothing else to give him, not daring to ask, *Why didn't you ever tell me she was autistic? Why did you tell me so little that mattered?*

"I could call my ex, but she hates it when I check in too much. She says I am undermining her, like I don't trust her." Seth looked back at me again, perplexed. "Why can't I just be worried about my girl? Why is she always so suspicious?"

Seth shook his head, as if coming out of a daze. "Well. What do I know, anyway?"

"You know plenty, don't you? Being a psychologist and all."

"Yeah. Plenty."

I saw his face twist up with bitterness, and I blinked and stepped back.

Seth held up his hand. "What's that? Did you hear something?"

Seth took off running, and I was at his heels, shedding the heavy afghan as I went.

He got to the doorway first and as he pulled the door open, we heard Trish's calls grow louder. Her voice was cracked and shaky, and we moved down the stairs as fast as we could manage.

My brain went frantic with input: Trish, bloody and limp at the foot of the stairs. The mountain range of stuff piled higher than our heads. The clutter on the steps themselves, one in particular covered by light pink cardboard boxes.

My hand shook on the stair rail.

Seth got there first and propped her up. "Breathe slowly, Trish. We've got you now."

I sat at her other side and took her hand. Her pulse skittered under my fingers. I stroked her hair away from her face and cringed for her at a jagged gash near the hairline. Her skin was pale and cold, still wet from the rain.

"Be right back," I said, and dashed up the stairs, looking for the afghan.

As I came back down the stairs, eyes on Trish, she cried out, "Mary, be careful!" just as I was remembering to step over the junk that must have caused her fall.

I snapped the afghan open and laid it across her. She was shivering in earnest now, but propped up on her elbows, under her own power.

"I'm going to find towels," Seth said, pausing before leaving to look me in the eye.

I nodded at him, giving him permission to leave us.

I moved Trish's hair again to inspect the cut. It was jagged, but not deep. "Where else are you hurt?" I asked her.

"Everywhere," she said through a sniff.

"Where is it the worst?"

Trish lifted her left hand out of the afghan. Her wrist was puffing up before my eyes.

"We should take you to the doctor."

"No, for God's sake. I'm not going to sit . . ."—her words were coming out in a stutter, whether from cold or fear or both I didn't know—". . . in some waiting room for hours on top of this. We can wrap my wrist. Ice it."

Seth appeared at the top of the steps, then came down to hand out towels. He had one around his neck. Goose bumps marched across my skin. I was still soaking wet myself.

"Let's get you up the stairs at least," I said.

At the foot of the steps we helped her to standing. Seth put one arm around Trish and guided her back up the stairs. I followed behind, reaching out my hands pointlessly. As if I could really save them if they started to fall.

T rish and I sat across from each other on her bed. We were both wearing her clothes, our hair up in towel turbans like we used to after a day swimming in the lake. Trish had added another blanket around her and only just managed to stop shaking. Seth had gone to make an ice bag for her swollen wrist, after we'd cleaned out her cuts as best we could.

"I kept thinking of Jack. And Mom," Trish gulped out.

A stab of guilt jarred me. How long had it been since I'd visited Mom? In the years since her death, I have often tried to grab on to the memory of when I'd last seen her. But the specifics were elusive, and the only memory I could conjure was a sense of desperation to leave her home, crammed as it was full of junk, cats, and the smell of cat urine.

I hadn't known it would be the last time. How could any of us have known?

Trish added, "Think how terrified Jack must have been."

I said nothing, sensing that I could only make her feel worse with any comment I could possibly have.

"What kind of mother does this to her children?" Trish groaned, holding her head in her hand, the blanket loose around her like a cape.

"You didn't mean for this to happen."

"So what. It happened. No, it didn't happen. I *did* it. That's what we could never get Mom to admit, right? That she did it? That it was wrong and she did it?"

"She was defensive. We put her on the defensive." I traced the floral pattern in Trish's bedsheets, and I couldn't help but wonder when she last changed them. "She probably knew what she'd done, deep down. She wasn't delusional. She just didn't want to be reminded."

Seth cleared his throat in the doorway. "Everything OK?"

"As much as it ever is," Trish grumbled, suddenly flushing pink. "Thanks for saving me."

Seth only nodded and handed over the bag of ice. Trish winced as the cold ice met her wrist.

"I still think . . ." I began.

"No."

"In the morning if it's worse, you really should go in . . ."

Trish groaned and lay back on her pillows. "I need Motrin and a book to read. Please?"

I left Trish in her bed and went to go find what she'd asked for. Seth was trying to dry himself off. We'd never found Ron's old clothes.

"Did you check on your daughter?" I asked him, heading toward Trish's medicine cabinet.

"Yes," he replied, eyes darting away from me. He walked away, calling over his shoulder. "I'm going downstairs to use the dryer on these clothes. Don't come down for a while unless you want an eyeful," he said, joyless despite the joke.

After the storm rumbled away into the night to menace some other town, Seth got in his car to drive all the way home, saying he'd enjoy the solitude. Trish remained in bed with her romance novel, magazine, and iced wrist.

That left me to pick my way across the muddy driveway and climb into the trailer alone. I thought about trying to explain myself to Trish, how yes, I could technically stay in Jack's room that we'd managed to clean. Only, all the clutter was right outside the door. And it was distinctly a little boy's space, and that made me uncomfortable in a way I couldn't articulate.

I closed the door of the trailer behind me and exhaled. It wasn't that cold inside. I wouldn't turn on the generator tonight and instead just sink into the silence.

I set about changing from Trish's old nightshirt into my own pajamas. I brushed my teeth, washed my face, and swallowed a Unisom with a gulp of bottled water. I settled into the small bed at the rear of the camper, with my booklight on over a copy of *Sense and Sensibility*, and waited for the chemicals to put me out.

Since I'd moved out of Mom's house I'd never been able to feel comfortable in someone else's space. I'd once tried staying at a hotel when George and I attended a trade show. I was jumpy the whole time, pondering all the feet that had marched across the floor, all the butts in the bathroom, hairs that had washed down the shower drain. That a housekeeping staff could manage to thoroughly clean a gigantic hotel every day was ludicrous. I'd had to take two Unisom and could barely function the next day.

I hadn't tried a hotel stay since, until Trish slapped me and drove me out of her house. George just took other managers to the trade shows.

If I stayed in Jack's room, I'd feel the clutter just outside the door, I know I would. I would feel it creeping up on me, bloblike, and I'd be the crazy sister, or at least just dumb old Mary, the awkward one.

I knew that Dad and his wife were meticulous about the camper's condition between vacation jaunts. I could thus pretend it existed only for me, and that it was miles and miles away from Trish's hoard and her warped, demon-possessed brain.

Despite Unisom, Jane Austen, and my aching muscles, sleep eluded me. Untold hours passed while I lay still and silent in the dark, waiting for yet another dawn.

Chapter 31

Morning came too soon, just like it does every damn day.

I'd set my alarm for even earlier than a normal workday. Mary had taken to rousing early in the trailer—still too prissy to sleep in my house, despite Jack's bed being clear, clean, and empty—and I needed once again to make this phone call without her listening.

I risked a foray across the clothing piles to peek through the mini-blinds in my bedroom to see the trailer. All lights off, still.

Branches lay across my lawn like that childhood game of pickup sticks. Yard work I could not begin to deal with, not now. A clean yard would not appease Ayana of Child Protective Services, who was due back today to check on me.

The sun was already inching up. As the shrubs and ferns and saplings had not yet leafed out to keep it at bay, the early sunlight set the dead leaves and mud in a wasteful gorgeous gold.

Magic light, my mom had called that first light of dawn, and the last light of dusk.

I carefully made my way over the tar pit of clothes, gasping once as I'd forgotten my wrist and leaned on my left hand for support as I crawled across my bed. I tiptoed down the hall, blinking away memories of my mother's demise that had been raked back into the forefront of my mind by my own stupid accident.

I dialed the number by rote and practiced a couple of coughs.

"Kendrick and Adams," Angela answered, barking into the phone, trying to make herself sound taller than five-foot-nothing.

"I'm"—here I coughed and hacked—". . . still sick. I won't be able to come in today either. Really high fever, too."

"I've got a ton of filing for you to do! And I'm expecting clients all day! Are you taking vitamin C?"

"I'm sorry, I really can't help it." I kept my voice raspy and low, as if I could barely muster the effort to speak.

"Hmm. A four-day weekend for you, then."

"I've been sick since Sunday. Not exactly a fun time."

"And spring break, too, isn't it?"

"My sons are both gone this week. No fun here at all."

It was so like the conversation we had yesterday morning I felt dizzy with déjà vu. Only this time the derision in her voice was not even the slightest bit concealed.

"Hmm. And not pregnant, either, you say. Well. If you're not better by tomorrow, you'd better get to the doctor, don't you think?"

She didn't give a damn about my health. That was her way of hinting she would soon ask for a doctor's note if I didn't get my ass back to work. I sniffed and faked a sneeze. "Yes, ma'am" and got off the phone as quickly as I could. I looked around to see if Mary had snuck up on me. She could do that, padding around quietly like some kind of monk. All was quiet.

Mary, as an Olympic-level worrier, would fret if I told her the truth. There was no way my boss would have approved a vacation for me at the last minute. Angela wielded the rules like an iron mace because, heaven forbid, as a woman who weighed less than my purse, if she showed any humanity she might be crushed by Men of Business. Not that I'd ever seen evidence of such men waiting to destroy her or her company.

But I needed this done, not only to show Ayana of Child Protective Services but my father, and Mary, and Drew, and everyone else who didn't believe in me, that I could do this, and I could do it quickly, too. And I had to show Jack that his faith in me was not misplaced after all. Someone would ruin his faith in people, I was sure of that. Someone would break his heart and betray him and make him wary. But it would not be me, by God. Not me. And not over stupid rules at a workplace run by a terrorizing bitch.

I swallowed a lump in my throat over the thought of calling her again tomorrow. Any minute she would demand a doctor's note for my supposed cold symptoms. And when I finally did get back to work, I'd have a cut on my face, and maybe my sore wrist would be in a brace by then, if it continued to hurt me as much as it had so far. How would I explain all that?

My phone chimed with a text from Drew. He'd finally confessed that he was house-sitting at his girlfriend's house and taking care of their dog. He claimed that Miranda's folks just wanted a family-only vacation and that it worked out well he could watch the dog for them, but I suspected trouble in paradise.

Want some help? Drew's text offered.

Sure, I typed back. I'd never say no to my son wanting to see me. I'd blinked and he grew up and suddenly was never here, and I still wanted to cuddle him and ruffle his hair. I couldn't even reach his hair anymore without standing on a stepstool. Mom once told me the nights are long, but the years are short. No joke.

A knock on the door sent my heart dropping to my gut, but I remembered it would only be Seth. Too early in the morning for Ayana.

I let Seth in. His eyes looked red and bloodshot. "You look terrible," I told him.

"Good morning to you, too. Mary up yet?"

"Not yet. Soon, I imagine. I'll make coffee."

"I brought some," he said, gesturing with a travel mug as he followed me inside.

I knew I should thank him, this stranger, for doing this for me, but in this early-morning moment, before it was time to confront my clutter for the day, I found myself instead overtaken by curiosity. What was his deal anyway? Why the hell was he here? I asked, "Did you and Mary ever date or anything?"

Seth leaned against my kitchen counter and half smiled down at his running shoes. "Nah. Her roommate was my steady girlfriend."

"Ah. And after you guys broke up, it would have been too weird, I guess."

"Well. We didn't break up until after college. One of those high school sweetheart things that we actually thought would last." He chuckled, shaking his head.

"So . . . what exactly brings you here, now, then? Unless you run a charity that provides free cleaning for crazy hoarders . . ."

Seth squinted into the distance as if considering his answer very carefully. Just then the door swung open and Mary appeared in my entryway, blinking furiously, the bright morning light behind her setting her in silhouette.

She was wearing her bathrobe and slippers and carrying a travel bag. "Oh. Morning. Could I use your shower?" She pulled the door shut behind her.

The robe was tied loosely, so that she had, in effect, a plunging neckline. Mary seemed too sleepy or dim to realize. I, however, noticed Seth noticing.

I waved her in. "Of course, ninny. You could sleep in the house, too."

She stepped past Seth, and I watched him watch her go. Mary really was pretty, and she seemed to have no idea. Common for women to underrate themselves, of course, but she had the worst attraction-detection system I'd yet seen.

* * *

Hours later, fueled by Mötley Crüe on my old tape deck, we'd cleared off the counters and floor in the kitchen. I could actually see my kitchen canisters, which were an array of blues from deep cobalt to spring sky. As Seth and Mary rested in the dining room chairs, I opened cupboards, marveling at their interiors: organized, spacious.

I'd culled all the duplicate appliances I had, which left breathing room right there, and I'd hoped would bring me some cash at a yard sale. For a time I'd had a weakness for appliances, believing the new would always be better, faster, nicer than the old, only I couldn't easily get to my old ones to replace them, so I'd put the new stuff in a bag on the floor or on the counter and get distracted . . .

With the best of the new appliances freed from their boxes and displayed, my kitchen looked new again.

I tried not to think about how much wasted money was gleaming now on my counter.

"What's done is done," Mom always used to say when we hassled her over something. She could somehow never find the receipts to return anything. I always suspected she threw them away on purpose at the doorway to the store for this very reason.

"Let's celebrate with real food," I said, dusting off my hands, though they were clean anyway. "Let's buy some actual produce and make a salad. Some deli-meat sandwiches. We can buy some pasta for dinner. If I had time, I'd cook a ham, I'm so happy. Let's head to the store . . ."

"I'll go," Mary interrupted. "You've been working so hard, you rest here and enjoy your new kitchen."

I put my hand on my hip. I could read through her like glass. "You don't trust me in a store."

She turned so pink she nearly glowed. Then she said, "The Target boots, remember?"

Seth stood up. "I'll go keep Mary company. You can call your sons and check in with them. Watch some TV and rest. We've still got a long haul."

I did want to check in with Drew, I realized. Since our texting this morning he had not arrived nor given me an update.

"Fine." I sighed. "Whatever." I sounded like Drew, spitting out a "whatever" as a substitute for "fuck you."

It would be good for Mary and Seth to talk anyway, because it seemed that this Seth character kinda liked my weird little sister. And we were only fortyish. That's half a life left, God willing.

After they headed out to the store, my exhaustion caught up with me in aching waves, plus my swollen wrist had begun to throb. I took my cell phone into the bedroom to call the boys.

First, Jack. I called Ron's cell.

" 'Lo," he answered.

"Hi, Ron," I answered, correcting myself from the old "hi, honey" I still wanted to say. "Calling to check on our boy." That was an endearing term I never intended to give up. No matter what else, that would always be true.

"I'll let you talk to him. He had kind of a rough night."

"What's wrong?" I sat up on the bed.

"Nothing serious. Homesick." I heard a tiny crack in Ron's voice, and I felt a sprig of sympathy for him, trying to enjoy spring break with his little boy, but his little boy wanted to go home.

He put Jack on, and my boy was trying to sound brave. "Hi, Mama. I'm fine."

"I heard you were a little sad last night, pal."

"Yeah," he answered, his voice gravelly.

I clutched my hand over my heart. "Honey, your daddy misses you, and he wants to spend time with you."

"I know." I heard him suck in a shuddery breath. "Hey, Mom?"

"Yeah, pal?"

"If you get the house all clean, can Daddy move back home?"

I curled over on the bed. "Um. Pal, it's not that simple. Sometimes two people . . ."

The words caught in my throat, all that *two people can't live together anymore* bullshit I spit out for days and days and weeks after Ron left. I cleared my throat and struggled to finish my thought. ". . . It's just not that easy, honey."

"Summer went home."

I sat up at this. "She did?"

"Yeah."

Don't ask him, I told myself. *Don't grill your son.* I blurted anyway, "Why?"

"I dunno."

"Well, never mind. Hug your dad if he's sad, OK? Is your shoulder OK?"

"It's OK. I'm tired of the brace; I want it off."

"You have a checkup after spring break. It'll probably come off then."

"OK." He sniffed hard. At this I knew he was crying.

"Pal? I love you, you know that? You'll be back really soon."

"I know. Is the house getting clean?"

"It's getting there. Mary's friend is helping. And Drew is coming over later."

"I wanna come, too."

Me, too. "Pal, your dad wants to spend time with you."

"I wanna come home."

"I love you, Jack. Let me talk to your dad, OK, pal? I'll call you later. And you call me anytime you want." I made a kiss noise into the phone and heard him still sniveling as he handed it over.

Ron took the phone back with a heavy sigh. "Hi."

"I'm sorry he's so upset. Honestly, I'm trying to be positive about it."

"I know, Trish. Maybe I should just bring him on home. He's not having any fun, and watching him cry to be home with you is no day at the beach for me."

"Oh, but, Ron, your special time with him. . . . And I know he's crying now, but what if he feels rejected by you?"

"I'm the one who feels rejected, honestly."

I bit my tongue not to say, *Now you know how I feel.* "Well, if you want to bring him here, of course you can. I'm not going to stop you. But try to make it fun, maybe if you guys went fun places . . ."

"It's the first week of April. It's too cold at the beach. He can't go to Chuck E. Cheese or any of those crazy places with a broken shoulder. He can't even go to the mall and play on those play things. We tried that and someone crashed into him, and he cried for ten minutes it hurt so bad."

"Well, if you have to. I'm just saying it's not what I want, you know that, right? I want you guys to have your time together."

"Whatever, Trish. It's fine. I'll call you when I decide."

We hung up with the simple "Bye" used between vague acquaintances.

I lied to Ron. I did want Jack back here. I was also glad that Summer chick bailed, even if it hurt Ron's feelings. As Jack and I always said, "Mommy's not perfect."

I called my other son, listening to his cell phone ring, trying to remember the last time Drew was eager to see me, his mother.

Chapter 32

A s we pushed a cart along the aisles of the store, it occurred to me how much we looked like a married couple. Like those people over there, the young woman with her fingers woven through her husband's as they stood considering what kind of milk to buy. Milk buying could be a hand-holding occasion for some couples, it seemed. I wondered if they had sex every night, too.

I wondered if George and Nurse Melissa held hands in the grocery store.

"You OK?" Seth asked.

"Why?"

"You looked kinda pissed off just now. I hope you're not upset with my bread selection. I find Wonder Bread fairly tasty, myself."

I laughed in spite of myself, something I remembered doing often in Seth's company, in our college days.

"Just remembering this guy I worked for. He owned the bookstore that just closed."

"Pissed off at him for closing it?"

I could nod. I could pretend that was the truth and hide the truth of my humiliating Miss Moneypenny act, but this was Seth here. Seth who never passed judgment, who had endless wells of compassion. At least, he always used to. It seemed.

"Pissed off at him for breaking my heart like a toothpick and pretending he didn't notice."

"He was your boyfriend?"

I sighed. "No, which is what makes it pathetic. I just let myself moon around and pine after him, and he flirted with me all the time, and never went any further. Stupid me thought it was because I was his employee. And the store closed, and I thought, at last! We could be together! Turned out he got engaged."

"He got engaged when his business closed? Wow."

"Family money. He'll be fine."

"Will *you* be fine?"

"What choice do I have?" We wheeled past the cheeses, and I nabbed some sharp cheddar slices.

"You didn't answer the question."

"I know."

"Are you sure you really wanted to be with him?"

"Why do you ask?" I decided that having a serious conversation in a grocery store was just grand. I was looking at the list, and all the products, and I could look anywhere but at Seth with his blue eyes and ridiculously long lashes, probably the only hair left on his head. I barely stifled a giggle at this thought.

"I would think that if the job was the only obstacle between the two of you, you could have solved that one on your side of the equation. You could have looked for another job."

"The economy's terrible."

"Ten years? It hasn't been terrible that long."

"Do we need mustard?" I asked, searching for the condiments aisle and pondering what Seth said. Had I deliberately stayed in a pretend relationship with my boss?

Seth picked up some mustard, stubbornly saying nothing, letting his challenge just sit there in the air around us.

"You're right," I said, folding my arms and suddenly feeling cold in the store's sterile aisles. "If I'd gotten a new job, I had no confidence he would still be interested. Out of sight, out of mind, as always with me."

"As always?"

"When I left home, my mother closed off from me, emotionally. After the funeral, Trish stopped calling me. Even you never told me anything important in all those phone calls. I was just some annual obligation."

I dared not look at him. I hadn't meant to say that.

Seth stopped the cart. I could sense him turn toward me, and step closer, but I remained staring at the pickle relish.

"I wasn't trying to close you out. I just didn't think . . ."

". . . that I might care? That I might matter? You only told me about the good stuff. Why bother talking at all if you're just going to edit out anything you don't like to say?"

I screwed my eyes shut tight and bit my lip. I really would drive him away at this rate. No more phone calls, no more postcards. No reason to remember my birthday at all anymore, except to renew my license plate.

"I wanted . . . I think I wanted you to think well of me."

I finally looked at him. He'd stuffed his hands in his pockets and was working the toe of his shoe into the tile, like he was trying to stub out a cigarette. He shrugged. "I wanted to seem like I had it all under control."

"Why would I think less of you because of your daughter's . . . Because of what you can't help? And your divorce?" And, I finished in my head, whatever else you haven't bothered to talk to me about?

"Maybe I also could let it not be real. Once a year I could be a college kid again, talking to you. Carefree."

I laughed, and he jerked his head up.

"I'm sorry, but do you actually remember college? Carefree my foot. You were working yourself sick with all your classes, and your dad had a heart attack all the way across the country. Every little mistake seemed like the end of the earth. And remember when Rebecca dumped you?"

Our eyes locked and I jerked away, remembering that drunken kiss that he might be remembering, too. I shook the memory out of my head and went on.

"Be honest with yourself. That's what you tell people in your job, right? You didn't tell me anything because I wasn't important. You tell important people important things. That's the way it works."

"Do you tell people important things?"

"I don't have any important things to tell."

"I can't believe that's true."

"What difference does it make now?" I could feel myself flush, wishing I could have just a moment or two of Trish's blithe confidence. She always knew what to say in a group of people, always seemed to be the bright center of attention at school, at football games, roller rinks, anyplace outside our house. Whereas I would leave a note for a boy in his locker and he'd avoid my eyes in the hallway and I'd know I stepped in it again, violated the invisible rules of the social world that my sister had absorbed somehow.

Seth began to navigate the cart toward the checkout lanes. He was silent, and his face had that look of concentration he'd get when he came over to our dorm room to study with Rebecca. Back then he'd have a highlighter always in his hand, tapping the back end quietly against the pages as he read.

"I don't know what I expected," I said, as he wheeled the cart into a checkout lane and started stacking groceries. I leaned on the handle of the cart, and my gaze skimmed the tawdry covers of the gossip rags. "I was just your girlfriend's roommate. It's not like I was special."

Seth paused in the act of dropping the bread on the moving belt. "Really? That's what you think? You weren't special?"

"Of course I wasn't."

"But that one time—"

"You were drunk," I said, too loudly, causing the people in front of us to swivel their heads backward a moment, then face forward so they could pretend not to eavesdrop.

"I didn't mean then," Seth said, quietly as he could manage and still be heard. "I meant when my dad had a heart attack. My supposed girl-friend couldn't be bothered to come back from her trip, or even take more than five minutes on the phone to talk. The guys I knew were all, like, 'Bummer, dude,' like I'd run out of weed or something. You were the only one who understood. The only one who made it better."

Then our groceries were at the front and the cashier said, "Paper or plastic, sir?"

As Seth answered and became absorbed in the mechanics of grocer-ies, I let his words echo in my head. *The only one who made it better.*

Chapter 33

This time, Ayana's smile seemed genuine. Either that, or today she was in better shape to fake it.

She stuck out her hand, but I turned around quickly, pretending not to notice. Honestly, did she think I'd be her pal now? I don't care if she did rent a Dumpster. With a few keystrokes she could send me to beg for my son in front of a judge.

"You've made some good progress here, Mrs. Dietrich," Ayana said, pulling my door closed behind her. Mary and Seth had taken some of the boxes from the front room and moved them to the garage. They were not yet sorted, but they were out of my living space.

It hadn't been so bright in here since before Ron left, and I could picture him at my dining room table so easily my breath caught.

"But," she said, something dark creeping into her voice, "you look like you've been injured."

I folded my arms to hide my sore wrist. I'd wrapped it in an Ace bandage and had meant to put on a long-sleeve shirt before she arrived. "I tripped is all."

"That's quite a trip that can do that kind of damage."

Ayana pointed at my head, and I grimaced. I'd forgotten about the cut and pulled my hair back in a ponytail, exposing it to God and the world.

"There's a lot of stuff here still, and I tripped on it. We've been working really hard."

"You make sure you take care of that." Ayana started to move down the hall, then stopped. "You sure that's how it happened? A fall? No one *made* you fall?"

"Ha! My husband doesn't even live with me, so no, he's not beating me. I'm a freak and a supposedly bad mother but not an abused wife."

"No one said you—"

"Yes, yes, I know. No one said I was a bad mother. Whatever. Let me show you Jack's room."

I could feel her prying eyes glinting at me as I passed. Christ, but she was nosy.

"Oh, so much better," Ayana said, scribbling on her notepad. "Now this is how a boy's room should look."

"I know that. I'm not stupid."

"I was just expressing how much better it is in here. How does he like it?"

"Very much," I lied. "He's so happy to have his own space."

"So he's sleeping in here now?"

"He's with his dad for spring break," I said, walking away from her. "Let me show you the kitchen . . ."

Ayana followed me, giving approving nods to the kitchen, writing more on her notepad. "But when Jack is here, is he sleeping in his room?"

"Yes, he is."

"Great!" Ayana chirped, like I was five years old and I'd just given her a finger painting.

"Now, have you made much progress in your own room, or in other areas of the house?"

I braced myself for the reaming I was about to get, though I knew she'd toss in a bunch of fake-sincere empty smiles and bureaucratic nonsense to make it seem all nicey-nice. "My room is next."

"I'd like to see it." She pivoted on her heel, and I noticed how she did not so much ask permission as announce her intent.

She peered inside. "I notice how some of the piles are disturbed."

"I had to dig for some old clothes the other day."

She consulted her watch. "I've got some time before my next appointment . . ."

"Another dangerous mother? Does this one feed her kid too much sugar?"

". . . And I've got time to help you sort. Why don't you get some bags?"

"My clothes? No, I'll make those decisions."

"Of course. I'll just hold the bag and talk you through it."

"I do not need a stranger's hands all over my private things!"

"Mrs. Dietrich, I'm trying to help you. If your things are so precious they can't be touched by anyone, why are they all over the floor? Why does it smell the way it does in here?"

"Insults, now. Some help you are."

"I'm trying to get you to challenge your counterproductive thinking patterns."

"What textbook are you quoting now? *Talking to Crazy Bad Mothers,* volume one?"

"I've never said you were a bad mother, and I don't believe you are."

"You've been bullshitting me every minute and don't think I can't tell, little girl."

Finally, I saw some reddening of her face.

"There's no need to be swearin' at me, and who are you calling little girl?"

I heard it again, that slight drawling sound. She recovered herself instantly with a tiny headshake. "Ma'am. I can see you're frustrated.

But if I thought you were a dangerous mother, I would have gone to the judge already."

"Well, thank you so very much for not taking my child away just yet."

"Why won't you let me help you?"

"Because I've got help. My sister and her friend are at the store for a few minutes. We can do it ourselves."

Ayana wasn't budging.

"Look, I appreciate your effort. Your intent might be just as you say, but it doesn't change the fact that it's my stuff, and it's hard enough to let my sister touch it, and her friend I barely know, let alone have a stranger come in here and handle my things. There's no way I can forget who you are, or why you are here. And whatever you might say to the contrary, you are not here to help me."

"But, ma'am—"

"You're here for Jack. Not me."

"We all have the same goal."

I rubbed my temples. Was she really so thick, or had she just swallowed the party line that thoroughly?

The doorbell rang, and I frowned. Wrong time for the mail, and I wasn't expecting packages, anyway. I'd given Mary a set of keys. Well, maybe she'd forgotten them.

"Excuse me," I said, and pushed past Ayana. She trailed me to the door like a clingy child.

I pulled it open to see Ron standing there with Jack.

Jack flung himself at me, gripping my waist and sniveling.

Ron wasn't looking at me. He was gaping past me at what had become of the house he built.

Ron and I ended up in his truck. He was silent, drumming his fingers on one thigh, his other arm over the steering wheel at the wrist, left hand draping loose. This was how he would always drive on the highway, seeming barely to be in control of the car, when actually in a half a heartbeat he could seize the wheel and wrench us out of the way of a crazy driver.

In other words, his casual appearance didn't mean he felt casual at all.

We'd left Ayana and Jack in the house together and stepped out for privacy. At first, when Ron got in his truck, I thought he'd peel out of here, but he beckoned me in.

"Say something," I blurted.

"You told me . . ." he began slowly, staring through the windshield as if he were driving. "You told me it was all crap, and that the accident was a freak thing, that he got hurt by tripping. You told me that it was all trumped up, and a misunderstanding. You told me it was already sorted out."

"I'm working on that. I've made progress."

Ron turned to me slowly, his eyebrows snarled together and his mouth hanging open. "You're telling me it was worse than this?"

"What! So there are some boxes in the living room, big deal. The kitchen is clean, the dining table is clean, Jack's room is clean. You know I've never been a perfect housekeeper."

" 'Some' boxes, Trish? There were probably fifteen boxes in there stacked as high as my head along the back wall. And look at that!" He jerked his finger at the open garage and Dumpster. "All that shit was in the house?"

The garage piles were spilling out onto the driveway. It did look like the garage had puked up my junk.

Ron slumped back in the truck and tipped back onto the headrest. "I didn't see our room. I don't even want to know."

"You don't get to say '*our* room.' You left."

"Small wonder."

"It was not this bad when you took off!"

"No shit it wasn't, cuz if it was, I'd have taken both kids with me."

"You wouldn't have dared."

"If I'd have known my little boy would get a broken bone in his own house? Hell, yeah, I'd have taken him with me. I still might."

"No. Ron, you wouldn't. You brought him back today because he was so upset to be away from me. You wouldn't do that to us."

Ron shook his head, staring out the windshield of the truck. "Trish, he's my boy. I can't let him get hurt. And look at you! It happened to you, too, didn't it? You tripped, or something fell on you."

"We're cleaning up!"

"I'm such an asshole. I can't believe I left the boys in this mess. I should have taken them with me in the first place."

"You don't mean that . . ."

Ron sat up in the truck and glared at me. "The hell I don't. If you don't get this shit cleaned up Trish, it won't be that little Ayana girl in there you've got to worry about."

I curled up in my side of the truck. "Don't say that. Ron, please."

"Please, my ass. What did you used to always say when the boys tried that? When you'd say 'No, you can't have Cheetos for breakfast' and they'd say, 'Pretty please, Mama?' "

My heart was pounding in my ears. All I could think of was Jack sobbing for me on the phone.

Ron answered for me. "You'd say 'Please is not a magic password.' Well, it ain't."

"I didn't mean for this to happen. I swear I didn't."

Ron ran his hand through his hair and gave his nervous cough. "I know. I don't mean to be so mad, but . . . my God, Trish. Look at that."

I wiped my eyes, my face, trying to recover some sort of decent appearance before going back in to see Jack. "Maybe . . . maybe you could help us."

"Are you outta your mind?"

I couldn't look at him. Couldn't face his justified fury. "I just mean . . . You could spend spring break with Jack, still, and . . ."

Ron shoved open the truck door. "You made this bed. You can fucking well lie in it."

The truck rocked with the force of the door slamming.

Chapter 34

T rish's driveway was cluttered with cars. To me, this seemed an ominous sign.

"I think that's Ron's truck," I said, as Seth pulled his car to a stop behind a different vehicle, a gray sedan I'd never seen before.

We shrugged at each other, and each took a couple of shopping bags up to the house. I had keys, but decided to knock, not wanting to barge in.

"Come in," I heard Trish shout in her exasperated, *you're so stupid* voice.

Seth shouldered the door open, and we walked into a four-cornered argument.

A young black woman with short hair and a coat too big for her was gesturing, trying to get Trish and her ex-husband, Ron, to be quiet, and Jack was trying to talk over the lot of them, but it was all babble.

Seth walked himself into the middle of the scrum and said, "Enough."

It wasn't loud, or even that forceful. But his voice took on a resonance that brought everyone to attention.

In the beat of silence that followed, Jack piped up. "Who are you?"

"I'm Seth," he replied. "You must be Jack. It's nice to meet you. I'm a friend of your aunt Mary."

The new woman spoke next. "I'm Ayana Reese; I'm a social worker here to help Trish clean up."

Ron cleared his throat and ran his hand over his hair. "I'm Trish's ex. Jack and Drew's dad."

"What a nice little party," Trish spat. "Let me just get out the cocktail weenies."

"Oh, I love those!" Jack blurted.

Trish flopped onto the couch and put her head in her hands. "I didn't mean that literally. It was just an expression."

"I love those, too, Jack," I said, just to say something. "Maybe next time. Let's go make you some food and let the grown-ups talk."

I noticed Seth stayed behind, and I was glad, not only for whatever mediating effect he would have. I wanted a few minutes with my nephew.

Whatever kids passed through my orbit tended to be brats in the store pulling books off our shelves and drooling on our train table toys. Or the children of coworkers who would be pulling on Mom's or Dad's hand, whining to get moving, or to buy a cookie from the café.

And here was Jack, who turned out to be an actual little person. Based on the warmth spreading through my heart at seeing him again, I must have really been missing the little guy.

"Want to help me make some pasta?" I said.

He pointed with his chin at his collarbone brace. "I dunno."

"You can stir, right? You can keep our pasta from getting sticky."

"Deal."

I pulled out one of Trish's new purchases—a bright blue pot—and set some water to boiling. After I stared at it for a minute or two—a watched pot will boil eventually, right?—I decided to sweep the floor.

The broom was handy, and the brushing of the bristles against the floor was soothing. I could overhear voices from the next room and heard Ron say something about lying.

I cleared my throat, desperate for conversation to distract Jack. "So you're back from spring break?"

He leaned against the counter and chewed on his thumbnail. "I guess. I wasn't having much fun."

"Sorry to hear that."

"It's hard to be away from Mom. I really don't want to move away."

"We don't want you to, either."

"I think my dad does. And Miss Ayana, too, cuz she said something about how she doesn't like it that I sleep with my mom. Why doesn't she like that?"

Oh-oh. "I don't know how to explain in a way that would make sense to you. Probably because you're old enough to sleep by yourself. You're a big kid now."

"We're not perfect," Jack mumbled.

"I know, kiddo. No one is." The water was boiling so I cracked some spaghetti in the pot. I pulled a chair over from the kitchen table, trying hard not to hear the tense voices bubbling over from the front of the house. "Here. Stand up here and you can stir."

I held out a hand and he took it, pulling himself up. He was surprisingly sturdy for a kid who seemed so slight. I watched him stir and noticed that he did have a solid build, like his dad. Maybe his situation was what made him seem fragile, from a distance. That, and his injured arm.

Standing on the chair as he was, we were shoulder to shoulder. I dared to put my arm around his waist. He leaned into me slightly.

Jack stirred and stared into the pot, thoughtfully. "It's changing states. The water, turning to steam? We learned about that in school. Matter changing states."

"Neat," I said.

"I didn't mean to tattle on my mom," Jack said, then, still stirring with frowning concentration.

"What do you mean?"

"I guess she told Miss Ayana that I sleep in my own room, but when Miss Ayana asked me, I told her I wasn't."

"Oh. But that was true, wasn't it?"

"Yeah."

"You're not in trouble for telling the truth, kiddo."

He shook his head and turned to me, chewing his bottom lip. On a chair, he was level with my face. I could see the long lashes around his eyes, and one wonky loose baby tooth at the front of his mouth. "Then why is everyone upset out there? I should never have told Miss Ayana those things at school, either."

"What things?"

"When she came to see me, I talked about the house and how I hurt myself. I didn't know all this would happen. I didn't mean for this to happen, Aunt Mary."

Tears pooled in the corner of his eyes. "Oh, kiddo, don't . . ."

I didn't dare leave Jack standing on a chair with only one good arm in front of a hot stove and a pot of boiling water to go fetch Trish, and he needed something right now, something I was ill-equipped to provide.

I pulled him closer. At this height, he could tuck his head right into my neck, on my shoulder. He cried quietly on my shirt. I patted his back and rubbed smooth circles like Mom always used to. "It's not your fault, no one thinks that."

With my other hand I turned off the stove burner, and then rocked slightly in place with Jack, flying blind and hoping I was doing it right.

"Jack!" Trish exclaimed. "What's wrong?"

She'd come in through the living room, her eyes bright and face flushed. Trish moved restlessly, seeming electrified and nervous. I assumed Jack would let go of me and leap to his mother, but he did not.

I looked at Trish while Jack continued to lean on me, shrugging. What do I say? Do I repeat all that just happened as if Jack weren't in the room? Do I let him tell it? He continued to snivel, and Trish grew more tense and furious with each second I didn't explain.

So I said, "He's upset because he thinks this is all his fault."

"Of course it isn't! Pal, of course it's not."

"I told him that," I said.

Trish made to take Jack from me, but he didn't budge. I watched the agony in Trish's face. She clearly wanted to take him right off the chair, but to do so might hurt his arm. I started to nudge him off my shoulder, but he didn't move. I wasn't about to peel him off like a dirty shirt, so I just glanced at Trish and shrugged again.

She closed her eyes for a moment, and sagged, then stormed down the hall to her room and slammed the door.

"See?" Jack whimpered. "She's mad at me."

"No, she's not. She's upset right now. She's having a bad day."

"She has lots of bad days."

Jack finally stood back from me. I wiped some wetness off his face with my thumb. "Your mom just needs a hug is all. Do you think you should go hug her? Because I promise she's not mad at you."

He nodded, and I helped him down from his chair. I watched him move off down the hall to knock on his mom's door, and I hoped to God my promise was true, that the demon in Trish hadn't turned on Jack, too.

I turned the water back on, waiting for the pasta to boil again, waiting for someone to come in and catch me up on current events.

Seth and Ron stepped into the kitchen.

"Ayana is gone, for now, but she said she'd stop by again Thursday," Seth said. "Anything I can help with?"

I shook my head. It was only spaghetti, not an Amish barn raising, after all.

Ron had a hat in his hands, some free cap that you'd get from a store. He was working it like a rosary. "I, uh . . . thought maybe I should stick around and help a bit."

Now, that was a surprise. I thought he had a new girlfriend to entertain him. "What does Trish say?"

"I dunno. We haven't exactly . . . We haven't had a chance to discuss that."

Seth and Ron were leaning against different countertops. I was beginning to feel watched, so I gave them a job to do. "Set the table, would you?"

Ron went right to the cupboard with the plates. Of course he would know where everything was. At least in the organized version of his house, which we'd managed to partially restore.

"So what was going on out there, if you didn't talk about helping?"

Ron coughed. Seth answered, "They were having some trouble sorting out a couple of things Trish said, which didn't turn out to be true." He glanced backward, down the hall.

"Oh," I said. "Jack told me she lied about where he was sleeping."

"And she also had underestimated to Ron the severity of the situation."

Ron appeared in my peripheral vision. "How bad was it, Mary? Can you tell me? For real?"

I closed my eyes. "Don't put me in this position. She's my sister."

"I just wanna know one thing. Was it as bad as with your mom?"

I bit my lip and considered what to say. Yes, I started to answer, thinking of the tiny little paths around Trish's living room when I first came in, the thick, choking dust and scent of mildew. Just remembering made my skin itch with the ghost of those hives. But again, no. Yes, her fridge had too much expired food, but it was all in her fridge, not all around her living room. She had no animal waste.

I settled for: "Not quite."

Ron dropped his gaze to the floor, considering this, perhaps remembering the last time he saw our mother's home, trying to imagine what "not quite" must have looked like.

"I wish . . ." he ventured, then shook his head, walking with practiced assurance to the silverware drawer.

Chapter 35

Many lonely nights I'd imagined having Ron back at this table, in a clean house. I never pictured, however, my son in a brace injured by my clutter, a social worker visiting me with the threat of a judge hanging over my head, and my sister and her old "friend" sitting silently like a couple of boulders at the end of the table.

I looked again at Jack. He caught me looking. "What?" he said.

"Want some more Parmesan cheese?"

He shook his head, and I pretended to concentrate on my plate. The sounds of flatware on my dishes was making me a little batty. Was no one going to talk, for the love of Christmas?

Jack seemed fine now. He'd knocked on my door and I knew from its quietness that it was Jack, and I almost absorbed him, I hugged him so much when he came in.

It had just been such a shock to walk into my house, finding Jack and Ayana deep in conversation and have her take me aside the way she did. She pinned me with this hard stare and asked why I had not been honest with her about where Jack was sleeping. I didn't mean to yank my head in Jack's direction, didn't mean to ask, "What did you say to her?" It burst out of me before I thought better of it, along with a surging sense of betrayal. Why was everyone against me? I asked her, and she'd scolded me right there like a wayward kid about how I shouldn't be upset with my child for being honest. Then she wanted to know if I was encouraging him to lie to her, to the authorities.

No! I'd stage-whispered. Ron was edging closer to our conversation until he was practically on top of us and I'd barked at him to get away, and then he demanded to know what was happening and Ayana said she needed to have this conversation with me privately and she'd talk to him in a minute, and Jack started trying to talk over us and then Mary and Seth came in and Seth acted like some big fat hero jumping in to restore order.

No wonder no one felt like talking anymore. We'd all been talking too damn much.

My phone chimed, and I snatched it up. I finally saw the old texts from Ron about bringing Jack home. I'd left my phone in the bathroom of all places, so no wonder I'd missed those messages. The new text was from Drew. *Sorry, got held up. Be there tomorrow after walking dog.*

Held up doing what? I knew better than to ask. He wouldn't answer and would just get indignant. I wondered whether other moms of teens dealt with this secrecy, or if it was just me, because I'd filled his room with junk and he'd left and believed I had lost the right to details of his life.

"So I think I wanna stay and pitch in," Ron said.

I dropped my fork, wanting so badly to spit his words back to him, the ones about how I could fucking well lie in the bed I'd made.

He knew me inside and out and read my mind. "I know what I said. But I already took the week off and rescheduled jobs and that. I can keep Jack company and also help out."

Once again a powerful urge seized me to throw the whole lot of them out of my house, to lock all the doors, draw all the shades, and sit in the dark with my ice cream and television and forget about all this shit.

I almost made myself chuckle thinking of Ayana clucking with disapproval at my *counterproductive thinking patterns.*

"Fine. But you don't get to throw anything away without asking me."

Ron frowned. "How's that gonna work? I mean, anything? That'll take a frickin' year."

"That's the rule."

Ron shook his head slowly, staring back at his plate. I could tell from the way he set his jaw he was pissed. "What, Ron? Just spit it out."

He cut his eyes over at Jack, who was still eating, looking between the both of us, eyes bouncing back and forth like he was watching tennis.

"Let's go outside a minute," I said. "I need some air."

He wiped his mouth with his napkin and followed me out. I heard Seth try to engage Jack in conversation about video games as I shut the door behind us.

The afternoon air was cheerfully warm, and I almost smiled in spite of myself.

Ron started to walk, hands jammed in his jeans pockets, kicking up dead leaves as he went. I followed along, knowing he always found it easier to talk when he was doing something else.

"You shoulda got these leaves up before winter. I woulda helped you."

"I don't care about the leaves."

"What the hell, Trish?" He sounded more weary than mad.

"Don't give me the wounded clueless bit, Ronald. You knew the house was a mess when you left, which is why you left, so don't act all amazed that it continued to be a mess when you were gone."

"You know it wasn't just that. It wasn't just the stuff."

"Bullshit," I retorted, but it was a knee-jerk answer and empty of conviction.

We walked farther in silence, our feet scuffing across the rotted, dead forest floor as the house shrank away behind us.

"So what was it, then?" I finally said. "In your estimation, why did you leave me and your sons?"

"You weren't you anymore."

"Gee, that's helpful."

"I mean, all you did was sit on the couch and watch TV all night long, and you never talked to me about nothing. You never made jewelry anymore, you never went out, you just . . . sat."

"I was tired! Doing all the books for your business, answering the calls, filing . . ."

". . . till you quit filing and just put the stuff in piles . . ."

". . . And then the boys would get home from school and I'd have to oversee homework and then cook dinner . . ."

"And I worked hard, too, and I'd still want to get a sitter and take you out somewhere and you'd say no."

I held my arms close against me. A breeze rustled the branches over our heads. We'd come to the back fence of the property. Out past the fence was a subdivision, where there used to be a field. Some of those houses could have been built by Ron, even. He hired someone to do his books these days. Kept his filing at the office.

"You know why I was depressed, Ron. You know damn well why."

He dropped his head, staring at the dead ground. "I know. It hurt me, too."

"Not the way it hurt me."

He turned to me. Touched my elbow, trying to get me to look him right in the face. "I tried to help you. I found those meetings for you, remember? The support group? I wanted to take you out on dates to get you out of the house, to bring you back to life. I offered to hire a cleaning lady."

I was refusing to turn to face him or meet his eyes. He continued,

"You know, come to think of it, you're the one who did the leaving. You just managed to do it while sitting on the couch."

"You thought a cleaning lady would help?" I scoffed.

"Dammit. What was I supposed to do?"

"Not leave me and your kids."

"I do have regrets on that score. I never shoulda left them in this."

"It wasn't that bad then," I said, cringing at the pleading in my voice, for understanding if not forgiveness.

"No, but I shoulda known. I shoulda checked up, instead of just parking in the driveway when I picked up the boys. I shoulda done some damn thing."

He took off, striding back toward the house, so fast I had to step double-quick to keep up. I stumbled on a root and muttered a curse. He turned back and offered his hand to help me. I held on to his hand for too long, staring at him, until he pulled his arm back and walked away, back toward the home he built for me.

Chapter 36

S eth and I stood elbow to elbow at the sink, washing dishes. Would we be doing these couple-type things all week? I wondered. And every time, would I think of George and his fiancée doing these things together?

I'd been checking my e-mail on my phone, and not once had George checked in with me, after all those years working together, all the secrets we used to share in the back office, on break.

After Trish and Ron got back from their walk, they'd eaten the rest of their meals with a joyless air, like inmates choking down swill. Afterward, Seth suggested going through the clothes in the bedroom, and after some thought and staring at her plate, Trish said she'd select her best and favorite clothes and everyone else could just shove the remnants in bags for donation. She'd excused herself to go select the clothes, while Ron and Jack went outside to play Frisbee. We could see them out the kitchen window, hear Ron's encouraging shouts, watch his exaggerated leaps as Jack sailed the disc time after time wildly out of his reach.

"Oops," I said, my hand brushing Seth's as we both reached into the dishwater.

He nudged me with his shoulder, and for a frightening moment I wondered what I'd done wrong. I looked up at him and spied his little grin. "Oops," he said.

I flicked water at his shirt. "Oops."

He dribbled soap bubbles on the top of my head. "Oops."

I flicked water again, this time at his face. "Oops."

He grabbed his eye, buckled a little bit, and I laughed, until he started wiping in earnest, then said, chuckling and grimacing, "Actually, I'm not kidding. You nailed me with soap in the eye."

I gasped, and then reached up with the dishtowel, trying to dab his face dry. "I'm so sorry. . . ." I felt my face flush hot. Was I doomed to forever sabotage everything good and fun?

He stopped blinking and relaxed his face. "That's better," he said, so quietly he almost breathed it.

I noticed his hand on my shoulder. Then it slipped down to my hip and rested there. I'd had to step close to reach his face with the towel. Only inches separated my chest and his.

The phone rang.

Seth stepped back.

It rang again, and I folded the dishtowel, waiting for Trish to pick up. She didn't, and I figured she must not have a bedroom extension. I never could stand to ignore a ringing phone.

I picked up. "Hello."

A woman's voice asked, coolly, "May I speak to Patricia, please?"

"Trish!" I called. "Phone!"

I heard her call faintly. "Is it Drew?"

"No!"

"Take a message!"

"She's a little bit busy right now, could I take a message?"

"Who is this?"

"This is her sister, Mary. Who may I say is calling?"

"Tell her if she still wants a job tomorrow, she'd better call her boss with a damn good explanation."

The phone went dead.

"Oh, no," I said. "Oh, God."

"What?" Seth said. "What is it?"

"She's gonna kill me. It's not my fault, but she'll kill me anyway."

Seth was trying to get me to elaborate, but all I could do was stare down the hall and try to imagine explaining to Trish what just happened.

W hen I came upon Trish, she had clothes in the middle of her bed, three piles, about a foot high each.

"I think that's it," she said, shaking her head. "I can't believe it. But these are all the clothes I ever wear. All the rest of these," she swept her hand across the room, "are either ugly, outdated, or they don't fit my big ass, or they just smell too funky. I thought I had so much I had to keep, so much I could use, but it turns out I was basically rotating the top layer of stuff."

"Your ass isn't big."

"Well, it ain't small."

I looked at her ass; I'd given the first answer out of female solidarity, not because I really knew. It was bigger than I remembered, certainly not massive.

"I guess the rest of this can go," Trish said through a sigh. "God, what a waste."

I didn't know if she meant waste of time, waste of money, or waste of energy. In any case, she was right.

Then she adjusted her ponytail and asked casually, "Who was on the phone?"

I scrunched my eyes shut, like I used to as a kid when our dad would yank out a loose baby tooth that I had no nerve to pull myself. "Your boss."

"Oh, shit." Trish turned away from her stuff to face me, eyes round like golf balls.

"She, um . . ." I cleared my throat. "She said to call back with an explanation if you still want a job."

"What did you say to her!"

I put my hands up, like in surrender. "Nothing! I said you were busy. She asked who I was and I said your sister. What's wrong with that?"

Trish flopped on her bed and put her head in her hands. "I've been telling her I have the flu."

"Not on vacation?"

"No. She would never have given me the time off."

"Well . . . call her back and say you were sick. You were busy throwing up and that's why you couldn't come to the phone . . ."

Trish muttered, "It's hopeless. She already didn't believe me; I could tell she didn't. She was just waiting to pounce."

"Maybe she won't fire you. Maybe she'll just get really, really mad and make you grovel."

"Oh, yay," she answered drily.

"I'm trying here! And why didn't you tell me, so I could at least cover for you?"

"Because you would have flipped out about me lying to my boss and tried to make me go to work so you could clean without me and then you'd throw something out I needed."

"I wouldn't do that!"

"Flip out? Or throw out my stuff?"

"Well, okay, I would have worried, but why do you keep assuming we'll throw away something you need?"

"Remember Mom's photo albums?"

"That's not fair. And for all we know she lost them years before. Whose side are you on? You were cleaning *with* us that day!"

"I'm just saying, accidents happen, don't they?"

"Do they ever."

"What's that supposed to mean?"

"Nothing, just . . . Nothing. Now what?"

"I guess I call her back and beg for my job."

Trish hauled herself off the bed like she weighed a thousand pounds and dragged past me to the kitchen phone. "Do me a favor and give me some privacy, will you? Go play Frisbee or something."

I watched my proud, hilarious, bold sister pick up the phone, cringing as she dialed. I fled outside, not wanting to hear her grovel to that nasty pint-size Scrooge she worked for.

Seth had already gone out. He was kneeling next to Jack, coaching him on his Frisbee throw.

"This way," I called, waving for the Frisbee, knowing I'd probably drop it and make a fool of myself, but at least that would feel normal.

Chapter 37

I replaced the phone on the charger in the kitchen and leaned against my cupboards. The conversation with Angela had gone exactly as predicted. She sounded gleeful as a six-year-old as she canned my ass.

"I'm afraid this is unacceptable behavior, and I can no longer work with you," she'd purred. "Your things will be in a box by the end of the day today."

I'd tried to claim that I'd been sick this morning and had slightly improved. But the presence of my sister and her statement that I'd been "busy" was enough to condemn me in Angela's view. Plus, I couldn't rise to her challenge to provide a doctor's note stating I was sick enough to be gone for two days.

I tried to find joy in the fact I didn't have to work for her again, but instead I sank into the cold dread of the unemployed in a recession. I thought of my credit card statements. I'd already been sinking in the muck of my impulse spending. It was only a matter of time before I was all the way under.

I rapped on the kitchen window, interrupting the Frisbee game. I beckoned them back in.

If I lost my job over all this, it had better fricking well get clean, at least, so I could keep my son while going bankrupt.

We formed a firemen's brigade of sorts down the hall. Mary and I stuffed clothes into bags—as best I could, anyway, with one screwed-up hand—and then we passed them to Ron and Seth, who ferried them out to a pile in the driveway. Jack, still being one-armed himself at the moment, decided he felt tired and volunteered to take a nap. I tried to hide my delight that he lay down on his own bed, in his own room. True, he didn't have a choice because we were working in his usual spot. Baby steps, though.

"What's this?" Mary asked, as she was doubled over, reaching to the floor to snatch up some of the oldest, crummiest clothes. She stood up with a brown book about the size of a record album.

"That's one of Mom's albums," I said, breathless with disbelief. "I didn't even know I had it."

Mary sat down slowly, feeling for the edge of the bed, her gaze so focused on the book she seemed hypnotized. "I thought they'd all burned."

Seth cleared his throat and said he'd go straighten the bags into a neater pile. Ron shuffled out after him, silently.

I joined Mary on the bed, and together we sucked in a breath as she opened the brown cover.

Inside the pages, it was about 1980 or so. A chuckle burst from us both at Dad's Tom Selleck–style dark mustache. He was puckering up to our mother's cheek in this picture, taken by one of us kids, based on the low vantage point of the camera.

Mary stroked our mother's face in the photo. Mom was making an exaggerated face for the camera, her eyes hilariously wide and her mouth in an oval of scandalized surprise. One hand she'd raised lightly to her cheek, as if to say, "Oh my stars, who is this man kissing me?"

Her curly hair was barely held at bay by a long, patterned scarf, the ends of which ran over her shoulder and twined around one arm.

Behind our parents' goofing off was the kitchen, all done in avocado green, burnt orange, and mustard yellow. The white countertops were not only visible but desertlike in how blank they were.

Mary let loose a quick bark of laughter at the next picture. We were sunbathing, she and I, back before anyone imagined the sun could be bad for you, short of crippling sunburn.

I was wearing a two-piece yellow suit, my little preteen boobs just popping up like spring bulbs pushing out of the dirt. I wore smoked sunglasses with lenses big as tennis balls, and I was up on my elbows, trying to look cute. At my side was a magazine, probably *Seventeen.* I was always trying to rush into adulthood. *Idiot,* I silently told the thin, smooth, perfect girl in the picture.

Mary was wearing a black tank suit, plain. Her sunglasses were at the top of her head, and she was squinting so much that her pale hazel eyes had disappeared into her long lashes. She had raised a delicate arm to ward off the glare. Instead of my self-consciousness attempt to look adorable—already knowing, as girls do, that how you look in a picture is of critical importance—Mary was slouched and her feet were splayed. A paperback, which looked to be a Sweet Valley High book, was propped on her stomach, and it looked like it was just about to slide off and onto the old bedsheet we were using as our sunning surface.

"I remember this," Mary said. "No more than one minute after Mom took this picture, Dad came after us with the hose."

Now it was my turn to laugh. I'd forgotten! We were furious for a few minutes, sputtering and wet, then Mom got this funny look and sauntered over to our laughing dad, who was holding the hose loosely in his fingers.

She snatched it with the reflexes of a ninja and turned it on him, and in an instant it was a girls-against-Dad water brawl. We'd had to buy the library a new Sweet Valley High book, and Dad replaced my magazine for me.

We leafed through a few pages with quiet smiles. Mary exclaimed as jabbed a photo with her finger, "I'd forgotten all about that!"

Mary had worn her hair so long as a girl that it was halfway down her back, and unlike me with Mom's ragged curls, hers was stick straight. One night I begged her with the tenacity of a barnacle to let me doll her up, and she finally caved, just to shut me up, I think.

The picture we stared at now showed us the results. I'd crimped Mary's straight hair into these funny waves with one of those crazy irons. Her hair was so long it had taken about six years, but then I moved on to her makeup. Mary's eyelids fairly glowed with electric blue shadow. Fuchsia splashed across her cheeks, and her long eyelashes were gobbed up with turquoise mascara. On her hands were my fingerless lace gloves, and I'd tied a giant lace bow into her hair. In the picture she was pretending a pencil was a cigarette, dangling it with improbable, unconscious sexiness from her fingers. Bangle bracelets encircled nearly her entire arm.

"You kept telling me how gorgeous I looked," Mary said, through disbelieving laughter.

"Yeah, well, I also thought shoulder pads were totally rad, so what the hell did I know?"

"It actually made me feel sort of awful."

"Huh? Why?"

"Because if I was so 'gorgeous' with all that stuff on, what did that make me normally?"

"Aww, Mary. I was paying you a compliment."

"Not me, you weren't. Not the normal me."

"Earth to Mary? That was decades ago now. It's okay to get over it. You take things so seriously."

"I'm just remembering, Trish. It's not like I'm carrying open wounds into my adulthood about blue mascara and a lace bow. Anyway"—she tapped her fingernail on the picture—"it was fun."

I turned to more album pages. "I always thought you were gorgeous with or without that stuff."

"You never said."

"Didn't I?"

Mary shrugged. "Nope. Pretty sure I would have remembered."

"Huh. Guess it's not the way sisters talk."

"Guess not."

I slowed my page turning as the album crept up in years. I knew without having to ask that Mary was noticing the same thing.

The kitchen countertop, behind this Thanksgiving dinner photo from the late 1980s, was buried under a collection of indistinct things. A few pages later, a shot of the Christmas tree showed—just at the edges of the frame, as if our mother tried to crop it out—piles of boxes, bags, and old bits of junk.

We turned one more page, and the two dozen or so remaining pages were empty.

Mary allowed herself to flop back onto the bed, her eyes up at the ceiling, unfocused, like a TV corpse.

I opened my mouth to speak to her, but light footsteps drew my attention.

"Mama?" Jack rubbed his eyes with his good hand. "Where's Daddy? Is Aunt Mary OK?"

"We're fine, pal. Fine and dandy." I walked him out of the room and tried not to think about how long it had been since I'd taken pictures inside my own house.

Once we reconvened and Mary had shaken out of her stupor, I popped some old-school music into my tape player to speed us along. We'd gotten the room nearly empty in under two hours.

As Bret Michaels crooned about every rose having its thorn, I paused in cramming some stained sweats in a bag, addressed everyone in general, and pronounced, "My God, this song is stupid."

We all laughed wearily. Mary's hair was looking stringy and I wanted to brush it. Ron said, "I never could stand that shit."

"Oh, please, I've caught you singing along, you hypocrite."

"If I did, it was that, watchacallit, 'Belgium Syndrome.'"

"'Stockholm Syndrome,'" Seth corrected, smiling in such a way that no one could take offense. "And I'm with you, Ron. Give me Sonic Youth any day."

Mary interjected, "Listen to you, acting all hard-core, when I happen to know that you loved Counting Crows."

Drew startled the bag right of my hands by appearing behind Seth. "Counting what? Are you kidding me?" He made a face at the music. "And this? Please, Mom, if you want me to stay, you gotta shut that off."

I punched the Stop button and came up to hug Drew. He permitted it for a moment before stepping back to look around the room. "Wow."

"Yeah," I answered, smiling, hands on my hips. "Wow."

The smile melted from his face. "Wish you coulda done this years ago."

"I'm doing it now. And you're welcome."

"I'm supposed to thank you for just now picking up years' worth of garbage?"

Seth said, "Drew . . ."

Drew whirled on him. "I don't even know you, so shut up."

I opened my mouth, but it was Ron who spoke. "I will not have you talking to people that way, especially people who came here to help, for no personal gain or nothing. You apologize to him, or I'll knock you to next week."

Drew scowled at the floor, but grunted out a "sorry."

I worked my jaw, trying to swallow down my resentment that Ron could ride in here after years of being gone and act like the hero, reining in my son. And for Drew to actually listen to him seemed miraculous, plus unfair. I'd stood up to Drew like that many times only to be blown off completely. And I was here! I hadn't left the family when it got rough!

I handed Drew a bag. "We're just bagging up all of it. I've already separated out what I'm keeping."

Without the music, the plasticky crinkling of clothes into bags was enough to drive me mad.

"Somebody say something for the love of Pete," I muttered.

"Something for the love of Pete," Mary answered.

This released a group chuckle. Mary had pinpricked the tension, and it seemed to be leaking away. I marveled at my gratitude for her presence and wondered what I'd missed out on all those years by not picking up the phone.

After the bedroom was cleared, we sprawled in the living room, aching with effort. You wouldn't think clothes would be that heavy. I said, "Oh God, I'll never go shopping again," head tipped back on my chair, face addressing the ceiling.

They all had the decency not to correct me. I'm sure I sounded like a hungover lush moaning she'll never again touch tequila.

Mary had passed out bottled waters and Diet Cokes and was preparing to read another of Mother's diary entries. Drew had said that sounded boring, so he took Jack for ice cream at the Lickety Split. Seth and Ron made to leave, but Mary told them not to bother, it was just a teenage diary, after all. I was too tired to argue and let her start reading with the men in the room.

May 1, 1961

Well, I just had an interesting night at the Van Linden house.

See, prom is coming up next week and I'm not looking forward to it like the rest of the girls are. I like my dress just fine, and Wally has been nice and all, but it just all seems so silly now that I've been helping Mom at the camps. Seeing how the migrant workers live crammed into these tiny huts, working for hours and hours in all kinds of weather with never a break, their injuries and illnesses going ignored until Doc can get there . . . That plus the news about the Freedom Rides, and down South where colored kids can't go to the same schools with white kids, where they can't swim in the same pools without causing violent riots, well, I can't seem to get excited about a corsage. I can't help but think that the amount spent on my dress would help buy some of these migrant kids some decent shoes.

So I said something like that tonight. Margaret was blabbing on and on about how she wanted some new shoes and Mother was telling her that money was tight right now, and Margaret whined I got to buy a prom dress and I couldn't take it one more second. I shouted, "You just be glad you have shoes at all. Some of those kids at the camps don't even have shoes, and they run around with bare feet. Doc had to pull a nail out of one kid's foot the other day and she screamed fit to die while he was digging it out."

Father yelled at me, saying I didn't need to act so high and mighty and if I thought I had better moral values than the rest of the family I could go to my room.

"*I* think I have better values?" I blurted out before I had a chance to stop and think. "You're the one always talking about how *those people* are lawless savages."

My dad stood up and he lifted his hand like he might smack me one, but Mother stood up and ordered me to my

room. Before I'd even pushed my chair back, she was arguing with Father. Margaret stuck her tongue out at me as I
left.

Those people are the ones my dad is always muttering
about as he watches the news or reads the paper. Usually
he's talking about Negroes, but I know he'd say it about the
migrants, too.

Oops, Mother is knocking . . .

Okay, I'm back. Mother said she told Father that I was
getting my period so that's why I was so emotional, but that
I had to come out and apologize to him for being sassy.

I wasn't going to do it. I told Mother I didn't want to
apologize, that I hadn't said anything that wasn't true. But
without using any words, she begged me. With the look on
her face. Then she said quietly, don't you still want to go to
the camps with Doc?

And I figured out that if I didn't grovel and apologize and
take back what I said that Father would make me stop going, and maybe Mother, too. That if he thought his precious
girl was being warped by the experience—I'd say expanded,
educated—he would put a stop to it.

So I did it. I slunk out there and gave my apology with
Margaret smirking at me the whole time. I told Father that I
was feeling out of sorts and didn't know what I was saying.
He patted me on the head and offered to let me eat the rest
of my dinner, which Mother had kept warm in the oven.

I said no, I wasn't feeling well. Partly that was to support
Mother's cover story. But it was also because I couldn't sit
there and choke down that food next to him after all that.

Well, the prom dress is already bought, reservations already made, and there's talk of going out to the lake after

the dance to have a bonfire. That sounds nice, to be out
under the stars. Maybe I'll even feel romantic toward Wally,
in the right setting. There's a first time for everything.

Meanwhile, I can change the world in college, out from
under my dad's watchful eye!

Mary closed the notebook. "I can't believe she never talked about
all this. It sounds like quite an awakening for her. And I had no idea
she fought like that with her father."

True. The Grandpa Van Linden of our memory was a sweet-natured,
indulgent old man who liked to give us chalky pink candy and taught
us pinochle.

I frowned up at the ceiling. I was so tired the air seemed to swim
in my vision like it does over hot concrete. "You know? I just remembered something. She told me she never went to prom."

"She did?"

"Yeah." I pulled myself up to address her directly. "Remember
when Jason reneged on his prom invite to me, junior year? Because
he found out the girl he really wanted to take was available? I cried
and cried like I thought I'd die. I asked her about her prom, if she had
something like this happen, and she said she didn't go. Said she wasn't
interested."

"Well, she doesn't sound very interested in the letters. Maybe something went wrong and she ended up not going."

Ron coughed, clearing his throat, and I sat up to look at him, wondering what he was nervous about.

"Not to change the subject, but . . . You know, it seems to be there's
just one major room up here we ain't done yet."

I gripped the arms of my chair. "No, not yet. We haven't done the
bathroom. Or Drew's room, either. We need to do Drew's room."

Ron said, "The bathroom just has some old shampoo bottles and some random papers. We can take care of that in no time. Drew's room won't be that bad, neither."

I shook my head, hard. "No. We can leave that one alone. We don't use that room."

I felt them watching me. Their stares had a physical weight, and I wanted to wipe them off like crawling bugs.

Ron said more gently, "No, we can't. It's high time we dealt with it."

"It's a spare room. Just close the door and leave it."

"You've been leaving it all these years and look where it's got you."

My heart started throbbing in my chest. I felt its pulse in my hands, my ears, my stomach.

I heard Seth suggest, "You guys aren't just talking about a room, are you?" Mary asked if I was OK. Ron said, "Trish?"

Their voices sounded distant and echoed, like I'd fallen down a well and they were all at the top, calling down to me.

Chapter 38

Seth stood before me in the yellow light over Trish's garage. I had my purse in my hands and was preparing to disappear inside my little trailer. Ron had just left for his bachelor apartment, and Trish was inside trying to bribe Jack into his own neatly made twin bed for a change.

I shifted from foot to foot, feeling weirdly like we'd been on a date. Only his shirt had sweat stains in the pits, and my hair was a rat's nest, and I smelled weird from embracing Trish's musty old clothes by the armful.

I had already decided to throw these clothes in the garbage.

"Sounds like that one room is going to be hard," Seth said finally.

"Yeah. I wish I understood why, exactly."

Trish had quashed any further attempt to raise the issue of That Room, but I sensed from Ron's glowering silence that we hadn't heard the end of it.

I told Seth, "I think you should know what might be coming. If anyone touches that room."

"What do you mean?"

I told him how she slammed me against the wall when I dared open that door. Seth's eyes widened, and he reached out his arm, as if the injury had only just happened. I stepped back before I knew what I was doing.

He dropped his hand and lowered his gaze to the gravel driveway. His brow wrinkled a bit: his "thinking" face. "Maybe there's something in there she wanted to barricade forever, some object that has such a painful memory she literally buried it in things."

I nodded. It seemed plausible.

He continued, "I'd bet that Trish, in her daily life, pretends that room doesn't even exist. And to have to acknowledge it, in fact confront it, must be incredibly painful. Do you know if something happened to her?"

"Other than her divorce?"

"It could be the divorce, I suppose, but it sounds like she started hoarding before Ron left, though maybe not to the same degree."

My face burned, having to admit to Seth how I'd let her set me adrift so easily. "We weren't in touch for years. After Mom died . . . I only found out about her divorce on Facebook."

"She never called you?"

I shook my head, tasting shame now at how I didn't pick up the phone, either.

All those years I missed as a proper aunt to Jack, and Drew. I looked away into the dark outside the weak circle of light.

"I wonder," I managed, my voice shaky in spite of myself. "I wonder if I could have made a difference. If I could have . . . stopped it. All this." I remembered small, vulnerable Jack pinned under an avalanche of clutter and felt just as culpable as if I'd pushed the pile down myself. "If Jack had been hurt more seriously, I never could have forgiven myself."

When Seth stepped forward and circled me with his arms, my instinct was to pull back from this startling closeness, but he didn't let go. He hugged a little tighter, just enough to be warm and caring, not enough to be weird.

I wondered again how other people knew how to do this; how to be affectionate enough without going too far, how to accept kindness without wanting to pull away.

I gave in and rested my head against his chest, turned sideways. My ear fit over his heart, and I felt it thrumming away. My arms were still locked around my own self, my purse an awkward lump between us. I let go of myself and my purse and wrapped my arms around him. I remembered him embracing me at the funeral. I recalled the quick, giddy hug we'd exchanged at commencement, my mortarboard falling off backward.

Seth said, "There's nothing but agony to be had if you review the years gone by and beat yourself up. In the end, Trish is responsible for Trish." I both heard his voice in my ears and felt it through my cheek, resting as it was on his chest.

He moved one arm up to stroke the back of my head.

"The only thing you can change," Seth continued, "is what you do from now on."

A noise inside the house made me recoil. I looked toward the door. No one came out. I pressed my hand over my heart as if I could slow it with downward pressure. I hurriedly wiped my face, ran my hands over my hair to smooth it back.

I felt queasy with embarrassment.

I sipped in the cool night air, and this time the chills I felt were definitely temperature related. This I could handle. Cool air causes cold skin causes goose bumps. This much I understood.

"So," I began. "Um."

"What's wrong?" Seth asked, hanging back.

"Other than the obvious?"

"What do you believe is the obvious thing?"

He was doing his shrink thing. Well, that is why I asked him here. But I'd expected him to do it only to Trish, not me.

. "I'm just tired," I offered lamely, praying he wouldn't pursue my obvious dodge. "But, look, I do think you should know something. A bit of Granger history."

Seth folded his arms and assumed a listening face, which he must have practiced across his desk many, many times.

"You knew my mother was a hoarder." He nodded, recalling our conversations in the dorm and over breakfast. He and Rebecca were the only ones outside the family I'd ever told, until George. And George never had the whole story. I was saving that for later.

"Yes?" Seth prompted.

I shook George out of my head. "Anyway. One day, when we were teenagers, my dad had this idea. That if only we could clean up while she was gone, then she could see how beautiful it all looked, and she'd be able to keep it clean. But we had to get to the baseline first, was how he put it."

Seth grimaced; no doubt with his training and recent research he could see coming what we, as naive young women, never expected.

"So," I continued, "he took her to Florida on a vacation, which was quite a treat for them. We never had much money for that kind of thing. And then my uncles came—my dad's brothers—and some cousins and my grandparents who were healthy enough and we cleaned like demons for days. We really tried," I said, aware I was defending myself though Seth wasn't accusing, "we tried hard to keep the special things, and to take care of her precious items. We did our very best."

"I can't imagine she reacted well."

"We were so proud. We were all standing in the lawn like soldiers for inspection. I knew she'd be shocked, maybe even a little upset for a minute, but when we showed her all her special keepsakes I figured she'd be mollified. But . . ."—I screwed up my face at the memory and sucked in a hard breath so I could go on—". . . she went bananas, just tearing through the house and screaming like . . . like she was being attacked. Like someone was physically assaulting her. There were some boxes around still, and she started tearing into them. She ripped drawers open, yanked clothes off the hangers. Trish and I hung on to each other and just shook. My dad charged in after her and grabbed her, trying to get her to calm down. She thrashed so hard in his arms that she broke his nose. He still has a bump there. Eventually she cried in his grip until she was limp like a ragdoll, with my dad's nose bleeding all over the both of them." I chuckled bitterly. "My dad was a cop for thirty years, and his worst injury was from my mom. He moved out shortly after. I moved in with him soon after that. Mom never forgave us. There were a couple of photo albums she never could find, plus a sweater that had been her mother's. None of us knew that sweater had been special. It looked just like a mothbally, out-of-date sweater. She haunted the thrift shop for weeks afterward, trying to find it, which she never did. And every time she'd come back with bags and bags full of more stuff."

"That must have been traumatic to witness."

"You have no idea. Well, I guess you probably do, actually."

Seth started to reach out, and I stepped back, and picked my purse up off the driveway. "The point is, we might have a repeat performance."

I started to head into the trailer. "Mary?"

"Yeah?" I said, foot on the little step before the door.

"Are you OK?"

"Sure," I said, stepping inside. "Why wouldn't I be?" I shut the door and closed out the world.

Then I collapsed fully clothed on the trailer's small bed, unable to stop seeing my dad's bloody nose and my keening, thrashing, unrecognizable mother.

Sometime past midnight I got back off the bed, and with shaky hands forced myself to put on pajamas and wash my face in the tiny sink. My eyes were puffy, the whites cracked through with scarlet lines. I wondered how different life would be if George hadn't closed the store. If, instead of accepting his family's largesse to start a new venture, he'd poured the money into the store, keeping it alive. How I wouldn't have been able to fly to Trish's side. I wouldn't be staying in this tiny trailer next to her hoard, collapsing on an old friend like some kind of ninny fainting heroine. I wouldn't be thinking about how I shouldn't have ignored my nephews.

Instead I'd be back in my old routine of morning treadmill jog, working at the store, errands, dinner, reading, and bed. The days had a sameness that I suppose to some might be dull, but it didn't feel that way to me. It felt like flannel pajamas and warm milk, my house like a cocoon. The opposite of my family home, where the walls were literally closing in on me by virtue of more things coming in every day, and nothing ever leaving. I left for school every day feeling lighter than air and came home with a trudging step to the cave our mother had built.

When I would come home to my own town house after a long day at the bookstore, I could feel my joints loosen, my forehead smooth out from whatever work-related worries might have been crowding my brain.

I imagined Seth in here now, asking me where George would have fit in with my exacting, ordered, comforting life.

Excellent question, Imaginary Seth.

Whenever I'd daydreamed a relationship with George, I imagined it happening within my town house, but with nothing else out of order, nothing disturbed, as if I could superimpose him on my life like in photo editing. That would never have worked, I could now admit. George would have come with his own habits and quirks, and they would have clashed with mine, most likely, because although Trish thinks I'm oblivious, I've always been aware that I'm odd.

So, Imaginary Seth answered, you kept up this faux relationship, at a distance, in your head, because you could keep your life intact, just the way you wanted. You could think you were in love without the mess of actually adapting to someone else.

With that thought rattling around in my brain, I flicked off the tiny light next to the little sink, and took the three short steps to the bed.

I dreamt I was buried in Trish's secret room, only the door wasn't there, just a smooth wall, and no one could hear me on the other side.

Chapter 39

The knocking that woke me up echoed in rhythm to the stabbing in my hip.

I pulled myself up from Jack's bedroom floor, squinting in the sun as it blasted around the edges of his window shade. Despite the pain in my joints from sleeping on a floor all night, I scurried to the front door before the pounding woke up my little boy.

I yanked open the door to see Ron standing there with a cardboard carafe of coffee. "I know you like this kind," he said.

"Thanks," I answered, honestly glad, but also irritated. "Why didn't you just use the key? I never changed the locks or anything."

He moved past me to the kitchen to deposit the coffee. "This isn't my house anymore."

I pulled a mug from my cupboards and offered one to Ron. "Jack slept in his own room last night."

"That's good," Ron said, pouring the coffee.

"Just good? That's outstanding."

"Outstanding. Gimme a minute before I do jumping jacks. I haven't been awake too long."

Maybe not so outstanding that I had to sleep on his floor to convince him to stay there. I hadn't intended to stay the whole night and in fact had never even brushed my teeth. I thought I'd rest there for a few minutes until Jack drifted off, only I drifted first, I think.

I dug around in my purse for an Aleve.

"You OK?" Ron asked, squinting at me as I swallowed a pill.

"Just sore. My wrist still aches a bit. This is hard work."

"No shit," he said, not angrily, just in the casual way Ron had of cursing. I remembered how hard he'd worked to break himself of that habit when Drew was little. He'd worn a rubber band on his wrist and snapped it each time he caught himself, or each time I caught him.

He tried so hard to change himself for us, and then years later he would leave. Senseless.

"You gonna be OK today?" he asked.

I shrugged.

"I'm sorry," he said.

He was leaning forward on the kitchen counter, hands wrapped around the mug as if it anchored him in place. He stared down at the coffee and cleared his throat roughly. "I'm sorry I couldn't help you."

I didn't know what to do with this. "Yeah, well."

"I'm really sorry, honey."

Honey. He hadn't called me that in years. "Don't."

"Don't what?"

"Don't come in here today acting all affectionate and sweet, now, years after it would have mattered, just because your girlfriend bailed on you."

He straightened up, let go of the coffee. "Hey, now."

"You don't get to be the hero today, got it? You had that chance and you missed it. You rode off into the sunset and left me to suffer alone."

"Now, listen here a minute. You say 'suffer alone' like someone else was hurting you. No one else filled this house with junk, T."

Another nickname brought back to life. "That's not what I meant by suffering."

"I tried. I told you I tried. You know I tried."

"You could have tried harder."

"You didn't want me to!" He folded his arms, scowled. "You got madder every time I got near you. What was I supposed to do? I gave you space, you felt ignored; I tried to take care of you, you bit my head off. All the while shopping and picking up stuff and never getting rid of nothing."

"So that made it OK to look up your old girlfriend."

"We just talked. And I already apologized for that about six million times."

"When I was already so vulnerable."

Ron leaned in over the counter, closer to me, lowering his voice in volume but not intensity. He stared me down hard, right in the face. "You weren't the only one who grieved that baby."

My heart felt like a trapped animal beating against the walls of a cage as I backed away from my ex-husband, toward the bedroom we used to share, past the door that I never wanted to open again.

I piled another box on top of the couch in the living room. It was full of school projects, CDs, notebooks, copies of *PC World* magazine, some old medals from band competitions back when Drew-then-Andy was playing the trumpet. The trumpet itself stood next to the couch.

"We've gotta trash some of this, T," Ron had insisted.

"It doesn't belong to me, it's Drew's," I'd retorted.

The first layer of stuff out of Drew's room had indeed been mine. When my filing cabinet downstairs had overflowed, I took to putting important papers in boxes and setting them along the wall in his room. Unopened mail that I had yet to deal with—some of it dating back to before the birth of Jack—was piled just inside the door.

Those things came out fairly easily, as I realized with bitterness that if there was going to be fallout from not opening the mail, it had already happened long ago. As for important papers, I let Ron guide the sorting. He'd become efficient in filing since he left me and had to do it himself, until he could afford an assistant. He was piling stuff in a gi-ant bag, offering to take it to his industrial-strength shredder at work. "You got a wood chipper? That might work better," I quipped.

Once we got down to Drew's things, though—all those emblems of himself as a funny, ironic middle schooler, before his Goth takeover—I insisted those be set aside.

I coughed as the dropped box spewed a cloud of dust. The door swung open behind me, and Drew loped his way in, followed by my father.

"Hi," he said. "I called Grandpa."

Despite our eventual and uneasy truce on Easter, for the sake of Jack and also for Ellen, who was on the edge of a coronary at the slight-est hint of conflict, my fury at Dad had only gone from full boil to continuous simmer.

"I see," was all I could muster.

"Well, we're doing my room today, right? I wanted more help."

An ally, I thought. *That's what you really wanted.* "Here." I pointed to the couch. "This is your stuff to sort through."

"I don't want it." He strode away and looked into his room, which was first down the hall so I could still see him easily from where I stood. He shook his head, folded his arms. "I forgot my walls were blue."

"Oh, shut up. The piles weren't that high. You could still see the walls."

"I just hadn't looked in here in so long." He tossed his blackened hair out of his eyes and shed his leather jacket, dropping it on a kitchen chair. I noticed with his short sleeves more muscle definition than I'd remembered. He was getting so strong, and I didn't even know how he was doing that. Protein? Exercise? It wasn't so long ago I was aware of every calorie, every activity, every hour of sleep my boys got.

"Drew," I said, my voice somewhere between pleading and bossing. "Come here and look through this."

He stepped back into the living room. "I said I don't want it."

"You don't even know what's here."

"I haven't seen it in months and haven't missed it. Everything I care about is at Miranda's."

Everything?

I tried a new tactic. "I can't let it go until you look through it. If you don't now, I'll have to store it until you do. I can't take it, throwing something away without looking."

He snarled and stomped to the boxes, whipping through the contents roughly. I couldn't watch so I returned to the room itself.

My dad was already inside, working briskly as if he'd been there all week. He pointed to bags full of clothes. "Clothes, never worn. Tags still on."

"Donate pile."

He pointed to some paint cans. "Paint cans, not sealed properly, probably all dried up."

Ron grunted from behind me, where he was hauling out a box of what looked to be Christmas decorations. "I can get rid of those at work. I got a special disposal permit for paint."

They weren't even looking at me. I drifted back to the kitchen. I heard rustling in the bathroom where Seth and Mary were removing papers and tossing things in garbage bags. Probably old shampoo bottles. I had a habit of keeping the last ounce in a bottle, not wanting to waste it, yet too frustrated to squeeze it out, so I'd start a new one. *Smack, smack, smack,* I heard as the bottles were tossed in a bag. How stupid was I to keep those? With all the other bottles around as evidence that I never used that last bit anyway?

"Fine," Drew barked, drawing my attention. He was stuffing some old composition books and a handful of his old band medals into the beat-up backpack he'd brought over. "I'm saving this."

"Not your trumpet?"

"I don't care about the trumpet."

"It was your grandfather's."

"I didn't know him."

I was opening my mouth to protest, something about the importance of legacy, which kids these days didn't give a rat's ass about, when I heard an oath from my father.

"Jesus, Mary, and Joseph!"

I walked into the hall and shrieked.

My father stood in front of the open door to the Room, the one I'd ordered them not to touch. At his feet was a pile, which looked to me like earthquake rubble. He was gaping at the interior.

"What were you doing in there?" I demanded.

He continued gaping. "I wanted some gloves and Ron said to try the spare room . . ."

"Ron!" I shouted. "How could you send him in there?" Then, immediately I knew why. "You did that on purpose. You wanted my dad to see."

Ron threw up his hands. He stood on my side of the rubble. "Naw, honest, T. I thought you might have some in there. That was always where you put extra stuff."

"Bullshit," I spat, my hands clenched. "You know I've got gloves in the garage."

"What the fuck," I heard Drew say through an astonished breath. He stepped over the fallen pile to join my father, still staring inside.

I couldn't see for myself, but I didn't have to. They were all staring at a wall of things as high as my head, with a door-sized arc just inside on the floor. Some of that wall was collapsed at their feet and would allow a glimpse to the farthest reaches of the room, things that hadn't been seen by anyone in years.

"Is that a crib?" Drew asked. "Really, Mom?"

Seth and Mary had come up behind me. I could feel their shadows and hear their breathing. I could feel their judgment.

I felt a flush of heat crash over me from my feet up. "What? I told you it was bad."

Mary, through her hands, said, "It was completely walled up. There's not even . . . I mean, how?"

"You've seen it before," I reminded her, my voice tight and gravelly. She shook her head. "It was just a blur. . . . I don't remember this."

"Christ almighty," my father breathed. He turned to me and his face registered disgust, but something else as well. Something I hadn't seen since the day Mom broke his nose: fear.

"Daylight's burning," Drew announced. "Go, people. Get bags. It'll take days for us to get rid of all this, so let's move it. We might need another Dumpster, even. Mom, would the social worker get you a second one? Can she do that?"

I shook my head, hard. "We're leaving it alone. I'm not ready."

"No way, Mom," Drew said, squaring his body to me, hands balled up tight. "No. We just can't. Do you know how long that would take you to do this yourself? There must be"—he looked askance at the door—"thousands of things in there. Maybe a million. If you have to physically touch and look at every single one, you'll never finish. Ever. We're here now, so let's do it."

"But there are special things in there."

"Yeah, so special you buried them in junk and shut the door forever."

"You know why," I challenged, speaking in code I knew he'd understand.

"That's the past. This"—he flung his arm at the wall of things—"this is sick. It's a sick way to deal."

Seth cleared his throat. "Drew, maybe we should go outside and talk."

"No one's talking to you, loser."

"Drew!" Mary interjected.

Drew whirled on her. "Oh, come on, Aunt Mary. This guy has all the free time in the world to hang out here and dig through a stranger's crap? Maybe he's living in his car for all you know. It's none of his damn business."

Seth wouldn't let it go. "Jack is in the room right behind us. . . . If we just stepped out and got some air . . ."

"Like Jack doesn't know what's going on anyway!" Drew bellowed. Ron stepped forward, and Drew held up a hand. "Everyone should have thought about poor Jack years ago when you could still walk through our living room. But Aunt Mary was nowhere, Ron took off and left us here in it, and Grandpa acted like he didn't know anything, never bothering to check up. Thanks a fucking lot, people, and now you're worried about his feelings because I'm finally sick of all the dancing around the subject?"

Drew grabbed a fistful of clothes, still with tags, half hanging out of a Target bag. He balled it up in his hand, stepped toward me, and shook it. "This is not going to bring your baby back."

A gasp went through the room like an electric charge: shock from those who didn't know, pain from those who did.

Mary turned to me. "A baby?"

My voice was gone, and my legs went to string. I leaned on the hallway wall, sank slowly down. Ron was the one who answered. "Trish was sixteen weeks along. At the ultrasound . . ." He coughed. "There wasn't a heartbeat. Some kind of blood clot problem."

Ron stared down at the floor and kicked the carpet with his boot. "This was supposed to be the baby's room."

I curled up on the floor, making myself as small as possible, feeling my stomach press against my thighs, thinking about how my pregnant belly had felt, how I'd stroked it all day long, already feeling the kicks.

The baby had started kicking so early, and I'd been overjoyed. So vital, so big, so strong already! Then the movement slowed down, seemed to stop, and the doctor wasn't worried but she had me come in for an ultrasound anyway, to put me at ease.

Of the many things I could never forget was the way the lines deepened around the tech's mouth as she swept the wand across the sticky gel on my belly, the way she excused herself without a smile to fetch the doctor. She'd turned the screen away from me before she left.

We got home, and I yanked that room's door shut, hard.

I felt someone crouch next to me and did not look up. Then I realized by the gentle touch it must be Mary. My dad would try to pull me to my feet, get me to buck up, and move on.

"Why didn't you tell me?"

I ignored her. There was no answer worth giving.

"I'm so sorry," she continued.

So what?

Drew, now, from high above me. "I'm sorry, Mom. I didn't mean it to come out like this. . . . I was sad, too. But this isn't right. What's here isn't right. We have to do it now, for Jack."

I said into the hollow created by my arms and knees, "Can't we just close the door and leave it alone?"

"No, because it's sick," Drew said. "It would be like an alcoholic leaving all his empty bottles around. And, no, don't say because the door is closed that makes it OK."

"I can't."

Ron spoke up. "Then let us do it."

"I can't do that, either."

My dad's voice boomed out in the narrow hall. "Enough of this. We are not debating. We are cleaning out this room, Trish, and you can help or not, as you feel able. End of discussion."

I looked up to see my father reach his long arm into the room and pull down more of the wall. Another cascade of things rained into the hall, dividing us from each other. Jack had appeared behind his father. Ron had one arm around him and was stroking the side of his good shoulder. Jack looked at me with big eyes, a puckered forehead. He looked wary. When we lost the baby, he'd been too little to understand and kept patting my squishy stomach for days after the D&C to say "Hi, baby," the memory of which to this day could still stop my heart.

"Is the baby in there?" Jack asked now, regarding the filled doorway with awe and fright.

"No, no," Ron answered for us. "No, the baby is gone, Jack."

"Gone where?"

"Gone to . . . heaven," he answered, his voice cracking over the word.

Jack looked up, as if he could see her floating there, a cherub on a cloud. "With Grandma?"

"Get some bags," my father ordered.

When a man's hand reached down to touch my elbow, I thought it must be Ron, but it turned out to be Seth. He helped me to my feet, led me to the kitchen. "Let's talk a minute."

Mary stayed behind, talking quietly to Jack.

Seth said under his breath, "I think you need to let us help you. Same as we've done before, setting some ground rules about what to keep."

"Not there," I said, my throat closing up. "Not in there. What if . . . I can't."

"Drew is very perceptive for a teenager. You should be proud of him."

"I am."

"It's not healthy to keep this room this way. It would be as if you had cancer, but we left a tumor in place because it would be too painful to get rid of it. It will spread if we ignore it."

"What are you, some kind of shrink?"

Seth folded his arms. "Now that you mention it."

I jerked my head up to look him full in the face. "Really? You're not serious. Are you serious?"

"Yes. I'm sorry we were dishonest."

"Mary told you to lie, didn't she?"

"You needed the help, and she predicted you wouldn't want me here if you knew what I did for a living."

Mary came out of the hallway then, kicking a stray plastic bag off her foot. She turned to Seth first. "You told her?"

"She figured it out."

A fiery rage charged through me. "You traitorous bitch."

"I was trying to help!" Mary yelled, putting her arm up like I had a meat cleaver or something.

Lucky for her I didn't.

"You orchestrated all this. Put Drew up to challenging me, made sure he called our father who would take over and refuse to listen. Had a shrink on hand to manipulate me without me being any the wiser." I whirled around to inspect my decimated house. "What have I gotten rid of that I didn't want to, because he tricked me into it?"

Seth protested, "Trish, I never—"

"Shut the fuck up, liar! I'll see you disbarred for this. Whatever they do to shrinks."

I heard rustling of plastic and turned to see my father and Drew energetically shoving things into bags. "No!"

I dimly heard people calling my name, even a "Mommy" from Jack. I yanked at my father's arm, but he was always strong and didn't budge. Drew had stepped into the room itself and I couldn't reach him, couldn't stop him.

With each thing they threw in a bag I felt stripped.

My dad waded into the room, sweeping his arm across the top layer, not even looking.

It burned, physically burned to see it. I saw the future then. I saw a crib thrown into a Dumpster, the tiny clothes I'd purchased with one hand on my rounded belly, a yellow blanket with duckies meant to swaddle my baby, bottles I'd purchased brand-new, saw all of it swept into bags, all traces of my lost child ripped away from me . . .

I couldn't hear my own screaming, but I saw it in the faces of my family.

Chapter 40

I clapped my hands over my ears. Seth reached for her, being closest, but she shook him off and tore through the kitchen, out the patio sliding door, and away through the woods. She wasn't even wearing shoes.

In the ringing echo of her shrieking, I heard Jack sobbing. The men in the hall were arguing. Blaming one another, maybe. Blaming Trish. Maybe me. As if that mattered.

I gaped at Seth. How could he have told her? Couldn't he have predicted what she would do?

He held his hands up in surrender. "I couldn't hide it anymore."

I rummaged for my shoes and headed past Seth toward where Trish was rapidly shrinking at the horizon.

"Maybe I should come," he ventured.

I ignored him and took off at a dead run across Trish's yard.

The only sounds were the scraping of my shoes across dead leaves and the puffing of my own breath. I couldn't go as fast as I needed to; the terrain was rutted and hazardous with roots and rocks and who knows what else. Trish would know it better than me, and she had a head start.

I was beginning to catch up, Trish's figure growing in my vision again instead of shrinking, when she reached the fence behind the new development. I saw her hop the fence like she did it every day and disappear into the newly planted shrubbery among all the little matching houses.

I tried to kick into a higher gear when it felt like something grabbed my foot, yanked me down flat on my face.

"Shit."

I detangled my foot from the root that had tripped me. Other than a little soreness from the fall I seemed intact. I tested my foot; ankle not turned. I rose, brushed off dirt and leaves. With my sudden stop a stitch had grown in my side. I breathed deeper, walked ahead.

I'd lost visual contact, but she wouldn't be able to hide in a subdivision. A woman with wild curly hair and a bandaged wrist, in sweatpants and socks wandering around among new houses with no obvious purpose—no dog to walk, no kid in a stroller—would stick out clearly. Unless she took it in her head to break into someone's house or hide in a toolshed, I'd spot her.

As per usual, good old Mary had screwed it all up. Having Seth around, yet making him lie about his job, turned out to be a disaster in waiting. "Duh," I said aloud to the greening woods. Birds chirped back at me.

I reached the back of the subdivision and opted for a house that seemed dark. Spring break, maybe they were gone. I climbed the chain-link fence and then snuck out to the front, letting myself through their unlocked gate, then hustling as fast as possible to the sidewalk.

I walked ahead, hands in the pocket of my hooded sweatshirt, concentrating on looking normal.

When I felt sufficiently far from the yard where I'd trespassed, I looked up and started searching for Trish again. The streets were winding, but I could still see for several yards. There were mothers walking with their kids, some boys on bikes. A couple of teenagers walking while talking and texting at once.

I got to a T-shaped intersection—between Fox Run and Pheasant

Ridge—and screwed up my courage to ask a young mother fussing with her baby whether she'd seen a woman my age with long, curly brown hair.

If the young mother was disturbed by these strangers in her neighborhood, she didn't show it, more preoccupied with her infant in a travel carrier attached to a stroller. She was fussing with a tiny bonnet. The baby seemed to be unhappy with both the bright sun and the bonnet, too. "Um, I did, actually. She went by on a bike. I noticed because she didn't have shoes."

The baby finally grasped a teething toy and jammed it in her gummy mouth. The young woman stood back, sighed, and straightened her own sweater with an air of satisfaction. "Is everything OK?"

"Oh, sure," I lied. "Thanks."

She headed off, no doubt her head filled with details about teething infants and diapers and what she'd have to cook for dinner later. I'd caught a glimpse of a platinum wedding ring as we talked, with a generous square diamond in the center. I trudged in the direction she'd pointed and wondered what it would be like for one's days to involve sunny walks and teething rings instead of bookstore inventory? Or, for that matter, unemployment?

What did it do to Trish to see babies everywhere?

I walked to the corner of a busy street, now having to admit I'd lost her absolutely. I'd left without my phone or purse and didn't know exactly where I was. I turned back in the opposite compass direction from my initial pursuit, along the busy street, assuming I'd eventually get to Trish's rural road, and I could turn back to her house and gather what was left of my family to figure out what would happen now.

I was hungry and sore by the time I returned to Trish's, which seemed distressingly quiet and dark.

A note on the door said: "Ron took Jack and Drew to McDonald's and the park to keep Jack's mind off things. Your dad and I went to look for both of you in separate cars. Call one of us when you get back so we know you're OK. Seth."

The note was vague, addressed to either one of us. They'd left the door unlocked, and I nudged it open, hoping to find Trish inside on the couch, watching TV.

No such luck. Nor was she in her newly clean bedroom, or Jack's room, or huddled inside the secret room among her baby's things. The house rang with her absence.

I drifted into the kitchen to find my phone, to text Seth that I was no longer lost.

As I passed the calendar I noticed Trish had circled tomorrow and written in red: "Ayana."

It would certainly not be a good sign if Trish hadn't come back by then, no matter how much progress we'd made on the house. It would look as if she'd abandoned her children. Well, maybe she did. It was hard to know what was going on in her head. How much was the hoarding demon, how much was my sister.

In the end it might not matter. Someone had to take care of her children who could provide them with a safe, stable home, who would not scream like she was on fire and run off into a subdivision at the slightest provocation.

I grabbed an apple from her fruit bowl and settled at the kitchen table to send my text to Seth.

In the unusual quiet, with only the ticking of a distant clock to distract me, I noticed we'd left Mother's diary at the table. I'd promised to read it only with Trish, true. But we'd all been promised lots of things.

I read through several pages of prom preparations and growing fascination with the migrant workers, particularly Inez, whom she idolized as she would a real big sister. As I might have idolized Trish, in another kind of life.

She was picking out colleges and was attracted to DePaul University in Chicago. She had an adorable crush on President Kennedy.

One entry described another fight with her father: a character in her diary so far removed from the Grandpa Van Linden we knew I could scarcely imagine they were the same person. He accused her of a sassy mouth again when she made a comment sympathetic to civil rights protesters and threatened her with having to stay home from college, where she might be subject to "dangerous and radical influences." As the fight escalated, he threatened to make her stay home from the prom, too, saying perhaps her "morality was becoming dangerously loose" based on her refusal to respect the commandment to honor her father.

Despite her earlier ambivalence about the prom, teenage Frannie, my mother, in her all her glorious teen stubbornness, was all the more determined to go.

The next page's entry was brief. Just three small words, centered halfway down the page, in scrawled blue ballpoint pen.

Lord help me.

Chapter 41

I walked the bike up the steep hill, my legs trembling with exertion, a trickle of sweat down my back and between my breasts.

It seemed exposed here, too new and raw. The sun was far too bright. I dropped the bike in the grass just off the path. In the distance a mower roared, but it was far from me at the moment.

I sat down on grass warmed by the sun and stroked the smooth granite with my fingertips.

FRANCES EVELYN GRANGER
BELOVED MOTHER, DAUGHTER, AND SISTER
1944–1996

Mary and I had argued about the inclusion of "wife." She'd wanted to say "wife," and I balked. Mom was no longer anyone's wife and I couldn't engrave a lie into permanence. We would feel the lie every time we visited, I told her. In the end, we left it up to Dad, who of course voted for accuracy and truth though I could tell it pained him. At the time I thought, *Good, I hope it hurts*. It should hurt to break your vows and leave your wife.

But then, more pain is the last thing any of us needed.

"Mom," I said. I could find no more words. I trusted instead she could feel me. My frustration, pain, confusion.

I would jump in front of a moving train for my sons. Throw myself in front of a mugger's gun. Leap into a rushing river.

Yet when challenged to throw away old things for their sake, I failed.

They should have known better, though. My dad especially, with his broken nose, should have realized you can't just reach into a hoarder's belongings and start ripping items away.

They cared so much about cleaning that damn room, but no one stopped to take care of *me*.

I put my face in my hands and cried through my fingers as I remembered the times I was cared for. Mom giving me ginger ale when I was sick and letting me watch cartoons all day. Bringing me a Ken doll to go with my Barbie, just to cheer me up.

Dad picking me up and brushing gravel off my scraped knee after a bike spill.

Ron holding my hand while crying huge, fat gobs of tears as I pushed out Jack. Tears such that I'd never seen, before or since. Even that time he crushed this thumb with a hammer.

"Why doesn't anyone care anymore?" I asked, of Mom, of God, of the air. "Why am I even here?"

If I'd stayed at home and taken care of her, maybe I could have saved her, cured her, saved myself, ultimately. Or died in the fire with her. But at least she wouldn't have been alone. I wouldn't be alone now.

I tried to imagine—as I had many times in the past standing here at her grave—my mother cradling my baby-never-born, the two of them keeping each other company in heaven. This never brought me the peace I hoped.

I curled up on my side, toying with a blade of grass, letting my eyes go unfocused past rows and rows of granite stones marking the end of everything.

* * *

Mary came around to my field of vision and sat down cross-legged in front of me, where I was still curled up on my side. I had a flash-memory of playing duck-duck-goose with her at some birthday party or something.

From my sideways view, all I could see was her old dirty jeans and running shoes.

"Whose bike is that?" she asked.

"I'll turn it into the police and say I found it."

"I'd better handle that. Someone may have seen you take it."

"Whatever."

"Everyone's worried about you."

"I'm sure."

The lawn mower had stopped, I noticed now. Birds tweeting, distant traffic.

"You should sit up, Trish."

"No."

"Looks like there's a funeral coming soon."

At this I rose to my elbow and followed Mary's stare. There was indeed a canopy over a grave several yards away. That meant soon a procession of cars with little orange flags would be pulling in. I dragged myself up to sitting. It would seem rather odd and disrespectful to look like I was taking a nap.

"I'm not going to apologize for getting mad," I said. "You lied."

"I know I did. I'm not going to apologize for that, either."

"It was wrong."

"I had to do it."

"No, you didn't."

She imitated her eight-year-old self and stuck out her tongue, prying a chuckle out of me.

"Stop being funny. I'm having a nervous breakdown and I'm not supposed to laugh."

"Oh, it's not in the handbook?"

"Ask Dr. Seth, secret shrink. He would know."

"That's not why you're really mad anyway. I know it's not."

"It sure as hell didn't help."

I picked at more blades of grass. It was so green already, so lush. How was that possible? Just a week ago everything was brown and mud.

"Dad still doesn't get it," I said. "Why doesn't he?"

Mary shrugged. "I'd better text the boys that you're OK."

"Go ahead, I guess."

Her thumbs working the phone, she asked, "You *are* OK, right?"

"No."

She slid the phone shut, looked at me again, inspecting. "You weren't hit by a bus or anything."

"I forgot, you've gone all literal on me. Yes, I'm physically intact. Well, my feet hurt from pedaling in socks."

"Now what?" Mary said, sighing.

"You know? You haven't even looked at Mom's grave."

She flinched, but still didn't look.

I asked, "Have you ever visited?"

She shook her head.

Of course not. After all, she abandoned her in life, too. "I can't say I'm surprised."

"How often do you visit?" she asked, looking past me.

I shrugged. "Once a month to once a week, depending on weather, how I'm feeling."

"Does it help?"

"Help what?"

"Anything."

She didn't seem to be challenging me. She was simply asking. Mary was one of those people who could often say, with complete honesty, "I was just asking," because she actually did not have an agenda. She wasn't usually conniving enough. Until she dragged

Seth out here pretending he was just any old friend. It's always the quiet ones.

"I don't know. I just know that I need to."

"And I don't. Need to, that is. I don't know why. I know it seems awful to you. But that's the truth of it." Mary finally risked a sidelong glance at the gravestone, then pointed at it. "She's not here. Not to me."

Mary then placed Mother's diary on the grass between us. She placed it there with both hands, as gently as if putting down a newborn baby.

"I'm sorry that I read it without you," Mary said. "I read some because I didn't know what else to do; didn't know if you were even coming back."

"And?"

"There's an entry," Mary said, tapping the cover. "There's a long entry, and the one just prior was only three words long. It said, 'Lord help me.' I didn't want to read more without you."

I reached for the diary and saw a flash of my teenage mother—looking something like me—scrawling page after page with tears plopping onto the paper. I riffled through our family history for a disaster that would have occurred in 1961, realizing quickly I knew of no such tragedy. Maybe no one else did either.

I started to pick it up and stopped, seized by a thought: "Wait, how did you know I was here? And are the boys going to come charging in here now?"

Mary shook her head. "I only texted you were fine and we'd be home soon, not where we were. I thought you'd need some time." She glanced away, at the canopy for the distant grave. "As for me, I just guessed. Even Clueless Mary has a hunch sometimes."

"Maybe Mother nudged you."

Mary grimaced. "Don't start that talk. It weirds me out."

I started to open the diary, and Mary interrupted. "We're going to read it now? Here?"

I looked at Mother's grave and nodded. "Yes. Yes, we should."

After a moment—maybe she considered arguing—Mary scooted around next to me, and we began to read silently.

July 14, 1961

I've made a terrible mistake.

I'm a tramp and I'm an idiot, with loose morals just as Father said.

That stupid, cursed prom. Wally was a very good dancer, as it turned out. He had nice breath. He wasn't wearing his glasses and looked nearly dashing, except for this unfortunate cowlick. He fumbled the corsage as he pinned it to my dress, and in his crooked smile and his adorable fumbling I finally felt that rush of feeling the girls have been talking about. Giggly and giddy, like when you're on the swings as a kid and you reach the very top and are suspended for half a heartbeat before you swoop back down.

I felt it again when his arms were around me at the dance, for "It's Now or Never," which I will never be able to listen to again now.

Is that why I did it? That feeling?

The trouble started after we all got bored at the dance, and Larry said he knew a spot on the beach that was secluded, where we could park our cars and have a bonfire and no one would bother us. And then Rich said he'd gotten some wine and brandy from his older brother. Even with the fire it was cold out on the beach and Wally put his coat around my shoulders, which was very sweet. I had a paper cup and they all kept refilling it.

Somewhere in me there was this little voice, sounding

like my sister, Margaret, actually, that scolded me. *You shouldn't be doing this.* That it was a bad idea to be on this secluded beach with this boy I didn't know very well, while drinking, too. And I knew my father would be so angry if he knew I was behaving this way. But then Wally put his arm around me and I laughed with all this warmth in my chest from the drink and I had my first of several disastrous and wicked thoughts: *I don't care what Father thinks. To hell with him anyway.*

People started pairing off. I didn't even notice until later we'd been left entirely alone, everyone else in their own little pockets of sand dune, or up at the cars. I looked up at the stars and they were so stunning and clear, and also spinning in this way that was sickening and delirious and wonderful.

He leaned in and kissed me, hard.

Here is where I should have pushed back. I should have pushed him back and told him to take me home, like Betsy did and everyone made fun of her the next day, but Betsy isn't in trouble, is she?

I didn't do that, though. I kissed him back. I kissed him hard, and I leaned against him and pressed my bosom into him and when he nudged me back on the sand—or did I lean back myself? I really can't remember, but it hardly matters now—I let myself go.

Then he was on top of me. It felt thrilling, and electric, and dizzy. I felt like the sand dune was whirring us off into space. By the time I realized he'd unclipped my stockings, he was kissing me so hard right then I could barely breathe. Then my panties were down around my knees, and suddenly he rolled back away and everything was wet and sore.

He said the weirdest thing. He said, "I didn't mean to come inside, you're just so gorgeous." And I thought, come inside where? I really thought that. And then I got scared and turned to one side and threw up.

I kept telling myself for weeks that we hadn't done it. These were the weeks I didn't write, I couldn't bear to admit even to myself in these pages what might be true. I wasn't even naked, and didn't you have to be naked to do it? That's how stupid I used to be.

Now I know you don't have to be naked. Because my period is gone and my breasts are sore and I'm tired and sick all the time and my skirts aren't fitting. I have to admit I'm a tramp with loose morals just like Daddy said.

The worst part is that he won't admit it. I got Wally to walk me home one day after school and I told him, and he got this look on his face, this look like I was garbage, and he said not to blame him because he didn't do it. I started to cry on the street and insisted that yes, he did so, and he knew it, and he said, "All I ever did was kiss you. It must have been someone else" and he called me a whore. He's scared too, and he's lying, only I can't lie my way out of my trouble like he can.

As soon as everyone finds out, he'll probably tell them the same story too, and I won't have any way to contradict him.

I don't know what to do. I have to tell my parents and I don't know how. I've ruined myself, I've ruined our family. I don't deserve to live, I really don't, but the only reason I haven't tried to kill myself is because I'm afraid to and also because it's not the baby's fault.

I'll pray. That's the only think I can think of to do.

August 1, 1961

My father was, as I predicted, livid. He was in a rage, screaming at me for being so careless and sinful and that he hadn't raised a whore. The same word that Wally used. I wanted to say that all the other girls had gone off with boys that night, too; they were just lucky enough not to get in trouble. That I didn't know it could happen so quickly, with my clothes still on. That no one told me anything about it, actually, except not to do it.

But I knew there was no point. My mother was kind to me, but only after Father left the house to go drive around the neighborhood. She fed me saltines and ginger ale and had me lie down with a cool cloth on my forehead because she could see I was trembling. My sister wouldn't even look at me, but that was no surprise.

I told Mother I wished I could undo it, and she told me there's a way I can make it all better. I was so relieved to hear her say that I didn't even think to ask what it was before I said yes, please, anything. She told me about these homes for girls who get in trouble, where you go off and stay there and have the baby, and they find a barren couple who wants a child desperately and then you let it be adopted. Then you come home and pick up your life where you left off, and the barren couple gets to experience the joy of parenthood they so desperately want. She said then I could start a family the right way, on my own time, later. She said it's a good Christian place, where kind people know how to help girls in trouble.

I told her I didn't want to be away, and she said it was only for a little while and that they'd visit. I told her I'd think about it, and then she put her hand on my arm and said, "Sweetheart, there's nothing to think about. It's what we're going to have to do."

And so I have no choice. I flip between grateful and terrified. Grateful that there's a way to go back in time, in a way, and that a nice married couple will get to be happy because of my mistake. But I'm terrified to be away from home, alone when I have this baby, and . . . I know this is a wicked, selfish thought, but this is my baby, and what if I wanted to keep it? I always enjoyed the little ones at the migrant camp. Couldn't I take good care of my own baby? Like Inez with her baby sister?

But I have to stop thinking like that. Because if I do, I will make myself crazy. It's not up to me anymore, and I don't deserve a choice because of the ruin I've brought on myself. I know I didn't mean to do it, but I was the one who got drunk and lay down in the sand with him.

Frances

August 13, 1961

I'm undeniably showing now. I'm not allowed to leave the house unless I duck down in the backseat until we're out of the neighborhood. That's humiliating, so I don't leave. It's easier. It seems like the town is buying the "sick" story my parents have been telling, or at least pretending to, which is sort of a relief because I was afraid Wally would run around calling me a whore. Maybe this way I'll have a life to go back to.

Though I can't imagine what that life will look like now.

Even if—when, I guess—I give up this baby, I'm not going to college. The home costs money, and my father says he's spending my college money on that, and whatever else is left is going into Margaret's education. Margaret doesn't give a damn about school; she just wants a husband. But Father thinks she'll get a better one at a better school, so off she goes. And what can I say? I did this to myself.

I can save up my own money, though. After all this is over I'll move out, get a job waiting tables or something, and start saving. I can go to nursing school myself and show Father, and Mother, and Margaret that I don't need them anymore. And then I'll date, but I'll never drink again, and never let one near me until I get married. Maybe I'll move far, far away after all this. I'll go to California, or New York. Somewhere no one ever knew that I was "sick."

I'm so bored. I wish I had more books. I've got nothing to do here but get bigger and think. I help with light chores like folding laundry, but otherwise I stay in my room watching the light rotate along the walls with the sun until I want to start ripping down the wallpaper.

October 22, 1961

A long gap in writing here. But I've got nothing of interest to report, and after I write, I get so morose and sad because I'm thinking about my situation. We leave for the home soon and I'm so scared and lonely. I'm bringing some yarn to knit some sweaters. I'm also going to knit a baby hat. I would like the baby to have something from me.

I think I've accepted I can't keep her. (For some reason I'm convinced it's a girl.) For a while I would try to plan out what I would do to keep her, but it all falls apart without the support of my family. Where would I live if not here? Because I could never make enough money to support myself and the baby while paying rent, too. And even if I could find an amazing job paying all this money, who would watch the baby while I worked if not my family? If I had to pay a babysitter, that would erase so much of my paycheck I'd be back to where I started. So how would I feed myself, the baby? How would we survive? We wouldn't, simple as that. There is no other choice.

This baby deserves a nice mother and a real father who will acknowledge her and love her as his own, a comfortable house, and a good family. If I kept her, we'd be poor or even destitute and she'd be known as a bastard child.

I get my mind all made up about this, and then she kicks me, and I rub her through my belly and I think I won't be able to do it, they'll have to saw my arms off to take her.

I may not write for a while. This is getting too hard.

February 15, 1962

It's a new year and it should feel like a fresh start. That's what my father tells me. With a girdle my stomach looks almost as flat as it used to. I'm back in my old room with my Elvis records and magazines and books, and I'll start school again soon, only a little bit behind the class, since I was doing so well before . . . well, before everything.

Only I'm dead inside. I have to be, because if I feel anything, I want to scream and scream and run back to the home and beat on the door and threaten them with knives until they tell me where my daughter is.

My mother said they'd be kind, but they lie to you. They don't tell you that giving birth makes you feel like you're going to split in two. They don't tell you that giving up your baby will be like ripping out your own heart. They only tell you that you have to sign the papers because this couple has been waiting and this baby deserves a family and what kind of life could you give it anyway? That the only way to redeem your shame and mistake is to sign. And they stand over you and they make you sign. And so I did, and I let go of her. Every time I think of that moment, when I let the lady from the home take her, I think I might die from the pain of it, and I kind of hope I do.

When no one was looking, I took some nail clippers and I snipped off a piece of her hair, which is dark and curly, like mine. I wrapped it in some tissue and now it's in an envelope. It's the only time—other than just now, writing here—when I let myself feel anything. Once a night I say my prayers, and I pray for Laura while stroking the only piece of her I still have. Then I cry myself to sleep and wake up dead again.

I may have to stop writing. It was like living that moment all over again to tell it here, and I thought I'd feel better letting it out but I don't. Not one bit. Plus I'm afraid someone will discover this book and Father will be angry with me again for being ungrateful about them solving my problem for me. Not to mention he'd be furious with me for keeping a record that might one day be discovered. In fact, if he found this notebook, or that lock of Laura's hair, I'm quite sure he'd make me destroy it. See, I'm supposed to go back to normal now. Everything just like it was.

Maybe I should burn it before anyone has a chance to find it. But if I did . . . I'd lose the last piece of my baby I can ever have.

Everyone else might pretend she never existed. But I will never be able to forget her. Ever.

Chapter 42

A trumpet blast startled me so much that I dropped the diary on the grass.

In our frantic reading, Trish and I had not even noticed the graveside ceremony beginning in another part of the cemetery.

A bugler was playing "Taps." The assembled small group clung to each other under and around the canopy. When the last bitter notes rang out into the air, the minister began speaking, but we were far enough way not to hear.

Trish whispered, "Oh, my God" again and again. She paged rapidly through the rest of the notebook, looking for more writing, perhaps, or maybe even the lock of the baby's hair. Nothing but clean, blank pages with blue lines bright as the first day of school.

I tried to access the same feelings Trish had, and failed. I was not a mother. Had never been pregnant. I understood academically that a mother was attached to a baby even in the womb, could understand in a clinical sense that it must indeed be difficult to hand over a baby for adoption, even when the baby wasn't planned.

But Trish seemed to feel our mother's pain as deeply as if it happened to her. I suspected she was also grieving her own lost baby. Lost differently, but gone all the same.

Trish needed my sympathy for what we'd just read. But she was my mother, too. Our mother who'd suffered this secret pain.

It hit me like a slap. We had a sister, whom our mother had named Laura, born in 1961 or 1962, sometime in the winter.

"No wonder," I said finally. Trish didn't respond. "Christmastime, remember? She was always such a nut about it. Then right after she'd fall into a funk that would last until Easter."

Trish raised her head at last, wiped her face with shaking hands. "Yeah, I remember."

Our mother considered the merchandise of Christmas to be at least as holy as the birth of Christ, based on the way she shopped. We could count on almost daily fights with our father, most of which he lost because she could always counter with the fact she was creating a happy holiday for the girls. Cheerful decor, cookie cutters, snowman-shaped baking pans, wreath-making crafts, a football field's worth of festive ribbon, more little houses for her Christmas village—it was all meant to make everyone happy.

I wondered if Trish was now also remembering the postholiday depression that would hit when we went back to school and the tree came down. We always thought it was just some winter blues, sadness at the end of the season.

She must have been trying to bury her grief in the holiday, but when the holiday ended, she would not be able to beat back the pain anymore, having all those empty hours again, just as her baby's birthdate approached.

My phone chimed for a text, and I regretted not switching it to vibrate. I glanced at it. It was Seth, saying the boys were anxious to see their mother, and worried about her.

"We should get back," I said.

"There is no 'back,'" Trish muttered.

"What?"

She pointed at the letters. "Back from that. From knowing that."

I paused. Considered. My world didn't feel so different. The fact that her hoarding may have been motivated by the pain of giving up a secret baby did not change the fact that she did hoard, and then she died.

"Regardless. We need to get back to the house. Your boys are worried about you." I stood, brushed grass clippings off my pants. "Trish? It's time to go."

She looked up at me, her eyes bright and wet. "Why didn't she tell us? She should have told us."

I pulled her gently to standing. "She was ashamed; it's all over that diary. That was years before the sexual revolution. Before the pill. Married couples had twin beds on TV."

"I can't believe Grandpa would have acted like that," Trish muttered, and I nodded. The father portrayed in the letters was harsh, unforgiving, in an Old Testament biblical kind of way. We'd known Grandpa Van Linden to be a sweet old man who ruffled our hair and called us "his girls." He never seemed fazed by Trish's big hair and miniskirts.

We walked back toward the stolen bike, at the same time as the mourners began to file to their cars. I picked up the bike and we stood back to let them pass, my car being away at the bottom of the hill. Their faces were somber, still.

"I don't feel any better," Trish said.

"Take a shower, get something to eat. That will help."

She huffed. "I don't mean right now. I mean . . ."—she pointed at the last car as it rumbled over the gravel past us—"any better than those people in those cars. Fourteen years later. Wasn't it supposed to get better?"

Trish looked askance at me, and I shrugged, having no explanation to give her.

* * *

I deposited the bike at the police station and joined Trish back in the car. She'd been slumped in the backseat in case anyone had seen her ride off with the bike. As we got back out onto the road, I assured her the officer had been only barely interested, taking down my name and asking a couple of questions about where I'd found the bike.

Trish remained prone in the back. She said, addressing the roof of the car, "Mom rode around like this when she was pregnant. They made her hide like some kind of fugitive. Made her stay in the house like house arrest."

"It was a different time."

"Don't defend them."

"Who said I am? The time was, however, different."

She sighed loudly. "Fine. Different. Whatever." A few beats of silence, then, "I wonder if she knows."

"Who?"

"Laura. The baby. She must be . . . gosh, almost fifty now. Kids of her own maybe. I wonder if she knows she's adopted."

"Probably so. I knew adopted kids in school. It wasn't a big deal."

"Not to us. To them, maybe."

"Yeah. Maybe. Trish? Not to change the subject, but . . . OK, I guess I am changing the subject. What are you going to do about that room?"

"I don't know." Her voice sounded strangled.

"Other than the basement, which we can probably ignore for now, or at least clear a path to your washing machine and leave it. And we should finish up Drew's room. But . . . it's the worst space. By far."

She didn't answer except to prompt me to turn right onto her street.

"What are we going to do?" I asked her, hearing my own irritation creep into my voice.

"Give me a freakin' minute here," she snapped. "Some of us are just a wee bit shocked by the idea we have a secret half sister. Some of us who aren't emotionless robots."

When I got out of the car, I tried to slam the door to broadcast my irritation, but in my exhaustion it only thunked quietly closed and didn't even latch.

Chapter 43

I walked in on the men in my life arrayed around my dining room table, a newspaper fanned out in the middle, with coffee mugs plus Jack's McDonald's cup dotting the surface.

At the opening of the door I saw their faces click from expectant to relieved to varying degrees of pissed off.

I looked to Ron first. His face had that resigned sag that always made him look like a hound dog. He looked like that when I busted him talking to an old girlfriend, later when he walked out the door, later yet in court for the divorce decree, and at every exchange of our children. Drew's face—what I could see underneath his hair—was snarled up in a tight scowl. He refused to look at me.

Jack was running to me and already clinging to my leg before I could fold down to hug him. Even he, though, was angry.

"Mom! You scared me when you left. You shouldn't do that."

Seth excused himself and said he and Mary would go for a drive. I just nodded as they wafted past me, silent. I met my father's eyes. They were damp and red.

"Patty Cake, I'm glad you're back."

"I'm sorry," I said to all of them, stroking Jack's hair. "I shouldn't have done that." I untangled Jack from my leg and crouched down to him. "Especially to you. I didn't mean to scare you. But—"

"Ah yes," my dad interjected. "The famous 'but.' Like Mom would always say she didn't mean to get so angry at us, *but* we didn't have the right to touch her stuff. *But* she worked hard and deserved a few nice things. *But* she meant to read those magazines when she had time. *But* she was tired and couldn't keep up."

With every "but" he'd knocked his fist against the top of the table.

It took effort to straighten myself carefully and choose my words, when I really wanted that broken vase back so I could hurl it again.

I looked again at Ron, who was pretending to read the newspaper. "Ron and Drew, please take Jack outside to play."

"Mama . . ."

"Jack, your grandpa and I have some things to talk about."

Ron told Jack they would go walk in the woods and look for bugs under rocks, and like any good country kid, Jack went along. Drew stomped past, never meeting my eyes.

I folded my arms and regarded my father, still seated at the table, one hand holding the newspaper as if he had to get back to the sports scores. "So how does the moral high ground feel? Are you light-headed from the altitude?"

"Come off it, Trish."

"It just seems to me that from where you sit, I don't get a vote in how I'm treated. Because I screwed up, I get to be wrong forever, is that it? I have to take what's coming to me."

"What's coming to you is some responsibility, and I'm sick of hearing the 'but.' And so were you, the whole time growing up. Don't tell me you believed every apology she ever gave. She wasn't ever sorry."

"Don't you dare act like you knew her mind."

"Like hell I didn't! We were married for thirty-five years and I knew her in ways you couldn't possibly. I knew everything about her!"

"So you knew she had a baby at seventeen years old and was forced to give it away? And that she wished she was dead from the pain of it?"

My father jumped back from the table like he'd been bitten by a snake. He knocked his chair over in his haste to stand. "What?"

When I'd spit out this piece of news, I was playing *Gotcha!* and thought I'd feel smug. Instead, I felt sick.

"That's not true," he said. "She would have told me. . . . Oh, God, Trish? Is that true?"

"I shouldn't have said it that way."

"How do you know this? And why are you only telling me now?"

"I found a diary . . ." I began.

As I told Dad the story, he slumped back to the kitchen table and rested his head in his hand.

"Oh, Frannie," he murmured, eyes down on the table, not seeing the newspaper anymore. "Frannie, honey, you should have told me."

He pressed the heels of his hands into his eyes, grimacing. The moment felt intimate, and I turned to go find the others, to let him sit with this knowledge and fresh grief.

"Patty Cake."

I stopped in the living room, turned back.

"Yeah, Dad?"

"Do you think she really did all that because of that baby?"

"Yes. Maybe. Not everyone who gives up a baby hoards, so . . . I don't know, it's complicated, I think."

"She never did want to let go of you girls. She carried you so much people joked you'd never learn to walk. She must have thought . . ."

He trailed off, folding his arms and resting facedown, like a kid at school told to put his head down on his desk.

I finished his thought in my own head. She must have felt someone was coming to take her new babies, too.

He picked his head up off his arms. "Patty? Do you . . . ? I mean . . . Did something . . . Other than what we know . . ."

"No, Dad. I don't have a deep, dark secret. You knew about losing the baby."

He wiped his face. He was looking older by the minute now, his complexion pale and eyes red and watery. "You seemed OK, though. After. You and Ron."

I shrugged. "We weren't."

"It wasn't such a mess in the house then, was it?"

"Not as bad. Not right away. It's complicated, Dad. I don't understand it myself."

He stood up and came around to me. When he folded me in his arms, I smelled aftershave and coffee and the laundry soap we always had at home. Ellen must still use the same kind, or it's a trick of my memory. His scratchy flannel shirt on my cheek felt the same as ever.

"Oh, Patty Cake. I'm sorry. So sorry."

I let him hold me and pretended I was little again and hadn't started ruining my life yet.

"My girls," he muttered into my hair. "My poor girls."

W hen my sons and ex-husband came back in from their walk in the woods, I silently prayed gratitude for this truce with my father, this moment where he put aside what'd happened and was simply Dad again, taking care of me.

They all got their waters and Cokes and sat around the living room. Drew stared at me with one eyebrow cocked, his face a challenge: *Well?*

"I'm still sorry. Genuinely sorry I got so upset. I need to explain something," I said, careful not to say "but," trying harder than Mom ever did to not make excuses.

As I spoke, I wondered if Mom had only ever been trying to explain, in her way. The only way she knew, because she didn't have an Ayana or a Seth or a state-paid shrink.

"We do have to deal with that room. But not today. This isn't something . . . It's not like ripping off a Band-Aid, where faster is better. It's more like . . ." I closed my eyes. Mary was always better at this, coming up with a good metaphor for something. It was all that reading she did all the time. "It's like a dam. A dam built holding back a river. If you blow it up, the water will explode out and destroy everything. We have to take it down slowly. Let things seep out gradually."

My father began, "You have a point," preempting Drew, already sitting up straight to argue with me. "I should've known better than to start ripping stuff out. Me especially, considering. I was . . . upset. Worried. I don't want you to . . . to end up . . ." He cleared his throat, heavily, twice. "Anyhow. Slow it'll have to be."

Drew sighed and sounded like a tire letting out air. "But you'll never be able to do it."

"Thanks for the vote of confidence."

"I just mean that real life will get in the way, and it will get harder and harder, and we won't be able to be here all the time."

"We'll just close the door and leave it for now. All the public spaces are cleaned up well enough to please Ayana, and today we'll finish your room," I told Drew. "It's time you moved back in."

He worked his jaw, wanting to bark at me, holding it back. I allowed myself a speck of relief he was trying to hold back, that he thought I was worth the effort.

"And you'll do that other room when, exactly?" Drew cocked his eyebrow at me again.

"You guys can't just force it. I know it doesn't make sense to you and I hate it, too. Don't you think that I wish I could just clean it all up like that, like magic?" I snapped my fingers.

"Ayana said that," Jack interjected. "She asked me what I would do if I had a magic wand and could fix anything. I said I'd magic my dad and Drew back in the house and clean it up, too."

Jack looked from his father to his brother, and to the cleaned-up living room. "Hey, maybe it worked!"

I kissed the top of his head. "No, pal. It ain't magic. Whatever it is, though, I'll take it."

"So I did OK talking to Miss Ayana?"

"Of course, sweetheart. Of course you did."

We all let the moment be, until Drew's phone went off. He replied with some quick clicking, then said, "That was Miranda. They're coming back early because her brother is sick. I have to go make sure their dog has everything it needs." He stood up and stretched, and I thought, *Here it goes. He's leaving me again.*

"I told her I had to get back, and that I'd be having dinner here. Should we get some pizza or something?"

I regarded him with wonder. "Sure, hon. Pizza sounds good to me."

"Hey, Pop," Drew said, and I saw Ron startle at being called that now, something Drew hadn't done since the divorce. He hadn't called him "Ron," but just hadn't really called him anything, starting conversations with a generic *Hey, what's up?* "You know there's a hockey game on tonight. Maybe we could watch it after dinner. If you'll still be here."

"Yeah. Sure. I'll stick around a bit."

Drew waved at his grandpa, ruffled Jack's hair, and said "G'bye, squirt, see you later"; then he was out the door with something that was almost a smile on his face.

"Glad to see him stepping up," my dad commented.

"Drew is just a kid, despite the fact he's six feet tall. He's been stepping up just fine I'd say."

"I just meant that he shouldn't have moved out; he is your child."

"He made the decision you and Mary made. To get the heck out."

"I'm an adult. It was different."

"Mary wasn't an adult. She was fifteen."

"*She* was different. She was . . . delicate. She couldn't have stood it any longer." Dad looked down at the floor between his feet. "The way you could stand it."

I considered teenage Mary, thin and awkward, trying so hard to stand like a sentry at the door to her room, keeping it pristine. The invading junk creeping in, relentless.

───── Chapter 44 ─────

As Seth backed his Lexus down the driveway, he reached one hand up and toward me. I froze, but he was just bracing himself against the back of my seat to turn around and look out the back. His intention wasn't to stroke my cheek or squeeze my shoulder to give comfort.

"I'm sorry I told Trish when I did," Seth said. "I could have picked a better time. But she called me out on my psychologist jargon. I never was good at that, dropping the job at the office. It's not just a job, you know; it's a whole way of thinking. It changes everything about how you look at people. I wonder if MDs have the same thing, if they see people as a collection of symptoms all the time."

"Is that what we are to you?" I asked, as I stared at the trees whipping past the window outside. "Symptoms?"

"That's not what I meant. I try, you know, because it used to make my wife crazy. She'd go, 'Just be human!' and I'd say 'I still am!' But I knew what she meant."

"You are human," I said. "I shouldn't have asked you to lie."

The growly sound of tires over gravel was replaced by the hypnotic smooth rumbling over pavement. "Where are we going anyway?" I asked. "Anywhere?"

"I want to see the ledges. It's Grand Ledge after all, right?"

"I've seen them," I replied. "School field trip." Nature never was my thing. I'm easily chilled or overheated, and I hate bugs. I toyed with a brochure I'd found on the dashboard, smoothing the existing creases and skimming cheerful descriptions of events like the Island Art Fair and Yankee Doodle Days.

Seth pulled up to a parking space in Fitzgerald Park. Through the windshield I could see a wide, grassy expanse, a playground, a large red building, and a paved path that led off through some scattered maple trees. Other than a father and his young daughter on the swings, this park was deserted on a chilly early April day. Seth got out first and led the way walking down the path. Sun spilled down onto the trail, impeded only slightly by the still-bare trees.

Seth wasted this walk on me. We could have gone to the mall or just sat in the driveway.

"What happened when you found Trish today?" Seth asked, as we approached a set of wooden stairs and railing winding down a steep embankment.

I steadied myself on the rail. Debated what to tell him. Decided it didn't matter what I told him. It wasn't my secret to tell, nor was it mine to keep.

So as we picked our careful way down, I told him about our mother's secret baby, Trish's pained reaction as if she'd felt it herself, echoing her own, different, loss. How Aunt Margaret, our grandparents, hid this from us all these years.

"Are you all right? Finding this out?"

"I guess so. My life is still the same." As I said it, a stair seemed to dip away below my feet and I stumbled. Seth seized my elbow from just behind me as a gasp escaped before I could help it.

"Is it?" he asked, releasing my elbow as I straightened up and brushed off my clothes, though I hadn't actually fallen.

I stared at the faulty stair, meeting Seth's eyes and looking down at it again so he'd see that it was angled wrong, that it was just a faulty step, not some deep subconscious freak-out. "I don't know," I said, continuing to walk. "Knowing the 'why' doesn't change the facts of the matter."

"You have a half sister out there."

"A stranger to me, though. We have some genes in common, but so do Trish and I, and look how we get along."

At the bottom of the staircase, he turned right, and we followed a dirt path along the riverbank for a few yards. I stopped short at a bridge over a branch of river. The concrete surface was bordered on either side with rusty pipe railings, which seemed too low to be useful. They were only hip height, and the bridge was narrow enough I could easily touch each railing without even straightening my arms. Across the bridge I could see a densely wooded path.

I said, "Why are we here again?"

"I thought you needed a break, and Trish needed some privacy."

"We could have just sat in the yard."

"I wanted to talk to you. When you weren't hauling boxes or preparing to dash into the trailer and hide."

"I don't hide in there," I answered, too quickly.

"I didn't want you to go into your trailer last night. I wanted to keep talking to you. And I was thinking about you the whole way home. And when I went to sleep. And this morning."

"I must be quite a complicated puzzle then."

I started to recognize how stupid I looked, standing there at the edge of this bridge and not moving. I crossed quickly, chin high, straight ahead. The river was glassy with stillness. Ahead of me was one of the sandstone rock formations, soaring high above my head, crowding the narrow trail. Moss, lichen, and even trees grew impossibly out of chinks in the stone. There was a narrow crevasse in the rock that looked small enough for a child, or thin adult, to slip through.

Seth had caught up to me and we resumed walking. "Well, maybe you are, but I wasn't trying to solve you. We've hardly said two words that weren't about Trish's house, or boxes, or cleaning products. I just wanted to talk."

"You're talking to me now." The sun was behind the rocks, and I wanted my warm coat.

"Even you aren't *that* literal, Mary."

I didn't reply. For a time we walked in silence, the path occasionally narrowed by a rock formation jutting out over the path, forcing us to walk single file. Once, Seth extended his hand behind him, and I stared briefly at his open palm before I took it, only long enough that we passed the rocks. On the river side of the trail, there were often steep drops right down to the brown water. Seth stopped to look at a maple tree, whose winding roots tumbled, naked to the air, down the rocky side of the embankment.

"This is like something out of Middle Earth," I said.

"I thought you'd seen it before?"

"I thought I had. I don't remember it being so . . . impossible. How is that tree even still there? Barely hanging on?"

Seth took a step closer to me, and I straightened up, tensed.

"Why are you doing that?" he asked. In the silence after his question I heard the clear twittering of birdsong. "Why do you always do that?"

"Is it Dr. Seth asking, or just you?"

"Just me."

"I don't know."

I moved on before he could ask me something else. He followed me down the path until we came to a railroad trestle soaring above us. The spindly structure of the trestle looked hardly strong enough to hold up a train, though I understood it obviously must. I hoped a train wouldn't rumble over, even so. Seth teetered his way down a slight rocky slope, toward the river.

"Come on," he said, holding his hand out again. I looked down at the stones, which did not seem to be meant for human travel. "What's the worst that could happen?"

I almost laughed at his question. With my mother dead in an inferno and his own daughter struck with autism, he should know better than to ask.

I shrugged to fake a normal person's casual attitude. With my hand in his, I picked my way down, feeling the muscles in his palm tensing to keep me balanced, until I reached a small level spot of rocky shore next to the sleepy, still river.

He did not let go despite my gentle tug back. He looked away from me, smiling at the scenery, still keeping my hand. It wasn't a fierce grip, nor was it light. "Isn't it pretty?"

"It looks like decay to me." Dead trees leaned over in the water like fallen men.

"Why are you so nervous?" he asked.

"I'm not nervous." I raised my eyes from the muddy water to meet his.

"What would happen if you let me get closer?" He stepped closer. "What do you think is so terrible about being close?"

He smelled good. Musky and spicy. I could feel his warmth, or maybe I just imagined it.

But as he closed the space between us again, my heartbeat felt labored, my breathing shallowed.

I jumped back, stumbling on a root or stone. "It's . . . too much."

"Too much what?"

"I don't know." I felt as if I'd just stepped back from a precipice. I scrambled back up the rocks, having to use my hands like a child climbing on a playground. Stones and pebbles slid away under my feet.

"Mary!" Seth called, his voice sharp with warning, or maybe reprimand.

"Is it such a huge strain to let me stand near you?" he asked breathlessly, scrambling back up the riverbank to join me where I stood on the path, arms folded tightly. "Why would that be?"

"I thought you were trying to be human," I retorted, walking briskly away from him.

He caught up to me with his long, quick strides. "I'm sorry," he said. "I didn't mean—"

"We should be getting back."

I led the way back to the car, and he walked just behind. Now and then I'd look back, making sure he was still there.

S eth and I returned to find the occupants of the house quiet and separate, like a tableau.

Ron and Jack were watching cartoons on the couch, nestled together. My father was repairing some piece of trim in Trish's dining room. Drew was nowhere.

Seth offered to help my dad, and I went off to find my sister.

I discovered her in the hall, stacking the things our father had torn down earlier.

I bent down to help her, and for a few moments we just stacked in silence.

"Where is the diary?" she asked.

"In my purse. It's safe."

She pushed some rows of things back into the room. "We'll have to move this before tonight. Ayana's coming back and she wants to see 'total freedom of movement.' "

"What is it, anyway? All this?"

"Right here, it's art supplies," Trish answered through a sigh. "Remember when I used to be an artist?"

I almost replied automatically she still was, but I caught myself in a rare moment of clarity about how that would sound to her: condescending, false.

I glanced into the room. It had big windows. With all the things gone, it would probably have nice light. "What if this became your studio?"

"One thing at a time."

"Seth thinks you could use some help. Not from him, that wouldn't be appropriate—"

Trish snorted. "I should say not."

"—but he can refer you to somebody."

Trish sat back from her crouched position, settling on the floor. "I'm already getting 'help.' Some state-contracted shrink. I had to sit through three hours of stupid tests and quizzes and analyzing chitchat last week."

"Oh. I didn't know."

"You didn't need to. It's embarrassing enough as it is, being forced into this. You know if they decide I need drugs, they will make me take them? Or refer my case to a judge? What kind of world is this?"

"Is it possible meds would help? I mean, maybe it wouldn't be so bad . . ."

"God, just shut up, Mary."

I let it go and switched to our other, newer problem.

"What are we going to do about . . . Laura?"

"What about her?"

"Should we . . . try to find her? Or something?"

Trish tipped her head to the side and rolled her eyes at me. "And tell her what. Hey, guess what, we found you! Only your mother died in a fire and was a lifelong hoarder because of the pain of giving you up. Welcome to the family!" she finished with exaggerated, mean-spirited cheer.

"I hate it when you do that. When you take what I say and exaggerate it to extremes to make me sound stupid."

"I made my point, didn't I?"

"I'm going to call Aunt Margaret. I want to hear what she has to say about it."

Trish rolled her eyes again, and I wanted to kick her. "Yeah, good luck with that. I'm sure she'll pour her heart out to you and give you every detail."

"I'm surprised you aren't curious."

Trish groaned. "Mary, I've got all I can handle right here. OK, so now we know. Leave it alone."

"Because that strategy has worked out so brilliantly already."

Trish jerked her head at me, and before I walked away I caught a glimpse of her openmouthed shock.

No wonder Trish was so fond of sarcasm. It brought a type of spiteful pleasure, akin to kicking a broken appliance.

I emerged into the living room to hear my phone ringing in my purse. I fished for it and looked at the caller ID. My apartment complex manager?

"Hello?" I said, wary and worried.

"Mary, I'm glad I could reach you. I'm afraid there's been a break-in."

"What?"

"You've been away for a while it seems, and . . . Well, someone broke in. We need you to come back and assess what's missing for the police."

My stomach began churning. "When did it happen?"

"Not sure. Your neighbor noticed your door ajar and contacted us."

I agreed to come back and hung up, then called to the first person who sprang to mind. "Seth!"

Chapter 45

I let Ron tuck in Jack. Listening to him read a story to his son made me want to cry and slap him at the same time. The sweetness of it made me want to cry, but then again he's the one who abandoned us. He's the reason I never got to hear him read to our boy anymore.

After Mary and Seth fled to inspect the damage to her town house, and Dad was convinced—with great reluctance on his part—to return home instead of trailing them to Ypsilanti to hover over the local cops, I collapsed on my couch and grabbed the remote, trying to sink into television.

Instead I shut it off and listened to Ron's voice with that rural twang trip over the funny names in a Harry Potter book. I kept murmuring the correct pronunciations to myself, which I knew because Jack and I had started watching the movies together.

So far Jack was not objecting to sleeping in there alone. Ron reported that when Jack stayed with him he had his own room, so maybe having his father tuck him in was the trick. Not that he could do this every night. Perhaps I shouldn't have let Ron do it at all; perhaps Jack will be confused now, thinking his dad is coming home. Life is confusing enough for the grown-ups who supposedly understand these things.

And speaking of confusion, it seemed we had a half sister now, out there somewhere. I'd believed all along that diary would reveal something I'd rather not know. But know it I did, and in reflecting on mother's pain in this, an old memory rose up out of the mists.

I sat up on the couch. *No wonder,* I thought. *No fricking wonder.*

When I'd told her about my pregnancy by Greg, she'd seemed stricken as one would expect a mother to feel for a twenty-two-year-old daughter living alone in a crummy apartment with a data entry job and few marketable skills beyond typing and answering a phone. We were sitting in my apartment in fact. I'd asked her to come over, pacing with the phone in one hand and the pregnancy test in the other. Stringing beads into pretty necklaces—my artistic attempt at a career—would hardly support a baby, and I believed her distress to be related to that fear: How would we get by? Not to mention the moral failing of my actions, though Mother never was one to judge such things harshly.

But when I wondered aloud whether I should give the baby up, to some other couple who wanted a child, she grabbed my hand in both of hers so hard it hurt. "Don't you dare," she'd said, her hazel eyes filming over with tears behind her large round glasses. "I don't care if I have to sell everything I own to support you, that child is my flesh and blood as much as yours."

I assured her I had no such plan, I was just thinking out loud, just scared, just wondering. The outburst had seemed overly strident, considering the circumstances, but in a moment or two I'd explained it away to myself: she'd simply wanted to know her grandchild.

But now. Now I understood. And nothing would seem simple again.

My front door swung open, and Drew sloped in, his eyes looking red under all that black. Bizarrely, his eyeliner was smudged. I couldn't wait for him to grow out of that stupidity.

"Look what the cat dragged in," I said, noticing it was hours later than he said he'd be. He'd missed out on the pizza, and the hockey game he was going to watch with Ron would be nearly over by now.

Drew came over and plopped down next to me. Not on the other side of the couch, but right next to me. Then he stunned me by leaning over and resting his head on my shoulder. He had to slouch dramatically sideways to do it, being so tall.

"Honey?" I asked.

"We broke up."

I turned to face him, and he let me hug him, awkward and sideways, as he rested his head on my shoulder. "I'm so sorry," I said, because I was sorry, though I never liked Miranda and had honestly been hoping for this day. But you never want to see your children hurt, even for their own good. I cried over their flu shots, too.

"What happened?"

"I don't want you to feel guilty."

"OK," I said, drawing the word out, prompting him to go on.

He sat back from me a bit, leaning sideways on the couch. He looked past me as if to see out the front window, though the light was failing and there was little to see but shadow.

"She started out saying she was sorry that she couldn't stay and help, and then she started carrying on about how weird you were, and how gross the house was, and I'm, like, really? This is my mom and you're gonna say this shit to me? So I called her on it. I told her that's not cool, that I know you've got problems, but still. So then she said it's more than just 'problems' and she's worried I'll turn out weird, too. And then I got kinda upset and said some things I shouldn't have."

I couldn't find the right words. How could I not take this personally? I wanted to wring her delicate little freckled neck.

"Oh, Drew," I said.

"I told her that people in glass houses shouldn't throw stones, because her sister is, like, ninety-five pounds and eats nothing but carrots and cottage cheese and everyone acts like it's totally normal. And how her dad goes through, like, six beers every single night."

"Wow."

"Yeah, wow, so who is she to talk? So, yeah, that didn't go over well

and she broke up with me." He laughed darkly. "For 'not being supportive.' Ha."

I reached over to smooth his hair. I couldn't reach it most of the
time, and I found myself surprised by its softness.

He shrugged, moved his head away from my hand. "I don't know
what she saw in a loser freak like me anyway."

At this I lunged forward for another hug. "You are not. At all. Don't
let that prissy brat make you feel that way. You're a straight A kid and a
whiz at computers and you're funny and caring and she's an airheaded
idiot who wants life to be like *Glamour* magazine. Tell Molly Ringwald
to go to hell."

"Who?"

"She was this actress . . . I always thought Miranda looked . . . oh,
forget it. Someday we'll watch *The Breakfast Club*. I think you'd like it.
And *Heathers*. We should definitely watch *Heathers*. You're more of a
Winona Ryder kind of kid anyway."

"Who?"

I realized he was teasing me when I noticed a little tuck in the side
of his cheek. I shoved him playfully, and we both laughed.

"Yeah, Mom, I know who they are. I've seen *The Breakfast Club* and
I do like it." He started singing the song from the movie. *"Don't you . . .
forget about me . . ."*

I sighed and smiled at him, basking in the echo of his laughter.
"Don't worry. I couldn't possibly."

Chapter 46

Seth put a hand lightly on my shoulder as I pushed open the door to my town house. Kitchen drawers were gaping open. My DVDs littered the floor. The television was gone. But none of that stopped me in my tracks like the muddy footprints across my carpet. The thought of someone else's hands pawing across my items, ripping open my drawers . . . I shivered and my stomach roiled.

Seth was stroking my shoulder with his hand. I walked out from under his touch and drifted down my hall, wincing as I approached my bedroom. My closet was standing open, clothing torn down and scattered. My books lay like battlefield casualties. My jewelry box was in the center of my bed, its contents spilled around it. I lunged for it, started sifting through the contents.

"Oh, God. No. No, no, no."

Seth settled himself carefully next to me. I could sense him trying to meet my eyes, but I couldn't look away from what I knew to be missing.

"Oh, God. They took it."

"What?"

"Mother's ring." I put my hand over my eyes. "Trish will kill me. She wanted it, but our father gave it to me. It was one of the few things rescued from the fire. He said Mom had wanted me to have it and Trish would never believe him. Now that it's gone she'll hate me even more."

"It wasn't your fault."

"It won't matter."

It felt like a pop inside my chest. Sudden and small, the cracking of a twig. Followed by an upwelling of pressure. I was a balloon, stretched ever more thin.

My wailing and sobbing sounded bizarre in my own ears. If I wasn't feeling the sobs clogging my throat, my hot tears burning my eyes, I wouldn't even think it was me making this noise. I felt myself rocking, which I must have been doing under my own power but that felt alien, too.

The mattress swayed as Seth joined me on my bed, sweeping aside the remains of my cheap costume jewelry, wrapping his arms around me. He said nothing, but rocked with me, holding me, as I let this emotion consume me, wondering at what I'd become.

I startled awake to everything feeling strange and wrong, and nearly screamed.

Then the nighttime amnesia vanished, and I remembered all of it. Trish's house, the clean-out, Seth, the break-in, Mother's ring.

Seth was stretched next to me. He was on his back, one arm thrown up over his head. We'd lain down—or melted down, almost—as my crying receded, wordlessly curling up together, clothed, on top of the covers. We did not speak as we let exhaustion overtake us.

I couldn't help but remember the only other time I'd seen him sleep, when he came to our dormitory looking for his recent ex-girlfriend, and I let him sleep off his drunk on the couch.

We'd come together in crisis—his breakup, my mother's funeral, Trish's hoard. I wondered if this pattern would repeat itself, and how often. That when my current disaster was smoothed over—somehow it would and some sort of equilibrium would return—he would go back to his own life and his patients and having his daughter on alternate weekends. We'd be back to our postcards and annual, lighthearted calls.

It was something, I supposed. To have such a good friend that he would fly to your side in need.

I watched his face, smooth in repose, and remembered the intensity of his stare in the park as he asked me why it was so hard for him to be close. Now, I wondered, more to the point, why he wanted to be close to me. Why anyone would want to.

The memory of Seth in the park today prodded another memory, this one older, and blurry with nostalgia. It was the day after his father's heart attack, and Rebecca had not yet arrived back to college from her trip. Seth was working in the student bookstore then, and on my way to grab a sandwich in town I'd stopped at the store to drop off a photocopied magazine article I'd found about technology improving longevity for heart attack survivors. He took his break when I got there, and we sat outside on a bench, as Ann Arbor paraded by. It was a windy day, I remember, and my hair was already a nest of snarls from my bike ride over.

He scanned the article, then folded it carefully, and tucked it into his jeans pocket. He turned to me with a wan smile, catching me in the act of spitting my hair out of my mouth. He reached up and tucked it behind my ear for me. I was reaching at the same time, and our hands brushed.

I chuckled and put my hands back in my lap, and the wind whipped my hair in front of my face again. I had to turn away from him to free myself from the tangle, to let the wind blow my hair behind me. In my turning away, something switched off that I hadn't noticed until just then. There was a warmth I'd been feeling, in his presence, and when he'd brushed my hand.

I heard him stand up, and I stood up, too, and he waved good-bye and went back to work.

Our parting was so casual I assumed I'd imagined that feeling, simply conjured it out of desperate loneliness, considering I'd found that magazine article in the first place while studying in the library on a

Saturday night, while everyone else was out drinking, dating, and having sex.

Now, here on my bed, drowsiness was creeping up on me again. I allowed myself a few sleepy moments to recall the pleasant sensation of his hand brushing mine, without actually reaching over to touch him, in the darkness of my room.

W hen I awoke, Seth was looking at me.

The daylight was muted, as if through fog. He had sleep creases in his bald head, which, despite it all, made me smile.

"Hi," he said. Then more seriously, dropping the smile, "Are you OK?"

"Yes."

"Are you sure?"

I considered. "No. But right now, yes."

He reached out to me, and with the gentlest touch I'd ever felt, like the brush of dandelion fluff, he moved a strand of hair away from my eyes. I did not flinch or shrink back. He said, "I'm sorry this happened to you."

"I'll live."

"Can I talk like a shrink for a minute?"

"If you must."

"Don't deny how you're feeling. Let it happen, reckon with it, acknowledge it. Even with the mess, I can see how ordered your place was. This must feel like a significant violation."

I rolled to my back, looking at my ugly popcorn ceiling and considering. Yes, violation would be the word for the first feeling as I crossed the threshold. Then a powerful sense of loss at the absence of Mother's ring.

I tried to put the violation and loss aside for the practical consideration of toothpaste and a hairbrush, but the feelings trailed me like little ghosts all through my morning routine.

Seth steadied me with a hand at the small of my back as I again regarded my living room in the muted daylight. Outside the sky was a pale, unambitious gray, as if the weak and early springtime couldn't be bothered to conjure up a genuine storm.

"It's pathetic," I said at last.

"What is?"

"This actually looks like a huge mess, but it's not. Push the drawers back in, put the DVDs back into the cabinet. Clean the carpet." I laughed bitterly. "Except for the ring, I had almost nothing of value worth stealing and not enough things to make for a genuine ransacking."

"It doesn't even look like you put up any pictures."

I pointed to a Georgia O'Keeffe print over where the television used to be. "I always liked that. But it's not very original, I know . . ."

"Why didn't you make this space your own?"

"Don't analyze me right now."

"Can't I just ask a simple question?"

I turned away from the wreckage to stare at him. "I don't know. Can't you?"

"Not everything I say has an agenda."

"Everyone has an agenda, don't they? Everything has a secret meaning, every dream means something. . . . Maybe I just like it neat, OK? Maybe I just don't like to put holes in the walls that I'll have to spackle over later. Maybe I don't like snapshots and maybe I don't have any. My work was my life and you don't go around taking pictures at work."

"Why are you angry at me?"

"Why are you interrogating me?"

"I'm not."

"You're not *just asking,* either."

"I care about you. And I worry about you."

"Well, stop. I'm the sane one, remember. I'm glad you stayed with me, glad you . . ." Instantly, the memory of Seth embracing me, of us drifting off together on my bed, filled me with queasy discomfort, in the same way as the memory of an awful mistake. "I'm glad you were there for me. I thank you. But I'm fine."

"You shouldn't deny—"

"Stop!" I shouted. "Leave it alone. God, I know how your wife felt."

The atmosphere shifted. I could almost smell the air go septic. "I'm sorry. I didn't mean that."

Seth was still, looking down at my carpet. I dared not speak; I'd said so much wrong already, so much wrong in my clumsy life.

Mute, he walked to my DVDs and began stacking them. He was neither gentle nor rough with them, nor did he look at me.

I could go to him. I could walk over and apologize, embrace him.

But the rigid set of his shoulders told me I'd done too much damage already.

I walked to the kitchen and began stacking flatware back in their spaces, letting the clicking of objects fill the silence between us.

Chapter 47

yana almost danced when she saw my house. She clapped her hands like a delighted little girl and then made to hug me.

I stepped back. Good for her to be happy and all, but I had a limited store of affection for bureaucrats with the power to get my children removed from my care.

"Jack slept in his room last night, too," I said. I saw Ayana start to speak, and I put one hand over my heart, the other in the air. "Hand to God. On my mother's soul."

She nodded, and I knew she'd ask Jack anyway. She had her job to do, and I'd already lied to her last time.

"OK, so that's the good news," I told her. "But it's not all good."

I beckoned Ayana to follow me, and I showed her the Room.

"Oh, my," she said. "Yes, I remember this from the first day. Some of the items look like they've been disturbed.

"You have a very good memory. I had a hard time yesterday when some of my family moved some things in here. Roughly. I got very upset and I ran off for a bit. But there were adults here to take care of the children, and I came back. You need to know that."

She was writing. I hated it when she wrote. "Thank you for telling me, Mrs. Dietrich," she said.

I sighed. "You can call me Trish," I allowed, tiring of hearing Ron's mother's name. "We're going to do this room. But later." I looked her hard in the eye. "It took years to get this way. And there's pain buried in there. I can't just grab it all out of here at once."

"No one expects perfection, Mrs. . . . Trish. We just want progress."

"So you've said."

"Do you mind telling me what kind of pain?"

"Yes, I mind."

"I hope you will discuss this with your psychologist."

I snorted.

"You'll need to be forthcoming and cooperative. I know it's unpleasant, difficult work, but it's necessary."

"Why is it *necessary* for me to be mentally dissected? It's not good enough for you that I cleaned all this shit up?"

"What if it all came back? After all this effort, what if it happened again?"

I leaned against the wall, and in my mind I watched a movie of my mother's home filling up on fast-forward, even faster than before the Florida trip.

That was different, I tried to tell myself, knowing it wasn't so different as soon as my brain formed the thought.

I sighed. "Everyone's pushing me so hard all the time. I'm so tired."

"I know you are," she said, reaching out to touch my elbow. Her hand felt absurdly light and thin, like a bird wing. "That's why I want you to have some support."

I heard her drawl slip in on the word *support* and wondered where she came from, what she herself had left behind. She was trying to hide it with her professionalism and her trench coat and messenger bag, I knew. But it would sneak out now and then, despite her best efforts.

"Where are you from, Ayana, if I may ask?"

"Detroit," she said.

"Where in Detroit?" I asked. Some suburban types would say Detroit when they meant Farmington Hills.

She cocked an eyebrow at me. "Detroit," she answered again.

She offered to help me sort in that room and I declined. Instead Ayana made arrangements for the charity truck to come get the things we'd purged so far, and for the trash company to come empty the Dumpster and start new. I hadn't admitted that I'd lost my job though I imagined she'd figure it out. She was sharp, I'd give her that. Young, but sharp.

"Bye, Miss Ayana!" called Jack from the kitchen table where he'd been eating a late breakfast. He'd woken up disappointed not to find his dad here, and I reminded him the magic wand wasn't real. Ron had stayed for a while and we'd talked, but we only talked, and he left the house with a simple wave, just like a friend would.

But before that, he finally told me how he grieved the baby we didn't get to have. How he'd drive out into the woods and sit, smoking, and sometimes he'd drink, too, until he swerved his truck nearly off the road one time and took to making sure to leave the beer at home.

So all the errands he was running back then had nothing to do with needing more milk, or a part for his truck. He could have told me, but then I didn't talk to him, either. We stood on either side of a widening sinkhole and watched each other get closer to its crumbling edge.

I listened for sounds from Drew's room, hearing no stirring yet. He was still sleeping, in that hibernating way teenagers can sleep for hours upon hours. Together we'd tossed stuff off his bed and forged a path through shopping bags, changed the sheets. It wasn't pretty, but it would do. I'd vowed to finish his room, to make space for him in my life, not just in my heart.

Now I allowed myself a moment to savor the house looking almost like it used to, with both kids where they belonged.

I noticed some papers scattered on the coffee table and scooped them up, starting to pile them on the kitchen counter—no. I have to sort, not just stack and ignore. One was about Jack's school carnival and I set it in my wicker basket for school reports. The others went straight to the kitchen recycle bin.

"Good job, Mom," said Jack with a mouthful of Froot Loops.

"Thanks, pal. Don't talk with food in your mouth."

"I'm not perfect!" he said, garbled around his half-chewed breakfast.

"Me neither, kiddo."

T wo hours later, Mary and Seth walked in as I was scrambling up an egg for Drew, who was by then hunched at the kitchen table, scowling at his phone, his hair still crazy with recent sleep. "She's texting me," he said, punching the screen with his thumb, I hoped hitting Delete.

When I saw Mary's face, I knew it was bad.

"What?" I demanded.

"They took Mother's ring."

The spatula fell out of my hand. I was betrayed when Father gave it to Mary, but at least it was in the family. Gone?

"Why didn't you have it hidden? Locked away? Or, I don't know, wear the damn thing like she meant something to you?"

Mary clenched her fists and pursed her lips, looking an awful lot like our prissy aunt Margaret just then. She started to turn around and I made to pick up the spatula, but then she whirled back and advanced on me, jerking her finger at me like I never could stand for her to do.

"She did mean something to me, and stop accusing me of having no feelings just because I didn't fill my house with garbage and go screaming into the woods."

"Mary . . ." Seth said.

"Shut up!" we sisters chorused.

"So that's how it is," I shot back. "Despite all my progress, that's how you're going to define me."

Mary grabbed the sides of her head. "Arrrrgh, just like with Mom, it's always about you. Like you're the only one who ever has problems."

"I didn't say I'm the only one, but I'm tired of being treated like the freak."

"And I'm treated normally? You have so much contempt for me I'm surprised you even bothered to let me help you. But you were desperate. Last-Resort Mary. And now I've helped you clean out your house—except, of course, the most important room—you're done with me. How convenient."

"Who said I'm done with you? I'm pissed at you over the ring."

"It's not about the ring! It never was. It's about you playing the victim and the martyr so we all feel sorry for you and no one ever confronts you, just like with Mom; all she had to do was cry and we'd all go to pieces trying to make her feel better. And look how much good that did."

"I don't have to play the victim when everyone attacks me. It's not playing then, Mary."

"So helping you is attacking you, but we leave you alone and then we're shunning you."

"How about treating me like normal, huh? No helping, no shunning, just like normal?"

"Because you're not normal!"

Sizzling and burning drew my attention. The egg was now blackened. A fire alarm started shrilling. Jack came screaming out of his room, and for several minutes there was the chaos of bashing off alarms until they stopped and comforting a startled boy.

While Seth tried to scrape the egg out of the pan I saw Mary shaking her head and walking out the door.

"Where are you going?" I asked her, following her out.

She paused in front of the trailer. "Most of the house is clean. You're not keen to do the last room, and you wouldn't want me helping in there even if you ever decide to deal with it. So I'm packing up to leave, and you're welcome."

"Now who's being a martyr?"

She slammed the door shut on the camper, but it swung back open again. As she banged it shut again, I caught a glimpse of her face, snarled up as if in pain, or anger.

Seth had appeared behind me and walked to the trailer to knock.

"Go away!" Mary called, sounding like a bratty preteen.

"It's Seth," he called, his voice full of hope, almost a question.

"Not now," she called out.

Seth stood there on the other side of the door, arms limp at his sides, hanging his head. When I walked back in to finish Drew's breakfast, he was still standing there on the other side of her door.

Don't hold your breath, I thought. *We're all on the outside.*

Chapter 48

In the end, I called a maid service to clean the place up.

Each time I tried to bend down to scrub the carpet, I would retch to imagine a filthy stranger—in my mind's eye he was grubby, long-bearded, cackling like a crazy person—touching my things. It felt like he was touching me.

I had just enough energy for introspection to realize this connection between self and objects was something in common with Trish. But not enough energy to call her and tell her about it. She had cast me aside, again, just like when we were teenagers and I moved out, just like after the funeral.

So that's how I found myself sitting again alone at my kitchen table, everything back to normal except for a potted plant where my television used to be. I prepared to make another round of job searches online, with no hope whatsoever. It's a lot of work to hope, after all.

Seth had gone back to his sabbatical, doing whatever it was he was doing before. When I'd packed my bag to leave Trish's house, he was standing on the other side of the trailer, knocking to be let in, but I couldn't bear it. Every nerve was jangling, every inch of my skin felt prickly and hot. He later left me a voice mail, asking how I was. His voice sounded cool, professional. I replied by text I was fine. He asserted that he, too, was fine. Ayana seemed to be fine with the progress Trish had made.

Jack's arm was fine, too, I was told later via text from Drew.

We were all just gloriously fine.

Before I clicked on the online want ads, my mouse arrow aimed at another bookmark I'd made: an adoption registry. It was the most passive form of attempted reunion there could be. You just had to fill in a profile and wait to be found. Or you could search other profiles, to see if your relative had already sent out her own version of a note in a bottle, cast into the cybersea.

I had not, as yet, filled out a profile of my own. This Laura person could end up being just another relative to argue with and feel awkward about, more so because we'd lived wholly separate lives. And, as Trish had pointed out, it's not like we would come bearing such wonderful news. It also seemed hopeless with the little information we had. On one site alone, dedicated to Michigan, over three thousand adoptees and parents were trying to find each other.

Yet I'd looked up this information. And there it remained, on my computer.

I had also called Aunt Margaret, which turned out as badly as Trish had predicted, and worse yet. At first she denied knowing what I was talking about, until I started reciting bits from the diary that were too detailed, too personal for me to have made up. Then she seemed to get angry with my late mother for leaving this, as she put it, "shameful record."

Then she'd relented, at last. I took grim satisfaction in how difficult it was for her to speak about it.

"We just didn't know anything else to do," she insisted to me. I would not give her the satisfaction of agreeing with her, or making sympathetic noises, so she went on. "It wasn't like it is now, where it's less of a problem, where there are programs and education and such. You didn't raise a bastard child yourself. You made another couple happy and that was that. I didn't know . . ." Here she made sort of a strangled, coughing noise. "I hadn't had my own children yet. I didn't know what it was like to carry a child. I was just a kid, and it wasn't my decision."

Here I thought, *No, but you certainly relished your position as the favored, virginal daughter.*

"And she seemed to be fine, Frannie did. She went to work in a steno pool, and then she met your father on a blind date and she seemed to be a contented bride, and she was a very good mother to you girls. And none of that would have happened if she'd kept the baby. Remember that before you go and judge us. You would not even be here to judge me." She paused, and I thought I heard her breathing hard into the phone. I wondered if she'd imagined this conversation before. If somehow she knew we'd find out and she'd prepared her defense in advance. She was probably right, I thought. I doubt anyone would have set my father up on a blind date with a single mother in the 1960s.

She wasn't going to say anything else, so I continued. "Yet you never told a soul. Even as Mother started hoarding."

"That had nothing to do with the baby. Your mother was always emotionally fragile, very excitable."

This did not sound like the mother I knew. To us, when Mother wasn't fighting with one of us about the hoarding, she was solid as a rock. Maybe because of the hoarding. Because that was the way she coped.

"Even after she died, you never said a word."

"Why would I? And she'd sworn me to secrecy."

"She had? Or your parents had?"

"We all swore to keep it a secret."

"Yes, and stuff her down in the backseat so no one would know."

"I tell you I was just a kid, too! Our parents, rest their souls, did the best they knew how to do. It wasn't our fault your mother opened her legs on prom night."

Here I'd made some sort of shocked noise.

"Well, it's true. This wasn't a lightning bolt out of the sky. It happened because she had sex out of wedlock."

Without any preamble, I repeated the story of that fateful night, about how that boy kissed her so hard she couldn't speak and was inside her before she knew what was happening.

Margaret cleared her throat. "Well. That was some detail she never shared with her sister."

"Would it have mattered? Or would you have blamed her anyway?"

"I don't know." And then again, softer: "I don't know."

Before we hung up, I pried the name of the unwed mothers' home out of her.

And with this information I sat as spring gathered strength and daffodils gave way to tulips, and the forsythia exploded in yellow then faded into its stately rich green, each day passing with neither Trish nor I picking up the phone.

I was filling out an application for a retail manager position at a clothing store when my house phone rang. I'd taken to screening the few calls I got.

I glanced casually at the caller ID, then seized the phone.

"Yes?"

"Mary Granger? This is Officer Sherman."

"Yes! Did you find the thief?"

"No, ma'am, but I believe we found the ring at a pawnshop. Could you come identify it, please?"

I ran out the door so fast I had to come back for my purse. And my shoes.

I drove straight to Trish's house, hands shaking on the wheel, with a wide smile on my face. They'd found the ring. It was indeed hers.

It was Mother's wedding ring, and engraved inside, thus unmistakable. And it was going to Trish. It had nothing to do with any deal we made earlier, but only to do with a powerful and rare intuition that I needed to drive there, right this minute, and give it to her. I'd never felt more sure of anything, and this confidence made me giddy.

I rolled the window down and listened to classic rock on the way.

I was struck with another impulse. I punched Off on the radio and used speakerphone to call Seth. Voice mail, but I sang out to his phone: "Seth! They found the ring! I had to tell you. No one else will get how much this means to me. I'm driving to Trish's house right now to give it to her." I paused, realizing I had no exit strategy for the message. "Well. Bye then."

Trish's car was in the drive. I realized I'd forgotten what day it was, the calendar rendered moot in the world of the unemployed.

As I stood on her porch and waited for her to answer the bell, I bounced on the balls of my feet.

She yanked open the door hard, the gesture already advertising irritation, frustration. My giddiness popped like a child's soap bubble, my presumption looming huge.

She froze with her hand on the door, gaping at me.

"What the hell are you doing here?"

Chapter 49

I walked along a twisting path through the clutter, until I reached the inner sanctum of the room in which I'd tried to bury it all. Now it had been exposed to the air, and despite closing the door, I could no longer pretend it didn't exist.

So each day when the boys headed out—Drew in his beat-up noisy car, Jack dropped off at school—I'd allow myself to be pulled inside, too weary from all those years of stuffed-down emotion to resist. In the back of the room was the crib, in the exact spot Ron had set it up all those years ago, when I was young and fertile and happy.

I ran my hand along the plastic guard on the top rail, remembering how first baby Andrew, then Jack, had teethed on it. We'd put the crib up in an early burst of nesting, a whirlwind at twelve weeks along when we'd gotten encouraging results back on a test called AFP, which showed a likelihood of a strong, healthy baby. I already had an adorable baby bump, and everything seemed fine, so I set Ron to the task of assembling while I started shopping in earnest. I went out and bought baby outfits, both for a boy and a girl, keeping the receipts. I bought a brand-new yellow baby blanket and draped it in the crib. There were duckies parading around the edge of it. I'd lugged in bag after bag of diapers, nipples, stuffed animals, wanting new things for this baby, not just hand-me-downs. This baby would not get stuck with a bunch of leftovers like poor Jack had to deal with: faded, worn-out things Drew had worn years before.

Then the active baby seemed to slow down and stop moving. And the ultrasound tech got those grim lines on her face. And I slammed the door to this room, opening it only to throw things inside.

And now, I was looking at those duckies again. To my left was a baby swing. Scattered around my feet were unopened packages of pacifiers, diapers, clothes—all those things I'd bought in a frenzy back then, feeling secure in the second trimester, the odds on my side.

Ayana and my state shrink say I should stop living so much in the past, to enjoy my children in the present. And I have tried, especially now that I can see *both* their faces at the table every day. I even promised Jack that when I find a permanent job we can see about getting a dog, though that means he has taken an unhealthy and irritating interest in my job hunt, which so far has only resulted in part-time temp work filling in for a lady on maternity leave at Michigan State.

Drew has developed his own unhealthy interest in my habits: asking me every day about my cleaning progress. I choked down my outrage, reminding myself that I drove him out in the first place; this is his home too. I cast myself back to my own teen years, with garbage all over the front yard, all the inner surfaces.

The doorbell rang and yanked my attention back to the present moment. I ignored the first chime, staying with the crib, but the evangelist or salesman stubbornly leaned on the bell. I cursed and stomped back to the front of the house.

And I yanked open the door to find my sister, of all people.

Her hair looked ragged and overly long. She was wearing plaid shorts, plastic flip-flops, and a top that didn't match. But she was grinning at me like a lunatic.

"What the hell do you want?" I asked.

By way of answer she rummaged in her purse and stuck something so close to my face I had to grab her wrist and back away so my eyes could focus.

The ring.

It had been years since I'd seen it, and it had been on Mom's finger then, before the divorce. I'd written it off twice: first in the fire, and recently with the theft.

"I'm glad they found it," I said, not taking it from her fingers, wanting to shove her off my porch for flaunting this at me.

"It's yours."

"Be serious."

"I am."

"You look like a nutcase, frankly."

"I feel like one, a bit. Something told me I had to drive here and give this to you now."

I raised a brow at her, wondering if I should take her pulse or have her breathe into a paper bag.

"Something told you? How very unspecific of you."

Mary's maniac grin was melting away. "You don't want it."

I sighed. "I don't know anymore. Come in, anyway, as long as you're here."

Mary refused to budge, still holding that ring at the end of her outstretched arm. "Please, take it."

I did then. I'd never worn it when Mom was alive, and then Dad gave it to Mary. So for the first time I slipped it on. Mom had put on weight in later years—who hadn't?—and it had been resized. It fit on only my middle finger. I walked back into the house and headed toward my bedroom and my jewelry box. I heard Mary close my front door and follow.

Halfway down the hall I noticed Mary's footsteps had stopped. I turned and saw her staring through the open door into the Room.

"You opened it," she said.

"Yes."

"Not cleaning it?"

"No. And don't start."

"I'm not going to." I could hear her disappointment, though. What did she think was going to happen?

I nestled Mother's ring into my jewelry box, next to my wedding ring. I slammed the lid shut over two ruined marriages.

W hen I came back down the hall, Mary wasn't there, and I knew right where she'd gone. I followed her into that one room. Its walls were mint green, painted by Ron when he first built me the house and imagined two more babies.

Mary looked at the array of baby things, a sheen of dust covering the diaper boxes. She crouched and poked in some of the shopping bags. "Oh, Trish," she said, pulling out a little lavender sleeper with flowers on the round collar. The kind of impractical detail utterly unsuited to normal use.

"I was going to take her home in that. Take pictures. There's a boy one, too. It's blue with sailboats."

I put the back of my hand on my forehead. "I can't do it, Mary. Getting rid of this is like throwing my baby away. I know, I know, it's not true. Knowing and feeling aren't the same."

Mary chewed on her lip, inspecting the bags around me. "What if you didn't 'get rid of' it. What if it was a gift? Somewhere specific, instead of just dumped in some big collection bin at Goodwill?"

"I don't know. Maybe."

I stroked the crib rail. I could smell the baby powder, feel their gummy mouths gnawing on my finger. It wasn't just the lost baby; it was all my babies I'd preserved in here. I still had my sons, but my boys as innocent little babies were gone forever.

"What does it hurt to have this here?" I asked, my raspy voice giving away the answer even as I asked the question.

"We lost the ring," Mary said, "for a time. And now we have it again. Did you feel like Mom was any more lost when we didn't have it? Is she back in any sense now that we do?"

"I never said it was logical."

"I'm not saying you should get rid of all of it. But this . . . it's a morbid shrine."

I wanted to yell at her to shut up and leave me alone. I wanted to bury my face in the ducky blanket and cry. I wanted to curl up in a sunny patch of carpet at our feet and stay there all day.

I did none of these things. Nor did I agree.

Mary moved first, walking with a defeated slump to the doorway. Surrendering, it seemed. Just as I had.

She stopped just at the door and bent to pick up a bag. "Trish?" She dug around inside the bag, then pulled out a sweater, tags still on. She also inspected the receipt, and I flinched before she even spoke. "You bought this a month ago. And put it in here."

I braced myself for the onslaught of anger and ridicule. Yes, I bought something, didn't use it, and threw it in my last hoarded room. Let the berating begin.

Mary crossed the room back to me and put her arm around me, her head on my shoulder. I was struck dumb with surprise at her tenderness.

Chapter 50

My fizzy, giddy feeling that drove me down the highway to Grand Ledge to present my sister with our mother's ring had hissed flat by the time I was back on my own pathetic little doorstep.

I glanced down at the pristine welcome mat with its insipid daisies and grabbed it off the concrete porch. I walked a few steps to the communal Dumpster and winged it inside, listening to it thunk hard against the hollow interior.

I inspected my doorway before walking in. The door was closed tight as it should be. I opened my door carefully and froze. I listened for unusual sounds and performed a visual sweep.

I latched the door behind me. The only sound was my own pulse pounding in my ears.

I hung my purse on its proper hook and turned on my laptop on my kitchen table, preparing to once again apply for jobs I would not get. I waited for the computer to come to life and wondered what I'd thought would happen because I drove to Trish's place. That I'd find her home miraculously clean? That the ring would cure her like an amulet?

My face burned as I mentally replayed the call I'd placed to Seth.

I probably sounded like a desperate, giggly teenager to him. He no doubt deleted my message with a scowl of frustration. After all, we'd hardly spoken since I'd said that awful thing to him at my place about knowing how his wife felt. I couldn't blame him, really.

Well. Trish had the ring. And she'd allowed me to place that call about the crib.

After searching the job sites, I searched my shelves for *Pride and Prejudice*. I had not alphabetized my books when I put them back on the shelf. This had been my one concession to acting like a real person.

My cell phone rang and I picked it up without looking, assuming it was Trish calling, perhaps even changing her mind.

" 'Lo."

"Mary."

"Seth?" I sat up on my bed, sitting cross-legged. "Hi."

"I'm glad you called. I'm sorry I didn't call back earlier; I was with a patient."

"Oh, your sabbatical is over."

"I think it's good for me to be back. It's been busy, and a little strange, but after a while I was so sick of looking at my walls."

"I know."

"Great news about your mother's ring. That's wonderful."

"Yes, it is."

"You sound subdued, compared to earlier."

"I'm a little tired is all."

"Like I said, I'm sorry I didn't call back right away. I was otherwise occupied."

"So you said." I sank into disappointment over our mundane small talk. All he'd done was return a call, which was, after all, the polite thing to do.

"After my patient, I was on the road."

"Mmmm." I picked up *Pride and Prejudice* and opened to the first page, expecting he'd be hanging up in a minute or two and I'd have yet more silence to fill. *It is a truth universally acknowledged* . . .

The doorbell? I sighed with irritation. "Hang on, Seth."

I carried the phone into the living room. I stuck Jane Austen under my arm and with my free hand pulled open my door, just a bit, for the delivery person, or Girl Scout with cookies . . .

He was there, on my porch, his phone to his head. "Should I call back? Sounds like you have company."

"What are you doing here?"

He reached over and took the phone from my hand, punching a button.

"You can hang up now, I think." He handed the phone back.

I stood there with my phone and my book and gaped at him, thinking he couldn't be real, Seth didn't just drive here in the middle of the week right from work.

He was wearing black pants and a crisp white dress shirt open at the collar, with his sleeves rolled up. No tie. His shoes were shiny and stylish.

"You could invite me in," Seth prompted. "Unless you'd rather not . . ."

"No! I mean, yes. OK. I guess. I'm not really prepared. . . ." I stood back to let him come in.

Seth pulled the door closed behind him. "Yes, I can see the place is a real mess."

My face burned at his teasing. I turned away from him watching me and walked into my living room. I sat on the sofa I never used and realized as I settled in how the cushions were much more springy and fresh than the big chair I always sit in. It's possible no one had sat here since I tested it out in the store.

Seth did not wait for me to give him permission to sit. He selected the chair I always use, leaned back, and crossed one ankle over his knee.

"Why are you here?" I blurted. "Why didn't you call from home?"

"I was afraid you'd tell me not to come if I asked."

"What gives you that idea?"

"You were pretty upset with my, as you put it, interrogation."

I looked down at my lap. This would be my penance, it seemed, to forever replay my worst outbursts, my clumsiest moments. "I already said I was sorry. It just slipped out."

"At first I was . . . hurt. But when I thought back on our conversation, I realized that I had been, in fact, slipping back to that old script. That illusion that I could use my training and knowledge to fix everything for the people I care about, when sometimes the people I care about needed empathy. That I should just shut the hell up and listen."

I continued looking down at my lap and my hands, folded loosely. I noted his phrase, "people I care about."

"You had just endured a terrible violation of your privacy and personal space, and a loss of an object that meant a great deal to your family. And I chose that moment to grill you about why you didn't hang pictures."

"And I let fly with the worst insult I could have deployed."

"Did you calculate that? Did you go out of your way to be vicious?"

" 'Course not."

"I know you didn't. I wanted to talk to you earlier, but you seemed . . . remote. You only answered my calls with text messages."

I tipped my head back on my couch. "It was all so much. The fight with Trish, my nephews, the break-in. It was . . . overload."

"But you sounded different today, in your message."

"So you decided to drive here? Based on that?"

"That's the size of it."

"Well. Thank you, then. I guess."

Seth leaned forward with his elbows on his knees, clasping his hands. He massaged his hands, working his fingers like he was preparing to play a piano concerto.

"There was a reason I was particularly sensitive about my job."

I could see his jaw working, like he was chewing something. "OK."

"I wasn't just on a sabbatical. It wasn't that simple. I . . . lost a patient. I lost a patient, Mary."

"Oh, I'm . . . I'm sorry." Part of me wanted to reach out to pat his arm or his hand, but he seemed stiff. Untouchable.

"I'd been getting so tired of hearing about problems. They call it compassion fatigue. I was so wrung out every night, but then I still had to field calls from my ex-wife about Aurora, or care for Aurora if I had her for the weekend, and I felt like I'd gone cold all over, in every way. I was telling myself that I still was doing a good job for my patients, that I was putting one foot in front of the other. . . . Then I lost Chris. A gay teen with suicidal ideation. Until it wasn't ideation anymore."

"Oh, no."

"It's happened before. In my field it does happen sometimes. But I couldn't help but wonder if he somehow knew. If he detected that I'd unplugged from him . . ."

"You can't do that to yourself."

"You'll be amused to know I'm seeing my own shrink."

"Not amused. It's good."

"It was you. And your sister that got me back to work."

"Us?"

He sat up, relaxed his pose, turned in the chair to face me.

"You and your sister were working so hard. And I'm not just talking about hauling boxes. You could have let Jack go live with your dad, or Ron, and stayed away. She could have done the minimum required, rented another storage unit, or tried to con the social worker. I watched that, saw you both were doing so much with few resources, and here I was, ready to throw away my career and everything I'd worked for,

everything good and right I've ever done for all my other patients because of one setback. So I went back."

"How is it? Is it OK?"

"Yeah. It's been OK. Hard, but as I said, I'm seeing my own
shrink."

"How's . . . how are things going with Aurora?"

"She's making some good language progress. Thanks for asking."

More trucks went by. Home alone, I'd never noticed how noisy the
stupid trucks were.

"So . . . why did you drive here? You could have told me that on the
phone."

"Yes. I could have. But I missed you, Mary."

This startled me into sitting absurdly upright, on the edge of the
couch. "What?"

"I missed you. I wanted to see you."

He smiled at me. Not his joking smirk, but a soft, genuine smile. He
was turned to the side in the chair, one arm thrown over the back of
it. He looked as relaxed as I'd seen him, maybe since college. Maybe
never.

"That's it?"

"That's it. Simple, isn't it? Sometimes things really are simple, even
for shrinks. I missed you, and now I'm here, so I'm not missing you
right now."

"I . . . don't know what to say."

"There's nothing you have to say."

"I'm not sure why you could miss me. Weird old Mary, who can't
stand normal human contact."

Seth smiled. "I don't see 'weird old Mary.' I see my friend, who was
kind to me during a tough time, when everyone else was too preoccupied or immature. I see my friend, whom I took for granted all those
years ago, too fixated on my high school sweetheart to see the nice girl

right in front of me. I see someone who put aside her own discomfort and pain to help her sister keep her children."

"Fourteen years too late."

"I think the only 'too late' is never. I think you were right on time."

I felt a flush creep up my face as he continued to stare at me. But what else was there for him to look at? My Georgia O'Keeffe print of a flower that looked like a vulva?

"Can I ask you a question?" he said.

I stiffened. Of course there would be questions. He'd ask about Trish's hoarding, or whether I alphabetized my spices. Whether I could track dirt in without having a conniption.

Seth said, "Could I see you sometime? For dinner or something?"

"Huh?"

"I'd like to see you again. Like I said, I miss you. The cure for missing someone is seeing them. Since I'll start missing your company as soon as I get home, it would be nice to know I had plans to see you again."

I shifted on my cushy, unused sofa. "Well. I don't know. Let's see if I can fit you in between 'nothing' and 'watching grass grow.'"

Seth chuckled, his grin now wide and amused, his blue eyes crinkled up. "When you find a clear space in your calendar, let me know."

I was inert with shock. Had this just happened? Further: I'd just cracked a joke that actually worked?

Seth's smile faded, and the light left his eyes. He rose to standing. "I should go. I've imposed too long. And I have to get back; I've got some reading to do tonight for a patient tomorrow."

He turned away and was heading for my door. In moments he'd be back on the road, back to his life, and there would be no more sound here but the trucks outside.

I leaped off the couch like I'd been stung and caught up to him in my entryway. He was already turning around, having heard my rushed approach.

I flung myself at him with my eyes closed, not unlike myself as a young girl when I'd jumped off the high-dive. I'd landed flat on the water then; it was like being hit by a heavy wooden board.

This time I wrapped my arms around his waist and buried my face in his chest, and I let him embrace me.

"Saturday," I said into his chest, my nose full of the clean-laundry smell of his white dress shirt. "I'd love to see you Saturday."

Chapter 51

I was just fine watching the diaper boxes and shopping bags go into the truck.

But when Ron and Mary walked by carting the crib—the crib in which Jack used to frantically bounce while holding the rail, the same rail that still bore baby Andy's teeth marks—I had to run back into the house. I sat at the kitchen table and stared at Mother's ring, which I was wearing on my right hand, with some yarn wound around the base of it to keep it snug on my finger.

I heard Mary approach, and she rubbed my shoulder. "Breathe deep, Trish. Keep your larger goal in mind."

"Have you been watching those stupid shows again?"

"Reading," she answered. "I got some books."

I shrugged her hand off. "Just . . . don't make a fuss, OK? This is hard enough, don't . . . draw attention."

"OK."

The front door opened, and we both turned. Ron stood in the doorway, the spring sun pouring in around him in a bright rectangle on the floor, broken up by his long shadow.

"You ready, T?"

I sighed, and by way of answer stood up and grabbed my purse.

We squeezed all three of us into the front of Ron's truck, with me in the middle. I had to squeeze my hands together to keep myself from resting my hand on Ron's thigh like I always used to.

My breathing was shallow, and three times during the drive my vision became speckled with dots of light until I reminded myself to breathe deep and slow, from the abdomen.

I'd kept two special sleepers. Mary had helped me wrap them in tissue paper and put them in a box marked KEEPSAKES. I could look at them anytime and always remember how we'd anticipated our baby, how we'd loved it even when it was just a bump and a flutter.

I remembered those sleepers, held them in my mind, and tried not to think about the other things in the truck bed behind us.

We pulled up to a church in a ramshackle neighborhood and listened to Mary read off a piece of paper to pull around behind, near some double doors.

A large black woman with corkscrew curls greeted us. Her name tag said "Serita." Behind her I saw Ayana, and I stiffened and folded my arms, flashing back to when all this started, with her on my porch holding out that business card, talking judges and unsafe living environments. Ayana either didn't notice or didn't care. She waved and smiled brightly.

"Welcome, and thank you!" Serita called out. "This is such a wonderful blessing. There's a girl having a baby next week and that child was gonna be sleeping in a dresser drawer as of this morning."

She ran up to me and hugged me hard, like we were kin. "Hi, honey, I'm Serita. I run this place."

Ayana said, "Hi, Trish. This was such a great idea your sister had. I'm so glad she called me."

I detangled from Serita's embrace. "I'm glad to be of some help." I coughed over the words, and I caught Mary dart a concerned look in my direction. She was halfway between Ron, who was lifting down the first boxes, and where I stood. I shooed her toward the boxes, wanting her to understand I was fine as long as she didn't keep staring at me like I was some volcano about to blow.

"We rely on donations like yours to keep going," Serita was saying. "I have such a heart for these girls. You know, in my day when a girl got herself pregnant there wasn't much like this around. The people who cared had nothing to spare, the people who had the money just didn't care. Thank goodness angels like you have some compassion."

"Hardly an angel, Serita."

Serita put her hand on her hip and looked down at me. "Who are you to say what an angel is?" She winked.

A man came out from inside and wordlessly started helping Ron with the boxes. Mary drifted back to me and was staring at me so hard I wish we'd left her at home.

As the boxes of my babies' things disappeared through glass doors into the darkened interior of the church, sweat tickled my palms and my heart tugged in their direction.

It will go away, I told myself. *This feeling won't last forever; they are just things.* I thought of the sleepers I'd kept, and all the dozens of pictures I had of both boys as babies, the fact that I had both my boys, still, in my nice clean house. In fact, now that the house was clean, I could make space to scrapbook those pictures and display them properly. Get them at last out of those dusty shoeboxes.

"You're doing so good," Ayana said, and I mentally corrected, *Well. I'm doing so well.*

I hadn't noticed a car pull up until a girl bopped out, then reached into the back to pull out a wiggly, chubby baby girl with a pink bow tied ludicrously into the tiny wisp of hair at the top of her head.

A toddler followed her out of the car as well.

"Hi, Miss Serita!" the girl called.

"Hello, Luz," Miss Serita called back.

"I gotta go potty!" shrieked the toddler, starting a potty dance.

The baby clapped, wriggled with her whole body, kicking her little legs where they dangled as young Luz had her in one arm, legs hanging free.

Luz said to the boy, "Didn't you already go? I asked you if you had to go."

The baby shocked me by reaching for me. The toddler was still begging for the potty. Luz groaned. "Miss Serita, can you watch Neveah? I've gotta get him to the potty."

"Looks like Miss Trish here can take her. Don't worry, Luz, I'd go kung fu on her before I'd let her run off with your child."

I was hot in the direct sun, but a chill raced over my skin, even so. Luz held her baby closer to me, the little boy yanking on her other arm.

I gulped hard. "Kung fu won't be necessary," I said, taking the little drooly thing in my arms.

It was the first time I'd held a baby since I'd lost my own. I saw Ayana watching me carefully, so I looked away, and focused on the child.

Neveah wiggled with delight as I made a funny face, then buried her own head in my shoulder. I patted her back and rocked slightly from side to side. Old habits never die, do they? I could see myself holding Drew's baby. Hopefully, years and years from now.

"Babies light up the whole world, don't they?" Serita said.

"That they do," Ayana said.

Mary came closer. Her eyes asked me, *Are you OK?*

I gave her a wan smile, nuzzled the baby's hair, and inhaled.

"Two babies already, that must be so hard," I said quietly.

"Oh, the boy is her baby brother. She's on babysitting duty while her own mama is at work." Serita paused for a peekaboo with the baby. "Luz is a sweet girl, and you know? Everyone makes mistakes."

"Nobody's perfect," I agreed, catching Mary's eye.

"Nobody but our Lord," Serita said, then stage-whispered, "And sometimes, I wonder about him." She burst out laughing then, confident that her Lord could take a joke.

Luz returned and held her hands out for her baby. The little girl kicked and wriggled away from me and happily grabbed a fistful of her mother's silky black hair. The boy clung to her knee. Ayana bent down to say hello to him, but he hid behind his sister's leg.

"Lemme get you those diapers, honey," Serita said, and excused herself.

The girl baby nuzzled her mom's neck, and Luz patted her back and rocked her in place, much as I had.

I pictured my mother holding her own newborn child, sneaking a few locks of hair, knowing the rest of her would be gone within days. I put my sunglasses on and blinked hard to regain control of myself.

Serita put the box of diapers in Luz's car. As I followed her progress, I saw Ron and the man from the church with the crib.

They marched by me, disappearing inside.

"No!" I shouted, chasing after them. Mary tried to touch my arm, and I shrugged her off. "I'm sorry, wait. I changed my mind. I can't." I was panting as if I'd run a distance, though I'd covered only a few yards.

Ron set down his end of the crib, squared himself to me, and folded his arms. "Trish. We talked about this."

Ayana started, "Trish, remember what's important is your children now, in the present day, who need you."

I wrapped my shaking hands around the crib rail. "I can't. It's all I've got left from . . ."

"Not all you've got," Mary said softly. "The sleepers. The pictures of the boys."

"I feel like I'm going to throw up. Or pass out. I can't do it. Not this. Not yet."

Serita appeared at my side. "Honey, if it's this hard, you don't have to give it up. You truly don't."

"Ma'am," Ron began. "There are special circumstances . . ."

Then I exclaimed, "Wait! They can't take it. This crib has been recalled. See?" I leaned into the side and the one rail dropped down. "They can't sell this kind anymore. And see how easy the side drops? Dangerous."

Ron scowled, his expression darkening. Ayana drooped in defeat. "She's right. We forgot to check the model number."

Ron almost yanked it out of the hands of the church volunteer, who had to step double-time to keep up with his angry progress back to the truck. Ron shouted, "I'm gonna need to bungee this down. Gimme a minute."

Mary tried to rub my shoulder.

"Not now, Mary."

Serita said, "Some things happen in God's time, not ours."

I didn't know if she was talking to me, or Mary, or all of us.

I went back outside and blinked in the bright sunshine, even with my sunglasses still down, trying to hide my crazy-hoarder anxiety. My heart was slowing down to its natural rhythm. I felt my world becoming stable again.

Luz had loaded the toddler into the car and had the baby in her other arm.

"Wait, young lady, can you hold on a minute?" I called out. "I'll be right back."

I ducked inside, spotting my boxes where they lined the hall. I dug through these boxes I so recently packed, and it took me three tries to find it. I imagined Ayana watching me through the church doors, frowning.

I walked back out into the hot parking lot and said to Luz next to her rusty Chevy, "Could you use another blanket at all? I just think this one is so adorable, I'd love for you to have it."

Luz took the blanket in her free hand, admiring the yellow duckies. She held it in front of her daughter. "What do you think, *mija*? Do we like the duckies?" The baby bounced so hard in place I thought she'd fall to the ground, and I made as if to catch her.

"Oh, I got her," Luz said. "She does it all the time. Thanks, though. For trying to catch her. And the blanket."

"You're welcome. Take care, now."

I watched that car pull out of the parking lot and down the road and remained watching until Luz and her baby had faded into the stream of traffic, no more than a speck among other moving specks, rushing through life.

B ack in my driveway, Mary unfolded herself gracefully from the truck and hopped down. I followed out her side, instead of getting out behind Ron. The whole drive home I could feel his radiating frustration about the crib.

We both went immediately to the back to look; it had survived the trip perfectly intact. I drooped with relief, not realizing I'd been tense. But Ron had fastened it securely in his truck, using blankets to protect its wood spindles where it was braced against the side of the truck bed.

"You did good, T," Ron said, but I could hear the downcast note in his voice. "I'll get this back in there, I guess." He started unwinding the crib with brisk, businesslike movements.

"I should go," Mary said, walking away from Ron and the truck, already rooting in her purse for her keys. "Let you two talk."

"You could stay," I said, but I realized I didn't mean it. I felt wrung out like a mop and desired nothing more than a nap after the morning I'd had.

"Nah, that's OK. You're tired."

We stopped in front of her sedan and stood there in a weird, prolonged silence, broken only by distant birds chirping and the clanging of Ron disentangling the crib.

"I'm sorry about the way I left. Earlier. After the ring got stolen," Mary said at last.

"Me, too. I mean, about what I did. Let's stop that, shall we? This fighting and not speaking? Mom wouldn't want that."

Mary nodded. "Of course. Definitely. Well. I should go, I guess. You look tired."

Ron called, "Ready, T." He opened the tailgate to the truck and climbed on, pulling the crib back where we could reach it from the ground.

I sighed with pleasure at the sight of the crib. I still needed it. Right or wrong, I needed it. "I'll help you in a minute," I called to him. He nodded, then leaned against the tailgate, looking down at his boots.

I looked down at Mother's ring and said to Mary, "I think Mom did this. Gave you the idea to come see me, so you could help me get this stuff out of here."

"Oh, come on." Mary kicked a piece of gravel in my drive.

"You never act on intuition, and yet this time you did."

She tilted her head up, as if addressing the birds in the trees. " 'There are more things in heaven and earth, Horatio, than are dreamt of in your philosophy.' "

"Horatio?"

"I was quoting Hamlet."

"Of course you were."

Mary squinted in the sun. "OK, speaking of intuition. I've got an adoption registry site all lined up on my computer."

My mouth fell open. "Me, too."

"Yeah?"

I laughed. "I can't tell you how many times I've stared at that site thinking I should call you. I didn't want to do it without you. I guess curiosity got the better of me, after all."

"So, OK then. Let's do it. Let's try to find Laura."

A swarm of arguments buzzed around my head, the same ones I'd considered as my mouse arrow hovered over the adoption site, nearly every day since my fight with Mary. Laura might not want to be found, she might hate us, we might hate her, it could throw everything up in the air . . .

"Tomorrow. Call me tomorrow and I'll come over and we'll talk about it. I'd like to see your place for a change."

"As long as you promise not to mess up my throw pillows," Mary warned, shaking her finger.

I gaped at her for a second, until her face broke into a sideways grin. "Gotcha."

We hugged each other hard, and I watched her drive down the driveway and all the way until she was out of sight. I chuckled to hear her singing along with Mötley Crüe, "Home Sweet Home."

I glanced down at my hand. Mother's ring bounced the bright sunshine back to me.

Acknowledgments

T hank you ever so much to my family, for putting up with my book-tour absences, my fretting, and for not once making me feel guilty for chasing this dream. Love you.

Thank you to my agent, Kristin Nelson, for having my back. Lucky gives his regards to Chutney. Thanks also to Lindsay Mergens for the advice on many things and assistance in writing book club questions, because you're much better at it than I am. Thank you as well to my Twitter comrade, Sara Megibow, and Anita Mumm.

Have I mentioned how lucky I am to work with Lucia Macro? Because I am. Thank you, Lucia, for making this book better yet, and for caring, about the book and the author, both. Thank you to many more wonderful people at HarperCollins: Esi Sogah, Tavia Kowalchuk, Shawn Nicholls, Pam Jaffee, Megan Traynor, Jennifer Hart, Liate Stehlik, Mumtaz Mustafa, and Christine Maddalena, who has moved on, but will be missed. You never forget your first (publicist).

I'm so grateful to Elizabeth Graham for her thoughtful early reads. You manage to be thorough, yet gracious and supportive, and that's like gold.

Huge thanks to my research sources, who help me seem very smart about lots of things. My friend Courtney L. Crooks, Ph.D., LP, helped me write a good Seth, and taught me the difference between a psychiatrist and a psychologist. Dr. Vern Boersma and Lu Reyes helped me understand the lives of migrant workers in the 1960s. Detective Pete Kemme helped me navigate the world of social services and write an accurate Ayana. Thank you to Maggie Dana and her friend, and to Danielle Schaaf's sister, Ann Johnson, for making sure I don't use the wrong slang for the 1960s.

Besides watching umpteen television documentary episodes about compulsive hoarding, I read the amazing and invaluable *Stuff* by Randy O. Frost and Gail Steketee. I highly recommend it if you want to understand at a layperson's level about compulsive hoarding. I also read the self-help workbook *Buried in Treasures: Help for Compulsive Acquiring, Saving, and Hoarding* by Frost and Steketee plus David F. Tolin, and *Overcoming Compulsive Hoarding* by Fugen Neziroglu, Jerome Bubrick, and Jose A. Yaryura-Tobias. For insight into unwed mothers who surrendered children for adoption in the 1960s and 1970s, I consulted *The Girls Who Went Away* by Ann Fessler. Thank you to Susan Ito for pointing me in the direction of that amazing and important book.

About the author

About the book

Read on

Insights,
Interviews
& More . . .

Meet Kristina Riggle

John Riggle

Kristina Riggle is a former journalist and one-time holiday temp bookseller, and the short fiction coeditor for the e-zine *Literary Mama*. Her debut, *Real Life & Liars,* was a Target Breakout pick and a Great Lakes, Great Reads selection by the Great Lakes Independent Booksellers Association. Her other novels have been recognized by independent booksellers as an Indie Next Notable book as well as a Midwest Connections pick. She lives in West Michigan with her husband, two kids, and dog.

Q&A with Kristina Riggle

Why did you choose to write about hoarding?

I've long been fascinated with compulsions. An early, unpublished manuscript featured a character with OCD (obsessive compulsive disorder)—tapping rituals, in the case of that book. Years ago, I watched an episode of *Oprah* featuring a hoarder whose physical appearance was stylish and neat. Her home was beautiful from the outside. She was intelligent, articulate, and composed. Inside her home, however, was a horror show of filth and debris. I was struck when she characterized herself as a perfectionist and showed the producers a clean, unsullied garbage can. She couldn't bear to put anything inside it and ruin its perfection. Astonishing. It's only natural that I would eventually write about something that fascinates me, so, here we are.

How did you research this novel?

The nonfiction book *Stuff: Compulsive Hoarding and the Meaning of Things* by Randy O. Frost and Gail Steketee was a tremendous resource, and I urge anyone interested in this topic to go read it. The same authors, along with David F. Tolin, also wrote a workbook called *Buried in Treasures: Help for Compulsive Acquiring, Saving, and Hoarding*, which is meant as a self-help guide for hoarders. I filled it out "in character" as Trish. That was tremendously helpful as far as figuring out exactly what kind of hoarder she would be. There are many varieties of hoarding. It is not a cookie-cutter disorder. I read other books, too (see the acknowledgments section for a list). Of course, I watched the hoarding reality shows currently popular on cable TV. I have mixed feelings about the shows. Seeing hoarders in action as they tried to part with their items was illuminating for me as a writer. They are educational and they seem to help some of the people featured. But the shows also feel exploitive and seem to oversimplify hoarding. In comparison, the books I consulted were more nuanced and realistic.

As for the character of Seth, I was lucky enough to have gotten back in touch with a former roommate who is a clinical psychologist. ▶

Q&A with Kristina Riggle *(continued)*

I already had the Seth character in the works when we connected again. A wonderful bit of serendipity! She helped me nail down his character and introduced me to the concept of compassion fatigue.

How did you choose the setting?

Trish's rural house is fictional, but the nearby cities of Grand Ledge and Lansing are real. It's easy to keep secrets when you have acreage and dense woods surrounding your house. I'll admit to having thought of my friend Jill's rural home when I came up with the setting, but she is very neat and has a lovely house! As for me, I live in an older suburb and I'm close to my own neighbors. It would be challenging to hoard on my block without someone noticing—not impossible, though. According to my research, hoarders are surprisingly good at keeping their secret.

Have you ever known a hoarder?

Not personally. Not that I know of, anyway (see above). However, in one of the places I've lived (I'm being vague on purpose to protect privacy) there was a house that the neighbors disdained for its outside clutter, along with clutter visible on the enclosed front porch. I have since realized during my research that this could very well have been the home of a hoarder. Some hoarders have neat exteriors, actually, but for others, the disarray extends to the yard.

I also reported in my newspaper days on the city's dealings with an elderly man whose house was packed to the rafters to the point that it was hazardous. I didn't think about it then, but now it seems obvious that he was a compulsive hoarder. I never saw the inside of his home myself, however. I can't remember why I didn't; it's likely he would have refused me entrance, though we did talk on the phone several times. I'd handle that story differently now, I'm sure of it, knowing what I know now.

Do you relate more to Mary, the neat-freak, or Trish, the hoarder?

I relate to them both! The older I get, the less tolerance I have for mess and disorder. I can physically feel more relaxed in a neat and clean setting. I'm more sympathetic every day to my mother, who used to insist on a clean bedroom—at the very least the part of my room she could see from the hallway. (My childhood room was at the end of the hall, so anyone in the living room of our little house could see straight in.) Nowadays, it makes me crazy when horizontal surfaces are treated as storage space for random clutter. That said, houses are meant to be lived in by real human beings, and that means messes will happen. Love and fun trump perfect cleanliness any day.

As for Trish, I absolutely relate. In recent years, we cleaned out every bit of our home and purged boxes upon boxes of old, unused items, some of which related to my children and had some sentimental value. It was so hard to watch my first child's baby toys be carted off at a garage sale! That being said, my house is meant to be lived in by my family as it is now, not exist as a museum to what used to be.

I will admit I still have my children's crib, though. Make of that what you will. ❧

Questions for Discussion

1. Before reading *Keepsake*, what did you know about hoarding, and the mental and emotional issues behind it? Do you know someone who hoards?

2. Have you watched documentary TV about people who hoard? Do you find these shows to be educational, and do you believe they genuinely help the subjects of the programs? What about the viewers at home? Do you think Trish would have recognized herself if she'd watched a show about hoarding?

3. Talk about Trish and Mary. Do you relate to either of the sisters, or both? If so, how?

4. What is your relationship with your own "stuff"? Are you like Trish, in that you might keep things you never use or buy unnecessary things in order to make yourself feel better? Or are you like Mary, in that clutter jangles your nerves and dirt upsets you?

5. Why do you think the sisters responded so differently to their upbringing by a hoarder parent? Why do you think Mary left to live with their father, while Trish stayed with their mother through the end of her adolescence?

6. In what ways is hoarding similar to a substance addiction?

7. Do you think Frances had a genuine choice in whether to keep her baby, or did the culture she lived in force her hand?

8. How different would their lives have been if Frances had kept her baby? Would Frances still have hoarded? Would Mary and Trish even have existed, or would keeping the baby have altered Frances's life so much that she never would have married the man she did?

9. Both Trish and her mother had husbands leave them because of their hoarding. Do you understand why they left? Could they have done anything to prevent what eventually happened to their wives?

10. In what ways is Mary's obsession with neatness connected to her discomfort with emotional closeness?

11. Mary's relationship with Seth started out as friendship. Have you ever had a friend for whom you've grown to have romantic feelings? Do you think that romantic ▶

relationships are best begun through
friendship, or do you believe in love at
first sight?

12. Discuss Seth and Mary's relationship. Why did
Seth not initially think of Mary in a romantic
way? Do you believe Mary can break down her
emotional walls long enough to connect with
Seth?

13. What do you think the future holds for Ron
and Trish?

14. Will Trish ever let go of the crib? Do you
believe it's harmful that she kept it? Have you
hung on to something for reasons that you
can't fully explain?

15. After reading *Keepsake*, do you have a deeper
understanding about what makes someone
hoard? ∽

More from Kristina Riggle

REAL LIFE & LIARS

Sometimes you find happiness where, and when, you least expect it.

For Mirabelle Zielinski's children, happiness always seems to be just out of reach. Her polished oldest daughter, Katya, clings to a stale marriage with a workaholic husband and three spoiled children. Her son, Ivan, so creative, is a down-in-the-dumps songwriter with the worst taste in women. And the "baby," impulsive Irina, who lives life on a whim, is now reluctantly pregnant and hitched to a man who is twice her age. On the weekend of their parents' anniversary party, lies will be revealed, hearts will be broken . . . but love will also be found. And the biggest shock may come from Mirabelle herself, because she has a secret that will change everything.

THE LIFE YOU'VE IMAGINED

Is the *life* you're living all you imagined?

Have you ever asked yourself, "What if?" Here, four women face the decisions of their lifetimes in this stirring and unforgettable novel of love, loss, friendship, and family.

Anna Geneva, a Chicago attorney coping with the death of a cherished friend, returns to her "speck on the map" hometown of Haven to finally come to terms with her mother, the man she left behind, and the road she did not take.

Cami Drayton, Anna's dearest friend from high school, is coming home too, forced by circumstance to move in with her alcoholic father . . . and to confront a dark family secret.

Maeve, Anna's mother, never left Haven, firmly rooted there by her sadness over her abandonment by the husband she desperately loved and the hope that someday he will return to her.

And Amy Rickart—thin, beautiful, and striving for perfection—faces a future with the perfect man . . . but is haunted by the memory of what she used to be.

More from Kristina Riggle *(continued)*

Kristina Riggle's *The Life You've Imagined* takes a provocative look at the choices we make—and the courage we must have to change.

THINGS WE DIDN'T SAY

What goes unsaid can sometimes speak the loudest . . .

What makes up a family? For Casey, it's sharing a house with her fiancé, Michael, and his three children, whom she intends to nurture more than she ever took care of herself. But Casey's plans have come undone. Michael's silences have grown unfathomable and deep. His daughter Angel seethes as only a teenage girl can, while the wide-eyed youngest, Jewel, quietly takes it all in.

Then Michael's son, Dylan, runs off, and the kids' mother, a woman never afraid to say what she thinks, noisily barges into the home. That's when Casey decides that the silences can no longer continue. She must begin speaking the words no one else can say. She'll have to dig up secrets—including her own—uncovering the hurts, and begin the healing that is long overdue. And it all starts with just a few tentative words . . .